ONE OF US

Also by Kylie Kaden

The Day the Lies Began

Missing You

Losing Kate

ONE OF US

KYLIE KADEN

PANTERA
PRESS

PANTERA
PRESS

First published in 2022 by Pantera Press Pty Limited
www.PanteraPress.com

A Cataloguing-in-Publication entry for this work is available from the
National Library of Australia.

ISBN 978-0-6486770-9-3 (Paperback)
ISBN 978-0-6487488-6-1 (eBook)

Cover Design: Christa Moffitt, Christabella Designs
Cover Images: Piter Lenk/Alamy, Jacob Lund/Shutterstock, wavebreakmedia/Shutterstock
Acquired by: Lucy Bell
Editor: Lauren Finger
Typesetting: Kirby Jones
Author Photo: Anna Gilbert Photography
Printed and bound in Australia by McPherson's Printing Group

The paper this book is printed on is certified against the Forest Stewardship Council® Standards. McPherson's Printing Group holds FSC® chain of custody certification SA-COC-005379. FSC® promotes environmentally responsible, socially beneficial and economically viable management of the world's forests.

To the boys I made from scratch,
Nate, Finn & Josh,
and to the amazing mums who helped me survive them.

Wildflower: *n*; uncultivated plant with conspicuous flowers growing without intentional human intervention.

Prologue

There was crowded, hurried, organised chaos as paramedics manoeuvred between police in paper booties. First responders in bottle-green overalls rushed to the victim on the living-room floor.

But the detective stood deathly still and watched.

The secret to finding reason in every crime scene was the detail. The debris of modern living was everywhere – a half-eaten yoghurt tub, crumb-speckled plates piled on the breakfast bar. The detective noticed crayon-scribbled walls, a scooter thrown in a doorway, a private-college schoolbag abandoned mid-hall. He scanned the happy snaps perched on the buffet, the smiles and laughter. Those images would soon be recoded, stored in the family's 'before' memories. Before this day, the day their lives were torn to pieces.

A shell-shocked, teary teenager sat hunched on the wing chair.

And there she was: the wife.

The attractive, middle-aged woman sat slumped in silence on the couch, hands splayed on either side of her like stabilisers. The show carried on around her in double speed, contrasting her stillness. She seemed not to have realised she was an integral player in the scene. That every reaction, or lack of one, was being analysed.

She was difficult to decode. Her expression remained blank, but her face looked as if a whole world of trouble was going on inside, her eyes fearful of some unknown terror.

This sort of thing played out between gangs in dark alleys, not around here. This place was ivy-league. The exclusive estate boasted twenty-four-hour CCTV whirring in the background, keeping the residents' artwork adorning their walls and their Teslas charging in their garages. Apple Tree Creek Estate – the name sounded as pure as the morning dew. Immaculate lanes, wide cul-de-sacs, shade-speckled playgrounds flanked by pockets of pristine gardens, springy lawns you had to sink your toes into – it was like a modern-day utopia.

The detective huffed, unsure.

Was the wife traumatised because she'd witnessed this low-life act, or because she was guilty of it?

Part 1

The Suspects

Chapter 1

Gertie

'But … we love each other. You adore the kids. You're *devoted* to them …' The dent lines on the doona spread out from where her husband sat and made the pattern become out of sync. Just like his words. 'I mean, I see your face when they blabber on with their long, boring stories and you don't look bored at all. You're never *token*. You actually *love* them.'

He nodded an impossibly slow nod. 'I do.'

Gertie shook her head. 'You're Super-Dad. Super-Dad doesn't *leave*.'

Ed's jaw twisted. He was feeling rubbish about it, she could tell. But this simply made no sense.

'My anniversary card said I was the love of your life. That I was the best mother in the world, that you'd marry me again …'

'I would.'

Her chin tucked in, disbelieving. 'And yet you're moving to Singapore.' The sentence had bumps in it, like the shaky breath filtering through her lungs. Gertie glanced at the framed family selfie she'd bribed the kids to smile for (after the forced removal of their screens on a Sunday afternoon to tackle the clifftop trail at Bondi). With all three inheriting Gertie's jet-black hair, dark chocolate eyes and wide grins, Ed's mousey colouring seemed tame in comparison.

'If it's just the job, we could come too … I know it's supposed to be a cauldron of humidity, but they have air-conditioning, surely? And schools, and specialists for Abe – he'd need some transitioning time, but we could manage if—' Even as the words left her lips, Gertie predicted their eldest, Kat, would collapse in a histrionic meltdown if Gertie even suggested their family emigrate to Singapore. *But the formal!*

Ed gently placed his hand across Gertie's lips, and she sat, stunned, mute, beneath his touch. 'It's not just the job, Gert. The job is just a vehicle …'

An excuse I can give to people to camouflage the fact that my rock-solid husband of twenty years is leaving me.

But she would not be told. She was married to a man impressed with logic, persuaded only by facts. He'd do anything for his family. He always had, before this strange mindlessness. He was the sausage-sizzle volunteer at the school fundraiser, the dad who knew which kids had crusts cut off.

Ed's eyes met hers for a millisecond. They were pained and watery, like the day after his company's end of year; tired, but a little relieved that the hard yards were over. Had they too been quantified, like a commodity? Did that broken look on his handsome face say that all the pros and cons of 'us' had been accounted for?

Ed gave his sympathetic head tilt, the one that used to melt her. The one that showed how kind he was. Gertie wondered if she had been naive all this time.

'Is this because of that show with the experiment where the guy takes a marriage vacation – is that what this is?' Gertie wagged her finger at him. 'Being part of the trend?' Ed had never been a follower before. He still wore chambray, for God's sake.

'Gert ...' He took her hand and gave *that* tone, the one usually reserved for disgruntled, blustering staff who were being 'transitioned outside the company'. It had a firm yet empathetic ring, and she had always been a little turned on by it – how it demonstrated the skill he had in finessing people at their worst. Now that he was using it on her, it sounded patronising. 'You haven't been yourself since Christmas. You're not happy. You haven't been happy for a while.'

'I am happy!' Gertie raised her eyebrows and stretched her lips in a manic grin to prove the point, but the tears streaming down on either side of it contradicted her efforts.

'Hon, you're not. You're always tired, stressed about the kids, unwilling to take time out to do anything for yourself or as a couple ...'

Gertie felt the frown arrive with her frustration. 'That's every woman with kids I know. The mental load's a killer. It can be a shit gig!' Half the time she felt as if her role was reversing the kids' mess just so they could make it again.

He hesitated. 'You're on anti-depressants.'

'Just a little one ... and they're for my back pain, I told you.' He was forgetting she'd broken her tailbone birthing Harry and never quite got over it.

'When we have sex, you are somewhere else.'

'No! I'm here! I'm right here!' She paused. 'Is that what this is about? Sex? Because I am open to ramping that up – just the other day Lou was telling me about this weekender—'

'This is not about sex, hon.'

Gertie was a little curvier than when they first married, and she didn't do actual exercise anymore, but her hair was still lush and shiny, her eyes dark and mysterious, and she scrubbed up okay for a nearly-forty-year-old mother of three. Gertie liked sex, she just found there were so many hurdles before getting to it – tiredness, washing piles, kids interrupting – that it always felt like a distant land that was no longer accessible by any means available to her. And when all the planets aligned and they did find themselves there, perhaps she *had* been mentally elsewhere.

One thing she did know for sure was that the tone of their relationship had definitely sullied since moving to Apple Tree, to this haven for Sydney's elite.

Gertie and Eddie Rainworth began married life with two bean bags and her mother's fridge. And yet when slurping two-minute noodles through disposable forks as they recounted the highlights of their day, she'd felt she was the luckiest woman she knew. They'd saved half of what they'd earned from their starter jobs straight from uni until they'd had enough for a deposit on a renovator, two suburbs away from where they wanted to live. It had rising damp and a leaky roof, but it was theirs. Dinners were cold or from a box (Ed had acquired the crusty old microwave from his dorm), but back in her days as a young nurse on her never-ending nightshifts, she'd count the minutes until she could return home and slip into bed beside Ed. In those early days, together in their house that smelled like wet dog, in their bedroom with vomit-yellow carpet, in a twist of cheap sheets, they had been enviably happy.

The set change for the second act of their married life had been unexpected – they'd won a charity prize home from a ticket stuck to a box of Cadbury Roses left for Gertie at the hospital's maternity wing by a patient who came in with suspected appendicitis and left with a newborn. The ward nurses had raided the chocolates but left the ticket among a nest of coloured wrappers. Gertie and Ed joked about those prize homes being pretend fronts for money launderers, that no actual families won nor managed to insert themselves (and their associated clutter) inside those picture-perfect lives.

But they *had*. And they *did*.

Apple Tree Creek Estate was minimalist in style with sharp contemporary lines and monochrome colours. The common area was landscaped to Botanic-Garden standard with contemporary plants like yuccas that had leaves as spiky and glossy as their residents. To Gertie, all that grey, all that formality felt like a prison block. It was carbon neutral, perfectly planned and designed for sustainability, but all that science made Gertie feel like an insect in a bug catcher. Each dwelling reminded her of the Lego villages her boys built, with lawns as artificially green as the baseplates the bricks clung to.

Locals complained when the village got the green light and carved its chromatic palate into the kaleidoscope of cultures that was greater Sydney. Tucked behind an estuary that fed Sydney Harbour, the estate's community boasted ex-PMs, Olympians, Instagram influencers and rock stars. But Gertie hadn't been worried. Before she'd trained as a midwife, she'd changed enough colostomy bags of famous people to know they were every bit as human as everyone else.

Was that the point where things had slowly gone downhill? When they'd moved to 12 Lily Court? How could she have thought – with their clearance-bin clothes and second-hand Tarago – that they'd ever fit in with the hat-wearing Range Rover club? Gertie was so petrified of being judged by the hoity-toity residents that she'd spent a large chunk of the gold bullion that came with the house on posh, impractical, provincial furniture to fill the damn thing. Then there was the 'stylist' who convinced Gertie she looked ravishing in gold shoes and resort wear, all of which had hung gaudily in her closet for years with the tags still on before she had donated it all to the Salvos.

Kat had been an all-knowing twelve, Abe an absconding three and Harry a red-faced bundle in nappies when Ed and

Gertie first visited the prize home in a cloud of disbelief, in awe that it was real.

Was that really five years ago?

The designers hadn't offered a better home. They'd promised a better life. 'What was wrong with our old one?' Ed had questioned. He would have preferred to sell the prize house and put the proceeds in a trust for the kids. 'Statistically, lotto winners are miserable.' Looking back now, he had sported a furrowed brow ever since discovering their windfall.

'We won't be miserable if we're together,' a naive Gertie had declared. Who'd refuse a free house? With a pool you didn't have to inflate before using! Not to mention it came with gardeners resembling jovial chimney sweeps and a security man with a shiny hat.

But a few months in, things hadn't been as glossy as the brochure. The pool cost a fortune to maintain, and unless you paid a fortune extra, the upkeep stopped at the property line. Not that she'd ever admit this to Ed, but Gertie had started to feel – and still felt – a sense of claustrophobia from the thick hedge of dense foliage encompassing the cluster of houses as if they were in an upmarket prison. She also felt something sinister in the dark shadow the hedge cast over her garden, killing her lawn, and a sense of unease in the sameness of the architecture on the estate. Even the interior plans were mirror images of each other. It was rather off-putting – as if her neighbours made tea at *her* sink, slept in *her* room.

Perhaps they'd been happier broke.

But this was where Sydney's elite chose to live – and after growing up in middle-class suburbia, Gertie always felt she had the cheap seats in the nose-bleed section of life. She was curious about what the rich got to experience with backstage passes. Her kids deserved the best. She wanted them to run free in a safe neighbourhood, attend the best schools, and climb in a playground without graffiti and the odd flasher.

'Change always brings growth,' Ed spouted, his voice tugging her back to reality.

Oh, God, it was those self-help books he'd bought from Amazon.

'It's only a twelve-month contract,' Ed said.

'Only!'

'I just thought if I take this job, it'll give you mental space, time to think – maybe even to consider moving out of this pretentious warren. You don't need *me* to be *you*, Gert. I'll make good money overseas, and it'll give you some time to figure out what you really want.'

'*You* are what I want! This *family* staying together is what I want!' Her tone aimed for confident, persuasive, but came out all bluster and bluff.

Could she be herself without Ed? It felt as if every memory she owned included him. Their lives were so intertwined, since childhood, really, when their mothers (nurses too, the both of them) would drink together, toes dipped in the shallow end of the Rainworths' kidney-shaped pool, and when, as teenagers, she and Ed would canoodle in the caravan behind the umbrella tree, acting as if their parents didn't know what they were up to. *I don't know how to be me without you.* 'Even if we're less happy now, we made vows!'

'Life's too short to think like that.'

She could see the weariness in his eyes, and it made her feel distant from him – small and distant from the biggest, most important person in her life. That wasn't a good feeling.

Ed continued. 'You were so deliriously happy in our mouldy old house when the kids were little. Tired, harried, but besotted. The only thing I've ever wanted was to make you happy. I think I did that, for most of our marriage. But not now. Not for a long time. I've accepted that. And if I'm not the person who can do that anymore, I don't want to stand in the way of someone who can.'

Could he seriously be this calm about his wife of twenty years finding someone else, or was this just a clever way to ease his guilt? Then it hit her, and the desperate need to cling to him like Teflon dissipated.

'Who is she?'

His eyes dropped closed, as if they'd reached an expected page of his script. The script he'd written in his head months ago, but had never allowed her to preview.

'You know there isn't anyone else, Gert.'

He was right. She kinda did. If Ed had been off with some other woman there'd be footage by now. The security in this place always seemed excessive for law-abiding citizens. Electronic keys. Apps that automated lights. Security vetting of housekeepers and pool boys and private physicians. Was it really necessary to stream footage of her front door to her mobile (as well as to digital panels all over the house, including near the loo, which the technician had assured her did not look both ways)? And while the urban planners had done a fabulous job secreting the bulbous cameras beneath the leafy hedges that adjoined the properties, Gertie felt they hadn't removed one crucial thing – an unnerving feeling of forever being watched. *Blink, blink, blink.* The irony about security was it robbed you of your sense of privacy. But it did mean she didn't have to worry, didn't it?

Besides, Ed was the same faithful dork he'd always been. Every second away from his family was accounted for – eaten up by work or soccer coaching or chauffeuring kids to their sleepover or karate class. It was physically impossible for him to have managed an affair unless it took place on top of the photocopier in his workplace, and she doubted that. She'd seen his colleagues.

But maybe he was *planning* an affair – in Singapore.

'You're so overwhelmed with the kids' lives, the kids' needs, you have no idea that you've lost yourself,' Ed said.

Gertie inspected her hoodie and threadbare leggings. Her sense of self – what she wore, what she did – was not exactly a priority. That had all changed the moment Kat was placed in her arms seventeen years ago, and it just got more ingrained with each child. Motherhood was a great leveller – any sense of self, vanity or privacy was punctured by kids crawling onto your lap when you peed. Her time was no longer her own. But she'd signed up for that. She was *grateful* for it. Gertie thought of her fertility-challenged sister, and how she'd amputate a limb for just one child.

'Eddie – they *are* me. I made them. Their happiness is my happiness. Their needs do come before mine.' *You can never be happier than your least happy child.* They were her life. Was that so wrong?

He nodded. Still so calm, still so unflappable. He'd rehearsed this for a long time; Gertie was ad-libbing, a manic dry run of a horrific scene she'd never thought she'd be in.

The creases across Ed's brow deepened with pity. 'The crazy thing is that's what makes me love you. That's what makes you such a good person, a good mum.'

But, evidently, a shit wife.

'After a bit of alone time we can regroup, and then focus on what's important – it will be good for us.'

He was talking as if they were eighteen, as if she just needed a nice trip trekking in Cambodia to find herself. *Men.* If anything, he was the one who had been a little off the past few months.

'Us? Don't make abandoning me be about saving *us*. What am I supposed to do when they need lifts here or there all at the same time?'

'That's the thing. With the role in Singapore, I'll be able to afford a housekeeper – a live-in, whatever I need to support my move as GM. It's a cushy job, Gert. Twice the salary—'

'You'll have a replacement to ball your socks – I'm delighted for you.'

'I asked for the allowance to be allocated to help *here* – instead of there.'

'I don't want a housekeeper! I want a husband!' she said between sniffs. 'You haven't got your share of attention? Is that the problem, Ed? Well, sorry if I've been busy raising your children! The children, as I recall, you more than willingly agreed to.'

'This is not forever, Gert. They can visit me. I get three trips a year, free, and my increased salary will pay for extras. I've already booked their flights over. There's a zoo, gardens. I could take Abe and Harry to the grand prix in September ...'

His eyes danced like Gertie hadn't seen in months. Ed was looking forward to this.

Her hand flew to her mouth. 'Oh, God, you're doing this. You're actually doing this.' Sobs pumped from her chest. 'When are you planning to tell the kids you're leaving us?'

Wrinkles gathered on his forehead. 'Gert, don't be like this. I'm not leaving you. I'm changing things up for a bit, seeing what falls out.'

Gertie raised her tear-stained face. 'And what if that's me?'

Chapter 2

Rachael

Two streets east and three gardens down from Gertie and Ed's, at 16 Lavender Lane, the loft window blushed as if everything inside was on fire. It was nearly midnight. Pink-nosed possums balanced on roof peaks, electric cars recharged in their garages and Rachael York left the lights on for her husband.

The lamp in the bedroom revealed a maze of designer furniture, a basket of crisply ironed sheets, and discarded pillows and throws. The scent of lemongrass and Persian lime wafted through the master suite, the oil burner masking the occasional whiff of new paint – a remnant of their renos.

Rachael York lay awkwardly in a twist of bamboo sheets, absentmindedly tracing the darkening line trailing down her growing abdomen. Carefully unwrapped gifts had been stacked high on the desk – ribbons dived over corners as a pale-pink bootie dangled loose from its pair. Her team at Beehive, her recruitment agency, had lavished her with such heartfelt well-wishes she'd cried ugly tears as they'd lugged bundles of rattles and bibs, onesies and throws to her Audi on her last day before maternity leave. She was physically exhausted, but her mind would not rest.

A headache of birthing books, prenatal vitamins and anti-stretch-mark creams cluttered her bedside table. She'd been clock-watching; hours had ticked by since she'd meandered through her nightly routine – stacking the dishwasher, reading six-year-old Noah to sleep and threatening to ban Ethan from the Xbox if he didn't shut it down. She was amazed how they lived in a different place but the daily tasks remained unchanged.

She accepted her fate; pretending she didn't have to pee was futile. She got up, legs wide, her swollen feet directing her towards the en suite. Her stomach fell forward as she lowered herself to sit to pee, forklift-like. Silvery stretch marks slivered down her belly. Not for the first time she wondered why they had paid a fortune for architects to redesign a bathroom with a full-length mirror that insisted she watch herself wee. Her sandy-blonde hair had grown coarse and thick, her cheekbones hidden under a rounded face. Was she too old, at forty, to pull off this pregnancy? Procreating was a young woman's game – that's why nature invented menopause.

The sight of her ridiculous belly, disproportionate to her small frame, overwhelmed her. Why did she marry a tall man with tall-person genes? What maniac designed the human reproductive process? Flashbacks to the magnificent, blinding pain of labour (that they said you'd forget but she never had) collided with this thought and kicked off a spiral of fear. She had no choice now. The baby was in situ, it had to get out. The fact that men become parents without having to physically *make* the humans never seemed so clearly unfair. *Let's have three*, he said. *It'll be fun*, he said. What was she thinking, bringing another child into an unsustainable planet that was melting, a world bubbling with violence and injustice?

Motherhood had never been on Rachael's agenda – too much to go wrong, too much she wasn't up to dealing with. But then she'd met Sam and wanted *Sam's* kids – the full-spectrum experience. She'd bravely ventured into parenting, surprising herself each day she'd kept another human alive and well and flourishing. Why would this time be any different?

Just breathe.

She panted her way through the panic like a contraction and waddled back across the solid oak floors to their lavish king bed. She had no right to feel overwhelmed with all she had. What sort of monster felt ambivalent, had anything but good thoughts about motherhood?

Sam should have been home hours ago. She didn't know why he'd agreed to the job now that he was coaching again. Maybe it was smart to milk his glory days – Sam being offered work as a keynote speaker had petered out as his notoriety had waned. In a similar way, it sometimes felt as if their marriage was living off the fumes of their earlier feats.

Their first kiss wasn't on the lips. Their first date wasn't dinner and a movie. Nothing about Sam and Rachael's relationship was the norm. They'd met at a charity ball; Sam devilishly handsome in black tie and Rachael in an emerald-green dress that set off her warm eyes. Broad, tall and perfectly proportioned, his charm and good looks had made him seem pretend, like a superhero figurine, not a living, breathing soul. Yet he'd lacked the arrogance and guardedness she'd come to expect from successful men.

When at one point she'd dragged herself free from his adoration, she'd googled him in a bathroom stall and discovered he was a professional athlete, a world-record-holding swimmer, training for the next Olympics in London. Seeing the red brick mansion with lavish green spaces in the background of the shot from his English childhood, she'd pegged him as a trust-fund kid with portraits instead of photos, housekeepers instead of

15

cleaners. By contrast, Rachael had practically raised herself on a farm, waking to the mew of dairy cows desperate to be milked and the sun peeking through the splintery sleepout slats. Hers had been a childhood in which weevils in the flour were expected and the weather controlled their fortune – her idea of luxury was scoring the bath before her brother peed in it.

She couldn't help but gape at his eyelashes (women would die for lashes that long), let alone the eyes beneath them. When he'd offered himself as a prize for the cerebral palsy charity auction they were drinking in aid of, Beehive made the winning bid.

'I'm sure having those biceps to help landscape the gardens at our new all-abilities playground will create a bit of publicity,' Rachael recalled announcing when she'd won the winning bid.

Sam had fobbed off the acquaintances interrupting their flirtatious chatter as they enjoyed a champagne at the bar, and it had felt as if she were the only woman in the world. Rachael had been sure it was just infatuation. She could see why those shoulders had graced the cover of men's health magazines, why that smile had gained sponsorship from the leading dental brand. Something about him had brought on a heady feeling and made Rachael want him immediately – not sex in broader terms, but his body, his smell, his lips.

He'd kissed her on the throat, and that had been the end of her.

He'd raised the partition between their limo driver and the back seat on the way to the hotel and warned Rachael that he was on the tail end of a messy relationship, that he came with a host of complications, that the online rumours about him were mostly true, and she'd admired his directness, his honesty. She'd also known she'd rather die than stop.

It wasn't until her silk dress had made a puddle of emerald on the carpet of the nearest five-star hotel that Rachael had believed it was actually going to happen. That this tall, perfect specimen of a man had chosen her – a drought-stricken farmer's daughter from out west. The newness, his physicality, the sheer want in her had created a flush of almost intolerable need.

Rachael had sunk deeper under his spell as they'd revealed secrets through the night. He'd shared his memories of boyhood in the quaint green knolls of country England before moving to Australia. The way he'd spoken about family, his traditional values and respect for his parents had made her swoon. Within weeks, she'd found herself enamoured of him. Their love-bubble was obvious even to strangers. They'd quickly eloped, despite Rachael's reputation as a discerning businesswoman. As a team their careers skyrocketed; their notoriety exploded.

As their relationship blossomed, she noticed his points of difference from previous partners. Her needs always came first in the bedroom. Sam would habitually walk on the roadside of the footpath to protect her. He loved to buy her designer clothes, and would set them out before a special event. She let him order at restaurants – he knew far more about food and nutrition. His focus felt chivalrous but his prowess between the sheets was anything but gentlemanly.

Being with Sam had made Rachael feel more feminine. She loved having a man take charge. She had always been the responsible one, even as a child, and in adulthood every business decision for her company rested on her shoulders. The magic settled over their relationship that first year like a protective shield.

All these years later, Rachael still felt gushes of those early love-drunk days, that all-encompassing sense that nothing else mattered. She'd put up with almost anything to stay in Sam's arms. Which was lucky, as he'd tested every boundary since.

Rachael consulted the security panel next to their bed – Sam's favourite gadget since they'd moved to the estate a few weeks ago. The screensaver was a picturesque shot of the oleander flanking Apple Tree Creek's gates beneath a glorious sunset. She navigated to the menu and clicked on 'home security'. Her husband's black Porsche GT3 was not parked tandem to her Audi. An eerie quiet settled over the house. She double-checked the alarm was activated in all sectors.

Apple Tree Creek. The name had attracted Rachael to the estate. It conjured images of wholesomeness, of vine-ripened fruit weighing down branches, crisp red apples firm to the bite and children wading in slow-flowing streams. It wasn't exactly quaint, but it was elegant and well designed, marketed as a luxurious, eco-friendly haven. It boasted world-class security, which was what her husband had wanted (for Sam to keep tabs on her, she'd joked to the salesman), yet they would be enveloped in a bubble of successful entrepreneurs – free of the riffraff best left outside.

What was left of the namesake orchards was a triangular grove boasting three varieties of apples and various fruit trees. The meticulous elegant gardens and vine-tangled surrounding fences made you feel as if you were inside a snow globe, sealed off, protected from the evils of the world. Rachael and Sam had had the delusion that no harm could come to anyone in the vicinity of those fruit-laden shrubs, behind those iron gates. And that was exactly what the York family had needed back then, with everything.

Since the move, her six-year-old, food-obsessed Noah was winning hearts at his new primary school and Ethan was topping Year 10 advanced maths at St Aquinas College. Sam had even landed a teaching job at the same school, much to Ethan's disgust. As an already awkward adolescent, all elbows and knees, Ethan avoided attention as a rule, and tried not to mention he was related to the PE teacher (he considered e-sport the only activity worth his time).

Sam's mother's Nordic genes were as dominant as his backstroke pull, and both Ethan and Noah had inherited his colouring. Rachael loved the boys' distinct eyes – hazel with flecks of amber and gold – that were as complex and enchanting as starlight in a desert.

Rachael thought back to their first night in the estate – she had wanted to unpack boxes, but Sam had found his dreaded spud gun in the move and had decided to make the evening memorable. He'd plodded around the small square of golf-course green lawn, covered from head to toe in protective gear, barely recognisable beneath one of the kids' stackhats and with cricket pads strapped on each limb to shield him from random flying potatoes.

Noah had been whingeing, 'How come Ethe always gets the good jobs?'

Sam had told Rachael she was a 'fun sponge' when she'd enforced strict safety instructions, demanding their six-year-old be nowhere near the PVC pipe when (a face-shield-wearing) Ethan sealed it off with a spud, filled it with deodorant and exploded the accelerant with a lighter. A roar and the spud had shot into the air at incredible speed.

'It's not fair! Ethan always gets to do it,' Noah had yelled at his father, ducking and weaving like a footballer as he anticipated the landing. 'He's your favourite child!'

'That's not true, Noah – I dislike all my children equally,' Sam had said straight-faced.

'You're mean. You don't even like us!' Noah had harumphed.

Rachael had narrowed her eyes at Sam's black humour. Her husband had made a beeline for his son, scooped the kid up on his shoulders with the prowess of a lead danseur, and had him in a fit of giggles within seconds.

'You know I love you, fart face.'

Ethan was reloading the spud gun, new muscles tensing in his biceps. 'Ready?' His voice was a little croaky, changing from boy to man like the rest of him. He grew more like Sam every day and was already wearing his dad's Nikes, but thankfully he hadn't inherited his overblown daredevil attitude.

'This is not the time to aim for your little brother, Ethe. Or my balls.' Sam had ducked as another potato shot into the air with a pop then crash-landed on the deck, splattering into lumpy mash.

Boof#2 — named after their original spoodle with curls that made him seem fat instead of furry — had galloped eagerly towards the mess. With a few slurps of his pink tongue, he'd licked it up, which had suited Rachael as she'd loafed on the hammock.

'Okay, E-man, fire her up again. C'mon, ya wuss. Be a real man and get serious with these shots, huh?'

Ethan had cringed at the macho name-calling his dad liked to dish out. Rachael blamed it on Sam's competitive ego, on playing in England's grassy meadows with his toff-nosed friends. His family had immigrated to Canberra's Institute of Sport when he was a promising thirteen-year-old, but he'd never quite lost the boy from Surrey. Rachael had hauled her pregnant-self out of the hammock and taken Noah's shoulders, directing him away from the gas lighter Ethan was clicking to ignite.

'What could possibly go wrong?' Rachael had said, waving away the musky smell of the Tommy Hilfiger body spray escaping from the pipe.

'You know you love it!' Sam's tawny eyes had locked with hers as he'd darted about on the grass like a peacock and planted a kiss on her cheek. All his faults melted away when he looked at her that way.

A hum, like a giant mosquito, had distracted her — she'd thought it was a remote-control toy at first, but realised it was a drone circling above their roof.

'Oh, that must be the six pm security patrol.'

'Should I aim for it?' Ethan had smiled, lining up the flying object with the pipe. His school shorts had looked ridiculous, too short for his ever-extending legs.

Rachael had glared her reply.

Sam had raised his eyes to the darkening sky. 'Reckon mooning the drone would be against body-corp regulations? They've got rules for every other bloody thing.'

'What's mooning?' Noah had asked.

Rachael shook her head. This was why they were in the tabloids so much — this streak of mischief she couldn't rein in. Life was never boring with Sam York.

'Last spud, Dad,' Ethan had called, lighting the pipe filled with aerosol. It had roared alight and propelled the spud high in the air.

'Strike three!' Sam had called.

Noah had cheered.

'I see all that shooting practice online hasn't helped your aim, son.'

Ethan had given him the finger.

'Just joshing, cobber.' As Sam had grabbed his first-born in a headlock, Rachael had taken a mental picture of the first night of their new beginning. Things were going to be different here.

But right now, she feared the loneliness that had plagued her at their last house had followed her.

The electric garage door thrummed. A moment later, six foot six inches of Sam York stumbled up the loft stairs, perched on the edge of their bed and loosened his tie. His thick, wavy hair, always ad-worthy, grazed his collar.

'How'd it go, Sam?'

He flicked off both shoes in quick succession before he stilled and pressed his thumbs into his closed lids. Tears flowed.

'Hon?' Air was sucked from her lungs as if she'd been winded. As soon as the light cast on his features, Rachael knew. It wasn't the first time she'd seen that look of all-consuming guilt. A cloud of dread swooped in on her.

'Blimey, Rach. I'm such a rubbish husband.' Those hazel eyes met hers with the sincerity of a mother's kiss. 'And you're amazing. I don't deserve you.'

She wished she hadn't waited up. She wished she could delay this moment even for just one day. She knew what was coming – her partner of over a decade had racked up another affair while she'd waited expectantly at home, growing his child inside her.

'Don't say it.' Her chin wobbled as she shook her head. She told herself she was wrong. She was happy to dig her head down deeper, forage for air beneath the sand.

But he went on with his truth. It had started with a leggy Californian and ended in a parking lot.

Rachael felt numb, as if he was discussing somebody else, but at the same time, knew it to be real, the details ringing true. Hadn't she expected this, marrying a charmer like Sam? Wouldn't she have left him the first time if it wasn't for the scandal that would follow, the fallout for the kids, for her business? Her feminist friends liked to judge women who stayed with men who strayed, but adultery was never as simple as it appeared from the outside.

'I'm a weak bastard, an utter prick.' His attempts to swear beneath his upper-class accent usually made her laugh, but not now. 'I have no excuse.' The agony on his face matched the despair in his words.

He was a contradiction; he had the determination to swim fifty k's a week for half his life, to push past thresholds of pain despite the lactic acid burning through every muscle, but somehow he couldn't find the strength to say no to a drunken party-girl.

She hated what her husband's athletic career had done to him, the obsessive routines and rituals when he was competing, the depression that plagued him after retirement. Once deemed *Cleo* magazine's 'Bachelor of the Year', the gold medallist's fall from grace was quick and painful, the unsustainable drug-like highs making the dreary existence of real life afterwards almost unliveable.

Rachael was so glad Ethan showed no interest in following in his father's footsteps. Ethan had always hated water; the drips felt like worms on his skin, he'd said.

Sam went on. 'And you, here, building our baby, taking care of our boys … I'm so sorry, Rach. I deserve a good bollocking.'

Sorry was just something he said to expunge his guilt. It didn't help her.

'Please forgive me. I need this. I need you.' He hesitated as he reached out to rest his hands gently on her swollen belly. He was co-creator and part owner of what grew inside – more than likely another golden-haired, perfect child. She couldn't find it in her to ask him to remove his touch, but neither could she offer support or forgiveness.

'Say something. Anything …' He noticed the pile of unwrapped gifts on the table. 'Oh, Christ, and it was your last day – how was your shower thing?'

She shook her head at his change of tone.

'Everything's going to be better now you've stopped work – more time for us.'

Stopped work? Running Beehive was the one thing she felt good at, the place she felt respected and valued. Her eyes narrowed, and she was unable to simulate the back-and-forth banter of any ordinary day.

Was this man, who only weeks earlier had been playing with their sons, throwing her a kiss as the dog tracked circles around the yard, the same man who now risked losing it all for sex with a stranger?

Rachael knew a better woman would demand better treatment. Would slap him, scream a torrent of abuse, evict his cheating, athletic arse. Yet all those options required so much emotional energy, and she was sick to death of being responsible.

The weight of the baby pressed on her lungs was suffocating. It felt as if her cerebellum was not receiving the energy to process words, and yet she tasted the salt from the tears gathering in the corners of her lips, as if her brain had computed the feelings without her permission.

She tried to conjure up thoughts of the charming blond bachelor she'd first met at that charity ball over a decade ago; the memory was yellowing in the corners like an old portrait, morphing into something more stifling than supportive.

His voice sucked her back to their room. To their life, in meltdown.

'I've just been driving around, knowing I couldn't bear coming home without telling you the truth. I know I'm a shit who evidently can't keep it in his pants, but the one thing I've always been is honest. And I'll do anything to make this right.'

This was his usual MO to smooth over the damage, but this time Rachael resented his attempt to dress up his betrayals as opportunities to showcase his devotion. This whole dreadful night, pacing around the loft, lights blaring, thoughts swirling, felt dreamlike. Staged. He sat upright, his face crestfallen, and waited for her reaction as if his world depended on it. Was the concern in his eyes an act, or did he really care? Which version was the real Sam?

They had moved here with the boys to escape this sort of scandal, not create a shinier, newer one for the media to feast on like hawks. She should hate him now. But hate took energy. And Rachael didn't have the emotional bandwidth.

She heard his breath catch as he waited for her response.

It was a rare moment where she held the reins, but she didn't want them.

'I'm tired, Sam,' was all that came out.

Chapter 3

Gertie

Gertie Rainworth's plan for getting through the week until Ed's departure to Singapore was avoid, avoid, avoid. When she *had* to see him, lurking in hallways, reheating dinner late in the evening, she seesawed between a pride-induced facade of being fabulous and unaffected in the hope he'd be impressed with her stoic resilience and change his mind, to a sneering cow reciting all the outstanding chores he had to do before she'd approve his leave pass. The strategy served her well until his boss granted him a couple of days off – big of him, considering her husband was unsubscribing from his life to relocate for the damn position – and Ed spent them flitting around her faintly concealed misery, fixing all the niggly jobs in readiness for his abandonment.

Gertie had never felt so torn. Part of her wanted to lunge at him with the shovel, which was waiting patiently for him on the lawn, to see how his head looked from the inside out. The other part was desperate to please him, fetch his favourite dinner, make him stay. He was the only man she'd ever loved, and he was leaving.

To make matters worse, they hadn't told the kids. Gertie had to pretend life was peachy and cycle through the daily grind as if nothing had shattered her core. It was like attempting to sip tea during a tsunami warning. She'd distracted her way through the week, ushering her raven-haired crew in and out of their Tarago.

Abe was Gertie's middle child, obsessed with emergency vehicles and garbage trucks, and who had a habit of saying inappropriate things at the worst possible time. With eyes as dark as his hair and a love of structure and logic, he had a sense of justice beyond his eight years. As long as Gertie stuck to his routine, managed transitions, made sure he was home to direct bin-collection day in their cul-de-sac and had a ready supply of toy cars and Itty-Bitty Bin bribery fodder, they managed. There was the fact that Abe only ate food that had not touched other food but Gertie was just relieved he ate something, unlike Harry.

Cyclone Harry, the youngest (and unquestionably the last Rainworth) was kind by default, had eyes full of mischief, and a perpetual rash of bruises down his shins. Stick thin, the Ritalin that aligned the tangle of paths in his mind to one manageable freeway worked a treat on his focus but destroyed his appetite. She'd barely seen him eat anything but white food for years. If Kat was the good girl who allowed her the confidence to be a good mum, Harry was the child who taught her not to judge other mothers.

Gertie's survival strategy was to tire Harry out with sport. So there she sat on the sticky bench at the school tennis centre, the faint funk of soggy sandwiches and old apple wafting from the bin, with all the other mothers trying the 'Exhaust Them into Submission' tactic.

Harry's eyes were cloaked under his cap, his arm stretching his racquet determinedly as he aimed for the ball and missed. It was Tuesday. And this was what Gertie did each and every Tuesday, marriage crisis or not.

'Next one, Harry!' Gertie had been saying that for years but still hadn't heard the ping of ball on string except once by accident – mid-sneeze.

Katerina Rainworth dawdled down from the senior school to sprawl herself on the rug, texting friends she'd only just left. She was headstrong but usually malleable, dark and lean like a young Sophia Loren. She sat with an elegance that, together with her love of high-necked vintage blouses, historical romance novels and high drama, made Gertie think she was born in the wrong century. Her glossy, dark hair was still perfectly tussled in a high topknot hovering over her head like a halo, her school shoes flung on the grass. Gertie envied her daughter's youth as her back ached from the hard bench. *Oh, to be seventeen again. To have unworn vertebrae cartilage and a pelvic floor.*

Kat pulled out a micro earbud to converse with her mother. She even made eye contact, so it must have been important. 'Mum,' she said, 'I've run out of art paper. The good stuff, like Aunty Lulu got me.'

Gertie rolled her eyes. Her super-organised sister was great at gifts. She had the knack of knowing what people wanted, where to find it and also had the budget to fund it.

As if she had heard her niece utter her name, Louise Underwood's face flashed on Gertie's mobile with all her cheekbones and perfection.

'Hey, Gert. Can you talk? I always catch you multitasking.'

That's because I always am. 'No, all good,' Gertie said, fearing this meant she'd actually have to say the words 'Ed is leaving' out loud.

Louise Underwood was three years older than Gertie and a sought-after criminal lawyer. But despite this success, she still rang her sister every few days with a list of life choices she seemed to need Gertie to approve before Lou accepted her selections were solid. Gertie was always suspicious of why Lou felt Gertie was qualified to do this.

The crowded frenzy of bell time had dwindled to dawdlers and path-kickers and worries of why Abe hadn't made it down from the Year 2 block. She zoned back in to her sister. Tilers. Plaster dust. Rain delays.

'The renos sound hectic, Lou ... but just picture you and Tim in that marbled double shower together when it's all finished, huh?' Meanwhile, Gertie had to be content with a bathtub of suspiciously mouldy squirt toys and a toilet that greeted her with a child's last deposit eyeing her from the bowl. But she wouldn't swap them. Well, perhaps she would swap them for versions of them who flushed.

The phone went quiet.

'Lou? You there? You okay?'

Despite insisting that she was, her sister began making a wheezing sound.

Gertie exhaled, feeling Lou's sadness infiltrate her bones. 'What is it, hon? Has something happened?'

Silence. Lou's soundless sobs as a kid were always a signal that she was about to blow. Gertie could see her, that pink doona gathered to her chin, trying not to cry as their parents fought down the hall. It had taught her to cry noiselessly. To find love with men that were easygoing – they both had learned that one.

'Lulu?' Gertie's mind ticked through the possibilities. The date. It was the last week of the month. The last week ... 'Oh, Lou. Aunty Flo came to stay?'

Silence, but she knew.

'Oh, hon, that cow. She knows she's no longer bloody invited.' *Oh, God, why'd I have to say 'bloody'.*

Lou's petite little sobs grew more audible.

'I'm so sorry, Lou. I can only imagine how heart-wrenching it is each month.'

Tim and Louise had been trying to conceive for years. Each luckless cycle hit them like a bus. Gertie noticed extreme moods in her sister when invited to gender-reveals or first birthdays; her lips would thin when exposed to evidence of other people's ability to procreate and jealous moods followed.

'The doctors told you nothing was broken – these things can just take time.'

'Not for you! And wouldn't we have the same egg factory? If I died tomorrow without being a mum, I'd be gutted.'

Since Lou's difficulty conceiving, Gertie had become so conscious of how much of her own self-image was linked to motherhood. How that level of love had changed her. And how the most well-meaning enquiry from acquaintances of 'so no plans to start a family?' left her sister broken inside. It was like mourning the loss of her dreams every twenty-eight days. Ironically, Gertie looked around at a crowd of mothers as they ushered tired children to their lessons, lathered them in sunscreen and retrieved lost hats, probably dreaming of pre-children days where their time was their own and not prioritised by the needs of their offspring, before they surrendered to self-sacrifice.

Kat pulled at Gertie's sleeve and whispered a suggestion that maybe she could drop her at the cool art store while Harry was playing and pick her up after, but Gertie shook her away in a half-headlock, half-hug, as she tried to hear Lou's pain. She spied Harry, slumped at the back of the line of fidgety, sweaty minions, met his eyes and saw they were a little sunken in the middle. She'd missed his shot. She'd mentally battled with her selves – the version of her that thought Harry had to be more resilient to function as an independent unit and not expect praise for every swing of his arm, and the other, marshmallow version that wanted to savour his sweetness, pad out his confidence any way she could before the cruel world sank its sharp teeth into him, her big-hearted, scrawny-legged Energizer bunny.

As Gertie continued to reassure Lou that all was not lost, that she had plenty of eggs waiting for their chance to become annoying little brats, she noticed Abe finally stomp towards the courts, backpack firm on his shoulders, hat square on his head. Everything had to be symmetrical and orderly in his life. Relieved, Gertie gave him a wave, but his mind was elsewhere. Probably counting cars. Probably oblivious to her. He threw his bag down on their picnic rug, evicted a few rogue ants and opened his scrapbook. It was like a pacifier. He flicked through pages of an array of vehicles (garbage trucks featured prominently). Transitioning from school to home was never easy, but having to resort to his comfort book already was not a good sign.

Louise's tone had morphed from pathetic misery to mildly paranoid. 'Maybe it's just the universe's way of telling us we're not meant to be parents.'

'Hon, shitty people are given babies every day, unvetted – that's not it.' Gertie may have been a midwife, but she also saw kids as being a bit like podcasts – just because they were easy to create didn't mean everyone should have one.

'Mum said shitty!' Abe called, pointing at her. 'No device time for Mum!'

The one time he'd listened. Gertie tuned one ear to focus back on her kids. Kat was placating Abe.

'Anyway, what happened today that was so bad?' Kat asked him.

Abe's lip quivered. The details came out in a torrent. 'The teacher told me to sit on the responsible-thinking chair for not sharing. I did what she said, but when they got back from break, she put me in trouble, anyway!'

'Wait,' Kat said to her brother, her face in a twist, 'you sat there through lunch?'

Abe's brow furrowed. 'She told me to stay there, so I did.'

'You didn't think to get up when everyone else left the classroom?' Kat asked.

'She said to stay until she said so! I thought I'd get put in more trouble!' Abe said, his dark brow furrowed.

'You're such a noob.' Kat ruffled his hair – another thing only his big sister could get away with.

Gertie's chest felt full as she pressed the confused eight-year-old into her side, her ear sweaty beneath the phone as she tuned back into Lou's voice.

'Look on the bright side – you can drink! Come round later for a wine. Didn't want to say anything, but you're a bit of a pain sober, anyway.'

'Ha-ha.' Lou's tone was lighter. 'Tim is taking me out to that new French place on the river for dinner.'

Gertie pictured it in her pipe dreams. A nice, quiet dinner without children. Gertie was jealous, yearned for just a speck of that sort of autonomy in her life.

When she released Abe from her arms his eyes were dark and steely. It was too late. He'd triggered. He started repetitively bashing one palm against his cheek and rocking himself in a rhythm. That lasted a few seconds, like a warm-up before his limbs had him bolting through the carpark. Teaching staff were huddled in scrums, venting about their troublesome students as he sprinted past, broad-shouldered, with elegant Kat sprinting after him.

Harry's tennis had finished, and he'd teleported to Gertie's knee, tugging her shirt. 'I got the ball, Mum! I got it in the right box, and you missed it!'

As Gertie patted Harry's head and apologised, brakes screeched as a car swerved in the main entry as Abe scuttled out of school grounds. Her breath caught.

'Lou, I've gotta go. The kids are out of control, drama fifty-five for the day.'

Lou huffed, and Gertie heard the resentment lurking inside it. 'You don't know how lucky you are, you know that?'

'Seriously?' Gertie exhaled. 'You don't know how lucky *you* are. Lulu — your time is your own. You can work. You can sleep in. You can spend all your money on shoes and marble toilets …' She scanned the street for Abe as she gathered up water bottles and hats. She couldn't even argue with her sister in peace.

'You're *so* ungrateful!' Lou said sullenly. 'You have everything you've always wanted — you won a house and retired in your thirties, stoic Ed at your side, three healthy babies without even trying. Sounds like it turned out okay to me.'

Gertie scoffed. 'Spare me the lecture on how children are a blessing, Miss Hot Shot Lawyer. You totally don't see what you have in your life either, Lulu. You got exactly what you always wanted — a career, a devoted man. Go enjoy champagne worth more than my grocery budget and have a romantic dinner with your hot husband.' Gertie turned away from her two remaining kids and lowered her voice. 'Meanwhile, I can't even keep mine in the country!'

Her sister paused as if planning her next offence, but then Gertie's words must have sunk in. 'What are you talking about?'

Gertie felt a surge of regret expand in her chest. 'I just have my own dramas right now — Abe playing on the road for one — and I don't have time for yours. I've got to go.'

Loading up school bags, racquet and rug, Gertie caught up to Kat and Harry and they proceeded to search the street for

Abe as if they were in a wonky conga line. Gertie towed Harry up the hill, feeling like a mother chimp at the zoo.

Where the hell are you, Abe?

'He wouldn't have gone this far – we're halfway home,' said Kat. 'And the art shop closes at four!'

'Can we stop now?' Harry whined. 'Where's the car?'

'Monkey breath, Mum parked back at school, we're looking for Abe. He's just having another Abe moment.' Kat rolled her eyes.

'Like when Mum messed up his car line and put them back wrong and he started breaking stuff?' Harry recalled.

Gertie patted his head. 'Yeah, we don't need to think about that day right now, hon.' Or all the others like it. Gertie had learned that parenting lesson swiftly – take detailed photos of the precise layout of Abe's precious toy cars before attempting to vacuum carpet, and never underestimate a kid on the spectrum – Abe had a photographic memory.

It had been twelve long minutes of searching. Did she call the police now? Set up a roadblock? Provide a recent picture?

Three minutes later, Gertie was making promises with the devil. *I'll give up wine and chocolate for him to be found unharmed. I'll do anything.*

'What are we doing again?' Harry asked, skipping ahead like a Mexican jumping bean.

'Looking for your brother. Abe ran out of the school grounds alone and you know that's not okay.'

He stopped in his miniature tracks. 'No, he didn't – he was helping Mr Newman. With the bins.'

Now it was her turn to stop. 'The bins?'

'He likes to line them up. You know, like the cars?'

Kat and Gertie looked at each other, then turned the convoy back in the direction of Hillside Primary (thankfully downhill) and there he was, her middle child, standing in the side street flanking the oval, helping the janitor roll out the wheelie bins. As they drew closer, she heard Abe's monologue droning on about the decision by council to change to single-purpose refuse vehicles, and the eco-friendly benefits of the fleet.

The janitor, in his fluoro vest and steel-cap boots, nodded at Abe, as if he was fascinated by the history of the garbage truck. 'I never knew that.' He lifted his eyebrows at Gertie as they approached, seemingly a little relieved that he'd found an owner for this particularly chatty lost property. 'Smart kid you've got here.'

'Yes, he is,' Gertie said, placing her arm around Abe's shoulder. 'Hon – you okay? We were worried.' The darkness had left Abe's eyes. His pupils had returned to their usual kind, intelligent way.

'They weren't straight. The bins. And it was only getting worse, so I helped him bring them down from A Block.' His voice was smooth, unhurried. The bin-mustering had calmed him.

'Okay, hon. All good now? Let's get home, huh?' It was five past four. 'Sorry, Kitty-Kat, we won't get the paper today. Can we try before school?'

'S'okay ...' Kat moaned. 'Hashtag used to it.'

An empty feeling Gertie couldn't quite label had troubled her all through dinner. She'd called Lou back after Taco Tuesday (all the weekdays had a set menu as there were limited meals Abe ate).

'Sorry-I-was-a-cow.' It had come out one-syllabelled, she'd said it so quickly.

35

'Already knew you were one,' her sister had replied.

But Gertie had heard the smile in her voice. Not for the first time, she'd found comfort in the no-bullshit nature of their sibling relationship. Even if part of her wanted to return to that time when pissing off your sibling was considered the Ultimate Achievement (with bonus points), not something that ruined your dinner with guilt.

Then Gertie had said the dreaded words out loud. 'Ed's leaving me.'

Lou had let the pause run on, sworn, then promised to be there in thirty minutes.

She'd made it in twenty. Harry and Abe were butting heads on the trampoline with Nacho, their salt-and-pepper wiry-haired mixed breed barking in delight when she arrived. The dog loved Lou best despite her mostly ignoring him. Gertie wondered if the same concept could apply to parenting. Meanwhile, Gertie left Ed with the dishes (first rubbing her cutlery straight in the taco sauce on her dirty plate for his benefit) and vented the story of the end of her marriage over warm goon.

'How do I explain it to the kids?' Gertie stage-whispered to Lou.

'Oh, Gert, kids are more resilient than you think with big stuff. That Easter camping with you lot taught me that. It's when you cut toast the wrong way that they crumble. They'll be more independent, and Ed will come back more appreciative, you wait.'

Gertie hadn't actually tried to consider the positives. She preferred her blame-Ed-and-drink-with-self-pity strategy. 'You think?'

Lou held her hand. 'I was your bridesmaid, remember. Never seen someone so besotted stupid in my life as that brainless dork.'

'Why do you two always think I can't hear you out there?' Ed called from the kitchen, a tea towel in his hand and an arched brow on his face.

They glanced inside, then at each other.

'He'll do his man-thing, and he'll be back. I mean, look at you!'

Wine spurted from Gertie's nose as she considered the soft-edged, greying-templed woman she'd become. Once a feisty midwife who loved a night out in hairspray and heels, Birkenstocks and tinted sunscreen were now her staples.

'You try your best to understate it, but I'm afraid your natural beauty shines through – it's infuriatingly unfair,' Lou continued.

'It's probably for the best he'll be gone soon. If that man leans on my kitchen bench another minute, chatting about how many flamingos live in Singapore Zoo, I swear I'll plunge that BBQ fork straight into his thick thigh.'

Lou's laughter deflated Gertie's rising fear for a moment, before she felt the hurt again, heavy in her gut.

On the day of Ed's abandonment, the suitcases were Gertie's undoing – lined up so neatly, so smugly on the drive. She'd bought those suitcases dreaming of a Canadian adventure – not for her husband to fill to the brim as he vacated their life. Ed's bags were as eager as he was to escape the place, the kids a wall of cuddles behind them. *Traitors.* The bastard had finessed the kids so well they barely baulked when the Uber arrived on the morning of his departure.

'But you'll be back for soccer on Saturday. Right, Dad?' Harry asked.

Ed patted his son on the head awkwardly then gazed at Gertie and mouthed, 'Sorry.'

'See you at the Grand Prix!' Harry called, his voice jumping as much as his feet, before hugging Ed's leg with all four limbs and his mouth, a signature drool mark remaining on Ed's pants.

It was clear Ed was torn about leaving them – gutted, in fact – but he also had a sparkle in his eye Gertie hadn't seen since he'd hauled his pack on his shoulders at the airport the day after their final uni exams. He was starting an adventure without them, writing a chapter of his life where their names would not be mentioned.

Gertie couldn't find the strength to look her husband of twenty years in the eyes as he said goodbye. She was too busy seething, too busy trying to make the gritted-teeth expression her jaw was doing involuntarily look like a smile for the kids' sakes.

'Remember, you don't need me to be you,' said Ed.

'Don't make this out to be about me,' Gertie mumbled as he was driven away. *When is anything about me?*

Three days after Ed left, Gertie woke to bickering crows and an empty bed. Her brain, on autopilot, explained Ed's absence by reassuring herself that he'd simply risen early to take Nacho for his walk, before the truth hit like a jet – her husband didn't live there anymore.

The reality kicked her chest, lead-footing the accelerator on her heart, lacing her blood with adrenalin. Her breaths turned rapid, her throat tightened, and a heaviness invaded her thoughts. After the initial panic, ugly sobs started. Gertie told herself she was owed a brief interlude of complete collapse.

Ten minutes to wallow in private before she'd don the Wonder Woman facade and get on with it. On with it – this life, these kids, alone. Gertie felt trapped. With parents interstate, and Ed as good as dead to her, she had sole responsibility for these kids' lives.

Of course, it was far better than Ed actually being dead. From the outside world, the day would unfold as any other. Ed still earned the money and she still used it to pay the bills. She still managed the day-to-day teeth-cleaning rituals and lost school hats. For the most part, the scaffold of her life was still intact. Perhaps she could focus on that? What did Ed *really* contribute in person other than be someone to help with the dishes and loaf next to her misquoting rom-com lines while she fell asleep watching Netflix?

Except he did provide more. His long fingers rubbed her frozen shoulder till it mobilised, he'd let her pilfer the best-flavoured squares out of the block of Snack chocolate as he'd listen to her monologues and long lists of misdemeanours the world fired at her. Frustrations that would now stay within to fester and rot her soul.

It hadn't taken long for Abe to realise the September Grand Prix was a lot longer to wait to see his father than he'd thought and he'd started a spreadsheet to count the hours. Gertie didn't know whether to be alarmed or proud. Harry was in shock when he discovered the six centimetres Singapore sat apart from Australia on the globe was six thousand kilometres in reality, as was Kat when she realised she didn't have her usual all-hours taxi service only a text away.

It was night when the loneliness fell, like a blanket that starved you of breath and cut out the light. The moan of timber beams contracting in the cool night air, the hissing of possums, territorial in the lilly pillies lining the front yard – suburban sounds Gertie was sure had been a nightly ritual, but were now insidious threats to more than her sleep. Regardless of the estate's ridiculous level of security, every niggling noise was a potential intruder, a signal of an imminent risk to her family, and there she was, lying frozen in her king-sized bed, hero-less.

When pangs of heartbreak blindsided her, she'd shun them away. What sort of woman pined for a man who considered leaving the country a treatment for whatever was lacking in their marriage? In *her*? Their favourite wedding photo – a candid shot of a younger them gazing at each other as they glided out of the church – now sprang from the hallway wall demanding attention each time she passed with arms full of folded T-shirts. Ed was right. All of a sudden, Gertie felt pathetic. She'd become an epiphyte, relying on Ed for support.

She didn't know how to survive without it.

Chapter 4

Rachael

Rachael found her Audi steering itself towards the office again. She couldn't face her empty house after dropping Noah and Ethan at school, or spending another hour aimlessly wandering in the cloud of indecision that had been monopolising her thoughts since Sam's confession. Work was the only thing she could rely on. Her marriage clearly needed triaging, but she feared the prognosis.

Sam wanted her to have a break from the hands-on management of her company, told her that family took priority. Rachael simply turned off her phone's location settings and failed to mention the visits. What he didn't know wouldn't hurt him.

There was a duck-egg blue Fiat in the last of Beehive's designated car spots, sitting in the speckled shade. It was strange, seeing another car in her space. As the doors of Beehive opened and she scanned the office, it was even stranger to see another woman warming her office chair. But there was the lovely acting CEO, tapping her keyboard, sipping tea from Rachael's polka-dot cup.

Ever since Sam had admitted to having sex with another woman (again), Rachael had been re-evaluating her life choices, trying to pinpoint when things had gone wrong. Had she selfishly spent too much time at this place? She had breastfed Noah from that chair while teleconferencing clients, missed a fistful of 'firsts' chained to that desk, that dream. Yet, observing the buzz in the Beehive office now, a week into her maternity leave, business was booming. The copier still running. The phone still being answered.

'Did you forget you're on leave, girl?' Gail, the acting CEO, joked.

Rachael felt foolish when they shuffled papers about to clear a space for her.

'I know everything's in safe hands, just thought I'd see how things are going ...' Rachael didn't recognise her voice, meek and quiet.

'Sure, ah, is everything okay? You just look a little ... windswept,' Annie, Rachael's old PA asked. Nothing got past Annie.

Gail and Annie swapped furtive glances.

Rachael looked down and realised she was wearing leggings, a moth-eaten cardi and yesterday's makeup, but the girls had seen her look worse.

They fussed over her, offering tea, recommending the staff-room muffins in a patronising tone. 'How 'bout we put you in the breakout room?' They appeared concerned, as if she was a vagrant caught sleeping rough in the front entry whom they had to remove without incident. 'You know you're welcome anytime, but is everything okay, Rae?'

It was then Rachael realised tears had escaped down her face. 'Hay fever.' She was doing the very opposite of what she advocated on 'RUOK' days. 'I'm fine, really.'

Her colleagues were like family, but something stopped her admitting the state of her marriage. The girls adored Sam, unconsciously greeting the Olympian with flushed cheeks and nervous stares whenever he paraded in. It would break their hearts if she told them what he'd confessed.

'Everything tracking well for the quarter?' Rachael asked Gail.

Gail's bright young face filled with pride. 'Ah, yes, since you've asked, we had a five-point-three per cent increase in placements this month.'

Rachael's face pinched before she had time to frame a masking smile.

Gail's alert blue eyes widened. 'Which I'm sure was just the flow-on from all that fab groundwork before you left. Satisfaction rates with jobseekers is also trending upwards.'

Annie coughed.

'All your progress sounds great!' Rachael said, feeling the pain in her back. It was surreal to see the business continue to blossom without her.

'You sure? Your face is weird,' Annie said.

'But all the clients miss you, Rach,' Gail added quickly.

Something unravelled. 'I worked through most of Noah's baby phase, so I've been Queen Bee here half my life. It's just strange to see someone else run the hive so well.' Rachael laughed. 'Eat the royal jelly, so to speak.'

'You're the founder, the concept owner, the lifeblood – you'll always be our queen,' Gail said, which came out a little brown-nosey. Annie noticed. She missed Annie's transparent ways.

Was this change temporary? Rachael felt a quickening inside and diagnosed she'd fallen victim to a bad case of FOMO.

She took a breath as Annie and Gail scurried away, giving her space to prep for an interview on a podcast. She needed to find the right headspace, needed her heels to feel something solid, which for Rachael meant focusing on her career. She'd make sure to use the interview to talk up Beehive and its success in finding employment for those who were often excluded from the recruitment space.

Rachael gazed out the floor-to-ceiling windows to the road. Was that the red car she'd noticed behind her on the way here? Was someone watching her from the driver's seat? She dropped the blind and refocused, telling herself she was just tired.

She turned to look out to her bright reception. The tawny hue of the décor had been a brave choice, but she loved their branding, the way the rich yellow set off the black uniforms of the office staff. Staring at the wall, she recognised the real reason she wasn't honest about her mental state and was embarrassed to realise it was shame. It felt politically incorrect to feel like this, wrong on some fundamental level, but a voice inside whispered it was humiliating to be seen as a victim. Her marriage to the Rio Rocket was so publicly envied. She was mortified at the thought of her colleagues pitying her if they knew the truth — that deep down she wasn't enough woman to keep her man happy. She couldn't fail them, tarnish the image of success she'd tried hard to build.

So, she did what she knew best. She soldiered on.

Later that day, Rachael decided to take Sam's advice and focus on their family. After dropping Ethan at his casual job at the local deli, Rachael decided to hover and pick up some supplies like a good homemaker should. She felt mildly stalkerish as she hid behind the display of organic sourdoughs hoping to catch a glimpse of Ethan in the wild, sporting his striped apron and hair net, politely conversing from behind the counter. Her heart pulsed with pride — was this the same permanently slumped, sullen adolescent who drank the milk straight from the carton at home? Maybe she had done something right after all.

Ethan was fifteen and an undercooked version of his statuesque father. It felt like only yesterday that he was a dimply-chinned infant. The fact that he now towered over her and wore a name badge was indisputable evidence that she'd finally made herself redundant. She'd mourned many incarnations of her son, the seven-year-old refusing her hand as they crossed the street, the twelve-year-old preferring not to be seen with her in public. Now the young-adult version had unfriended her on social media and rarely answered her texts. Parenting was like discovering the love of your life and then being broken up with, slowly.

A short, frazzled, brunette was next in line for him to serve. She had that harried look about her, the commercial-grade exhaustion only long-term parents recognised in their own kind. Her clothes were off-beat, arty, but also old and faded, as if she was clinging desperately to an earlier stage of life.

Ethan weighed and wrapped the rattled woman's order and tallied the total in his head like the human-calculator he was. 'Nineteen dollars fifty, thank you, ma'am.' His spindly arms held out her order like a gift.

She didn't take it.

It couldn't be the price. Ethan never got a cent wrong.

'Ma'am?' His tone was strange. *Was his voice still breaking?* His eyes darted about as if this was a practical joke. 'Ma'am?'

Rachael hovered near the specialty cheeses to observe the customer's face, while trying not to reveal her own. But this woman was not focused on anything but the pork chops wrapped in Ethan's hand. Everyone in the store was staring at that butcher-paper-packed bundle willing her to take it and move the queue along.

'Five. I ordered five.' Her hand covered her lips as the sobs spewed forth.

Ethan looked horrified. 'This is five ... like you said. Do you still want them? I can put them back, or get you a different five, even?' His face blushed, his eyes darting about looking for someone to save him. *Oh, bless him.* The woman was just having a mental-health moment.

'There are five in the family ... I always get five.'

Murmurs of frustration grew from the lining customers, who were only seeing her as the reason they were delayed. They had no empathy for the woman. No understanding that this wasn't about the chops. Rachael knew how it felt to be that woman, knew everyone struggled – hell, she was floundering even now, but was just less authentic than this woman, not brave enough to let it show.

The customer absentmindedly scooped up the chops, cradled them like a baby, and started to walk out without paying.

Panic flooded Ethan's face. 'Ah ...' He pulled his earlobe like he did when he was overwhelmed.

Rachael came out of hiding and waddled towards them. Ethan saw her and screwed one eye closed in protest. She approached as quickly as her pregnant belly allowed, threw a twenty-dollar note on the counter, and shepherded the woman out via the cheese tower to provide cover from prying eyes. *Nothing to see here.*

Trustingly, the stranger let Rachael guide her out. The woman seemed to come out of her trance, and embarrassment replaced her vagueness. Rachael wasn't sure which was more difficult to appease. She guided her to a shady bench on the footpath out of view of the store and placed the chops into the reusable shopping bag looping the lady's arm.

'Oh, God. I'm such a git. I forgot to pay. Sorry, I have the cash …' The woman fumbled through a quirky green purse with a red leather heart in the centre. Coins fell to the pavement in a sprinkle of chimes.

Rachael went to pick them up but struggled to bend over her round belly.

'No, don't you dare, you know your ligaments are ripe for injury in the last trimester …' the stranger said, scrambling to pick up her coins, mumbling something under her breath about midwifery in a previous life.

There was something unmistakeably likeable about her, something open and kind in her face, along with a sense that she was as lost as her coins.

She returned to the seat and caught her breath with a long sigh. 'Sorry – I've never shoplifted in my life. I was daydreaming.' Both women's eyes fell to her shoes. She paused, noticing they were mismatched – perfectly respectable ballet flats in slightly different designs. Chop-lady noticed Rachael noticing. As she laughed with gusto, the emotion the woman had been closeting leaked out. 'And look, I can't even dress myself. Who am I kidding? I'm as clueless as the kids. Not sure who has the most meltdowns – them or me!'

'Don't worry.' Rachael rested her hand on the other woman's shoulder. 'I was crying over an insurance ad this morning. We all have moments in our family – the trick is avoiding them happening all at once. Besides, I got my sandals to match but look at my feet, they remind me of stringed pork – plump and strapped in for roasting.'

The woman's smile split her face, and a whole new person peered back. Her hair and clothes were a mess, but her face had an understated beauty, warm brown eyes and an alert gaze. Her laughter waned, and she sighed out the rest of her fears before saying matter-of-fact, 'My husband left.' She blurted it in that way people could to strangers.

Her vulnerability, so rare and precious, compelled Rachael to disclose her own secret shame, as if it was the only way to absolve it.

Rachael shrugged. 'No judgement. I don't have the guts to leave mine …' Saying it out loud felt better than she'd expected, but still scared the hell out of her, and her throat ached with the grief of it.

The woman smiled and Rachael returned it in kind. In a torrent, she vented Sam's dirty deeds with the candour reserved only for those you never expect to see again. And for about twenty minutes, the curvy brunette with the thick bob listened. Rachael expelled every feeling about her philandering husband until the well of sadness ran dry.

Then, as if she'd passed the stranger a talking stick in an AA meeting, the chop-stealer held a stony gaze and said, 'It's like I've forgotten how to breathe without him.'

If it wasn't for the belly budged between them, Rachael would have hugged her. The women gazed at each other, an much was said in that look.

A moment later, it was as if they'd arrived at the end of a cleansing ritual.

'Can I offer you a lift?' Rachael asked, launching her pregnant belly from the bench.

'I'm fine. Honestly − flip-out concluded,' Chop-lady said. 'And thank you for …'

Rachael nodded. Assured the stranger was feeling better, she watched her leave with her five chops and her warm smile. Rachael felt strangely drawn to her.

She'd learned her secrets yet didn't know her name.

Chapter 5

Gertie

Ed and Gertie used to call Penelope Crawley from Lavender Lane the original Stepford wife. With her ruler-straight bob, sweetheart necklines and baked goods, her Sunday-school-teacher vibe had them fooled that a swear word had never whistled through those cherry lips. But that all changed a few years back at the estate BBQ when their neighbour had one too many and let the facade slip. She cut the act and the cussing, gossiping, mojito-sipping Penny materialised, and was highly preferred. As long as that version came to the forefront (and not pretentious Penny), they all got on splendidly.

Back when they were all in the throes of early parenting, inebriated Penny told Gertie she'd made a mint monetising her site, Womb with a View, which (before podcasts superseded blogs) was renowned for old-fashioned expertise on all things kids – from back-to-school routines to how to hide vegies in bolognese. The blog's point of difference was that she was rather politically incorrect, scathing about modern child-focused parenting strategies. Basically, her values were back in the fifties along with her hairstyle. Gertie still read some of Penny's unchristian-like anecdotes for entertainment value alone (such as how she slipped her toddler Phenergan to ensure a romantic dinner with her husband), but at times it was hard to reconcile real-life Penny, pruning her hedges to perfection, with the other version making trouble online.

It's a scientific fact that looking like death increases the chance of running into people you know by ninety per cent. Gertie spotted her neighbour's polka-dot dress flash through the local bottle-o carpark, her French bulldog sporting a tulle collar, tugging on her blindingly over-blinged leash. Penny was harmless, but you had to be in the mood for her exuberance, which a newly husbandless Gertie was decidedly not.

'Gert, is that you?' Penny took off her oversized cat-eye sunglasses as if to get a better look at just how unkempt Gertie appeared. 'Didn't catch you at the body-corporate meeting on Tuesday. I hope you're not unwell?' Penny held the crucifix dangling from her necklace between her finger and thumb as if she was ready to point out sinful excuses.

'Ah, no. Just ferrying kids about at that time, you know how it is. Harry had the optometrist, I think. That was it, yes.' Gertie couldn't face her as she lied.

'Oh? Glasses, huh?' Penny bent to scratch the ear of her drooling dog.

'So it seems. Just when I felt guilty for my genes predisposing Harry to a lifetime of never finding his towel on the beach, the optometrist blamed his poor eyesight on screen time. Still my fault, of course.' Something about their eyeballs not getting a chance to stretch with all the close work kids did on devices. The optometrist recommended Gertie encourage more outside time, the opposite of what the dermatologist had prescribed.

Penny nodded. 'Oh, bloody screens. Wasn't it nice when we gave them a cardboard box and they'd stay busy for hours? Did you see my article on screen time? We've rationed Spencer's time with the latest software. It's very clever – allowing access for homework but limiting gaming. I can't complain, really. My little mouse-potato *is* doing well at school, topping Digital Solutions at St Aquinas …'

Gertie's eye began to twitch involuntarily when Penny started to humble-brag. There was nothing as boring as hearing about someone's perfect world. Penny's life was as blemish free as her face. Gertie almost hoped she'd get a flat tyre to spice up conversations.

'… although not as well as your daughter. I saw "Katerina Rainworth" on the awards list – clever young lady, topping half the subjects.'

'Thank God – couldn't afford the exorbitant college fees if she lost her scholarship. Even with Ed's new flash job.' The words came out squeaky and Gertie regretted mentioning her other half. How ridiculous that saying was – 'other half'. Was she not considered whole without a partner?

'Finally,' Penny said. 'Well done, Ed! I did always pity you getting round in that pre-owned van of yours. You know it's still got an oil leak? I could recommend a mechanic if you like.'

Gertie offered a tight smile. She knew Penny found her lumpen, but she also knew her one-upmanship stemmed from insecurity, not menace. Another thing Penny let slip after too many mojitos was that she'd grown up with a dad who spent his dole on booze instead of food. Penny believed money was the true path to happiness and – now her husband's finance business had fleeced Sydney's rich and greedy – felt the need to remind everyone she'd outrun that broke girl she despised.

'How is Ed? Still in HR?' Penny attempted to frown, but Gertie could tell the botox was making that impossible. 'Is that why he was Ubering off the other morning – saw him on the security footage. Business trip?'

'Mmm, Singapore.' Gertie couldn't elaborate. Saying he'd 'left' out loud again would make it the norm. Saying it to Penny would make it common knowledge.

'How lovely! And how are the boys? Still a handful?'

Curious, spirited, vivacious. Gertie had heard all the labels to describe her challenging offspring (often by the likes of checkout supervisors while racing to open a lane to expedite their departure from their store). Take Harry. It wasn't as if his behaviour was extraordinary, there was just so much of it. He had to be moving, foot tapping, mouth humming, eyes darting. And Abe was Abe; quirky in his mannerisms, concrete in his thinking, infuriating in his logic.

'They're fine, but I'm buying plonk at ten am, so perhaps not choosing the best coping strategies.'

Penny touched her arm. 'I'll have you round for a girls' night, then, especially with Ed away.'

No need to rush.

Penny didn't leave.

Gertie grabbed a new topic. 'How's the cupcake store?'

'Just lovely. You know what they say: find a job you love and you'll never work a day in your life. Just made a batch of velvet creams for the new estate family – Rachael York, you know, Young Australian of the Year a while back? Founded that disability-recruitment franchise?'

Gertie nodded but had never heard of her.

'They're another dual income, sorry to say.' She made a face. A face that disapproved.

Penny and Gertie had been stay-at-home mums for most of their children's formative years. Penny seemed to think that made them kindred spirits, encouraging Gertie to join her in shaming working mothers, as if they were the enemy.

Gertie was more of the philosophy that the kids were their real adversaries and mums had to stick together.

'Martin says I'm being harsh, too traditional for my own good, but career women don't see what I see – the sad faces as the kids are marched off to after-school care like little orphans. I was so fortunate Martin earned good money so I could stay home. I'd hate getting a watered-down version of the day, a hurried fumble of dinner, homework, baths – maintenance tasks instead of quality time.' Penny tut-tutted.

Gertie had done a couple of stints back at work when Kat, Abe and Harry were little to keep her nursing registration current, so she considered herself a 'hybrid'.

'Hang on, you and Martin both work now, Penny,' Gertie said facetiously.

'Only when Spencer started high school. Now he's on his computer so much he barely notices when I'm home – probably prefers when I'm not.' Penny's watery eyes looked elsewhere before she turned back with her happy mask securely in place. 'Anyway, the new estate wife is married to that hot Olympic backstroker from Rio.'

'They're Brazilian?'

'No, the Australian gold medallist! Rather easy on the eyes. Oh, you've probably met him at the aquatic centre. He's just started teaching PE at the college, which is a little surprising after all the scandals, but you can't believe everything in *Who* mag, can you? Isn't Kat in the swim team? He's starting soon as the new head coach.'

'Oh, yes.' Gertie had no idea, but there was no harm in appearing more involved with her daughter's life than she was. Kat had always been a natural butterflier but reckoned swimming gave her man-shoulders and bad hair so was hard to motivate.

'Martin's already managing Sam York's investment portfolio.' She rattled on about a promising pharmaceutical startup.

Gertie found it hard to stay awake once people mentioned money.

'Oh.' Penny flicked her perfectly French-polished nails. 'Which reminds me, be a darl and watch Eva for me while I pick up Martin's Cinzano, would you? The bitch gets antsy if I leave her tied to the post. P!nk is a new client and she's coming for drinks tonight.'

'Ah …' Gertie hesitated as Penny looped Eva's lead around her wrist. 'Sure.' The grumpy bulldog looked ridiculous in her tulle collar. Gertie cringed for the poor creature's self-respect. She wondered why Penelope and Martin never had more children. 'Sorry, Eva, I guess you're the daughter she never had, huh?' Gertie whispered as her fellow hedge-dweller rushed inside and grabbed her order.

Gertie waited, contemplating her own beverage list. *Had it come to this – planning a weekend drinking alone?* The canine started to hump Gertie's left calf. She tried to rebuff the dog's advances by sticking her head inside the store and noticed Penny's credit card had been declined. She wondered if she should offer to pay or pretend not to notice and went for the latter.

Penny grabbed another card, turned back to the counter, before twirling around and smiling. 'Silly me! Wrong card!'

Gertie smiled. But when Penny returned to grab her precious pooch a moment later a little bemused, Gertie decided not to refer to the fact that her neighbour was empty-handed.

Gertie made it by a bee's dick to the school gate to pick up Harry and Abe, wearing the same chocolate-stained leggings she'd slept in the night before after falling asleep during her third attempt at a full episode of *The Affair*. Ed and Gertie had watched it religiously together, but since his disappearing act she'd kept watching without him. *Take that, Ed!*

'Muuuum.' Gertie knew that tone. Harry and Abe arrived at the pick-up line, all tears, dirt and high emotions. 'Abe stole my favourite stick and poked me with it and it's bleeding and now he won't give it back!'

What was with boys and sticks? 'Oh, sweetheart, let me see.'

A bloody, dirt-edged scrape blemished Harry's knee. She dabbed at it with a tissue.

With her knees pressed into the gravel on the footpath, Gertie spied the pregnant stranger from the deli at the gate. Gertie was torn. She'd connected with the woman, but was it a case of what you said in the deli stayed in the deli? Before she'd decided, the woman approached holding out a ziplock bag of tissues, Band-Aids and manuka-honey spray – the supplies all organised mums carried.

'I see your little man's had a scrape. I'm Rachael.'

'Hello!'

Here she was, helping again – was she part of a guardian-angel network? Gertie's two dark-eyed boys fell silent for once as she gingerly tended to Harry's graze. Then the kids began complaining at the twenty-second delay, as if their life was lagging like bad Wi-Fi, and they wanted to go home.

Abe sized up Rachael like a perv at a pub. 'Are you pregnant or just fat?'

'Abe!' Gertie's eyes widened at her son, but luckily Rachael just laughed. 'I'm Gert. Gertie Rainworth.'

'Rainworth?' Realisation dawned on the woman's face. 'Oh, so this is the Harry I've heard so much about. Noah's been begging to arrange a play date.'

'Arrange to play with *my* Harry?' Gertie heard the disbelief nestled in her words as soon as they were out, and they were ugly. *Bad Mum.*

'Noah tells me he's the funniest boy in class.' Rachael leaned forward and lowered her voice. 'And it would help me out,' she continued. 'I'm trying to fill up the attention tanks before the baby comes. I've been ignoring him, interviewing nannies all week.'

Her blonde layers streaked with honey set off her golden skin perfectly. She had a pop of apricot hue on her lips and her eyebrows were so neat, as if she'd taken a ruler to them. Gertie realised she was staring, embarrassingly.

'My mum doesn't believe in nannies, but my sister, Katerina, used to babysit for one of The Wiggles before – he used to live in our gated community – it's just for people with money. And my sister – she's on a scholarship at St Aquinas. Scholarship means she's easy to teach so we don't have to pay,' Abe blurted out.

Rachael nodded at him. 'Oh, that's my big son's school, too. Actually, Penny mentioned a Katerina was the best babysitter in the estate, wants to be a midwife – is that your daughter?'

'Guilty.' Something about Kat's lack of self-consciousness, the way she threw herself into imaginative play made her a natural, and her voiceovers while reading picture books had everyone in stitches. Gertie wanted Kat to focus on school, for her to swing for the fence as Ed would say, and study obstetrics, but Kat had other ideas. 'Kat's been fascinated with babies since becoming a big sister to these clowns.' Gertie smiled.

Rachael smiled warmly, then put a finger to her lips. 'If Kat's not too stretched, are you open to her childminding for us?'

Gertie was surprised. Hedge-dwellers hired renowned nannies with YouTube channels to raise their little cherubs, not students with 5SOS obsessions.

'Kat has been dreaming about a phone that costs more than my first car, so I'm sure she'd be keen for a bit of extra income.' *And by the look of that diamond on your finger, you're not short on cash.*

Abe strode ahead to the carpark. Panicked because of last time, Gertie followed.

'I'll be in touch,' Rachael called as she waved them off. Gertie knew the woman's life was not as perfect as it looked from the outside, but was she really as lovely as she seemed? She was mixed in her signals – warm and self-assured in her manner yet with an underlying fragility Gertie couldn't quite explain. What had Barry on security mentioned the other morning about the new celebrity couple in the estate? She wished she'd taken more notice when Penny was gossiping about them.

Gertie steered the boys towards the van, figuring Rachael was just being polite. That she was probably a professional-grade people-warmer, someone with a knack for making you feel singled out as special, but that time revealed she was all empty platitudes and she wouldn't get in touch again.

But she did.

Chapter 6

The Security Guy

Barry, the security guy, fastened his brass button, brushed a rogue petal off his lapel and sized up the newbies as they drove towards the gates. He'd googled the Yorks when they'd moved in a few weeks earlier. She was some philanthropic business lady, willowy-limbed and pretty in a high-maintenance way; he was that Olympic putz who spoke like he grew up in Downton Abbey. He'd bet the pretty boy only drank bottled water and had three middle names. The chump adjusted the collar of his crisp white polo and checked himself out in the rear-view mirror as he slowed to have the numberplate scanned. It was personalised. Barry figured *Yuppie Fuck* mustn't have fit on the plate.

Barry had bored himself senseless working in security all his life and still couldn't even afford the replacement key for one of those beauties. He couldn't even afford to get his wandering mum into a nursing home that didn't drug her to play nice. He shoved the sneer he suppressed into a catacomb in his mind so it didn't blow him apart.

Mrs York gave him an impeccably white smile and lowered the window.

Be professional, Bazza. 'Welcome back, Mr and Mrs York. Beautiful day to be alive, isn't it?' He fumbled for his hat, nearly knocking his Coke all over it. He hated that hat. It was pretentious and the patent leather showed up oily finger smudges after he finished his sausage roll. He only donned it when a resident drove up, otherwise it indented his forehead.

'Barry, I just wanted to check you got the security info from when we moved in,' the woman said in an unexpected country-girl drawl as her annoyingly buff husband pointed his finger at him in a gun salute.

'Everything's in order, the signatures for the fobs, the emergency contacts and such.' *And such.* Barry had started saying that after his last performance-appraisal feedback, hoping it made him sound clever. He felt like a bit of a dick, though.

Mrs York nodded compliantly, and after a muffled exchange between the pair, she stepped out of the Porsche. Outside the car, he noted she was with child. That was not mentioned on Google. The swimmer left her and continued through the iron gates, exceeding the 10 kph limit. The bastard couldn't wait? Barry shook his head. Plenty of marriages hit the skids in this warren. It was the cameras – uncovered things couples chose not to see before. But Barry was a meercat. Barry saw everything.

'The flowers are in bloom already,' Mrs York said.

'Oleanders. Beautiful, aren't they?'

Mrs York frowned – most of the wives couldn't do that on account of the botox, and he liked her a little more. 'Oh, I thought Oleander was poisonous.'

'Urban myth.' He wasn't sure it was, but it sounded reassuring. And that was his job. To reassure. All he knew about Oleander was that the blossoms smelled like unripe tomatoes. 'Do you have a cleaner to authorise?'

'No, ah, I just wanted to make sure you'd noted our exclusions.' She opened the leather document holder she'd had tucked underarm and pointed nervously at the long list of names.

Barry recognised some from the tabloids on his Google search. 'Exclusions?' He laughed. 'Mrs York, there's no need. I can assure you not even an Uber breaches these walls without approval. You can register guests via the app – it's all in the Welcome Pack.'

She swallowed then held his gaze with a vulnerability that compelled him to obey. 'I'll log them in the system pronto.'

He tipped his shiny hat.

'Oh, and while I'm here, I wanted you to remove the notifications for when I arrive and leave the estate to list on our display – we don't really need to record that.'

He held up his palm. 'Oh, you can do that from the app—'

'Oh, yes, I know. I mean permanently remove.'

He frowned, and by way of explanation, Mrs York said, 'My husband already thinks I shop too long – he doesn't need proof.' She laughed and her apricot-glossed lips turned up at the sides.

Barry knew a put-on grin when he saw one. He gave one every day. Like his hat, it was part of his disguise. 'Certainly, Mrs York.' He went to alter the settings on the main laptop. 'Just for *your* fob, then, not the other users?'

'Just me, thank you, Barry.' This wasn't the first time Barry had been asked this. Usually, it was by scoundrel men and usually to mask extramarital activities. It made him feel complicit in their dirty deeds, but generally the tips made it worthwhile. For some reason, this request made him feel squeaky clean. *Good for her.*

'Ah, Mrs York? I just wonder if the … the other users might notice if your data is not listed at all.'

She tilted her head to one side and frowned.

'I could always provide you with a spare fob – an unregistered fob, if you could promise it didn't fall into the hands of an unauthorised person, of course.'

She looked out over the sleek, leaf-free driveway and nodded.

He placed the spare fob in her soft palm, tapped his nose twice and she nodded again.

A brilliant cut diamond bulged on her finger as she pocketed the secret fob, touched his hand in appreciation and ambled through the iron gates. Her husband was probably waiting for his dinner.

A butterfly fluttered after her as if she was in bloom.

He gave them six months.

Chapter 7

Rachael

At 16 Lavender Lane, Gertie Rainworth's wide grin appeared on the security camera and Rachael felt a burst of expectation.

'Hey, there!' Gertie blurted, pointing to her shoes like a goof. 'Decided I'd go with a matching pair today for something different.'

'Mum, you're so embarrassing,' the pretty teen behind her shoulder mumbled. Katerina Rainworth wore her hair pinned high like an extra on a Jane Austen film, and a vintage top paired with shorts so skimpy they'd make Mrs Bennet pale.

From the corner of her eye, Rachael was momentarily distracted by a car rolling along the road behind her guests.

'Everything okay?' Gertie asked, waiting to be invited in. 'We can reschedule if ...'

'Sorry, now is perfect.' Rachael gestured for them to come through to the kitchen. 'I'm just wondering – you don't know anyone in the estate with a red Alpha, do you?'

'Our friends don't drive anything that cool unless they nicked it.' Gertie frowned, scanning the street. 'Sure this is a good time?'

Rachael didn't know if she was joking about her friends. 'Of course, the Alpha – it's just similar to one of Sam's fans we had some dramas with a while back.'

'Like a stalker?' Gertie's eyes lit up. 'I guess marrying an Olympic hero is not as exciting as it sounds.'

Rachael realised Gertie wasn't a stranger in a deli anymore, she was a neighbour, and a school mum, and perhaps blurting out her dirty secrets was no longer wise. Gertie's kids filed in from the front porch, enthralled.

'We had someone hide a motion-detector camera in a pot plant years ago so they'd get a pic when Sam left the house,' Rachael said. 'But thankfully, he's old news now.'

'And to think I took for granted the fact that I have a life of no interest to anyone,' Gertie said.

'Not true.' Rachael shrugged. 'I'm interested.' She ushered them through to the kitchen.

The two younger boys bolted to the trampoline, while the others settled on stools at the breakfast bar. Ethan was slumped over the fridge, which was pinging in protest as he kept the door open. His cheeks coloured as he noticed Kat's ridiculously long legs. His crumpled St Aquinas shirt hung over *Big Bang Theory* boxers, but thankfully they were hidden behind the island bench.

'Aren't you house captain?' he asked Kat.

'Yeah.' Kat crossed her arms. 'Aren't you the new kid who brought his laptop to the athletics carnival?'

'Yeah.' His shoulder rose almost imperceptibly. 'So what?'

Kat shrugged.

Rachael tried to make herself invisible, gathering snacks, watching the teens awkwardly converse about school and music and teachers. Sam and Ethan used to pay out on her by making helicopter gestures when she was caught 'hovering'.

'You in a band or something?' Kat gestured to the drumsticks lying on the kitchen bench. 'The drums?' she clarified.

He shrugged. 'Don't play much. Kind of prefer gaming. You play *Miner's Haven*?' Ethan said nervously, eyes flicking to Kat as he slipped onto a stool.

'A bit.'

He hesitated. *Was Ethan nervous?* 'You remind me of Lara Croft from *Tomb Raider*.'

Kat looked unsure if that was a good thing. 'More into tabletop RPGs. I like the stories.'

'*D&D*?'

'I *love D&D*.' Kat's eyes rolled with pleasure, as if she was eating cake.

Ethan narrowed his eyes. 'I didn't think anyone that looked like you played *Dungeons*. What's your Discord tag?'

'KittyKat04. Wait, you can play *D&D* through Discord?'

He laughed. 'You're such a noob.' He nodded. 'I'll send you an invite to my server.'

As Ethan bounced upstairs to his gamer cave, Rachael figured she'd witnessed the millennial version of writing your number on a guy's hand.

Rachael carried drinks, and she and Gertie sat in the shade of the back deck watching the kids play. She imagined an aerial view of the estate would appear like a giant hedge-maze. Yet that same ivy wall bordering each block gave you a false sense of seclusion – to make the best use of prime land so close to the harbour, the homes were tightly packed. Rachael had heard Penelope – the fifties housewife from next door – stir her tea early one morning. She was mindful of what might be overheard.

Silence hovered as the younger kids settled into their games. Rachael became concerned about what she'd already confessed. This stranger could do real damage with that knowledge.

Happy noise and off-beat questions (*What temperature is lava? Is the sun too hot to walk on even with shoes?*) splintered their attempt at conversation. The mothers eyed their sons, playing in sync, smiles all round. Kat was bright, fun and eager to please, but something about her niggled. Rachael tried to hush her concerns about trusting a teenager with her kids; she was the first to admit she was OTT with safety.

'No pool?' Gertie asked. 'I thought all the houses came with a private plunge.' She spoke with a plum on the *unge*.

'Not this one, thank goodness. Too much worry with little kids.'

Gertie nodded. 'How are you feeling about the birth? Keeping calm?' she asked.

'Sam has the birth plan sorted – another C-section.'

'Is he having the baby?' Gertie smiled.

Rachael wished she could admit it felt like she was just the surrogate carrying Sam's property. That she was reluctant to bring another child into the world, the way it was. But what sort of mother admitted out loud that she was often less than thrilled about carrying her husband's baby? 'He's incredibly involved,' she said instead.

Chimes of giggles billowed through the afternoon breeze. Kat had transformed into a tickle monster and the boys scattered across the lawn in hysterics.

'Well, if Kat's not keen to babysit, I might just have to borrow Harry to occupy Noah.'

Gertie looked at her incredulously. 'Glad to be of service. Harry can be full on for some, bless him, but he means well.'

Gertie's little Harry idled high. It was exhausting watching him flit from one task to the next – innocently spilling drinks or bonking heads by simply moving too fast with little thought. Noah watched Harry with astonishment – as if the spectrum of colours in the rainbow had become more vivid since he'd arrived. Did the kid live on additives or was he just naturally spirited?

'How's your week going otherwise? Rescued anyone else from a mental-health crisis?' Gertie asked.

Rachael nearly choked. 'I'm hardly qualified to save anyone – things feel like they're imploding in my world.'

'That's not how it looks from the outside. I hear you, though – motherhood's relentless,' Gertie said. 'I've learned to just set the bar low. I used to preach to new mums that I was a disciple of the CTFD method – only way to stay sane.'

'Sane sounds good. What's CTFD?' Rachael asked, remembering Gertie mentioning she had been a midwife so likely knew her stuff.

Gertie checked the kids were out of hearing range. 'Calm the Fuck Down parenting.'

Rachael erupted. 'Don't make me laugh. I'll pee myself.' She had forgotten how good unguarded joy felt.

'The method has a lot of applications. If you're worried that you're not a good parent – CTFD. Idiots get away with it all the time. If you're stressed about whether your toddler needs flashcards – CTFD. Just read to them, it's the best predictor of academic success. I'm not advocating neglect, but kids are wildflowers, not prized orchids – they take a bit of establishing, but give them the right conditions and they'll survive in a crevasse all on their own with a bit of loving.'

As long as you pick the right seed in the first place.

Gertie picked a grape from the bowl. 'Keeping it simple is the best way to stay sane. Midway through the Christmas holidays, I'm usually ready to lose it,' Gertie went on. 'On the first day back to school, the teacher asked how my "break" was. Should've seen her face when I said, "At least I didn't sell any of them." Imagine if I'd referred to them as "little arseholes" like I'd wanted to.'

Rachael nearly sprayed ginger beer over Gertie. She hadn't made new connections other than business contacts for years. The need for friendship outside her marriage had felt unnecessary. But something about Gertie made her realise you were never too old to forge friendships, that new beginnings were possible even in a life that was rather established.

As the shadows grew long on the lawn, Rachael felt her concerns about hiring a teenage babysitter loosen and dissolve. She observed Kat's vigilance with safety – rehoming hats when they flung off, zipping the trampoline net, allowing harmless silliness but intervening when things turned rough. It put Rachael at ease. She had thought only people like her – people who had felt the sting of tragedy – understood that never letting your guard down was crucial. Did she need to *Calm the Fuck Down*? It just seemed a little reckless – not for worriers like her – and likely to create more anxiety than it prevented.

She should have seen it coming, what happened next.

Kat, Harry and Noah – the three of them linked in what looked like a drunken conga line – snaked inside through the kitchen, lightsabers swinging, sound effects blaring, Boof#2 barking at the frivolity.

'Boys, I spotted the dragon behind the shed …' Kat called in an attempt to return the sword-swinging back to open space. Through the French doors, Rachael saw that Harry and Noah ignored her and hurdled the couch, their slashing weapons pulsing with noise, flashing with light, until all was silent. That was never good, and she went inside after them.

The two boys stood, statue still. Petrified.

And there it hung, askew, desperately clinging to the wire Sam had painstakingly hung it with just weeks ago; the Gunnar

Gundersen – Sam's favourite Nordic abstract artist's latest canvas painting, a slice cut out of it like a piece of pie. Sam would be ropable.

Inwardly, Rachael wanted to laugh. She hated that piece, had joked that their little Noah could be the next Gundersen when he'd let loose with a lipstick on her bathroom mirror. But she felt obliged to feign disappointment at her son's carelessness.

Kat raced to help see if it was salvageable, looking mortified. 'I'm so sorry, Mrs York – I tried to keep them outside.'

Gertie assessed the slashed canvas the boys had run from, and called with a fury Rachael was shocked her warm-hearted visitor was capable of. 'HARRISON RAINWORTH!' Then she quietened to a tearful whimper. 'Oh, Rachael, I'm so sorry. I feel so awful!' She kept placing the flapping section back into position as if that would turn back time. 'There's a reason we call him Cyclone Harry – I love him to bits, but he leaves a path of destruction wherever he roams. I'll pay for it! God, I hope it wasn't some rare priceless artist!' She gasped. 'Tell me it was on clearance at IKEA.'

Rachael shrugged. 'Never liked it much, and to be fair, I'd say that my little angel was just as much to blame. And in the end, they're just things ...'

Gertie teared up with relief. It was clear to Rachael that this devoted mum already lost too much sleep over her son's transgressions as if she was the one bounding through the house, arms flapping. After taking on too much guilt for Ethan's rather aloof manner, Rachael had learned to try to separate her behaviour from that of her children, but it was hard not to feel responsible for their actions.

Dark-featured Harry reluctantly crab-marched towards his mother, while flaxen-haired Noah took his hand in a gesture so sweet, Rachael's heart melted.

'Sorry we ran inside,' they said in unison, eyes darting towards Kat waiting in the wings.

Rachael tilted her head. 'Thank you, boys. I know it was an accident, but can we leave our running feet outside, please?'

The two six-year-olds nodded wide-eyed in disbelief they'd got off without a lecture. She picked up the canvas. 'It was just a local upcoming artist Sam supported at a charity gig.'

'Is that the same artist?' Gertie pointed to an adjacent canvas.

Rachael could see why her guest thought they were alike. It resembled two stick figures waving three-fingered hands beneath a ball of yellow sun.

'That's my brother's – a rather *less* accomplished local artist.' Rachael laughed. 'That's meant to be me on the right.'

'Oh, how sweet, a keepsake from when you were little?' Gertie asked.

Rachael swallowed. 'Liam was twenty when he painted it. The year before he died. Sam never liked me putting it in such a visible position.'

Gertie's smile fell, but she didn't shy away from meeting Rachael's gaze. 'Oh, hon …' Gertie said, grabbing her shoulder for reassurance.

Rachael shrugged. 'In a way, Liam's who motivated me to work so hard. Sam's always resented the hours I put into my business, but in my youth my brother was the fuel in my engine.'

'I read about your success – I'm in awe of it, if I'm honest.' Gertie's already large eyes widened. 'I've always been someone of simple pleasures. My toast and tea in the morning, the heat of the shower on my muscles at night, tucking in my kids. The life of a stay-at-home mum doesn't seem very accomplished when women like you do so much with your time. And you've got kids, not to mention being married to an Olympian! You know you're amazing, right?'

Rachael didn't feel amazing. She felt like an imposter most of the time, afraid at any moment someone would discover she wasn't as brilliant as her bio would have people believe. 'I like those things too, and I'm in awe of anyone who can manage kids day in, day out without paid work to break it up. Sam's rather traditional – never quite approved of me working.'

Gertie's brow furrowed. 'Ed's probably the reason I quit work too, after kids. Not that he'd ever admit it, but he liked having them bathed and fed when he got home so he could just kiss their damp little faces and enjoy them. I admit, things are simpler when the roles are defined. It got so muddy when we both worked.'

'While we're on Sam ... probably best if you don't mention to anyone what I said the other day ...' The affair part alone would be enough fodder to stir up a world of trouble in the media.

Gertie waved her hands, hushing her from finishing.

Rachael's stomach relaxed. She trusted this one. 'Thank you. Lots of energy goes into avoiding the wrong people hearing the wrong stories. It's half the reason we went for all the security of this place.' She focused on the ceiling so her tears wouldn't escape down her cheeks. When she said her life was imploding, what she'd meant was it was already in tatters.

'Hon, it's totally normal that things are still raw after ... what happened.' Gertie's eyes were bright with concern as she took her hand. 'I am here to listen, or offer a spare room, or anything you may need.' Her face softened. She left space for Rachael to elaborate if she needed to.

But as much as Rachael liked Gertie and didn't regret spilling all outside the deli that day, she couldn't find the words to elaborate further now that Gertie was no longer a stranger. Not yet. Not with the kids a wall away.

Rachael glanced over to see Harry traipsing squashed cherries the length of the hallway.

He paused, looked down at his shoes and his face pinched. 'Sorry …'

'Kids. Who'd have 'em?' Gertie sighed, said they should make tracks to get Abe from chess club but they'd love to catch up again. 'I'd understand if you wanted to charge a bond next time – that is, if you're game enough to invite us back.'

When Sam arrived home from coaching, he asked Rachael how her day was the way he always did, kissed her hello the way he always had. But today, the assumption implied in both irked her. He assumed everything would go on as usual. That she'd make his dinner, organise his life, pack lunches for his children (not to mention, make another from scratch), while he did whatever he liked, with whomever he liked – as long as he apologised. Was he any better than the boys today, leaving a wake of destruction with their impulsiveness?

She was torn. Rachael hated parts of Sam, hated what he'd done, but still admired his very image, his sexy stubble, the way he moved with such grace and confidence. The way he adored her. Sam had a natural way of gazing at her so directly, listening so attentively; no matter how long his gaze caressed her cheeks, wandered over her brow, it always felt snatched away too soon. She only needed to remember the all-consuming look on his face as he'd whispered, *No one will ever love you the way I love you*, as he thrust inside her, to know why she forgave him last time. She'd feel dead, stifled, if she'd married an ordinary, dependable bloke void of all charm. She had to expect this came with the territory.

Unshaven, bed-head Sam was Rachael's favourite because it was the version saved only for her. Not the celebrity swimmer. Not *Cleo*'s Bachelor of the Year. Her husband, in all his familiar, flawed, ordinariness. She tried to conjure that image to replace the version her protective instinct habitually streamed into her consciousness lately – Sam with another woman – and the thoughts of Sam choosing a stranger over her, of not being enough to keep Sam York from straying.

Sam filled a glass with ice from the freezer and started cutting fruit for his smoothie, one eye on some financial-looking graph on his phone. 'Spotted Ethan at school today – little bugger ignored me!'

Rachael wanted to keep giving the bastard the cold shoulder, but it was getting harder to maintain, so she responded without warmth instead. 'He's a teenage boy. Ignoring parents is in his job description.'

'Thank goodness.' Sam smiled. 'Imagine if we had to actually spend time with the greasy kid.' He gave her a look of fake disgust. 'The other time I ran into him in the hall, I asked him to stop calling me Dad at school, told him people might start to believe him.' He laughed at his own joke.

Her pride stopped her from joining in. What would it say if she did? She couldn't decide whether she should carry on, or make him pay. Was her indecision in allowing him to stay forgiveness by default? She knew that the best way to deal with emotion was to process it, then move on. She wasn't doing either.

'You're cruel. You know Ethan doesn't get sarcasm.'

Sam held his palm to the ceiling. 'Who said I was being sarcastic?'

Rachael rolled her eyes. 'I'm actually worried we aren't engaging with him enough. And once the baby comes, we'll be even less accessible.'

Strong neck muscles tensed as Sam's white teeth crushed on ice. 'You make us sound like a public building with no ramps. He doesn't want accessibility. He wants to take the stairs on his own and pretend we don't exist.'

'He barely leaves his room. If we're not engaging with him, he's likely to obsess over screens even more. You don't think that's a problem?'

'Not for me.' He stroked her arm seductively.

It made her shiver. Made the parking-lot woman pixelate in her mind and also made her want to throw up.

'Plus, you've outsourced that problem, removed any guilt by getting that screen-time app. It'll give us a bollocks-parent alert if we're being irresponsible gatekeepers, surely?'

Rachael narrowed her eyes as he pulsed the juicer, green mush dancing with each press, like a wave of nausea.

'Did you have a gander at the agency nannies, babe? Any promising talent?'

And his voice. That British accent beneath the Aussie drag melded a delicate mix of easygoing larrikin with an undertone of class. His ability to hit the truth head on, to never shy away from his faults – although always with an excuse at the ready. She told herself what he'd told her – it was only ever physical with the carpark woman. It was the only way she stopped herself from throwing things.

'I've lined up someone to do a trial on Friday when we've got our thirty-seven-week check-up.'

'Given the events of late, I'm guessing she's over sixty with a bushy moustache? Gout, perhaps?' He puffed out his cheeks as if to demonstrate. So casual about something that still made her sick to her stomach.

'Would that slow you down?' She laughed, then lamented – where was this burst of candour coming from? 'She's beautiful, actually, and seventeen.' Realisation dawned about the niggle that had rippled through her when she'd first met Gertie's daughter. The shiny black hair, the bright-blue eyes and alert intelligence. Katerina Rainworth bore a striking resemblance to the woman they never spoke of. The reason they'd felt the need to escape the world in the first place.

His eyes narrowed. 'Are you taking the piss? *Seventeen?*'

'She's great with kids, been helping with her younger brothers for years – she's responsible, Sam.'

His face pinched. 'She's barely older than Ethan and he's clueless.' Rachael knew she had poked the bear and that he'd now find fault in anything she suggested. 'You may as well get him to look after her, blimey.'

Rachael exhaled, her breath shallow with a baby curled around her ribs. 'I'd never put that responsibility on his shoulders.'

'Yeah, I get it, but I'd have thought your history would've also made you a little more discerning.' He swallowed hard.

'Excuse me?'

'Bollocks, sorry,' he mumbled. 'That was a low blow.'

She flinched when he touched her shoulder – she wasn't ready for affection from him. He snaked his arms around her swollen belly and she prayed he couldn't feel her tense. She gazed at her feet, swelling by the second, and he huffed, then took his smoothie to the stairwell. Reaching the hall, he paused at the print she'd found in the shed to replace the ripped canvas, thinking it would draw less attention than a blank wall.

'What happened to the abstract piece?'

Rachael froze. *Now he decides to notice things.* 'I leaned the vacuum on the wall while I cleaned up a spill and must have knocked it down, scraping the painting,' she lied. Better she take the brunt than Noah.

'Don't talk tosh.' The gravelly tone she hated.

'I'm sorry, it was an accident.'

His jaw clenched. She panicked, went unscripted. 'Hive had a good quarter. I'll buy you another at the next launch – call it a bonus.'

He shook his head and she saw her misstep. In public he bragged about his entrepreneurial wife, but behind closed doors he hated any mention of her income, any reference that she was the primary breadwinner.

Sam stepped towards the adjacent painting, her brother's childlike scrawl, yanked his keys from his pocket and slashed the canvas.

She had known Jekyll would eventually be usurped by Mr Hyde, but somehow it always shocked her when it happened.

Rachael's body knew better than to react. She stilled as he took the stairs and left her alone to think about what she'd done. Instead, she found clarity. She felt it expand inside and welcomed it as much as she dreaded what it meant. She had to deal with her husband before he begged for her forgiveness and she once again questioned the need to leave. Rachael was an educated, wealthy woman. Sam was never violent or abusive – it was nothing like that – so it should have been easy to orchestrate a simple separation from a cheating husband.

But nothing about this felt easy or simple.

Sam made butterflied lamb rack and cauliflower soup the following night. He had fresh peonies in a vase and crème brûlée in the fridge. The kids had helped and the music was loud as they danced laps around the island bench. Noah giggled from his father's shoulders and Ethan crawled out from his room to play along on his drum kit, a natural smile forming on his lips when his dad walked on his hands and flipped across the lounge. The pressure had built, released, and they were back to the playful mania phase that felt hopeful again, like when they'd first moved to Apple Tree Creek.

Sam's powerful arms lifted Noah onto his broad back as if he was weightless and carted him to bed in hysterics singing 'The Grand Old Duke of York', then finished the dishes on his return shortly after in the meticulous, perfectionist way he did everything.

Rachael stifled a sob when she turned her stool around and noticed a familiar picture adorning the wall again. He'd found the original of her brother's drawing in the attic, had it printed on canvas to replicate the one he'd sabotaged in front of her eyes. The skit had served its purpose of reminding her who was in charge, and Sam could reap the reward of reparation.

He noticed her notice and crossed the room to envelop her hands in his. 'Noah told me he damaged the Gundersen. I'm sorry I lashed out at Liam's painting. I was a real tosser.'

But now the replica drawing was a memory of her bullish husband's childish spite instead of her brother's unconditional adoration.

'Forgive me, angel,' he whispered in her hair, the heat in his musky breath sending goosebumps down her arm.

Sam's tall, firm frame pressed against her back, his cheek rough against the soft flesh of her neck. He promptly swivelled her on the stool and kissed a line from ear to breast, and she felt her body respond. In the past, Rachael had explained it to herself as stemming from a shallow, primal yearning, something dirty and sexual in origin. She'd always taken his denigration like a pill that remedied all her ailments. But since his latest betrayal, since her fledgling friendship with Gertie, it was becoming harder to fool herself. As if his influence had begun to fade, as if she was seeing her life through a different lens. She could see it clearly through the fog, her addiction to this. Was it really all physical, her incessant want, her relentless, animalistic need to be taken by a strong, capable man? Or on some unconscious level, did she want someone else to take charge? To be responsible so she couldn't be, wouldn't be to blame.

The slosh of warm water, cool skin against wet tiles.

Even with a baby on board, Sam's powerful shoulders didn't waver as he scooped up her slight frame, cradling her safely up the stairs, and put a spell on her once more.

Chapter 8

Gertie

Gertie Rainworth fiddled with the antique handle on her front door and considered the stranger on her porch. He looked barely older than her daughter, but it was hard to tell these days. Everyone looked twelve to her, even doctors who she figured logically had to be at least twice that. He carried a rucksack and a suitcase, and had a bent, dusty Akubra (a real one, not a city-slicker try-hard one), which when taken off revealed a flat mop of reddish hair with a damp ring of sweat above his ears. He was friendly, but a little scruffy in a manner not unlike the hobo who lived outside the IGA.

'But I don't need a nanny.' In the background there was a high-pitched scream, followed by a nasal *Muuuuum*. Foggy memories of melting down in the deli pinged in her brain, but she shut them off like too many obsolete screens on her iPad. She was fine!

'Yeah, nah.' His voice was languid, unperturbed. 'He said you'd say that. That's why he put my name on the gate.'

'Who?' Gertie asked.

'Your husband. He *is* your husband, right? Old mate Eddie? Big unit – sturdy fella, kind of quiet but sure of himself at the same time.'

Gertie's focus on this country boy narrowed. That was the best description of Ed she'd heard. She frowned at him, surveying his bulging bags. Plural. Did he think he was moving in? That seemed extreme.

A familiar swamped feeling hovered above Gertie's head – the one that made her feel like a water bottle overflowing in the sink that nobody noticed was already full. Her house, her life, her problems were already full.

As if he could read her mind, the guy said, 'Look, I've kinda already been hired. And the direct credit of my wage is already set up, so … I could just take his money and bugger off, but the thing is, I don't have anywhere to stay, and I'd feel bad. Plus, this backpack is killing me.' He plonked it on the deck, and Gertie swore a puff of dirt wafted up from it in a cloud like in a cartoon.

He had a suntan and a straight smile, and something about his heart-on-his-sleeve honesty made her open the door and invite him in.

Her phone chimed. A text from Ed informing Gertie that her 'backup' arrived today. She snarled at it. Surely if Ed had assessed him as suitable, he would have already asked for a blue card, diploma in child care and first-aid certificate as a minimum. But somehow, this kid didn't seem the type she'd pictured when Ed talked of a house-helper. She had imagined Mrs Doubtfire or a friendly Fijian grandma. Someone less … dusty. Maybe that type cost more.

As he lumbered his luggage up the toy-scattered hallway, his rusty bob pushing out from under his hat, he shared with her his surprise that he'd won the position.

'Why's that? Haven't you worked with kids this age before?' Gertie asked.

'Haven't had a paid job before.'

'Right.' The word came out through her nasal cavity as more of a squeak. *Why exactly had Ed chosen this young fellow to babysit for them?* 'And how did Eddie find you, then?'

'Mum and Mr Ed got chinwagging – mates from way back. I'm doing teaching at uni and she kind of nagged me into it, said it would be really good experience, something for the résumé. Didn't know the joint would be this flash, but. Winning!'

Gertie had known Ed since she was in plaits. She knew everyone he knew. 'And your mum is …?'

He turned away. 'From T-bar.'

Gertie wasn't sure what he was on about, this stranger in her house.

'You know, Toowoomba.'

'Ah, right. Schoolmates.' That woeful semester Ed had boarded in Year 11. He'd never said much about that time, other than that he'd hated being a whole state away from her. Who wouldn't? She was hot and fun back then.

'Yeah, he'd just got word about having to move OS when Mum ran into him in Dalby when he was on some business trip, and she told him I needed a place to crash in the big smoke, earn some coin before uni. Turns out I was way cheaper than the agency mob.'

That sounded right – thrifty was Ed's middle name. He made her reuse tea bags when they were saving for a house deposit. This was making more sense.

Harry had stripped off to his undies, abandoning his juice-soaked shorts and shirt in a sticky pile on the kitchen floor. An overturned cup floated in a puddle next to it like a tugboat.

'Abe's the one lining up garbage trucks …' Gertie said. The bloke barely flinched at the weirdness of that statement. 'And this is Harry. He's six.'

The manny nodded but looked perplexed. 'Would've said seven – with the missing front teeth. My sisters didn't lose them till grade two.'

'You're very observant. How many sisters do you have?'

'Only three.'

'Only?'

'I'm the oldest of the four boys.'

'Seven kids!' Gertie shrieked in shock. 'God, your poor mum.'

His head tilted, the freckles on his forehead drawing together.

'Sorry. That was rude. I'm sure she's immensely proud.'

He did have a certain unflappability about him. He'd need it, around here. If he stayed, of course, which he wouldn't.

Gertie went to boil the kettle before hat-boy swooped in and took it and filled it at the sink with a splash.

'He said you're addicted. To tea, I mean. That I should learn how to make it right. Strong with one big sugar, yeah?'

She slumped in the dining chair, watching this stranger move around in her kitchen looking for the mugs, picturing her bugger of a husband listing off her peculiarities, her quirks to this stranger, and didn't know whether to feel grateful, or patronised. All she was sure she felt was longing for him to come home. *You should be here making me tea, Ed. You bastard.*

'Thank you ... um ...'

'Fred.'

'Fred?'

'Yep. Why?' Fred said.

'Oh, nothing! A lovely, masculine name! There're so many Jacks and Olivers and, you know, not so many Freds, don't you find?' *Not under the age of seventy, at least.*

'That's good, though, right?' He said it like he'd never noticed until now.

81

'Absolutely! I mean, Prince Frederick did okay for himself nabbing our Mary.'

'S'pose ...' He was looking at her as if she was strange.

Am I strange? Is that why Eddie left? The cloud of overwhelm swooped in again.

Gertie had floury fingerprints on each side of the old maternity dress she'd thrown on that morning before dashing to the school run – a soft cotton sack that, to wear, felt like coming home. She'd vowed never to be seen in it again by those external to her family, but there she was. Being seen.

'Pool, Mummy?' Harry asked.

'Not now, sweetie, I'm just showing Fred around.'

'Pleeeeeaaseee,' Harry said.

'Nah, that's no wuckers.' Fred flicked off his shoes, then his sweat-soaked shirt. 'Swim sounds peachy. Melting out there. Usually have a swim in the dam every morning, so happy days.'

'Righty-ho, then!' Gertie grabbed the Banana Boat, then hesitated. Sun-screening Harry was a rather indelicate routine involving chasing him around the yard and lecturing him on skin-cancer mortality rates before cornering the kid like prey and holding him down with her elbows, while he acted as if she was coating him in hot wax, not SPF50.

Gertie figured there was no point hiding the truth – that they weren't a nice, normal family.

Fred squatted to Harry's height. 'Let's do it together, hey, Mr Harry?' He inspected the bottle's fullness and said, 'Nearly empty. Bet I can make this tube fart.'

Fred had been in Gertie's home ten minutes and had already stripped off and said 'fart'. He was going to fit right in.

At first, she wondered if this was an impromptu audition for the position and once he was 'approved' he'd do nothing but wee on the seat and leave wet towels on her floor like the other males in her life. But it was so effortless and authentic, this stranger's connection with Harry, that Gertie failed to believe it was contrived for her benefit.

For a moment, she had a fleeting vision of returning to the workforce and arriving home to her man-wife with dinner on the table, and a teeny kernel of pleasure planted itself deep inside. Would this crazy arrangement work?

Fred drew white stripes across Harry's cheeks, the brim of his nose and length of his arms, then on his own. 'See, we're both tigers now.'

Gertie feared this was a chink in his routine – that Harry was six, too old to be amused by zoo animals.

'Roaaar!' Harry yelled with enthusiasm, defying her. She ushered Harry through to the pool as Nacho bolted to the front door to welcome Katerina home.

'Hi, hon! We're out here,' Gertie called.

Kat looked up from her book at the random young man in their pool. *Was this a mistake?*

'This is Fred, hon. The home-helper your dad hired. He's studying education this year.' Fred waved.

'For real?' Kat whispered.

'For real. Your dad figured I'd need backup.' Wasn't that what partners were supposed to be?

Fred started a game of Marco Polo with Harry, and even Abe paused from lining up his car convoy to see what all the fuss was about.

'How was your trial at the Yorks'?'

Kat stole Gertie's tea. 'Trial? They never said it was a trial. I thought I was hired.'

'Okay. Sure.'

'It was glorious. They love me. Rachael's, like, the best. And she gets free stuff from stores begging her to use their products. She's, like, a proper celeb.'

Gertie's lip curled at the ridiculousness of commercialism. 'Was the dad home – the big swimming star?' She was curious about this man.

'Coach? He's great.'

'What's he like?' Something wasn't quite as it seemed in that house. She put the feeling down to the obvious – Sam York was a cheating shit and Rachael wanted to make sure that stayed private.

Kat shrugged. 'He's completely OCD, but I guess that's what it takes to be an Olympic champ.'

Gertie narrowed her eyes.

'Mum, he won two gold medals. For, like, a moment in time, he was the fastest backstroker in the world – and he lives two blocks away. How lucky are we to have him as our coach? Noah's a little champ and Ethan's pretty sick, too, actually; knows everything about *D&D*.' Kat got a dreamlike quality in her eyes. 'I'm babysitting again tomorrow.'

Would that tall, mini-Sam be alone in the house with her daughter?

'We agreed only a few hours a week. And keep your marks up, okay?'

Kat rolled her eyes and spewed forth an avalanche of enquiry regarding Fred. Who was he, why was he here, where was he going to sleep, and could she have a lock on her door?

'Hon, be reasonable.' Fred did look more grown up with his clothes off. *Should I get a lock for her door?* 'It will allow me to do more things.' Gertie was convincing herself with each word.

'Things? Like what?'

Gertie shrugged. 'Paint! Swim! Knit!' Her voice got all high and chirpy. She wasn't fooling anyone.

Kat looked at her blankly. 'But you hate that stuff.'

'Do I?'

'Yes. Remember that knitting-bee fundraiser you got roped into by Olivia Travis's mum? You only went because it had free wine – and do you even own a pair of swimmers? You said it'd be illegal to show your thighs in public.'

Instinctively, Gertie's hand pulled her dress over her legs – legs once smooth and golden, which were now speckled with hail damage. 'I said that out loud?' But by now, Kat had seen enough tears in the kitchen, hungover Sundays and hormonal outbursts to know the real Gertie. The facade that parents were faultless had left the building years ago (probably around the time the tooth fairy got drunk at a Christmas party and failed to make a delivery).

Gertie thought of Ed's kind, earnest face as he had gently explained his reason for taking the overseas post. That she had lost herself. That she wasn't the woman he'd married. That she needed time and space and independence to find the joy in life again, outside the family. Was he right? If her family was a stage production, she was the support crew (not to mention head marketer, psychologist, chauffer, costume designer and clean-up staff) and her kids were the protagonists. Had over-servicing her little stars encroached on her potential as a woman, as a wife?

Gertie had kept up with the occasional professional development course to maintain her skills, despite Ed thinking it was unnecessary, but if she didn't return to midwifery soon, her registration would lapse. It meant something to her. She had even had a stint in management, but she'd barely sunk her teeth into the role before she left to have her babies. Maybe it *was* time? Maybe Fred *was* her ticket to do that?

'... and how much do we really know about this guy, Mum?'

Gertie realised Kat was still talking. 'Hon, he's right there ...' Fred and Harry were oblivious to them, water-pistol war in full battle. Harry got shot square in the eye. Gertie waited for the tears, but he rose above it, and squirted Fred back with gusto.

The afternoon heat haze still hovered over the pavers, fogging Gertie's head. Sweat dripped down the soft curves of her torso and she glanced at Harry; so fresh and cool as he paused for a moment on the shady step of the pool.

His head tilted a little as he stared at Fred. 'How come you have three boobies?' Harry asked, a shot of water bullseyeing a small dent on Fred's breastbone.

'Harry ...' Gertie said.

'But he does, Mummy! Look!'

She had to look twice at Fred's glistening chest but saw that Fred, indeed, had three boobies. A regular pair peeking out through clusters of hairy freckles, and a third, smaller version squatting unassumingly mid-chest. There wasn't much Gertie hadn't seen as a nurse for fifteen years. Harry was now poking it like it was a magic button, just waiting to be pressed.

'Harrison!' Gertie called with a flush of embarrassment.

Fred slicked pool water from his nose and mouth, smiled and said, 'You know how you've got two nipples?' He shot Harry back on his own boring number of nipples, a stream of water hitting Harry's left boob then right, as he giggled with the absurdity. 'Well, I got three – lucky, huh? Pair and a spare.' Harry nodded at the logic and they dived in the churned-up water with the anomaly forgotten, continuing to dive and dash about with abandonment.

Hand covering mouth, Kat was flushed, sneaking sideways glances as Fred stepped out of the water to bomb-dive once more.

Gertie elbowed her daughter. 'Don't stare …' Sweat dripped down the seams of her bra. God it was hot, even for February. 'It's not appropriate.'

'It's usually only kids who notice it,' Fred said from the water. 'Most people are too busy worrying about their own looks to bother with mine.'

Gertie thought of all the times she'd skulked into the water, pulling down her T-shirt to cover whatever sin she felt needed concealment, and just how much attention she'd most likely drawn to the very parts she'd hoped to hide. Hit by an insane need to *not be that woman*, Gertie peeled off her sweaty house-dress-that-should-never-be-seen and was relieved to discover she'd chosen a black sports bra and opaque knickers that morning. She opened the pool gate and jumped.

The water was soft, wet and wonderful.

'Mummy!' Harry called, his shiny face splitting with joy as he hurtled towards her and curled his scrawny arms around her neck.

'Hey, beautiful boy,' she whispered into his slick black hair as she twirled him around. He had been a toddler in a safety vest the last time Gertie had swum with him. The last time her thighs had seen daylight. She nuzzled in to blow a raspberry on her youngest's neck and he responded with an agony of giggles.

Hearing the shenanigans, even straightlaced Abe ventured from the house, arms folded, but interested in the newcomer. 'Mum – how come Harry's talking to the man? We don't know him. That means he's a stranger.'

'Fair call, dude. I'm Fred,' he said to Abe. 'And your mum tells me you're Abe and I know you like cars. See, now we're not strangers anymore. Cool?'

A tick set off Abe's right eye. 'I have a question. Do you have a beard over your penis?' he asked Fred. 'See, my dad does, but I don't.'

Fred laughed. 'Dude – I said we weren't strangers, doesn't mean you can ask me anything ...'

'Jump in, Abe ...' Gertie said.

'I'm in my uniform.' He was torn.

'And?' Gertie smiled.

In an unprecedented act, Abe broke the rules and dived in to join the family swim. Fred reloaded his water pistol and squirted the back of Gertie's head.

'Is that appropriate, Fred?' Gertie gave her best mock-evil stare, but he wasn't buying it. Gertie laughed out loud. The joy emanating from inside her made it impossible not to feel free, not to feel anything was achievable.

For the first time since an Uber drove her husband away, Gertie felt hope. She'd christened herself in her own damn pool and felt as invigorated as an ad for Evian.

Chapter 9

Rachael

The morning sun wove between the shutters and curved a checkerboard of light against Rachael's cheek. She lay still, making her breaths long and slow. She thought of the determined look on Sam's face as he'd flicked his wrist, his key cutting the canvas she adored just because he could. It was petty and mean. She'd run out of energy for excuses. The confidence she'd once clung to, intoxicated, mesmerised, now felt more like a curse she could no longer live with.

Sam was leaving early for his annual boys' trip – a few days away with his brothers in some remote estuary – and she was a little relieved. As he left, his lips grazed her forehead in that way she'd once found tender and intimate – he'd pause a little as if to savour her, breathe her in. Now the gesture felt creepy and she naive for not picking it before. How long before Ethan saw too?

It was clear to her now that every day she spent with Sam she died a little more, drifted further away from who she wanted to be. It had to end.

She checked the security panel to confirm he'd left. She had three days alone. Three days of Sam being off-grid. It was more exquisite than having her own secret fob to come and go without being tracked.

Adrenalin charged her limbs. She rose too fast and felt giddy as she strained to reach the suitcase high in the wardrobe. There was something underhanded about escaping while his back was turned, but it might be her only chance. Sam's suits were colour-coded, his shoes lined up with meticulous care. Why had it taken years to see it? That his need for control was built on the foundation of making her believe she couldn't cope without it?

She tossed in basic clothes, toiletries. She made a mental list of the essentials – school uniforms, Noah's swimmers for Wednesday. She wasn't due for two weeks – surely she didn't need to pack baby things? Christ, she'd buy it all again if she had to.

Her children would always be her priority. But how would she explain to the boys when she picked them up from school that they were leaving their dad? The news would crush Noah – his dad was his hero. She imagined Noah's wide, trusting eyes asking why. Where would they stay? A dozen questions without answers threatened her resolve.

Rachael perched on the side of the bed and checked their joint savings account online, but she found it almost drained. She remembered Sam mentioning investing with Penny and Martin's firm. Was that where the funds went? Or was he playing games with her again? The only account she had that he couldn't control was her business account, and she arranged withdrawals to cover emergency expenses. She googled 'short-term accommodation' and jotted down a few options. She called a real estate agency advertising a furnished three-bedder near the school and explained she needed access today.

'Yes, it's still vacant. How long do you need the lease? Three months? Six?'

Forever? If she had to reveal the truth to the boys – that she was a quitter, that she'd given up on her marriage – there was no taking that back. Noah could be fooled with a story of a holiday away, but at fifteen Ethan was too old to be placated with vague platitudes. Would being honest undo the years she'd spent buffering Sam's moods?

'Oh, God, sorry – I haven't really thought this through,' Rachael said to the estate agent, her own voice sounding unfamiliar.

The estate agent was silently waiting on the line. 'Are you okay?' The woman's voice was laced with concern.

Rachael nodded, then squeaked out an unconvincing, 'Yes.'

'Can I help? Are you in danger?'

Rachael blotted the path of a tear that trickled down her cheek. 'No, he's not like that. He'd never hurt us.' He was just a cheat, not a monster. She had no right to even think of herself in the same category as women who really were battered and bruised. There it was – her fallback excuse for never before advancing this far on the 'steps to leave a husband you love' checklist. Rachael hung up, feeling stupid, impotent and alone.

The image of Sam's warm smile lit up her phone as she threw it on the bed. *What was I thinking?* Sam York had many faults – a vile temper, old-fashioned views on women and an inability to deprive himself of anything. But he was honest and funny and the father of her children. The public image of their relationship was enviable – Sam's magnificent bare shoulders draped in the flag, the poster boy of the Rio Summer Games; a glamorous full-page family portrait in *The Women's Weekly* just after Noah's arrival. But no one's reality was flawless, and when you signed up for marriage, you didn't get to choose which parts to take on; it was all or nothing. For better and for worse.

Just when his errant behaviour was more than she thought she'd ever put up with, he'd counteract the horrible deed by an equally potent act of generosity.

Deep down she knew she wasn't happy and may never be, but could she live with being to blame for tearing their family in half for her own selfish needs? If she initiated a split, the guilt would eat at her every time she shuffled kids back and forth or brushed off questions about the reasons why. The fear of that guilt had kept her planted, all these years. She was already burdened with enough guilt. She couldn't carry any more.

Her delicate hands cradled her stomach – another chain connecting her life to his.

Rachael unpacked her things and hid the suitcase away.

Later that morning, the tyres of Rachael's Audi pinged as they rolled across the drive flanked by an expanse of immaculate lawn blanketed by the morning dew. Her hair fell in soft curls, her smile wide as if it was any ordinary day, not a day where she failed to escape her life. Somehow that made the day worse than every day that came before it, even though in principle it was identical. Home from drop-off like any other day, she dipped her Gucci sunglasses to glance next door and spied Penny, mollycoddling her bonsai. Gertie had mentioned Penny was a good egg underneath the humblebrags, but Rachael hadn't made up her mind yet about her closest neighbour. In her purple dress and green shoes, she was camouflaged among the garden blooms and appeared to be pruning already perfectly spherical shrubs.

'Rachael – I was just going to call you.' She waved Noah's navy school hat like a fan. Had she been waiting for her since she'd left for drop-off? 'Found it on your driveway. If I had a dollar for every extra trip dropping off Spencer's retainer.'

'Oh, thanks, Penny.' Rachael took the hat, garaged the Audi then returned to chat, emptying the letterbox and perusing her mail.

Penny glanced furtively at her Rolex. 'It'll be first break soon. Does little Noah have a spare? You know the rule – "no hat no play".' The sing-song voice didn't hide her obvious disapproval of Rachael's disinterest in driving back through Sydney traffic to the school for something Noah should have taken responsibility for.

Rachael thinned her lips. 'It sounds harsh, but I don't drop things off – if they forget to pack something they learn the consequences.'

Penny's pruning shears stilled; she mumbled something like *but he's so little*. She assessed her progress, determined to sculpt that fig into whatever she considered perfection. Rachael gave a thin smile, flipped through the mail before her attention was pulled to a red hatchback speeding off past the pencil pines. 'Friend of yours?'

Penny glanced towards the street. 'Just the florist. Fresh blooms in the house make it so homely, don't you think?'

'Hmm. It's just I could have sworn I saw the same car at school pick-up yesterday.' Rachael could hear Sam telling her she was overthinking, explaining away the tightness in her chest by the fact that a human was kicking her ribs from inside, not that she was onto something.

'Doubt it – no kids. Oh, Martin mentioned Sam's away, so sing out if you need any help with drop-offs or anything. You mustn't have long to go now till little one arrives.'

'Two weeks.' Rachael stroked her belly. 'I do *hope* she's little given her father's size-thirteen feet. A troubleshooting guide would be handy.'

'If only.' Penny laughed. 'You know I managed a rather prominent motherhood blog – Womb with a View – with tips from when Spencer was little. Sparked a lot of comments – lots of unchristian judgement pegging me as rather old fashioned and controlling, but I stand by my principle that strong boundaries allow children to feel safe – shows they're important enough to worry about monitoring.'

Rachael sighed. 'I don't know – the more controls I put in place for Ethan, the less trustworthy he becomes. He's hacked through the last screen-monitoring program I installed – if only he could use his skills for good instead of evil.'

'Oh, Spencer wouldn't dare – he'd know that would upset me. I wrote about that, too.' Penny approached her collection of Japanese bonsai. Rachael felt a little sorry for the tiny pot-bound plants, wondering what could become of their branches with a little more freedom. Penny switched to a smaller tool yet slashed too harshly and baulked at the result.

'I'd never have the confidence to write an advice column. I find it impossible to know if I'm making the right choices. It's not as if my sons' behaviour is a barometer of my parenting. I'm used to business meetings where you get immediate feedback – with kids growth takes so long; you don't have to wait until your clients have survived adolescence for any indication that you're doing okay.'

'True.' Penny sighed. 'Well, just don't fuck it up.'

Rachael flinched, the words so unexpected.

Penny flicked the pruning shears into her vintage gardening trolley. 'I s'pose, given your condition, a mojito is out of the question? Apparently, that's a no-no now.' She screwed up her nose as if Rachael had got pregnant just to piss her off. 'Shame. I'm far better at advice after one – not that I'd admit that online these days. Bloody trolls – whores the lot of them.'

Rachael held her stomach as she laughed, scared she'd wee all over her shoes.

Her curiosity about mud-mouth Penny piqued, Rachael googled Womb with A View. Penny's blog was the first hit on her search engine and included years worth of content, life hacks and articles for busy parents that at a glance seemed rather useful. 'No one warned me that my thirteen-year-old son who used to greet me like a doting puppy, would turn into a cat.' Rachael could relate – Ethan used to bounce over to welcome her home and now was aloof, only seeking her company when he needed feeding. She dug deeper into the archives. 'The five-year age gap becomes problematic around bedtime ...' one post read. Wasn't Spencer their only kid? Perhaps they had a child at university, or had something more tragic played out in that house? Rachael got the impression Penny pandered to Spencer like a prince, cultivated him like her pot-bound bonsai. Was this the reason? She felt an unexpected connection with her perplexing neighbour.

Rachael knew Ethan had visited next door once, gaming with Penny's son, and quizzed him about Spencer Crawley over a vegan smoothie after school.

'His computer's so sick it needs three external fans to run. Got the latest graphics cards and his monitor has zero lag. And get this, Spencer's got the new iPhone, a back-to-base drone, an independent microphone ...' Rachael tried to appear impressed. To her, he just seemed spoiled. 'They must be loaded. He's even got a remote-control tarantula he takes to school. Think that's why everyone calls him Creepy Crawley.'

'I hope *you* don't call him horrible things like that. We have to live next door to these people.'

Ethan shrugged. 'Yeah, I get it, don't shit where you eat.'

'Language ...' Rachael smiled at how far he'd come in understanding social norms.

He slurped the last of his shake. His face had lengthened, his cheekbones becoming more prominent in the last year, as if finally growing into his father's masculine features. 'He is kind of a dick, though.'

Rachael scoffed. 'That's an official diagnosis? After one afternoon?'

'He takes the bus, too, so I've had a few weeks to gather evidence – stuff like him rating how hot girls are, writing down their best features, what they wear 'n' stuff.'

Rachael frowned. She hated anyone assuming they had a right to comment on anyone's body, complimentary or otherwise. Despite her concern over Spencer's moral fibre, Rachael liked Ethan sharing elements of his day. She ached to know him. To connect with the boy who used to hold up his hand for her to cover with hers. He still existed, beneath the pimples and stubble, behind those eyebrows growing bushier by the day.

'Think I preferred his rat, actually – Bart was pretty cool. He's totally obsessed with Fortnite.'

'The rat plays Fortnite?' Rachael joked.

He made a face at her attempt at a joke, but she could tell they were both more relaxed when Sam went away. 'He, like, monitors everyone's gamer ranking.'

'Ranking?' She felt a twinge zap through her lower back and had to sit down.

'Fortnite ranking. World ranking – depending on your kill rate, solo wins and stuff.'

Rachael didn't want to know Ethan's kill rate, but hoped it wasn't good, as that would indicate he didn't spend every waking moment on it as she feared.

'It's also freaky how their floorplan is the same. Oh, except for one bit – I opened the wrong door when I went for a piss – ended up in a weird sort of bedroom.'

Rachael shrugged but was intrigued. 'Probably just a spare,'

'Dunno, had like, trophies and men's clothes.'

'Maybe Mr Crawley snores and sleeps separately. In any case, it's none of our business.' *Maybe they have another child hidden in the basement whom they let up for air?*

Ethan did a double-take at the hall wall. 'What happened to Dad's painting? He smash it?'

Why would he say that? 'I did, actually.'

''Cause it was so fugly? Spencer also went on about Dad like he's a celeb. Gave me the shits. I mean, if they saw the tosser he was at home, drooling on the couch …'

'Ethe.' Was her son's growing insight revealing more about their marriage than she'd hoped?

'The world dotes on him like he's a god, it's so stupid. Kind of glad he's pissed off for a few days. We can just chillax.' As a young child, it only took a Happy Meal to smooth over any wrongdoing – it was far harder for his father to be forgiven for his moods now that Ethan was a little wiser.

Barry the security guard's round, cheerful face appeared on the digital panel near the door. 'Mrs York? You decent? Delivery.' Ethan padded to the door in his socks and grunted to Barry in his starched uniform as he handed over a beautiful arrangement of red roses.

Rachael sighed. The card's message read, *Miss you already. S xx.*

'Only time my missus gets spoiled is when I'm in the doghouse.' Barry chuckled, adjusting the belt looping his wide girth. He had a red line across his forehead where his hat usually sat. 'So, what's Golden Boy done now, eh?'

She wondered what Barry knew.

Rachael ignored the incessant urge to bake and reorganise her pantry the following Sunday. She hadn't felt right when she'd dropped Ethan at the deli for his shift. It wasn't sickness – she felt energised for once, but also frustrated and overwhelmed, as if all her errands were taking too long to achieve. Was she lost without Sam forever hovering? It wasn't until the dragging sensation in her pelvis became sharper and knocked her off her feet that it became clear – she was in early labour. A sudden searing pain shot through her abdomen in a sharp wave. She noted the time – 4.32 pm.

Sam was likely ankle-deep in mangroves, out of mobile range, and at the peak of his annual three-day drinking bender. She tried the satellite phone number he'd arranged just in case – it didn't connect. A second contraction shuddered through her, and she breathed through it, noting it was three minutes since the first – too early to be so close together. Panic rose in her throat. There was no way she could drive, but an ambulance would take forever.

Rachael called Gertie – she'd tell her they were just Braxton Hicks – but her mobile rang out. Rachael did her best to not let the latest in a swift line of menacing contractions floor her as she called Noah to help, then waddled down the street towards Gertie's place, Noah wheeling her overnight bag beside her as if they were going on a mini-break.

'Did you bring snacks?' her son asked.

Steadying herself against a tall fig tree, she breathed in and out, letting the pain shudder through her like an earthquake. 'Sweetie, run along to Kat's house on Lily Court, number twelve.'

'The one with the old bus?' Noah's wispy blond fringe curtained his eyes.

Rachael nodded. 'Tell her the baby's a bit early. That I need a lift. You're such a good helper.' Rachael couldn't breathe, couldn't speak through the pain, but told herself lies just to get through them. Was this a punishment – brought on by the stress of attempting to leave Sam?

As her son raced towards the Rainworths' place, Rachael screamed out the pain she'd been pretending wasn't there. She hugged the tree for grim death, with what seemed like only a breath's reprieve before another contraction was upon her. They were coming thick and fast. *I am not delivering this baby on the footpath.*

Moments later, the chilled young guy who'd helped her assemble the cot the day before on Gertie's orders, bolted across the street to where she clung to her tree. 'Hey, Mrs Y, lucky we got the cot sorted, huh?' He spoke loud and slow.

'I'm pregnant, Fred, not deaf.'

'Yeah, no wuckers. Gertie's bringing the car. You'll be sweet, Mrs Y.' His face said otherwise, as a gush of bloody amniotic fluid darkened the pebbled path beneath her bare feet. Fred pulled off his hoodie, grabbed Rachael's elbow and led her to the thick, soft grass beside the tree and lowered her carefully onto the hoodie. He sat behind her, hesitated, then rubbed her back. 'Ah, not sure how this works, exactly – I've only delivered calves.'

Noah and Gertie pulled up in the Tarago. Rachael was sucked into a world of pain once more, clenching her teeth to muffle a scream.

When it faded to a throb, she locked eyes with Gertie and cried, 'This can't be happening. Sam's away. I'm not due for two weeks.' She felt the urge to hitch up her skirt and push.

Gertie placed her hands on Rachael's stomach as the contractions tightened her skin. 'Ah, Rach, yes, it seems this little lady didn't get that email. I need to examine you, if that's okay?'

Rachael nodded, all modesty forgotten, and watched as Gergie gloved up.

'Looks like she's in a hurry – you're crowning.'

Rachael's breaths came thick and fast as she shook her head. 'I can't do this, not here. It's too much. I don't do labour well at the best of times.'

Gertie took a deep breath but stayed entirely calm as she announced, 'I beg to differ. You're doing so well.' She turned to Fred. 'Call an ambulance, tell them we have an expectant third-time mum—'

'Second,' Rachael clarified.

Gertie did a double-take then nodded. 'Second-time mum … thirty-eight weeks, seven centimetres dilated and get me those towels.'

'No, no, not here. Sam had everything planned,' Rachael said between pants.

Gertie rubbed her back, telling a frightened Noah it was okay, that Mummy was tough and brave, but Rachael didn't feel either of those things. She felt untethered from reality, as if she was being ripped in half by a great white shark who was still circling, about to return for another bite, and she'd do anything to swim to shore to escape the next wave.

'Rachael, honey, you're almost there. There's no sign of breach, you've totally got this! Just look at me, don't focus on your surrounds.'

Rachael gazed into her friend's dark eyes, and the whole world reduced to their confidence, their warmth.

'Okay, I've done this a few times, hon, and I think you'll be better sitting up …' Gertie reached over and helped Rachael upright to a crouch position, taking her pulse as she supported her wrists. 'That's perfect. Gravity is our friend. I had an old birthing kit in the boot – we used to give them out to expectant mums in regional towns, just in case.' There were gloves, wipes, a clamp-looking thing at her side, and Rachael tried to breathe through the panic.

'The ambos want to speak to you,' Fred told Gertie and proceeded to relay a few facts to the officer on the phone.

Gertie turned her head away from Rachael and whispered into the mobile, which only made Rachael listen harder. *It's a nuchal cord but there's no evidence of occlusion.*

'What's that mean?' Rachael asked

Gertie just gave a one-handed thumbs up. 'I think it's loose enough that I can slip the cord over baby's shoulders and deliver through the loop.'

'Is something wrong?' Rachael cried, tears flowing, snot dripping, her legs trembling as she crouched on her knees on the grass.

'Absolutely not. This is quite common, and I've done this all before, so I need you to just breathe, and trust me, okay?'

Her breaths raced like they were playing tag with the one in front.

'Pretend you're blowing bubbles in a milkshake through a straw. Keep breathing out. Can you see the bubbles, Rach?'

'I can't see any fucking bubbles!' she screamed through gritted teeth.

'Okay, Mama-bear, we just need one big push with the next contraction, and you might be ready to meet your daughter. Are you with me?'

'Bloody Sam, I'm going to kill him for missing this!'

'You can do this without him, Rach. You are a warrior. You can do anything you set your mind to. Bub's getting impatient,

101

so we need one big push so we can meet the precious girl. We're on the home stretch now, hon.'

Rachael stared into her friend's eyes, leaching the confidence from Gertie's words with each second, and nodded. Seeing Gertie take charge so competently, she couldn't help but feel calm. She clenched her jaw, groaned from the depths of her toes, and pushed, a scream so raw, so guttural it could have been from a wild beast cooked alive.

With the next push the baby's head was born.

Gertie's expression turned serious, her hands moving decisively. 'We'll just tuck this out of the way …' She swiftly looped the cord around the baby's shoulders, and with one last burning push one slithery baby girl was delivered into Gertie's open palms.

Rachael fell back onto the ground in exhaustion and turned to face her helpers with sweat-soaked hair slick on her forehead. Gertie's gloved hands placed the plump, writhing pink bundle onto Rachael's dress.

'Welcome to the world, little lady, and well done, Mum.'

With lush thick grass curved precisely along the path in a quaint little clearing in the shade of a fig tree, it could have been a Sunday picnic — if it weren't for the scattering of bloodied towels and used gloves.

'Noah,' a love-struck Rachael announced, as her stunned-to-silence son crouched beside her, 'meet Indiana Gertrude York, your baby sister.'

Gazing at her daughter, at her helplessness, her indecision about her marriage simplified into an obvious choice. Having children together wasn't a reason to stay. This baby girl was the best reason in the world to leave.

Gertie stayed with Noah as they wheeled Rachael into the back of an ambulance. The six-year-old had grown bored of his new sister and started asking for snacks.

'Gertie?' Rachael extended her free arm to grab her hand, worry etched on her face.

Gertie squeezed her hand and smiled. 'Hon, it's just precautionary, we'll see you there soon.'

'No, it's not that,' Rachael whispered, and Gertie frowned, leaning in. 'I need you to help me leave my husband.'

Chapter 10

Gertie

As twilight bled into night, Gertie buzzed with adrenalin. After receiving a tearful call from a relieved Rachael from the maternity wing and taking an exceedingly long bath, Gertie found herself wide-eyed on the couch, with Fred, reliving the day's unexpected roadside delivery over a drink.

'You were so bloody fearless, delivering that kid,' Fred declared to Gertie, still reeling. He sipped a beer Gertie assumed he was legally old enough to drink.

'It's birthed.' She sipped her wine. 'Delivery is something you do with a pizza.'

'Right. Yep. I mean, it was so amazing, but also so … gross. Who knew there was so much gushing and squirting and—' He paused, his young face lighting up with bewilderment. 'But hats off – what you ladies do – that is amazeballs.'

Gertie laughed, sure she'd scarred the poor lad for life.

'You were so calm, and you just looked like you were made to do it, you know? You should go back to it. Being a nurse, I mean. You're good at it. And if you don't mind me saying, you looked kind of sick out there today – you had a real *don't mess with me* vibe going on.'

Gertie spat wine down her clean PJ top and spilt the rest over herself in shock. 'Sick?'

'Sure. For an older chick, I mean.'

'Ah, thanks, Fred. I think.' Gertie considered sucking the spilled wine from her shirt but decided to wait until Fred had left the room.

'No wuckers!' he said, giving a strange gesture with his hand that resembled a cross between a peace sign and the bird.

Gertie chuckled. His navy eyes crinkled in a familiar squint, his muscle-shirt showing off his broad shoulders. Fred smiled at her in a way that set off a spell of déjà vu, a carefree feeling she remembered from her youth. A safe birth and some false flattery from a young fella – she hadn't felt that pumped in years.

Gertie thought back to when her children's bodies were a mere extension of her own, and when they'd arrived – holding each of them in her arms with Ed by her side – and missed him like sleep. Some days she thought she was killing this single-parenting thing, barely giving Ed's betrayal a second thought, while other days a wave of despair hit like an asthma attack, a dragging physical pain pummelling her chest, and she'd wonder if that's why poets talked of dying of a broken heart.

And did Rachael really mean what she said in that ambulance, or was her post-partum brain oversensitive to oxytocin?

It was hard to resume normal programming the next morning. Lunches, drop-off – it all seemed like Groundhog Day.

Fred read her mind. 'I've got the lunches sorted, Mrs R. After all that awesomeness yesterday, why don't you have the day off?' he chirped from the sink.

The concept of a day off from motherhood was so foreign she had no idea what that resembled. For example, this twenty-minute window was usually spent matching socks or finding swimming caps. What else could she possibly do to fill the void? With Fred controlling breakfast she escaped to the bathroom, keen to curl her hair like the working mums without burning her ear-rim. Harry came in.

'Morning, cherub!' A musical note she didn't recognise threaded through her words.

'Your voice is weird.' He looked at her funny via the mirror. 'And why are you ironing your hair?'

She hugged and smiled and waved as the kids marched out to the Tarago but felt displaced as Fred took her position in the driver's seat. That feeling grew louder as the house filled with silence. Gertie was ready, makeup done, hair blissfully fuzz-free, but she sat frozen on the couch. Why was the concept of a day off so frightening, the pressure so fierce? Perhaps she'd just stay home and get that washing folded, reorganise the overflowing pantry, bake something for the kids when they arrived back.

'And don't even think about staying home and doing jobs.' Fred read her mind again when he returned home.

This is getting weird. 'You think I'm *that* pathetic?'

Forced to leave home to maintain her self-respect, she decided there was always shopping to give life purpose, and bought too many gifts for Indiana Gertrude York, found Kat the art paper she'd been asking for all term and felt proud for solving her dilemma of having free time. Next, she spotted a quaint child-unfriendly cafe (cluttered with knick-knacks Harry would likely smash in seconds) to waste another hour consuming banana bread she didn't have to bake, and coffee she didn't have to brew.

But after twelve minutes, scanning the room full of chatting mums with their bubs sipping babycinos, Gertie had never felt so alone. Rachael would be recuperating, bonding as a family now that Sam was home. She called Lou, thinking she might meet her for lunch, but her sister's phone was off – she was likely in court. She tried three friends – all of whom were working or too busy to answer – then felt a wave of mother's guilt for not spending her time on her children's needs.

She had a manny – she was meant to be a lady who lunched, goddamn it!

She was about to return home within two hours, forgo this independence thing (*Tried it! Didn't suit!*), retreat to the safe walls of home where her role was defined (*Mum, toilet paper, upstairs loo, right now!*), the expectations clear (*What's for dinner? Where's my sports shirt?*), when she remembered how magical it had felt to help bring that precious baby into the world.

Except for birthing her own children, nothing Gertie had done since leaving midwifery had ever provided the same rush, offered the same sense of purpose. She'd gone to such lengths – through morning sickness and bouts of mastitis, to learn the skills required to do what she did. She'd missed it like air, and in that moment when Rachael's baby had taken her first breath and she'd cradled that miracle and handed it over, Gertie had felt the world shift. Her soul had reawakened.

She knew kids took a hit when parents returned to work – the missed sports carnivals, the mad morning rush – but life was bigger than her family, than what she saw each day, and she wanted to be part of it once more. To be her full self again.

Gertie opened up her contacts, scrolled through a long list of entries like 'Jack's mum,' and 'Sienna's mum,', before she found it – the number for the supervisor of her old midwives crew.

Gertie thought for a moment. Could she really go back to living with a body clock all out of whack, being awake when her family slept, to the emotional and physical pain that came with nursing?

Gertie didn't need to think, she knew the answer.

She was going to get a life.

The reality of returning to paid work proved less magical than Gertie had planned. The first shock of the brave new world came when she discovered, after years of post-grad study in midwifery, she hadn't kept up enough hours to continue her dual registration, so was relegated a casual position in a general ward. *Shouldn't having your own babies count towards something?* The second shock was seeing they'd put a frumpy, middle-aged woman's picture on her ID card to replace the hot young nurse that had smiled back at her before. But that didn't stop her. Ed wanted her to find herself, didn't he?

Not everyone left with a healthy newborn, but the maternity wing had always been her happy place, a village fuelled on hope. The throng of green- and blue-uniformed staff, the clipboards and lanyards and kitchen sinks stacked with empty vases, the over-instructive signage and astringent scent of ammonia. Gertie had always taken comfort in hospitals as proof that civilisation and kindness would prevail.

Fred had the nerve to attend lectures two mornings a week, and the small task of wrangling four pairs of matching shoes and socks and shunting everyone in the van by eight each morning seemed insurmountable with the additional challenge of getting herself decent, too. *How did people do this year in, year out?* She'd been late already that week, having to drop off kids before starting her shift. She didn't want to make a habit of it.

But that day, Abe was facing an existential crisis. Clocking twelve minutes in the two-minute zone wouldn't have drawn as much attention if Gertie Rainworth didn't have the only Tarago in a line of BMWs. Despite Harry bolting into the school grounds as ebullient as ever, Abe refused to disembark. His belt stayed firm, his back rigid, as he sat in his seat, frowning at the school gate as if he couldn't pass its threshold until he'd made an important decision.

Gertie waved and smiled as the au pairs beeped their horns. 'Aren't they friendly today?' she said.

Abe was too scared to sign up for coding club, despite being obsessed by all things tech, as he'd convinced himself the teacher had it in for him. The form was due that day if he wanted to secure a place.

'I really think you should join,' Gertie encouraged with not a hint of the frustration she felt, wondering if she'd missed her calling as an actor. 'You love coding, and you're so clever at *Scratch* at home!'

'She won't pick me to join the club, anyway. She hates me!' Abe cried, a grid of worry lines running across his forehead.

'I reckon the only people that could possibly not think much of you are those silly, sour-faced, judgey people who don't actually know you. Does she know how honest and clever and loyal you are? Has she ever actually spoken to you for more than five minutes?'

'No ...'

'So, she's new. An unknown.'

He nodded.

'Well. I find that if I approach new people with the assumption that they *do* like me – which, let's face it, usually is the case once they know how awesome I am – I have a much better chance of them taking a liking to me, than if I presume they don't. Because a funny thing happens when you assume people like you – you become likeable.'

He still didn't move, but the frown lines were noticeably shallower. She tried not to look at her watch. Despite knowing it would make her later, she crawled into the back seat to aid her campaign and held his warm cheeks in her hands.

'In summary, everyone I know loves you, Abe. How could they not? You are the only eight-year-old who has memorised the manual to every appliance in your classroom. So even if she doesn't *yet*, why don't we just pretend she likes you, until she does?'

He gazed suspiciously at the coding permission slip on the bench seat. 'Maybe ...'

Gertie kissed his cheek, unable to hide her motherly glee as he disembarked, backpack bigger than him, curling the sweaty note in his fingers. She was beginning to feel less like an imposter. The longer she got away with clunking and tripping inside Ed's shoes as well as wearing her own, the more it felt like the new normal.

'Hello, family dearest!' Gertie called upon returning home after work, lumping her bag on the kitchen bench.

No one so much as looked up from their dose of toxic, eyeball-stretching gadget viewing. Fred was scooping leaves from the pool, three nipples on display in the morning light, and gave a friendly wave. Kat grunted without her gaze leaving her phone, her pointer finger flicking back and forth in curls and dips intently, and the two boys barely realised she was there. It seemed like only yesterday that her kids trembled with anxiety when she left for work, but now they couldn't care less.

'How was school?' Gertie kissed each child on their apple-scented heads. 'I've got groceries in the back to bring in. Aunty Lou and Uncle Timmy are coming for dinner. Much to do.'

No one moved.

'Where are my helpers, huh?'

The kids didn't budge. Didn't even look up.

'What's that? Smoke? Flames?' Gertie mocked, pointing towards the perfectly fire-free kitchen.

No response.

'Okay! That's it!' Her back ached. She had a whiff of vomit on her work shoes that no disinfectant could erase (this time, from a dad who got too close to the business end in the labour ward where she was helping out) and she hadn't slept in thirty-two hours. She stomped over to the router and disabled the Wi-Fi in one swift flick.

Their attention was instant and sharp.

'Mum! I'm in the middle of school stuff!' Kat cried. *Utter BS if ever I heard it.*

'I'm downloading something!' Abe's eyes teared up. He screamed as if she'd torn off a limb.

Harry was slower on the uptake, only realising the reality when his game crashed. Wide-eyed and with balls of steel, he calmly stepped over and turned the Wi-Fi back on. Gertie proceeded to turn it back off, then they fumbled about like a game of thumb war, battling childishly to see who could press the button fastest, her large thumb squashing his tiny finger as she forced the bloody thing off as Harry pressed it on.

'Fine!' Gertie raged.

She stomped over to the lounge, recovering with some dignity from tripping over Nacho's chew toy, grabbed the mini and large iPad and Kat's phone in one swift swoop, and paced over to the study, where she proceeded to place their precious gadgets in the Lock Box (her old filing cabinet), turned the key and pulled it from the lock.

Three jaws dropped. No Wi-Fi was one thing. No devices *at all* was another.

'But, Mum! I was just about to beat the Ender Dragon!'

'You didn't power mine down and it's on five per cent charge!'

Even Kat was in a panic. 'What the! You can't do that – I'm texting Sienna!'

'You won't be getting these back this year!' Gertie shrieked. She tried her darndest to view the stress she felt positively, like the motivating force it was meant to be, but it wasn't working.

Harry burst into tears. Abe didn't panic – sure she'd never follow through.

Gertie felt the need to backtrack and not use hollow threats. 'Or ... well, at least until we've had some bloody family time – outside!' Quality, sunlit, eye-muscle-stretching, skin-cancer-causing outdoor time. Gertie felt a sting and realised she'd been gripping her keys with such tension one had punctured the heel of her hand. A line of blood tainted her lily-white palm, as if in warning.

She felt she was failing on every level. Normally she'd have bounced this frustration off Ed, but where was he? Visiting the zoo on his days off? Entertaining clients over Singapore Slings? Perhaps she didn't have this in the bag. Perhaps it was time for Ed to re-enter the stage and play his part. Gertie was out of lines.

Chapter 11

Martin

Martin Crawley parked in the side street just before the estate gates, his Cobra idling softly. He couldn't go home. Not yet. Not to the hard smile of his wife, disappointed again by something he'd done (and she didn't know the half of it). Not to the watchful winking of the CCTV hidden in the vines, in the hedge, in the hallways. Not to the son who barely grunted his way, eyes mesmerised by the pixels on the screen talking to people he'd never met. His mind just needed a moment to process all that had transpired. Everything he did was for Penny and Spencer. He'd been the sole provider for this family for over twenty years. Was a moment alone too much to ask?

Martin's shoulders felt squashed against the racer-back seat. If he'd known he'd spend so much time transitioning from work to home sitting in his car he'd have opted for a model with more room. At least he had no hair to be windswept by the lack of roof.

His mobile chirped the ringtone he'd set only for his wife so he'd never miss the call. 'Yes, love?'

'Darling, dinner's ready. You still at the office?' Penny asked.

Penny, his loyal, complex wife who would one day know everything. But he'd wait until the last possible moment to burst her bubble. If she was prickly now, he couldn't imagine what she'd be like to live with when she found out.

If his marriage was listed on the stock exchange, he'd be selling off quick.

Martin had read somewhere that people could sense your smile in your voice over the phone, so he grinned like a twit. 'Just approaching the gates now, Pen, be there in a jiffy.'

The Cobra purred as he slid it into first and drove on.

Chapter 12

Penny

Penelope Crawley had just started to forgive her husband for being late to dinner. She had even started to hum along to Celine Dion as she had stacked the Royal Dalton in the dishwasher and folded washing in precise piles to return to lavender-scented drawers. She'd even knocked before entering her teenage son's room with his pile.

The problem was he didn't hear her.

And oh, did Penny wish he had.

One horrifying minute later, she stumbled into her own dimly lit bedroom, her eyes fixed on the mobile phone she had just confiscated from Spencer. Jaw slack, she couldn't work out how she felt about the vile images on the screen. Shocked? Appalled? She tripped over Martin's ghastly slippers, but he barely noticed – too focused on his own damn screen. No doubt searching for yet another Cobra accessory they had no room for in this too-small, overpriced concrete box. Aubergine pillows supported his stocky frame, his laptop perched on yet another. She considered not involving him in what she'd caught Spencer doing in his room at all – something was off with him and he was increasingly late home from work, but the urge to share was too great. She wanted to write a blog about it just to vent all the emotions it triggered.

'Martin!' She perched on the end of their bed. She poked his toes when he ignored her, and he gasped, but at least she had his attention.

'What is it?'

'Martin, what have we done? Allowing him this bloody phone in his room all night, exposed to God knows what filth! Look at what I just found your son watching!'

After all she'd done for that child. The money she'd spent on counselling, being there for him at every turn – not to mention the school fees for St Aquinas (along with the 'unofficial payments' they'd had to make).

Martin held the phone at arm's length so he could focus without his reading glasses, then rolled his eyes. 'So, he's watching porn. Most teenage boys do. I would have too if they'd invented the internet back in the eighties.'

Penelope punched him in the leg again. 'Not just watching it …'

Martin twisted his lip, dismissive, then reached for his specs and had a good perv. 'Jesus.' He laughed. 'That looks a hell of a lot like the swimmer's missus from next door.'

Penelope glared. 'That's because it is!'

Martin scoffed but kept both eyes peeled in interest and she wondered just how familiar Martin was with this vile smut. 'Yeah, right.' The look of horror on Martin's face only grew as the video counter ticked along in the corner of the screen. 'What? Spence recorded this? Well, you can't blame him, really – that sort of thing going on outside his window.'

'He wasn't in his room – he's used a drone! Look! They're branches! He's stalking them, hiding behind a tree! And look at the way he's choking her, pulling her hair! How can I look at her now without thinking of her, down on all fours, being disrespected like a laneway whore? Surely only farm animals do it like that?' Penny's jaw went slack at what this meant. 'God, Martin, like we haven't had enough trouble with this sort of filth.'

Penny and Martin had been bursting with passion for each other when they'd first met, but had waited until they were married, and been faithful to each other with a rather healthy sex life ever since. They were decent, honest, hardworking people. Every instinct she'd ever felt, every decision she'd ever made as a mother. Was every one of them wrong?

God, I need another drink.

And how could she look that woman in the eye, after seeing that much of her? She genuinely liked Rachael, even though it was clear that her immediate neighbour preferred Gertie's company over hers, despite doing everything she could to make her feel welcome. Penny tried her best not to be jealous when she saw them toddle back and forth from each other's houses, without either of them ever inviting her to join them. Oh, God – maybe they were swingers? No, they couldn't be, surely. Penelope was certain Rachael and Gertie loved to mock her – she'd heard them snort-laughing like teenagers at the playground together and felt like a schoolgirl left out of a game of tiggy. *You can't play. The game is full.*

Should she come clean? Reveal her son for the pervert he was, or hide this forever?

Chapter 13

Gertie

Gertie woke the next Sunday to the sight of Harry inches from her face, dressed in his uniform (he thought it was a school day, bless his clueless heart) complete with toothpaste stains down his shirt. It was like the times she'd open her eyes in the wee hours to find Harry's face millimetres from her own, muttering something alarming like 'I did poos' or 'I turned all the taps on' that required immediate action.

'It's after six. I've brushed my teef. You said I could play!'

When she realised she wasn't having a nightmare, Gertie replied, 'Okay, hon. I'll get the key to the box. Give Mummy two minutes.'

After discovering the freezer defrosting and slipping on grit from the sandpit, two minutes blew out to five. She heard Harry yelling for her and hurried to put out each fire as quickly as possible.

Then she heard the alarming sound of rubber bashing steel. She entered the study to find Harry attacking the Lock Box with abandonment.

The Rainworths' family Lock Box had its roots in a moment of frustration-induced insanity, but it had become a rather useful resource. It offered a level of control over her children (and husband) she hadn't enjoyed for years. *'I will not open the box until you're dressed for school and brushed your teeth!'* They'd never found their shoes so quickly.

The only downside was when the key was MIA.

'Harry, let's just find the key, shall we?' Gertie offered.

Harry continued to kick the cabinet with an aggression reminiscent of drug addicts desperate for a fix. The contents of the top of the Lock Box spilled onto the tiles. Pens rolled. A pot smashed. Dirt scattered. Was this him acting out about his father's abandonment? She wasn't sure but figured she'd blame it on Ed in any case.

Like a human straightjacket, Gertie stilled his flailing arms by hugging him close. 'Harry! Stop!' she said, calm and firm. Both of them fell to the floor as one eight-limbed creature, but he kept kicking. When his feet repeatedly missed her, he reassessed how to maximise the impact of his tiny body and went for the headbutt, straight into the bridge of her nose — a tried-and-tested disarming method that he'd learned when he was two and had filed away for later use.

'It's after six and I'm dressed! I've brushed my teef!' he repeated as if in a trance.

Gertie tried to breathe through the pain pulsing through her head. She pressed her finger on her nose, warm blood trickling into her mouth. 'Sweetheart. Take a breath, remember your milkshake breathing? Stay calm, stay clever. In — one, two, three ...'

He kicked on. It wasn't that he was ignoring her, he simply couldn't hear her. His concrete thinking never bent for anything. He was a slave to his impulses. Nothing mattered but accessing that cabinet.

'Harry. I am not getting the key until you calm down and clean up the mess you made and apologise to Mummy for hurting my nose.'

'No!'

Gertie held her six-year-old's shoulders firmly. 'Sweetheart ...'

For the first time, he looked at her. He saw the blood. Shock danced in his eyes and he collapsed in tears, admitting defeat. Gertie grabbed another tissue and blotted up the blood. She held him for a long beat.

'Was that from me?' he cried, remorse replacing the anger.

'It looks worse than it is, kiddo,' Gertie lied, as pain zipped through both eyes.

A knock at the door startled them both. A glance through the peep hole found Mr Harris's red flannel robe. His bushy eyebrows reminded her of the gruff old man from *Up*.

Gertie opened the door, a fake smile thin on her face. 'Good morning, Mr Harris. Sorry about the commotion.'

'Is that what you call that racket!' Spit bubbles formed in the corners of his mouth as he spoke, and she couldn't help but focus on them. He was one of those strange men who wore Brylcreem to secure a spiral of long hair in a circular pattern to hide his balding scalp, but today the engineering feat wasn't fooling anyone.

'We're having a bit of a difficult morning, aren't we, champ.' Gertie turned to Harry and noticed him walking through thumbtacks, but as he had school shoes on he was unperturbed.

'A difficult year, more like it. This happens all the time, Mrs Rainworth. What in God's name is going on with that child of yours? He's off the rails!'

Gertie exhaled. 'I can assure you that although it sounds as though I'm breaking bones, we're just having a disagreement over his iPad ...'

'A disagreement! I fathered five lads and not one of them would dare leave me with a bloody nose or they'd know it. That's the difference between children raised with boundaries and children left to run wild through the streets, like this one.' He made a circular motion with his finger in the general direction of Harry.

'Mr Harris, I apologise for the noise, but I'm doing my best.' There was a wobble in her words she didn't intend. 'Harry is still learning to control his impulses. He has special needs, so—'

'Special needs! Phh! Sounds like an excuse! All that boy *needs* is a good dose of discipline! And over a bloody video machine! No wonder the child has no manners when you let him spend all day babysat by the inter-web while you toddle off to work!'

I will not take judgement from pensioners who never had to manage children in the digital age. Sure, they didn't have it easy with a couple of world wars, but this was a different world. A world where hardcore porn was freely available on every kid's mobile. Where paedophiles hunted children online like lions stalking gazelles. Where bullying and belittling continued uninterrupted on social media well after a child escaped home from the tyrants at school. Gertie wondered how many of the older generation *wouldn't* have thrown an iPad at one of their kids at 6 am on a Sunday morning if it meant an hour of peace to churn the butter or cut the wood.

Gertie Rainworth squared her jaw, wishing she had the guts to say half the thoughts spinning through her mind.

'Now if you wouldn't mind controlling your child, I'll try to get some sleep!' her neighbour spat at her.

Sure, Mr Harris. I'll just click the 'mute' button on my son.

She was wishing she could sink into the floor when she heard Harry inside.

'Got it!'

Mr Harris and Gertie both turned.

Harry, problem solver that he was, had picked the lock of the cabinet with a nail file Gertie hadn't known they owned, and was now holding up his iPad, his blotchy face, still wet with tears, now split with a triumphant grin.

She could almost see the rage rise up from Mr Harris' neck. 'And you're just going to let him have the bloody thing, after that little tanty?'

Effective parents are confident parents. She chose to tune out both Mr Harris and the little voice in her head that occasionally sneered disparaging remarks suggesting she was an imposter in her own life.

Mr Harris expected a reply and Gertie's stunned silence rattled him. She let Harry run off with his hard-earned device.

'What sort of parent *are* you?' Mr Harris asked, rhetorically, she presumed.

Gertie shook off her self-doubt and stood up straight. 'I'm his. And you, Mr Harris, decidedly are not.' She glimpsed the sight of his jaw dropping as she closed the door.

It was close to midnight. After a few red-eyed night shifts at the hospital, Gertie's circadian rhythm was fried. She imagined she was jetlagged from a trip to the Maldives instead of exhausted from life as she walked herself tired around the prison yard.

Fairy lights twinkled along the hedges, sprinklers misted the mondo grass, and pink-nosed possums ran the gauntlet along the hedges. Despite the crimson-brushed leaves declaring autumn had arrived, Mr Harris still had Christmas lights up – she figured Penny was too scared of him (still convinced he was a retired spy) to order them down.

As Gertie walked, she realised she hadn't thought about Ed half as much since returning to nursing. She'd started playing a game with herself, mentally noting the time that the first thoughts of him intruded on her day, and she had a PB of nearly twenty hours Ed free. If she was grieving a dead husband she'd consider this progress, but did she have something to grieve? She had no clue, and, she reckoned, neither did he, so there really wasn't any point in asking.

Gertie actually caught herself in the bath the other night, thinking about the sepia-skinned paediatrician from the PICU she'd worked with (and lined up behind twice at the coffee cart on purpose). Dr Shan had even commented about her bedside manner being second to none, which was a professional way of saying she was a goofball with the kids, but she'd take it.

Gertie was waiting for Nacho to do his number-twos, still thinking about the fine hairs on Dr Shan's forearms as he inserted a dosage into a patient's central line, when she heard a smash of bottles followed by a spray of swearing. She pulled her scruffy dog into the stinky alleyway where the rubbish of the rich went to die. 'Everything okay in here?' she called into the dark corridor.

'Gert? That you?' Penelope Crawley, slightly slurred.

'Pen? You okay?' Gertie pressed on the timed light switch, illuminating a polished cement floor, a row of council bins, and one faux-fur-trimmed silk-nightgown-wearing body-corp president stumbling to gather scattered bottles. For once, her hair lay flat and lank on her makeup-free face. In five years at Apple Tree, Gertie had never caught Penny without her face. Now, with all that normality showing, she was far less threatening.

She stared at Gertie as if choosing whether to throw up or speak, and Gertie hoped it was the latter. 'No, I am decidedly not okay.'

'What's up?' Gertie let Nacho go (he had nowhere to run in this snow globe but home) and crouched to help pick up the spilled vodka bottles. *That's a lot of potato juice.*

'I was hiding them. From Martin. He thinks I have a drinking problem, can you believe that?'

Gertie thought Martin might be on to something.

'Tell me why it's posh to have a cellar full of wine, but a drawer full of Vodka makes me an alcoholic.' That sentence was still rather coherent, but it went downhill from there as Penny spewed forth a jumble of drunken phrases that didn't quite fit together – failing as a parent, crossing lines and something about a dead rat? '... and the last straw – I found what was left of poor Bart in the garden! Ethan was the last to see him alive. It all turned to shit when the Yorks moved here.'

Gertie really hoped that Bart was the pet rodent. And what did Rachael and Sam have to do with these tears?

'Take a deep breath. Start at the beginning.' Gertie rubbed Penny's back as she sniffed and snorted.

'I can't even begin to ...' Penny leaned against the refuse-centre wall, grim-faced, her arms flailing about. 'You know when you think you're doing okay as a mum, then your kids do something awful, something that crosses the line, you know? And you question every decision you've ever made.'

Gertie remembered Abe plastering their TV with fence paint. Totally not cool. But Gertie didn't think that was the sort of trouble Penny meant.

'Only every day. We all doubt ourselves. Don't be silly ...' Gertie was about to say Spencer was a fine young man, but then remembered Ed catching the little sod clubbing baby birds out of their nest years ago, so went with, 'You're a great mum!' But she wasn't sure what that meant. All Gertie ever hoped for was 'adequate'.

Gertie finished picking up shards of broken bottle, slid them down the glass-recycling chute and sat with her neighbour.

'It can't be as dire as it sounds. You're devoted to your son – and this whole community for that matter.' Gertie didn't read the P&C or body-corporate newsletters, but if she did, she was sure Penny Crawley's name would be splattered all over them.

That said, Gertie had seen enough families in crisis to learn that being a decent parent was not always a guarantee your kid would turn out the same way. In fact, she was famous for scaring new mums with the reality – that you were naive to expect raising a child wouldn't involve at least one major challenge, but you could also expect to love them enough to rise to it. Kindness was found in the realisation that everybody struggled with something and it was hard to parent well without being kind.

'You don't know the half of it. And to think I lectured readers on raising kids in that fucking blog. I haven't got a clue,' Penny cried, flopping her lifeless arms beside her.

'Sometimes you just have to let kids find out who they are, be who they were meant to be – be the truest version of themselves,' Gertie mused. She'd read it on a magnet and it sounded wise.

Penny frowned. 'But what if their true selves are little arseholes?'

Gertie tried not to laugh, and the fire in Penny dwindled. She gazed up at the moon shining down the alleyway, seeming to sober with the awful smell of rubbish.

The woman yawned. 'Makes me think of Tyson. I can't help but feel awful. What if I miss the warning bells again?'

'Tyson?' Gertie asked. *Was that the rat?*

'And while we're on failures – it's official. Just like my blog, my bakery business is the walking dead.' She did a surprisingly

125

convincing impression of a zombie with her hands out front and her tongue lolling to one side.

'Oh, Penny, your cakes are heaven in a patty pan!'

'Martin tells me the problem seems to be something about the ingredients costing more than I charge.' She dismissed the idea with a flick of her wrist and almost hit herself in the face. She was as uncoordinated as a newborn. 'Turns out the quickest way to sabotage your passion is to monetise it.'

Gertie saw tears forming in the woman's eyes and felt a glut of sympathy for her. She'd seemed lost since Spencer hit adolescence and no longer needed her constant hovering. The cake business was her second baby, her little mid-life adventure.

'So, I drink tea and carry on, because that's what Crawleys fucking well do. And Martin's been driving around in the Cobra, which is what he does when he's angry at something, who knows what.'

'And what does any of this have to do with the Yorks?' There was still much Gertie didn't know about what was underneath Rachael's shell. Was her whole life a sham or just her marriage?

Penny's mouth opened, then closed like a goldfish. 'Let's just say all is not what it seems in that house! And that man – don't be fooled by that adorable accent and sweet little dimple. The way he treats his wife ...' She shook her head. 'He's at my place now, arguing with Martin over his portfolio – good time to escape the place.'

Having met the Rio Rocket briefly, Gertie could understand how his lean, elegant physique was famous for pushing those strong limbs through the pool, as if the water would do anything to oblige him. Seeing how different Rachael acted during the odd occasion when he was near, she was concerned he had that way with people, too. But it was clear he undeniably adored his wife. The chemistry between them was palpable, even with the problems she knew they had. Gertie admitted she had felt an internal shift when in Sam's company. He certainly had a way about him, but Gertie was unsure what kind of way, exactly.

The walls were thin in Apple Tree, and the driveways close. Penny must have learned about Sam York's carpark romp. Was that all she'd overheard? And what had Spencer done to disappoint her?

Penny went quiet. Gertie felt a soft thump on her shoulder and figured she'd be stuck with a comatose lump if she didn't get Penny moving soon.

'C'mon, Pen. It's like what you told me about spray tans – it'll all look better in the morning. Let's get you home.' Guiding her up to standing, she directed her slim neighbour out of the refuse bay, over to the cobbled street, and towards the fairy-light twinkle of Lavender Lane.

Nacho was waiting at her front door, tongue lolling from his twilight adventure. Gertie pressed her fob on the entry panel and Nacho ran inside, sending a whirring sound through her house.

'Balls to that.' She'd forgotten the alarm automatically engaged at midnight (she hadn't reset it since nightshift had changed her habits).

A moment later, a bleary-eyed Kat appeared and entered the pin to ameliorate the alarm. 'Wait, aren't I supposed to be the one sneaking in late?'

Gertie kissed her daughter on the forehead. She adored sleepy Kat, looking so benign in her Minnie Mouse PJs and bed hair, her attitude failing to wake with the rest of her.

'So sorry, hon. Go back to sleep,' Gertie said, but was glad when Kat dawdled behind her into the kitchen.

Kat turned up her nose. 'You smell like a pub.'

'How do you know, missy?' Gertie washed the alcohol stench off her fingers, put the kettle on and found the drinking chocolate. 'Took Nacho for his walk – finding it harder to sleep without your dad's snoring.'

'He's such a dick.' And there it was – Kat's attitude, awake and in sync.

'Don't talk about your father like that.'

'He is, but.' Kat opened the fridge and found a packet of Tim-Tams concealed beneath the Odd Bunch of carrots in the crisper – the one hiding place Gertie thought the kids had never discovered. 'And btw, you need a new spot for your snack stash.' She smiled and bit down on a biscuit with a grin.

Gertie poured two hot chocolates and added marshmallows. 'This is nice. You're barely home now – Miss Indy too scrumptious to be away from?'

'She is the best baby ever. The Yorks are great. You should see how Ethan makes mochas.' Kat smiled. 'He melts real chocolate into cream – it's di-vine.'

'How is that possible? That entire family has no body fat.'

Kat shrugged, growing quiet as they blew on their substandard hot chocolates. 'Mum. With Dad. How old were you? I mean, when you knew he was the one … back in the 1900s.'

Gertie choked on her drink. Was her daughter falling for the mini-Sam? He was a little young but certainly had his dad's looks, and she'd seen them looking cosy walking from the bus together. 'Sorry.' Gertie coughed. 'Hot.' She wiped a drip of froth off her lips. 'Ah, I guess I was your age – but our families were close, so we'd known each other for years by then.' *And somehow my seventeen was older than yours.*

'So, you've never been with anyone but Dad. Isn't that, like, weird? I mean, wouldn't it make sense to know what it was like with other men before choosing one partner for life?'

Gertie's eyebrows arched. 'Works for penguins? No, seriously, kid, when we were young your dad was always enough for me, and now, well, life is so busy, that side of things becomes less important.'

'That's kind of lame, Mum. I mean, all the novels, all the lyrics about love being all-encompassing, how could it not be like the most important, transcendent thing in your life? To have your heart flutter like a bird caught in a cage.'

Kat's eyes danced with wonder; a wonder Gertie hadn't felt for years. Maybe the girl had a point?

'Are you speaking from personal experience? Something I should know?'

Kat rolled her eyes, not willing to reveal any more. Gertie felt far older than she had before this heart-to-heart.

'It is amazing, hon, but love takes many forms.'

Kat nodded, finished her drink, said goodnight and got up to leave.

'Wait a sec – tell me what the Kat files have on the Crawley kid.'

'That freak …' She turned, thinking for a second. 'Um, well, he's a spoiled brat. His mother buys him the latest iPhone every birthday – just in case you wanna keep up with the Crawleys I'd be happy to oblige …'

'Not happening.' Gertie tried to look casual. 'Any other goss?'

Kat's face pinched. 'He's way too fond of his rat for my liking.'

'Is that Tyson?' Gertie asked.

'Bart. Spencer made him a YouTube star. He's a total dero — addicted to porn, apparently. Caught in the storeroom a few times.'

Gertie turned her nose up. Was that what Penny was so upset about? Did she catch her son watching smut online? 'The internet has a lot to answer for.'

'Der,' Kat said. 'Porn changes neural pathways, expectations of relationships, of women. Research shows it's even to blame for the increase in sexual violence. Child porn is the fastest growing business online.'

Gertie raised her eyebrows, in awe of her daughter's insight at such a young age. She also felt a little ill.

'But get this, he doesn't only watch it. He's got a drone. Apparently, he caught some Instagram influencer topless in their penthouse pool near the boardwalk.'

Gertie's eyes widened. *Penny's son's a perv?* 'Why didn't you tell me this?'

'Everyone knows. Sienna's dad's the principal and she reckons Spencer's the reason the school filled in beneath the stairwells.'

Gertie frowned. 'Stairwells?'

'He used to hide underneath, record up our skirts. Why do you think we call him Creepy Crawley?'

'Creepy Crawley?' Gertie squinted, unsure whether it was bullying she should discourage or clever assertiveness against a tosser who deserved it.

'Anyway, why the sudden interest in that waste of space?' Kat asked.

'You should have told me. Now I feel like I've breached the mother code by not warning Penny what her son is up to.'

'She knows. Spencer only avoided suspension 'cause the Crawleys donated a shitload to the school. You've never had to buy me out of trouble – and my scholarship's saving you heaps – seems reasonable to repay my good behaviour with a new iPhone?' Kat showed her dimples. 'Or a Jeep, even?'

Gertie viewed her bright, articulate daughter, and hoped that her awareness of the evils of the modern world would protect her from them.

Chapter 14

Rachael

Feed, rock, change, feed, rock, change. Rachael felt as if she'd done nothing else for days. She even found herself rocking the trolley back and forth in the grocery aisle. So drained from night feeds, simple things like what day it was often eluded her. She once decided to pack the boys' lunches while she was up for the 3 am feed, only to discover it was Sunday. She was bleeding and leaking milk and trapped at home. Her breasts felt like engorged melons, her nipples so raw the water falling from the showerhead felt like nails on her skin. As for her house, her bin was overflowing with smelly parcels, her kitchen a shrine to takeaway containers and her laundry, full of buckets of soaking pastel onesies recovering from poo explosions.

Rachael burst outside the four walls of 16 Lavender Lane and took a moment to breathe. In and out. With a baby whose cry turned heads and cleared a cafe in less time than it took to order a flat white, she couldn't take her anywhere. Indy hated the pram. Hated the baby capsule. Rachael had everything she'd ever wanted and more, and yet she was a prisoner in her home — her six-week-old controlled her life, practised sleep deprivation as a form of torture, and kept it going twenty-four seven.

Lucky she was the sweetest thing on the planet.

But the thought of going back inside, trying once again to settle her baby's inconsolable cry filled Rachael with dread. Her daughter might as well have been screaming *failed mother*. That's how it felt. Like every cry signalled how badly her daughter's needs were ignored. Indiana was allergic to sleep.

In the bright sunlight, Rachael noted a suspicious mustard-yellow smear on her sleeve, which went well with the furry strip of stubble tracking down her left leg. More alarming was the fact that she didn't care.

She sniffed and snorted, letting out the day's frustration for a moment. Perhaps she needed Kat around a few more hours a week so she could feel more herself? Rachael's eyes closed, dislodging spent tears that slid down her cheek.

A hedge of lilly pillies separated their yard from the neighbours. It was thick and lush, but you could still see movement, flashes of colour and shape between branches when someone loitered behind. Was someone watching her? Sam was forever telling her she was a catastrophe inventor, so she tried to ignore the feeling.

Her phone buzzed in her pocket, an Instagram notification. She knew the shiny, curated images on social media would drag her mood down lower, but she couldn't resist the distraction, the reminder that there was a whole world out there. She had dozens of DMs from new followers, and scanned through the messages praising her, asking for tips.

Rachael laughed. She wasn't feeling inspirational. A photo message from Beehive appeared – a unique native floral bouquet had been delivered. Her co-workers had strict instructions never to release her private address and Gail offered to drop the flowers to her. Rachael wondered which client had sent them, and felt a little less miserable after a brief glance through a window to her old life.

Another rustle in the bushes. Through the gaps between foliage, Rachael saw a well-groomed Penny with her retro washing cart that looked more like a pram, towered high with neatly folded linens. Then her attention was caught by an avalanche of colourful words billowing from Penny's upstairs window. The window where Rachael often noticed Spencer at his desk late in the evenings, face aglow with glare from multiple monitors. Was every millennial addicted to gaming? She wondered if things were as rosy as they seemed in the Crawley house.

'Penny?' Rachael approached the gap in the hedge, pointed her toes to see over into their immaculate rose garden and caught a flash of Penny's bright skirt as she escaped inside. A moment later the shutters snapped closed.

Rachael eyed off the thick cream cheese Gertie was spreading on the fresh bagels. 'You know I'm still five kilos over my pre-pregnancy weight. Sam has taken over my diet plan, making fun of my softer belly.'

'Rubbish. You're scrawny. How's week six going?' Gertie moved a basket of unfolded washing off the coffee table and plonked festering dishes in a crowded sink. Something about the disorder at Gertie's house made Rachael feel better about the state of her own.

'I feel like the walking dead, but I'm getting there. Sam's not coping so well – he's a bit OCD about his routine and babies don't quite fit in to his schedule. I sometimes wonder if we were ready to add a third child to the mix.' Rachael swallowed. 'Then I look at her and melt and feel bad for even thinking that.'

'It's okay not to be okay, hon. It's a rollercoaster of extremes. And the sleep dep is a killer – but it will get better.'

'How do you do it – juggling work and kids on your own?'

Gertie laughed. 'Is that what it looks like? I'm a mental case. I may look normal, but underneath I can't even remember my bleeding pin number.' Gertie did have a mildly crumpled look about her, but somehow it was part of her unpretentious charm. 'Truth is, sometimes I arrive at work and cry in the disabled toilets, other times I feel like I'm cheating on my kids with my job, but we're getting there. Fred's worth feeding now, keeps the kids alive while I'm at work. I still miss Ed, though. Wish I didn't.'

Rachael adjusted Indy in her arms. 'Have you guys had contact since he left?'

Gertie shook her head. 'Unless you count asking what the iTunes password was or him texting to ask how the manny is getting on.' She attempted a brave smile, but the wobble in her chin revealed the truth. 'I mean, Fred is nice and all, but often it takes so long to explain the intricacies of who hates crusts and what fruit each kid prefers that I could do it myself in half the time.'

Gertie was jiggling Rachael's camomile tea – she knew precisely how she took it without asking, and something about the fact made their friendship feel as safe and comfortable as soft old sheets. That and the fact that the woman had seen her vagina.

Gertie grew quiet, then hesitated as if editing her words. 'I seem to recall new babies not being conducive to marital bliss, but I guess you guys have been there, done that twice before …'

'Well, once.' Rachael braced herself.

'Ah, yes, I was wondering if you'd get to that story.'

'Sam wasn't as well known when we got married – no one's picked up on the fact that Ethan was walking when I entered his life. Ethe's mum, Charlotte, died when he was a baby – I never met her, but I hear she was young and troubled. Sam had just started teaching and had full custody of Ethan when she died.'

'I had no idea. Poor kid.'

Ethan wasn't Rachael's flesh and blood, but he felt like part of her now. Fused, not like ownership, but a permanent lease she was thrilled to keep signing. 'I adopted Ethan when we got married and he knows this, of course, but the media haven't clued on. I've always referred to him as my son because I love him like one, have since he was two.'

'Of course.' Gertie joined Rachael on the couch.

'But raising another woman's child had its challenges. Thankfully, the grandparents were over the ditch in NZ and have since passed, so we raised him as our own – didn't take long for the little munchkin to crawl under my skin.' She stroked Indy's tiny fingers. 'I feel a bit cheated that I missed knowing him when he was this small – but I've had two of my own since, so I'm blessed, really. So that's that ...'

Gertie nodded. 'Speaking of kids, how's that daughter of mine?'

'A godsend. She's got an old head on those young shoulders of hers.'

'You know you can send her home anytime. I'm starting to forget what she looks like. And can you please stop lavishing her with beautiful cheese and bottled water? She's beginning to expect that sort of extravagance at home.'

Rachael laughed. 'Actually, Gert, I think something's going on with her and Ethe. He's got a bit of a crush. I'm not certain, but they do chat a lot over homework in his room. And, well, the other night when I opened his door they were both on his bed – fully clothed I might add, but with a sheepish look on their faces.'

'Kat has been a little off with the fairies lately – feared it was either pot or a crush, so that's a bit of a relief. I saw them together in the playground the other day, actually. They were with a friend of yours. Rosa, I think her name was – long dark hair.'

Rachael felt a tightening in her chest. 'I don't know any Rosas, except for an old client. And how would she have gotten through the gates?'

Gertie shrugged. 'She said she was a family friend, had just started a florist. She gave me a card.' Gertie's brow furrowed, looking for it among a pile of permission slips and junk mail. 'Ethan seemed to know her. And she asked about the baby, so must know you.'

Rachael's legs felt wobbly. She had thousands of followers on Instagram – anyone could find that out. Something felt off. Gertie handed Rachael the card – Blooms by Rosa with a mobile number.

'When was this?' Her voice was pitchy.

'Ahhh, last week?'

On the card, there was a photo of an arrangement with a unique cylindrical vase, lined by a large leaf – the same design as the delivery to her office that day.

'Hon, is something wrong? She was lovely. I wouldn't worry.'

Rachael felt stupid. She could tell Gertie thought she was paranoid. Delusional. All the things Sam told her she was. Maybe they were right.

Her mobile chimed and she put down her tea. She'd turned her phone location services back on and her doting husband had noticed she'd strayed outside the 'home' bubble he'd set up on the GPS app.

Going out? Sam's text read. In her exhaustion, Rachael had forgotten to use the spare fob. She must have grimaced as Gertie asked if all was okay.

'Just Sam, checking in. It's just for security, in case anything happens.' In truth, it reminded Rachael of the cattle grid her dad had across the farm gate so the cows couldn't venture too far from his paddock.

'Does he do that often?' Gertie said it casually, but Rachael had begun to know her face. She had a way of saying something judgemental in such a nice way you almost forgave her.

'Meaning what?' Rachael met her eyes.

Gertie held them. 'I think you know what I mean.'

Rachael's throat tightened. All she'd divulged to Gertie – before she even knew her name – was that Sam had slept with someone else. Was she judging her for staying with a cheat? If they were judging each other, Rachael feared Ed was probably doing the same thing in Singapore.

Rachael felt an urge to defend her choice to stay married, as if it validated it. 'Sam's a little possessive at times, but he's a good man. He doesn't hit us, if that's what you're implying.' She had failed to keep the defensiveness out of her words, but hadn't she been ready to leave him only weeks ago?

Gertie was silent, and for a beat, Rachael feared her zombie-tired brain had misinterpreted her friend's intent, but then Gertie shrugged and said all nonchalant, 'That's not the only way men hurt.'

Rachael sat tight-lipped, torn between the pure relief of finally having someone see her clearly, someone she could share her truth with – all the reasons she should leave him, all the reasons she never could – and the terror of what was at stake if she did.

'Rach?' Gertie's eyes narrowed. 'Do you remember what you said after Indy arrived – in the ambulance – about Sam?'

Rachael had no idea what she was talking about. Indy's birth had been such a whirlwind, so exhausting, she could have said anything.

A deep, vibrating rumble emanated from inside Indy's nappy, so long and loud it cut the growing tension in the room. Rachael used the moment to slip her bag over her shoulder and her baby against her chest, and made for the door.

'It's her nap time soon, anyway. May as well just change her at home.'

'Rach – please don't go. I'm just trying to—' Gertie's eyes were kind and sad, but Rachael didn't care.

'Help? I don't need any.' She choked back tears.

As soon as she dealt with one email, another skulked into her inbox. Rachael had only asked Kat to stay until five. Perhaps she did need more help than she'd asked for. She shut the lid on her laptop. She'd ask Kat to stretch her shift another hour until Sam was home. But Kat was not in the nursery. She checked the kitchen – often Kat tried to help deal with the dishes and set Indy up in the sling. No sign of them. She double-checked the cameras, the external alarm.

That's when she heard the terrifying sound of splashing. Panic darted through her chest. Rachael paced to the main bathroom and found what she feared – Kat holding her newborn in the baby bath.

'I didn't ask you to bath her!' Rachael screeched, lurching for Indy, clawing her from Kat's wet hands. She grabbed a towel, drying Indy down more vigorously than necessary, the tears falling as she rubbed. 'You had no right to do that!'

'I'm sorry,' Kat cried, in visible shock. 'She did one of those explosive poos, you know the ones that go all the way up her back, and I just wanted her to be nice and clean for her next feed.' The poor girl was almost in tears as she justified her actions. 'She's fine. In fact, she loves the warm water. It calms her down.'

'You're too young to manage a squirmy newborn in a bath! Don't you know how dangerous it is?' Rachael snapped.

'You never said. I was going to ask, but you looked so stressed. I mean, I know how to bath a baby. I checked the temperature with my elbow and used the baby hammock. Mum has been letting me bath my brothers since they were little.'

'Well, she shouldn't!' Rachael was sobbing now, crying into Indy's warm little body, all snuggled in her towel pressed firmly against her chest.

Kat looked horrified at being in trouble but touched Rachael's shoulder and asked, 'Is everything okay?'

More sympathy she didn't want. She just wanted to be left alone. 'Please, just go. Sam was right. I should've known better than to leave a teenager in charge. I think we can manage things from now on. I'll see that we pay you for this shift, but let's make this your last.'

Kat bolted from the steam of the bathroom, grabbed her schoolbag and left.

Rachael's regret over her outburst only deepened when an hour later, the smoke alarm was triggered by her burnt risotto. 'False alarm, Barry,' she told the security guard when she set off the oversensitive sprinkler system. After mopping up the water with a baby strapped to her chest, she attempted to help Noah with his homework, which ended in him snapping his pencil and her patience. She tried to settle a grumbling Indy with an extra feed but was so tense her milk refused to let down. Indy butted her breast in protest, and again Rachael understood that breastfeeding wasn't the invisible cord between mother and child, natural and straightforward.

Everything in motherhood was harder than it looked and she was doubting her ability to manage it more than ever, and now she was refusing all help. With Sam still out coaching squad, she figured she'd at least appease the boys by scooping out the top layer of risotto and plonking a stodgy lump in each bowl.

'Dinner!'

She waited. No one came.

'Ethe? Noah? I won't call you again!' She slammed down her fork and huffed as their dinners sat untouched on the table. She scraped her chair out and sped down the hall. 'Ethan!'

He was perched on his bed and startled as the door yanked open. She was sure he'd hidden something behind his back. His room was dark, and it was hard to see with his monitor the only light source.

'Don't you knock?'

'What have you got there?'

'Nothing, I'll be there in a sec!'

Rachael felt a tremor in her lip. Could this day get any worse? 'Is it drugs?'

Ethan screwed up his nose, hurt swimming in his eyes. 'As if!'

Rachael swallowed hard. 'Just show me what's behind your back.'

He jumped, pulled his finger to his mouth and something scurried up his arm. Rachael flinched. Two shiny circles peered at her through the gloom.

'Oh, God, is that what I think it is?' A spotted white-and-brown rat stared up at her in answer.

'It's Bart. Well, I prefer to call him Bartholomew – I thought it suited him better. And before you crack the shits – yeah, I stole him from that freakshow, but you should have seen the way he treated him, Mum. Doing cruel experiments. Getting him drunk and filming him for his stupid YouTube channel. I had no choice but to rat-nap him. Spencer's a waste of space.'

Rachael exhaled. 'I'm sorry. I believe you.'

His brow furrowed. 'Huh?'

His surprise at her trust in him hurt. 'I believe you. Gertie mentioned he's not the nicest of kids and I know you are.'

'His mum found some random river rat after Bart went missing and now they think I killed him. Spencer blames me 'cause I was the last to see him.' He shrugged. Rachael wondered if this was why Penny was avoiding her. 'Spencer hates me anyway, banned me from his gamer server, so whatevs. I think his mum's pissed at Dad, too, for something.'

They were silent as they perched on the end of Ethan's unmade bed in the dark. Her son's fringe flopped over his face and needed a wash, but Rachael resisted telling him so. She stroked the rat's fur and found it was soft as silk, his nose pink and clean.

'Kat said we should change his identity, dye his hair like a fugitive. Got me an old birdcage from when Harry's budgie died. She's been bringing him food.'

Rachael gazed down her nose at him. Was that what they were getting up to in his room the other night? Feeding a rodent? 'He could live just on the crumbs from your desk.'

Ethan's smile reached his eyes. 'He really likes her; she's the only one he lets feed him.'

Rachael sighed. 'Have you worked out if she likes him?'

Ethan groaned. 'You've sacked her now, anyway. Kat texted me. She's really upset.' He carried the rat to his wardrobe and opened the door of the cage he'd been secreting for weeks. Bart scurried in and nibbled on what looked like Ethan's lunch.

'That may have been an overreaction. I'll see if she'll come back. Maybe you should ask her out.'

He shrugged. 'What's the point?'

'I guess she's a senior, will be off to uni next year, maybe that's sensible,' Rachael said. 'Unless there's someone else you like? Gertie said she saw you with a dark-haired lady called Rosa.'

'Rosa? I don't know any Rosas. Why would she say that? No, I mean, what's the point with any chick?'

'What? I don't see why any girl wouldn't like you, Ethe. You're smart and kind and you've got your dad's good looks.'

Ethan flopped on his bed with a thump. 'Good with rats.'

Rachael pushed into his side affectionately. 'Sorry about Kat. I'm just so tired, I haven't been myself lately. I think everything works better when she's here, don't you?' Rachael glanced at the way the light from the kitchen danced on his face. There was sadness there and it broke her heart.

'Nah, relationships aren't for me.'

'Because your mum and dad didn't last? You think all your relationships are doomed?'

'I know what he did, Mum – I hear you fighting. I'm not a kid anymore. And what if I turn out to be a tosser like him?'

Rachael's breath caught.

Kids. They see more than you think.

143

Chapter 15

Gertie

With an armful of folded washing in hand, Gertie plodded up the hall of thick pine floors towards Abe's room. She spied a PJ-clad Harry, an unenthusiastic Kat (reeling from something that happened at the Yorks'), and blank-faced Abe as they slumped in a line on the edge of Abe's bed, as if a family meeting was in session without her. Harry was straight from the bath, all damp-limbed and squeaky-clean, dark hair spiked like a tuft of feathers in the middle, while Abe controlled the laptop's camera angle. Kat was squeezed in between the boys, a strange look on her face as she picked at a seam on her pleated uniform skirt.

Then Gertie heard his low voice. The most familiar voice in her world. She'd been so desperate to hear it after he'd left, she'd resorted to watching old videos on her phone just to hear snippets. Now that she'd become used to not hearing it, there it was, live, in front of her without warning.

'And your mum? How's she going?'

Kat's eyes narrowed. 'Why don't you ask her? Should I get her?'

As her daughter gestured to the hall – she'd spied Gertie skulking in the doorjamb – Gertie raised a finger to her lips to keep Kat quiet. She wanted to slide, invisibly, into the room, catch a glimpse of his bulk, his wide, open smile (secretly hoping it was absent and he was miserable) without him seeing her conflicted face, yearning and resenting in equal measures. She wanted to tell him about her new friend, Rachael, how she'd delivered her baby in the street. She wanted to tell him she'd returned to nursing, that she did Pilates now, that she was trying to think about what he said about losing herself since parenthood and found herself noticing tiny pieces of the old Gertie scattered in the weirdest of places, as if her independence had been a coin lost in the dryer you never thought you'd see again. She'd noticed loads of Gertie-esque behaviours that had been in remission – blaring music in the car, taking random photos of trees, making pesto (Ed hated basil), soaking in a candlelit bath, listening to audiobooks in the car.

His voice again: 'No, no, Katerina, it's okay, I'll catch up with her later. But ... she's doing okay?'

Gertie froze like a coward. Kat's eyes stayed on hers.

'She's, you know, frazzled, drinking copious amounts of tea, so, the same, I guess. She got her hair foiled so she looks less mumsy now.' Kat and Gertie had an unspoken alliance as the only females in the household (even Nacho was no bitch). They had each other's backs. She questioned whether this was fair, for a seventeen-year-old to be the wingwoman for her mother. 'She's back nursing, you know.'

'She's working?' Surprise marbled his voice like blue vein through cheese. *Are you proud of me?* 'Already? But, what about you kids? How does she do night shifts?'

'We have Fred.' Kat rolled her eyes. 'You know I don't need a babysitter – I *am* a babysitter.'

'Yes, you did mention that, love.'

'And Mum only does a few shifts a week.'

'Well, I guess I did tell your mum to explore life a bit more. I was thinking a yoga class, though, not a career.'

Gertie felt a surge of pride. *Take that, Ed.*

'What's Fred like – getting on okay? He's going to be a teacher, you know.'

It was nice for Gertie to hear their familiar banter. But also, horribly painful. Despite a couple of absurdly polite texts, asking things like if he knew where the TV remote might be, she'd had little contact with her husband since he'd marooned her in their life. Through the tinny laptop speaker, she heard him go on to describe the beautiful landscaping in his little ex-pat village (not that unlike the community where he'd left), the old housekeeper that organised his shirts by colour, and the bright-pink hue of the flamingos in Singapore Zoo, while Gertie stood on the outside of her family, looking in.

As they chortled on, still not bored with the novelty of their dad in two dimensions, connecting with him despite the distance, she felt her cheeks colour as she muttered to herself, 'This isn't fair.'

Gertie walked to the lounge and plonked the washing piles on the cornflower-blue couch beside her. Bitter thoughts – that he'd chosen another path, that he didn't deserve their sweet little faces – jarred in her mind, and she cringed, desperate not to become like those high-horsey divorced soccer mums who thought nothing of withholding their children from their partners as punishment for their philandering ways, rationing their time as if it was rare. Because Edward Rainworth was not a cheater. He was simply lost. And they would be here for him, discoverable again, when he found himself and came home. He might just find she was a little different if and when he did.

Gertie's eyes shot to the plantation shutters they couldn't believe were theirs when she and Ed discovered they'd won the major prize. And even though the house was theirs, Ed still worked hard to afford the rates and electricity and exorbitant body-corporate fees. Sure, she didn't like the ridiculous hedge or most of the pretentious neighbours, but the house was rather grand and central. Her fellow nurses commuted over an hour to get to the hospital. What would become of this place if he did, indeed, prefer his Gertie-free life?

In terms of their relationship, Gertie felt stuck, in transit from one life to another, oblivious to how long this limbo could last. Gertie didn't do limbo well – she needed clarity in her thoughts, simplicity in the foundations of her life. She could convince herself of anything but just needed to know what to aim for. Was he just being kind, bringing her down gently? Was this forever?

She arrested the thought. Ed had been clear. This was simply a hiccup.

But every reminder of their separateness hurt – the single toothbrush on their bathroom sink, their joint email account 'GertAndEd' seemingly a lie. Regardless of the conclusion to this experiment, the bare facts were she now slept in that super-king bed alone, and had a dusty redhead in her spare room that she was only now knowing what to do with.

When would this all be finished?

Pushing and shoving were heard from the hall before all three kids filed out, the Zoom call concluded.

Gertie hovered, like the drones above their roof lines. 'How's Dad?'

'Good,' Harry answered. He was generally the only one who still replied. Gertie expected him to join the non-responsive ranks by age seven, like his siblings had. 'His hair is weird, but,' he said, contemplating the concept with deep concern.

Abe shoved past screaming, 'Nerf war!' obviously less affected by his father's absence and weird hair. Harry chased him like a shadow, no doubt to get the best weaponry. Nacho waddled behind like an afterthought, claws chinking on the floorboards, sniffing an invisible trail.

Cleared to enter, Gertie strolled into Abe's room with folded uniforms and balled-up socks, and saw the evidence of their treachery – the ruffled doona, the laptop still open on the bed. A close-up image of her husband's shorter, salt-and-pepper hair crowded the screen, bobbing left and right as he swore under his breath.

She froze, but then felt the need to signal her presence. 'Ed?'

'G?' His forehead now, at close range. 'Er, hi, I'm, I – I was just about to disconnect the bloody thing, once I work out how … we're using Zoom now, you see.'

She stood, makeup-free, hair needing a root touch-up, frozen with the realisation that her own image was minimised at the top of the screen. 'Okay …' *This is not the image I want my uncertain husband to have of me for the remains of this ridiculous farce.*

He cleared his throat. 'How are things, anyway?' Ed asked, his face a little twisted with what she could only guess was guilt. 'Kat said you're back nursing – wow. You didn't tell me that.'

'When would I tell you that, Ed? Isn't that the point of you living alone?'

'I wouldn't have thought you needed the money – with the rise and everything.'

'It's not just about the money, Ed. I'm a good nurse. I'm even doing stints in paeds, which I think I love almost as much as midwifery. The kids are inspirational.'

'Of course, hon. You're the best. But – isn't raising *our* kids rewarding too?'

'I'm still doing that, Ed, in case you haven't noticed. I'm doing it for the both of us.'

'Of course, sure, so, ah, how are you doing? Are you okay?'

Gertie felt the tendons in her neck stiffen. No words came out. They were too busy being filtered by her pride, her fear, her self-consciousness. This man. This man that knew every part of her, had seen her body peeled inside out in labour three times, stood by her while lactation consultants twisted her breasts, held a cool cloth to her head when she was feverish. This man had seen Gertie at her worst, yet she'd never felt uneasy or embarrassed. But in this moment, all she felt was awkward. Unwanted. Disconnected. They had never had to articulate their feelings in words like this. After so long together, their communication was so engrained it was like a well-rehearsed dance – second nature.

But despite the rush of terror at seeing his face, being expected to convey her emotions to a man she hadn't seen for months, she'd ached to talk to him and hated herself for it. She missed him silently slipping the perfect tea on her bedside table while the crows bickered in the soft morning light. She missed his stubble on her face as he kissed her goodnight. She missed the way he was polite to tele-salespeople, and patient with their children even when they accused them of being arsehole parents. She missed the bulk of him, crowding her kitchen and monopolising the couch. The way she could think of nothing else when his whiskers brushed against her cheeks.

Softened by his memory, her eyes met his once more, and the intimacy threw her. It felt strange. He was perched on a strange bed, in a strange room, in a country she'd never set foot in. *He should be here.* A rush of bitter and twisted nerves overwhelmed her. Gertie knew every inch of this man. Every core memory in his life since they were kids had happened together. He was the only man she'd ever been with. The only man she'd ever thought she needed. On the screen, he looked like an illustration of a man she used to know.

'Gert? You there? The screen seems to have frozen and I can't hear you. Look, in case we lose connection, I wanted to tell you – I'm flying home. For a training course.'

'Home? As in here, home?' Gertie was still getting over seeing him. She didn't have the processing power to compute the words he was using as well.

'Yep. Stupid management thing. Next week,' Ed said. 'I was hoping to stay there while it's on … if that's okay.'

'You want to stay here?' Gertie knew she sounded deranged, repeating everything Ed said like she was on a translation loop, but it didn't make sense. He'd said her sentence was a year. That next to no contact was to occur to give their relationship the chance to 'breathe'. She hadn't expected visitation rights. It was week eight in the school term. He'd called the kids incessantly, but he'd missed about a hundred lunches and school runs, a few dozen meltdowns, thousands of nags, and a lot of dishes. Gertie had put up with the backlash of his absence from Harry and Kat, had wiped the tears away from Abe's cheeks at night as he pondered why Ed chose to live alone when they were all here, missing him.

They'd adjusted. Gertie had a job. She had a lanyard! And a lunchbox like a real grown-up in the real world. She had a Fred. He had finally started packing lunches that got eaten by the right kids, knew how to forge Gertie's signature on permission slips. They had a new kind of warped normal. Ed coming back now, unless it was permanent (which Gertie knew it wasn't), would simply rip the scabs off the half-healed wounds.

She wasn't sure she wanted him back. She wasn't sure where he'd *been*.

And Kat. Gertie knew there was a lot going on with her – babysitting and exams and she seemed distracted and daydreamy. Could she really like that mini-Sam boy? Gertie had tapped on the shell of her daughter, tested Rachael's theory that Ethan and Kat had a thing going. But the more she tapped, the harder the barrier seemed to become.

Home. Together. A month ago, Gertie would have cried with glee at the thought of Ed uttering those words, but now they pinged from the hard metal shield she'd cocooned around herself and she felt a sense of pride in her resilience. In her cold indifference.

'The kids are end-of-term-feral. I don't want your visit to disrupt Kat's exams. Our daughter's doing senior in case you forgot. Remember that pre-med thing?'

'It's *you* who wants her to get into obstetrics. She wants to be a nurse.'

'Well, that's not going to happen,' Gertie declared. It had been settled after she'd made Kat a doctor's coat when she was five.

That dream did look rather 'pipe' after what Gertie discovered in Kat's schoolbag that afternoon – a D scrawled in red ink on one of her assessments. Gertie had exploded, blamed all the time she spent at the Yorks'. 'I just misunderstood the topic, it's no biggie,' were the words that came out of Kat's mouth when she confronted her, but her miserable face said otherwise. Academia used to be a reliable staple, a source of pride for Gertie, a source of confidence for her daughter.

'She won't be at uni at all if her grades keep dropping. I mean, a D!' Gertie mumbled without thinking.

'What was that? The audio wigged out. For a minute, I thought you said Katerina got a D.'

Gertie thought it best to just be still. He might think the video had frozen and hang up.

'She got a D! How's that even possible?' Ed asked. 'She's never got a D in her life. Are you letting her babysit too much? She's always talking about that rich family – and that Dungeons and Dragons boy.'

Gertie huffed. 'You think it's my fault? Couldn't possibly be yours, Ed. All the change. And I'm the one having to deal with it. I think I'll see the teacher, see what I can do.'

He huffed back louder as if to prove a point. 'You can't protect them from every minor blip. It's her responsibility.'

'Easy for you to say, you're over there! What if she loses her scholarship?'

Gertie heard Ed sigh as if he'd expected the niggle. 'She's a bright kid, Gert. She'll be fine. Let her sort it out herself. Or let me help when I'm back. I miss the kids and I can't wait until the grand prix. It's a perfect opportunity.'

'For what?' Those were the words that came out, but what she meant was that she had no idea what status their relationship was in. She wouldn't know how to behave. Edward Rainworth could not reset her heart remotely and expect it to reboot the same way. 'An opportunity to ravish the kids with dinners out and show them a good time for the weekend so I can pull their tired bodies back to reality on Monday and nag them to do their homework and take the rubbish out?'

'I know I don't have any right to ask you to do this. I've been awful and absent and I've left you with all the responsibility while I work through this. You don't have a new bloke or anything, do you?'

'A new bloke? Of course not. When would I have time?' Although the paediatrician with the brown eyes *had* suggested they meet for coffee to discuss her working in the PICU more often.

'Good. I was just checking, I didn't want to assume …'

Part of her wished she *had* found a new bloke just to shove it in Ed's face. How dare he assume she couldn't find a date if she wanted one!

'Gert, I think we need this reboot. I'am not sure this is working the way I hoped.' His voice was imploring. He may even have been crying. 'Please?'

'Agggghhh,' Gertie said, knowing she had no chance of holding her ground once tears were involved. Manly tears. Abe was lost without his father and resented Fred's attempts to befriend him. He'd gladly readjust the macros in his spreadsheet to calculate an earlier arrival date of his one and only dad.

'What – you expect me to go to a hotel when my kids are elsewhere?'

Did she even want to see him? She felt she'd just be a grumpy cow the whole time – that's what he deserved. 'Fine. But you'll have to bunk with Fred, and be warned, that kid eats a lot of onion rings.'

'How is Fred? You getting on?'

What's it to him? But she thought about it. She wouldn't be at work if it wasn't for Fred. Abe would be more out of his routine, Harry would break more stuff.

'He's a good egg.'

She saw the first genuine smile land on Ed's lips. 'I miss you, hon. I just want to see for myself that you're okay.'

'You know what? You don't get to know, Ed. You chose not to know about my life.'

He blinked quickly, as if in shock. He ran his thick fingers across his cheeks, over his mouth, and Gertie noticed his skin was pale, his hair too short, his eyes too close together. Were they always? Through the lens, across the miles, he looked and sounded very much like Ed, but a tweaked version. An imposter. Did she even know this man on the screen? She knew one thing for sure; the man she married would never have made a choice like he did, a choice that hurt her, disregarded their life, the life she helped him build. He wasn't exactly charming, he couldn't really dance, but he'd always been kind. This wasn't kindness.

Ed gazed at her with forlorn eyes, uncomfortable and shamefaced. Had the reality of his choice to run finally hit home? Sixty-three days he'd been gone, and the connection they'd had for over twenty years was severed, perhaps irretrievably, like a hat lost from a ferry. *Is it worth turning around for? Will it ever fit right again even if we do? Can't you just find another hat?*

A surge of sadness engulfed her. 'I think you're right. We shouldn't do this.' Gertie Rainworth slammed the screen down, her fingers covering her mouth as a rush of tears fell. The worst part – she wasn't sure if they were for herself, or for him.

Chapter 16

Rachael

Later that night, Rachael looped the block three times before guiding the pram into Lily Court. The main culprit of her wad of worry was too hard to name. Did it stem from Penny's sudden avoidance of them, her diva-like behaviour with Gertie and Kat, or the fact that Ethan wasn't as sheltered from his father's sins as she had hoped?

Rachael had assumed staying with the father of her children was the right thing. She had been naive to assume Ethan would never pick up on the emotional fallout. He was nearly sixteen. Rachael googled it. *How to ruin your child's love-life – have an affair! Your parent's infidelity might be causing your trust issues*, and, reading further, the damage was more enduring the older the child was.

She pushed past an abandoned scooter and kicked a soccer ball off the Rainworths' front path, feeling nervous as she pressed the buzzer. Things had been prickly when she'd left in a hurry the other morning.

Fred appeared at Gertie's door.

'Mrs Y,' he stuttered, his face reddening. Her recent impromptu doula's eyes flitted about awkwardly, adding to her nerves, before Gertie appeared at his shoulder and he scurried away.

'I'm sorry to trouble you this late,' Rachael said.

It came out so formally that Gertie smiled warmly.

'Don't be daft, woman, come in out of the cold and get that beautiful thing in here so I can eat her up.'

Rachael felt relief in her toes. It had been subtle, the way Gertie and Kat had become sources of joy and support in her day. They'd become her last salvations – warriors on her side of a battle she was yet to begin. Kat had been a godsend, knowing just when to help, when to pull away and let her be Indy's mum. She knew it was critical to explain her outburst with Kat and the bath, but the very thought of reliving the reason for her anxiety filled her with shame.

'I've never seen Fred blush.' Rachael pulled the pram wheels over the entry and took off her scarf.

Gertie nestled the baby in the crook of her arm, still cosy in her muslin wrap. 'I think Fred's still processing the fact that he saw more of you than he'd bargained for.' Then her face fell. 'Are we okay? I'm still feeling awful about speaking about Sam like that. You know I'm here for you no matter what.'

Rachael's marriage was still in the too-hard tray, so she dodged the question with a smile. 'I actually came to apologise to your daughter if she'll listen. I'm sure she told you what an ugly cow I was today.'

'Not in those words. She seemed more concerned about you, and not being able to hang out anymore. She likes you a lot better than us, you see.'

The warmth in Gertie's smile made Rachael feel better already.

'I'm sure that's not true.'

'And I hear you're still exposing her to cool stuff like organic eggs and starfruit. Now she demands them on my watch, and I simply can't keep up with your brilliance.'

Rachael's shoulders relaxed. 'I'd love to have her back if

she'll forgive me. Any chance I can blame my outburst on post-natal hormones?'

Gertie smiled, but it didn't reach her eyes. 'Is it something you want to talk about? Or were you just having a crap day?'

Rachael exhaled, and pressed her back into Gertie's couch, as if it would swallow her whole. 'You know about Beehive, my business, right? It finds niche positions for unemployed and under-employed people with disability. But most people don't realise the personal reason behind why I started it. It was my brother. Liam suffered a hypoxic brain injury from a non-fatal drowning when he was eighteen months and spent his life in a wheelchair as a result. Twenty seconds and a few inches of water is all it takes …'

Her thoughts sank into that shallow, soapy bath with her baby brother, reminding her with blood-curdling fear what could happen if an infant was left alone. Wrenching Liam's little body from the suds, arms drooping, lifeless, Rachael remembered sweeping his hair from his eyes, like her mum did. She'd carefully placed her brother's body on a dry towel, barely able to lift the slippery tot with her spindly arms, and wrapped him tight, rubbing his limbs as if she'd annoy him awake.

'I thought he was just sleepy, so I sang "You Are My Sunshine" like Mum used to. When that didn't work, when something in my three-year-old head told me something wasn't right, I called triple-zero, and the lady on the phone told me what to do until the paramedics barged in and brought him back to life. Well, brought a different brother back. He was never the same cheeky boy he'd been before that fateful day.'

'Oh, Rach. That's just heartbreakingly awful. That drawing at your place was his, right?' Gertie's eyes were warm and kind. 'I swear we had no idea baths were a problem. I can totally understand you flipping out finding Kat with your baby in a scene that brought you so much pain in the past.'

Rachael's eyes were fixed on a point in the distance. 'I was three. My mother told me to watch him – a child should never be burdened with that sort of responsibility. That's why we'll never own a pool, why I never let anyone bathe them but me. It's also probably why I'm a total control freak with the kids and have felt like a grown-up all my life.'

'Understandable with something like that. But you're still close with your mum, you said. Your family stuck together despite such a trauma? That's kind of amazing.'

'Liam passed when he was twenty-one. My parents never really recovered from the strain of the accident, of caring for him, and I'm sure my father always blamed her. They separated when I was young, but Mum and I have stayed close.' Rachael turned to Gertie. 'She got an alarm wristband, after that day. And never babysat for us alone when the kids were little. It scarred her. She has epilepsy and that daydream quality came over her that afternoon – even at three I could tell. She knew she was going to fit, told me to watch Liam and ran to grab the phone to alert a neighbour. We lived on a property in country Queensland and the ambulance was so far away. That's part of the reason I'll only live near cities now. We were broke from the drought so could never afford to travel to Brisbane for the specialists, so she never quite got the care she needed.' Rachael paused, caught her breath. 'She fitted on the kitchen floor with the phone in her hand. My parents had taught me what to do when it happened. I left Liam to try to help. I wedged a pillow under her head – all while he was drowning in the next room.' Rachael felt as if she was witnessing the scene unfold in the here-and-now instead of thirty-seven years before.

Gertie took Rachael's hand and held her gaze. 'Rachael, you listen to me – you did nothing wrong. You stopped your mother from injuring herself. You had the sense to call the ambulance with all that going on – probably saved your brother's life. I'd be so proud if I had a three-year-old who was that aware under the circumstances.'

Rachael had heard it before, but this time she felt something uncoil inside.

Indy started to grumble, bringing her back to the present. 'I should really get going. I just wanted to check on Kat – please tell her how sorry I am. And to pop around anytime if she'll forgive me.' Rachael let out a breath and stood to leave, feeling lighter than when she sat down. Gertie placed Indy safely in her pram.

'You know, I'm chuffed you're back at work doing something you're so good at. It's inspiring to see you embracing a new life in Ed's absence – and new highlights I see! They suit you.' She elbowed Gertie in the side playfully. 'God, you'll be on Tinder before you know it.' Gertie seemed petrified at the thought. Rachael just smiled and hoped Ed wasn't already on it. Then tears welled in her eyes. 'My God, I'm such good value as a neighbour, aren't I? If I'm not dropping babies on your footpath, I'm freaking out about stalkers or crying about childhood traumas on your couch.'

Gertie's brow furrowed. 'You think the woman I saw with Ethan was the stalker?'

Rachael hesitated, then realised there was no reason not to tell. 'I told Sam and he looked into it and found the woman was Penny's florist, just drumming up business by giving you her card. I think she also messaged me asking for business advice.' Rachael shook her head. It sounded so weak. She'd accepted it when talking to Sam about it that afternoon, but explaining it to Gertie now, she couldn't believe her own words. 'What am I saying? I saw her photo online. It was her.'

'Her?' Gertie asked.

'The troublemaker from years ago, following me again. I'm sure it was her. She's the reason we came here.'

Rachael paused, but Gertie nodded at her to continue.

'The first time I saw that woman she was in my bed. She was wrapped in Sam's arms in a scene so much more confronting than if they'd been in the full throes of passion because I knew it wasn't just about sex. There was real intimacy there, before I slammed the door and threw an adult tantrum, of course.'

'As you would. Hell, Rach.'

Rachael huffed out a laugh that held no humour. 'It didn't help that she was brilliant and beautiful and hopelessly in love with him, to the point of threatening suicide if Sam was to leave, which he finally did, to marry me. I mean, it helped me forgive him, seeing how hard she made it for him to separate from her – total and utter manipulation, the lengths this woman went to. And she wasn't a crazy cat lady, she was a professional woman. Annabelle Alesi, you know, the prize-winning journalist – striking woman with dark hair and big eyes?'

'You think this Rosa woman could be that old ABC anchor? I can't say she looked familiar when she was at the playground. How did they even meet?'

'She'd interviewed Sam when he was competing in the Pan Pacs, responding to the "drugs in sport" scandal. Like, I'm talking seventeen years ago before I'd even met him. They dated. He dumped her. She never got over it. He must have made an impression.'

'Goodness, but how'd she get inside? Barry wouldn't let her in here, would he?' Gertie asked.

Rachael wondered how tight a ship Barry ran. 'We've restricted her access here, of course, but I was sure I saw her follow me and Ethan at pick-up a few times, and once at work, and when I saw that car the other day, I couldn't help but worry that the very threat we'd taken cover from had followed us through the gates we'd hoped would keep us safe. I think Rosa isn't the florist's real name and she found a way to get to us. Of course, Sam just said I was paranoid. That Annabelle lives in Melbourne. That it's just someone who looks like her.'

'Wait, I'm a bit confused.' Gertie squinted, deep in thought as she held Indy to her chest. 'Are they two different people, or do you think the woman I saw somehow orchestrated Penny as a client just to get close to a man she hasn't been with for like, over a decade?'

'Penny told me her florist passed her a card in her cake shop, so maybe Annabelle discovered where he lived and saw Penny being a client as a way to get into the estate regularly. So, Rosa is Annabelle. But yes, when you put it like that, that it was so long ago. It sounds like Sam is right – I must be paranoid.'

'I didn't mean it that way, just trying to understand.'

'She got the message for a while when we were married and was out of our life for years – when Ethan was little – but then she started following Sam again a year or so back, popping up at public appearances, that sort of thing. She just never got over him. It got so out of hand, we went to court to get a restraining order. We had no proof, but I'm sure she baited our first dog to show what she was capable of.'

'Oh, that's evil. The poor kids! Poor you!' Gertie squeezed Rachael's hand.

Rachael rolled her eyes. 'It does sound a little OTT, but while he's far from perfect, Sam does have a way of making you feel like you're the only woman in the world, the only one he'll ever need. So much so that I was stupid enough to believe that she would be the one and only time he'd stray. And now I'm afraid Ethan's paranoid he'll turn out like him.'

'You wanted to believe in the man you loved – no crime.'

Rachael raised one eyebrow. 'I swear, one day he'll drive me to commit one.'

Chapter 17

The Janitor

The janitor felt privileged to be employed at his age, even if it was blowing leaves off paths for rich white people. Even if the leaves fluttered straight back as he left, he got paid. He needed to pay his family's bills back in Naxos. So, when Barry ordered him to blow the leaves, he blew the fucking leaves.

He'd even answer to Charles. His name wasn't Charles. It was Faidon. The Charleses of the world found work easier than the Faidons. Apple Tree Creek Estate paid well and didn't report him to immigration, so answer to Charles he would.

The leaf blower stalled, the nightmarish noise abated and he was thankful. Time for a smoke. For a moment, the janitor enjoyed hearing the gurgling stream meandering over the hedge, and at this time of day, the cicadas if he listened hard.

Was that the swimmer's lad with his breaking voice he could detect over the hedge? He'd caught him and Katerina stealing from the orchard and sneaking through the gap in the hedge more than once. He had no intention of dobbing. Then the hobnobs would fix the hole and he'd have nowhere to take his smoke break.

Now he'd have to wait till they were gone to have a puff.

The same dark hair flashed between the foliage, over by the creek with the swimmer's son, but it didn't sound like the Rainworth lass with the polite greetings. She sounded older, polished, cautious. Was this teenager already breaking hearts?

A fish's child knows how to swim.

Charles worked hard, blew the leaves, and kept his mouth shut.

Chapter 18

Gertie

Ed's plan to return for a few days had upset Gertie's equilibrium – just when she'd found some balance in her life, she felt the full mother-load on her shoulders. Since re-entering paid employment, she'd felt the world expected her to work like she wasn't a parent, and parent like she didn't work. Having a husband for a few days wouldn't solve much – what she needed was a clone.

She decided she'd make sure she wasn't on night shift the few days Ed was back – she didn't want accusations of not trying – and it would be nice for the kids to see their parents together, regardless of the state of their marriage. She hadn't given Ed a chance to relay his flight times before she'd ended the call in a huff. To avoid the knot in her gut at the thought of speaking to Ed again, she rang his Sydney office branch, figuring they'd have details.

'Oh, Gertie! Hello! What time is it over there?' the general manager's PA, Elena, asked.

'Over here? You mean near the harbour?' Gertie laughed. Had her call been diverted to Singapore?

'Oh, have you come back to Sydney – visiting your sister?'

'*Back* to Sydney?' Gertie was confused.

'You're not with Ed in Singapore? I'm sorry! I thought that was the reason he'd asked for the transfer. Don't you have family over there?'

Asked for the transfer? And aren't you paying for Fred because we opted to stay?

Elena coughed awkwardly. 'How are you, anyway?'

'I was just after details of the course Ed's returning for so I can align my shifts at work.'

'You're back at work! How great that you're feeling up to it. Let me check our team calendar! Won't be a sec.' The PA put Gertie on hold just long enough for the concern over what lies Ed had fed his colleagues to swell in her stomach. 'Ah, Gertie, I might need to check with my boss – there are no training details in the calendar yet, so might be a last-minute thing.'

'That's okay, Elena, I'll call Ed and sort it out, thanks.'

What on earth was Ed playing at? And if work wasn't the reason he was flying home, what was? Her husband had lied to her about the move overseas, to his workplace about his family, and about why he was coming home. Her life was unravelling. Harry was in trouble at school for biting, Abe was reading his vehicle scrapbook more than ever and Kat seemed to be suffering some sort of teenage meltdown. Gertie had a rumbling feeling that she was slowly but surely fucking things up.

Gertie's knuckles knocked on Kat's bedroom door, dinner balanced on one hand as if she was a room-service attendant. 'Kitty-Kat?'

Like an artistic expression, Kat's room was an accurate articulation of her life. She morphed seamlessly between exam-period Kat, with piles of textbooks and gaudily highlighted calendars for what-was-due-when, to socialite Kat, represented by impossibly loud music, makeup-stained sink and discarded clothes layering her carpet. But this week her room had become a cave of adolescent angst. Not a crack of light had infiltrated her bedroom in days and it had begun to radiate a decidedly unpleasant funk. She'd even got Fred to fix that lock on her door after she'd caught Abe stealing her charger again.

'It's Pad See Ew.' Gertie pressed her ear to the door.

Steps were heard, a bolt slid. The door cracked open as if it belonged to a haunted house and Kat was a puffy-eyed bed monster.

To Gertie's surprise, Kat allowed access, her eyes squinting at the brightness seeping into her woman-cave. They sat on her bed as she picked at her food, and Gertie resisted the urge to make jokes about requiring a hazmat suit or rush to deal with various disasters – a porridge-crusted breakfast bowl or the balled-up sports uniform Kat needed for tomorrow. Gertie agonised over the right words to connect with her daughter's suddenly lost soul.

'Can I help? Be a sounding board?' she finally asked.

Kat shrugged, but Gertie considered this progress. She wondered if Kat was still reeling from Ed moving to Singapore, that his return might cure her blues, but Gertie honestly felt the teen had barely noticed, too caught up in her adolescent world.

'Is it that D the other day, or something else? Boy related, maybe?' Gertie looked down her nose at Kat, her red-eyed, pallid daughter a mere shadow of the spirited, irritatingly opinionated teen she usually embodied. 'Or … girl related, even?' Gertie twisted her lip, casting as wide a net as possible.

'Mum! I think the fact that I'm into boys is fairly well established.' There *were* a lot of hetero romance novels on her shelves.

Gertie smirked. 'Year Ten Henry was rather effeminate ...'

Kat smiled, nearly choking on her noodles. Gertie felt like she was in, but then Kat scowled again and chucked her plate on the desk with a thump and retreated to her pillow haven.

'You haven't sat for the Yorks this week. Rachael not offering, or is schoolwork mounting up?'

'I'm done with them, told them I was sick. They don't want me around anymore.'

'Is this still about the bath thing? She apologised.'

'Sam never wanted me there, apparently, said I was too young. I can't be bothered with anything anymore. Nothing's the same.'

'That doesn't sound like you.' Gertie sat on the bed beside her. 'I'm pretty ancient, as you remind me often. I've faced lots of stupid situations – maybe I can help.'

'Things are different now to the olden days.'

Gertie resisted an eye roll. 'There's always an out. Maybe we can find it together.'

'There is no "out", Mum. I've been doing nothing but think about all of it and there is literally no way to fix this tragic situation. It's just a waiting game now, waiting for things to get worse or die.'

The words hit Gertie like bricks. *Get worse or die?* Kat was never this defeatist. She was a drama queen, but always spoke as if she was invincible. Gertie had raised Kat to believe she *was*. Her daughter's plans were sky high, and she'd never doubted she'd get there. Was it drugs or some sort of online bullying? Was Ethan pressuring her for sex? Nothing flagged as the right reason for her misery. Gertie became the big spoon, pressed close to her daughter, felt her sobs and wished she could muster some *Freaky Friday* magic to let herself slide into Kat's body, soak up her daughter's pain and fix her life. She had no doubt

Kat would probably do a better job at fixing Gertie's while she was at it.

Finally, Kat slept the sleep of the emotionally exhausted. Gertie savoured the silence, the warmth of her skin. But soon, curiosity took over.

Whatever was going on with Kat, there would be evidence hidden in her phone, the external hard drive to every millennial's brain. She thought back to Rachael's control over Ethan's devices, her constant hovering. Was she on to something? Was that necessary to protect our young in the digital age?

Gertie adjusted her arm with incrementally small, retreating movements until she was out from under her daughter, who was still sleeping soundlessly. Gertie had never been a snooper, had never had to be as Kat always had her life so put together. But the phone was glowing, egging her on.

Gertie fumbled to navigate the iPhone, came across a thousand selfies of trout-mouthed teenage girls looking disturbingly like Victoria's Secret models, and moved on to texts. Guilt ebbed through her and Gertie considered placing the phone down before she noticed a message thread from 'Yorky', who had a profile picture of Chewbacca. The thread was long, going back weeks, with obscure emojis, jokes and summaries of each other's days. Gertie scrolled further, and noticed some intensely personal stuff, insecurities, self-doubts and embarrassment about still being a virgin. *Oh, thank you, Mother of God!* Gertie hadn't realised how intimate things had become with Ethan.

There was a gap of days in their contact, then one last message from *Yorky.*

Wish you'd change your mind. ☹

Maybe it was Kat who'd done the dumping. Part of Gertie was relieved – a teenage breakup didn't seem too insurmountable a crisis. But was that all this was?

An 'F' was scrawled in pen on Kat's assessment sheet, and Gertie became that mother she swore she'd never be. That annoying parent who went in to bat for her kids when they flunked. She knew Ed was probably right. That if her daughter failed, she needed to learn to try harder. But the thought of Kat losing her scholarship, not living her dream, made her nauseated. She'd do anything to shield her from the harsh reality that was the world they lived in. That was her job.

Deciding to take a more active role after the 'D', Gertie had read over this particular essay before Kat submitted it and marvelled at her daughter's comparison of strategies to combat the rise of type 2 diabetes in Australia's greying population. She was no teacher, but she knew it certainly didn't deserve a mark that would seriously jeopardise her scholarship.

'Was this why you locked yourself in your room all weekend? Hon, this is not good, but we can manage it.'

Kat was silent. When Gertie pushed her for an explanation, she grunted, saying she just got the date wrong, and that's the mark you get if you don't submit in time.

'Coach York marks written work?' Gertie hadn't realised he taught. 'I thought he just paraded around in boardshorts and gold medals, a poster boy for the school's marketing material.'

Kat rolled her eyes. 'Mum, he's got a teaching degree and a diploma in dietetics. Why don't you like him?'

'I don't even know him.'

But what she *did* know she didn't like. She *did* know he tracked his wife like an offender with an ankle bracelet. But maybe Gertie had him wrong? Maybe this stalker bizzo was a real thing in celebrity land and he was simply being chivalrous?

'I can see why he won medals – his hands are like giant paddles. And he is rather easy on the eye. Ethan's got the same exotic Nordic look, too, don't you think?' She winked a little, trying to get a rise.

'Gross, Mum. You're like, old.'

Yes, old enough to know how to fix things.

The next day, when 'Mr York, Health Science classroom teacher' didn't reply to Gertie's email about Kat's fail, Gertie loitered at the pool after drop-off to catch him. He was stacking kickboards underneath the grandstand when she caught his eye.

'If it isn't my daughter's namesake – sorry I didn't get back to you, Gertie – computers and chlorine don't mix, so I play catch-up after training.' He touched her arm. 'I hated doing it, you know, that F. She's such a good kid.' He smiled with his eyes and she felt that shift inside her again. Like he was there for her, that she just had to tell him what she needed and he'd make it happen. He was like a hallucinogen. 'But you're a professional, you know what uni lecturers are like – they're cutthroat when it comes to this sort of thing.'

Immediately, Gertie's confidence waned. 'What sort of thing?'

His eyes crinkled at the sides. 'She didn't tell you what we spoke about?'

'She said she turned it in late.'

Sam tilted his head. 'That doesn't sound like Kat, does it?' He had a point. She had a colour-coded study timetable on her desk planner. 'She's one of a kind, your daughter, a brilliant student and butterflier, and Rach and the kids just adore her. But given we see her outside of school, I can't be seen to turn a blind eye to plagiarism.' He leaned his back on the railing, put the boards down and gave Gertie his full attention.

'*Plagiarism?*' Kat wasn't that stupid. 'But I saw her research notes, she had referencing – she wrote it.'

'St Aquinas uses the best plagiarism-detector software on the market.'

Gertie's throat tightened. 'Kat has no reason to cheat. She has plenty of her own opinions so doesn't need to mimic those of others. In fact, she rather arrogantly thinks she can write better than most.'

Sam nodded. 'I can see you've got her back – you're a brilliant advocate for your daughter – but it's our school policy. Look, I know it's hard to accept when our kids disappoint us, so I'll let you see for yourself. Follow me to my car and I'll grab the report. Sound okay?'

Gertie fell into line as he turned off the pool lights, wrestled with the padlock and then they made their way to the staff carpark. A Porsche sat idle in a VIP park. He'd been nothing but reasonable, yet the interaction made her feel like a powerless child. He unclipped a soft brown briefcase and flipped through a report which had highlighted passages known to be published phrases. The student name on the coversheet was Katerina Rainworth, with hearts dotting the i's in her handwriting.

'Oh, God. It can't be.' Gertie flipped through it. She leaned on the shiny black paint of his sportscar. 'I can't believe she'd do that. I mean, I've been struggling a bit, with Ed away, and I do put a lot of pressure on her about becoming a doctor – pre-med entrance scores being so competitive.' *Had she expected too much? Was this her fault?*

Sam's kind eyes focused on her, listened to her woes, reassuring her it wasn't a big deal, that perhaps he could talk to the dean, look at her resubmitting it if he was sure Kat understood the consequences of copying the work of others. He was utterly charming and understanding, his eyes crinkling at the corners as he smiled.

'Thank you. I'll get her to redo it and see you before class tomorrow.'

Had she piled so much expectation on her daughter to achieve that she felt compelled to cheat in order to do well? She and Ed were the risk-averse, toe-the-line, pay-bills-on-time kind of boring. How did Kat get so ballsy as to try to get away with cheating? And now she'd been caught, was it more important to protect Kat from the consequences, or make her take responsibility for her mistakes? This could ruin her.

Chapter 19

Penny

Penelope Crawley returned home in her pearls from the St Aquinas P&C meeting and slipped off her bra from under her shirt the second she closed the door. She turned to find her husband, Martin Crawley, stony white in the wing chair. She was about to complain that she was the only person to vote against Coach York's contract being extended – the rest all charmed by the two-faced misogynist, blinded by his 'unprecedented results training upcoming stars' – but the stunned look on his face made her stop. Sweat beaded along his lip. The phone was pressed to his chest like a bible.

He spoke softly, explained.

Penny was utterly confused. 'What do you mean, gone? How can all our money be gone?' she asked, laughing as she dropped her keys and bag on the counter with a clink. 'I did get suspicious when a few things declined, but I thought that was just you rearranging again.' She flopped in the one-seater next to him, legs akimbo, her heart beating faster than was normal. 'You're as safe as houses, that's what your reputation says.' She made a sweeping gesture with her hands like an airline steward. 'Crawley Investments – As Safe as Houses.' She pictured the logo, the advertising pamphlets – a roof line with a chimney.

'Yeah, well, our house may be gone, too, Pen. I'm so sorry.'

'What are you talking about?' She laughed. This did not happen to the Crawleys. She refused to be poor like her parents. She would not lower herself to their primitive-level existence again.

'I took a risk. You're always telling me I never take risks, and you're right. I'm a boring sod who plays it safe. So I changed it up. I invested big in a pharmaceutical startup Mr Fucking Olympics suggested. Turns out he used to dabble himself years ago. Some media friend of his with Russian contacts was in the know about using stem cells to enhance performance, and created a drug that wasn't on the banned-substance list that was untraceable and perfectly legal and miraculous. Everyone was going to want it, Pen.'

Penelope did not want to be pulled into this, but she had to know how big a sod he was – if there was any truth in what he was saying. 'What? A drug? For athletes? But isn't that immoral – wouldn't they have an advantage over the others? That's hardly fair, is it, Martin? Why would you sour your reputation by getting involved in that sort of behaviour? It's against the, I don't know, spirit of sport.'

'How is it different to better access to coaches or affording private dieticians or being born with bigger feet? I'm not on the Olympics board. I'm an investor, and the tip he gave me was solid – the research checked out, the patents were secured. I'm not a total idiot. The science was there, Pen, published in reputable journals. Sam was so sure he re-mortgaged their house to find the capital to buy big – they wanted a minimum of 500k to invest.' Martin paled as he stared at the wall. 'He talked me into doing the same, plus some. I thought everyone would want this supplement – everyone could take it, not just athletes. It was legal! Harmless!'

Penelope's glare was piercing. 'How could you re-mortgage the house without me even knowing?'

'All in my name for tax. Remember when we rented it out when we holidayed in France for that summer? We transferred the title.'

'Oh, yes, the tax thing.' Penelope's mind was already muddled. Reality dawned. Her safe-as-houses husband had gambled their house away.

'So, what went wrong with this foolproof scheme of yours? This untraceable, perfectly legal performance-enhancing substance?'

'They reckon there was a corporate spy at the lab. Someone tipped off the International Olympics Committee and now all the doping authorities are onto it. Look, the less you know the better, Pen. But let's just say the manufacturer now has a few million dollars' worth of product that is worthless and you and I and the Yorks are their biggest investors.' Martin splayed his stubbly fingers over his cheeks. 'I'm so sorry, love. All I wanted to do was provide for you and our family. To leave them something so they didn't have to struggle to buy a place of their own. Now all those years of building the business – all gone with one stupid, idiotic mistake.' He hung his head in his hand and sobbed.

Penelope sat, shell-shocked. 'But, but you're always doing fancy things to protect people – offshore safe havens and foreign bank accounts. Surely you've implemented some sort of safety net for your *own* family.'

'Why did I listen to him? He just sounds so confident, you know? So sure of himself with his London lilt and his sparkly eyes and his connections. Say it with enough confidence and suckers like me will believe anything. He has a mesmerising way about him, Pen, a way of making you doubt your own judgement and follow him blindly into a snake pit.'

Penelope began to process the reality of what her husband was admitting. Their apartment on Manly Beach, their time-share villa in France. Spencer's tuition fees. Her mani-pedis and weekly flowers and botox – gone, gone, gone. Would any of it be safe from this cock-up? Her stupid husband's ridiculous, illegal scheme that backfired, spitting smoke and grime all over them.

'But your clients love you. Your business will be fine, won't it? You've still got that. You can make more money!'

'Everyone knows, Penny. I'm a laughing-stock. Who wants advice from a financial guy who lost his family's savings? It's over. I'll be doing tax returns in shopping-centre cubicles just to make ends meet. And that's if the Tax Practitioners Board doesn't strip my licence for sheer stupidity.'

She shook her head at him in disgust. 'You had one job, Martin Crawley! One job! I raised the boys, looked after the house, made sure you had clean socks and hot food on the table. All you had to do was provide financially. Was that really too much to ask?'

'I'm sorry, honey.' He was crying miserably now.

'You're pathetic, Martin Crawley! And there is no way on earth I will accept that you've lost all our money!' She grabbed a vase from the side table. She'd never liked it much, anyway, only bid for it at auction because she *could*, and that part had made her feel good.

Martin's despair turned to anguish, and he tensed his fist. 'Bloody Sam York! I'll be lucky to avoid bankruptcy and it's all his bloody fault!'

'What rubbish, Martin, you were the professional,' Penelope yelled, poking her index finger firmly between her husband's ribs. 'You should have known the risks!'

Martin backed away, frightened like a mouse. 'Penelope! What are you doing, Penelope? It's the swimmer's fault, I swear.' His face, all chubby cheeks and flapping chins, ducked behind his forearms.

That's when she hurled the vase straight towards his balding head.

Chapter 20

Gertie

It was late, but Gertie wanted to be alone. Alone with her ruminating thoughts. She often sat outside at night, sipping tea from her *#1 Mother* mug, and gazed over the perfectly manicured lawns, fairy lights twinkling in the ball trees and the snaking streets of the estate like she was a king. But tonight, thinking about Kat's alleged plagiarism (Kat had lied to her face and was adamant she hadn't cheated), and about Ed misleading her about his secondment to Singapore, she was in no mood to look out at the rich and famous and their attempt at community living. She wanted her own island. In the Maldives.

What exactly had Ed mentioned about these imaginary training dates? She logged into the old laptop the boys used. She'd seen Abe re-watching recorded Zoom calls with his dad when he missed him. Now that she no longer believed Ed's secondment was out of his control, the thought of Abe in pain because of Ed's selfish need to be rid of them made her even angrier than she had been. She clicked on the recording from the previous night, and sped through to the end few minutes when they'd spoken like awkward strangers.

As she blotted tears with the corner of Harry's Pokémon pyjamas she'd never got to put away, waiting for the part where Ed said what date he'd be back, her stomach sank with inertia as she took in footage of Ed's new bedroom in Ed's new life. A dresser, a full-length mirror, and in the seconds before she'd gone all diva and closed the lid, Gertie noticed the unmistakable flash of something dashing out of view. A curtain of silvery-blonde hair. Not something – a some*one*.

A spike of rage jittered through her. *You utter prick.*

She shut down the laptop, told herself she was tired, that she was looking for evidence that he was a shit. But the image of a nameless somebody ghosting across Ed's bedroom pinged in Gertie's brain. She tried to ignore it, but it seemed to be getting louder.

She re-opened the screen, and frame by frame, she paused, rewound and repeated. 'Definitely a person!' she declared to nobody as she pointed menacingly at nothing, focusing intently on the magnified pixels.

If immigration was in the business of asking honest reasons for passengers' travel, 'mid-life crisis' felt like the most accurate answer in Ed's case. He'd lied about his reason for leaving. He'd given his boss the impression that his family had moved with him. And what had Elena from his work said about being glad Gertie was 'feeling better'? He'd specifically denied having someone else. Now he had a blonde in his room. The evidence led to only one conclusion – at the very least, Ed was a liar.

When Gertie married a dependable, honest man, she'd thought she'd insured herself against this feeling. This feeling of being utterly betrayed by a cheat, of watching her family fall apart and having no clue if it would be taped back together – or even if it should be. She'd overheard Harry asking Abe over Cheerios if 'Mummy and Daddy were getting divorced and were they going to have two Christmases like Jack does'. It felt worse than she'd ever imagined – or was it that she *hadn't* imagined it? She had always been a little smug about the fact she'd found a good man.

Headlights arced across the shutters and the security light triggered again. Was this Rachael's stalker? She felt bad for not taking the new mum's paranoia seriously. She'd googled and discovered more than she needed to about Sam York's love–hate relationship with the media – not to mention too many pictures of pecs to ever look him in the eye at parent–teacher meetings (no wonder Fred had issues seeing Rachael since the birth) – and thought Rachael might be wise to keep vigilant. She tilted open the shutters and caught the taillights of Rachael's snazzy little convertible Audi doing the loop of the cul-de-sac. She stumbled down the front entry just as Rachael zipped past again, gesticulating wildly to the back seat.

Ah, Indiana won't sleep. Gertie continued her out-of-character behaviour by running up the street beside Rachael's car, stretching her T-shirt over her leggings, feeling the ever-watchful cameras on her back as she paced along, Barry likely having a chuckle at her expense in his tiny gatehouse with his tiny hat.

'She's almost asleep,' Rachael stage-whispered to Gertie through the open driver-side window. 'Sorry I can't stop. I just need to give her a few more minutes in case she doesn't transfer. If you want to hop in, you'll have to do a running jump.'

Gertie shook her head, almost tripping over a bed of lavender, but she hurdled at the last second, and raised her hands in the air at her triumph. Rachael stifled a laugh as she observed her strange antics.

'It's okay, I need the exercise!' Gertie puffed.

'It's nearly three am, Gert – new shift? You alright?' Rachael asked as she slowed a little, trying her best to steer and talk simultaneously. Even in the dead of night, the woman looked ravishing in her PJs and straggly hair.

Gertie planned to nod that she was fine, but instead the truth slipped out. 'Um, not really, no.' Rachael squinted as if she'd misheard, so Gertie clarified the situation. 'Ed's having an affair.' Rachael's car swerved sharply, her tyres mounting the gutter before stopping dead. Gertie could hear Indy's little pissed-off cry from the street. She felt the same.

Rachael scooped Indy from her capsule, hushing her gently as she approached Gertie on the footpath. 'Are you serious about Ed?' she asked, sympathy etched on her face. 'C'mon, let's work through this.' She yawned. 'Your place is closest.'

Gertie paused a few metres into their walk back. 'Oh, Rach – look where we are!' Both women glanced over their shoulders to the clearing, to the old fig tree where Rachael's waters broke, and she subsequently gave birth to Indiana Gertrude York. 'See, there's a dead grass patch from the amniotic fluid!' Gertie observed with such fondness. 'And claw marks in the bark from you gripping on for dear life! You were so brave.'

Rachael threw back her head in mock laughter, exposing her throat. 'Now I know that part's not true. I was petrified, swearing like a trooper.'

Gertie looked at her friend with narrow eyes, wondering if she'd remembered pleading for help to leave her husband from the back of the ambulance that afternoon, and if she still felt the same. 'Being scared doesn't mean you're not brave, quite the opposite. It's the decisions we make because of fear that matter. And I remember a mother fighting against pain for her young. You don't know what you're capable of until you have no choice.'

Rachael had tears in her eyes, but that wasn't unusual lately. She put her arm around her friend and hugged her as best she could with an infant peeking up between them as if she was taking in every word with wonder. 'You really were born to be a nurse, Gertie Rainworth. Now can you stop the pep talk and weave your baby-settling magic to get this girl of ours back to sleep so you can explain?'

Once warm inside, Gertie held Indy tight, and made shooshing noises while stroking the soft pocket between Indy's eyebrows in a well-practised routine. She didn't stop shooshing until she'd performed the transfer and extricated her arm. As if sedated, Indy was out cold. Rachael stood by, drop-jawed.

'I don't know what you call that, but whatever it is I want to patent it.'

'It's white noise. Analogue radios off station work the same way, but like everything else, I hear there's an app for it now.'

Rachael unfolded a blanket from the armrest and prepared for Gertie's sordid tale. 'I'm listening, but talk fast. She's dormant now, but I'm not sure how long till she erupts again.'

'I need to show you.' Gertie left Rachael and Indy in the lounge room and returned a moment later with the treacherous laptop, cued the recording and pressed 'play'.

'See – it's a woman! In his bedroom!'

A figure – slight, short, most likely female with a curtain of platinum hair sashayed past the door to Ed's Singaporean bedroom towards – Gertie could only assume – a walk-in robe or en suite. 'Not a room a workmate would frequent, especially late at night, and who else does Ed know in Singapore!'

Rachael still seemed sceptical. 'I'm confused – didn't you say he's rushing home, that he's miserable, that he misses you? Does that sound like a man seeing someone else?'

That did seem odd. 'He wants to keep his options open, is all,' Gertie figured. 'Why not have your cake and eat it, too?'

Rachael's brow furrowed. 'And your affair theory is based solely on this video?'

'Of course not!' Gertie defensively rambled off all the reasons the entire set-up was off: how he hated planes, didn't like Asian food, had cut his hair too short and bought new clothes, how he was reading self-help books and simply wasn't being himself. She went on to explain the woman at his work thinking they'd all moved to Asia, that she had been under the impression Gertie had been unwell, and there was no training course as he claimed, which proved he was a liar.

'I know it in my gut, Rach. It all makes sense. The sudden, guilt-ridden way about him just before he left. I bet he's doing a trial run with this woman, making sure the relationship's got legs before he comes clean and tells me it's over. Then I'll be shipping my kids off to Singapore half the year!'

'Oh, Gert. Have you thought of asking him? Perhaps there's a logical explanation. Are you sure it's even human?' Rachael tilted her head and watched the footage again, as if from that angle the figure would materialise as a Samoyed or a large long-haired Persian and all would be right in the world.

'See this frame, here?' Gertie directed. 'Definitely woman.'

Rachael winced a little, confirming Gertie's fears.

'Am I right?'

Rachael's face twisted. 'Well, it certainly does look like a short, light-haired woman. But you're drawing a rather long bow to assume firstly, he's having an affair, and secondly, that said affair will result in forever replacing you and losing your children.'

Gertie's hands sprang up to her throat, as if the air was being drawn from her lungs by a ventilator. 'Oh, God. The very thought of my Ed kissing a stranger. I don't know how I can ever look him in the face again! I'm not the sort of woman who'd put up with that!'

Rachael grew quiet and her face fell. 'Sometimes it's not that simple.'

'Oh, shit, honey, I didn't mean anything by it. Every marriage is different, but I know it's a game changer for me. We've spent our whole lives together – building a family, sharing a bed, a mortgage, our dreams. I've shown him every part of me, and for him to ... to throw that away, betray it all to be with another and lie about it, set up this whole stupid work facade to enable his affair – I could never forgive that level of deception.'

Rachael lurched back a little. 'God, when you put it like that ...' Then she leaned forward, conspiratorially. 'Gert, just because I've chosen to try to make it work doesn't mean I don't totally understand that feeling. That sense of utter betrayal. Maybe you're braver than I am, but leaving Sam always felt too hard – the scandal, the kids, splitting the finances – being alone. But I'll admit – do you know what my favourite thing to do was that first time Sam cheated on me? I'd imagine all the ways I'd kill the bastard. I had him driving off cliffs, drowning at sea – I'd have to stop myself plotting some nights, scared if I thought too hard the ideas would establish their own blood supply and start to feel real. The anger, the bitterness – the more you love them the deeper that betrayal feels. And I really did love the silly bugger.' She sniffed back tears.

'You said *did*,' Gertie pointed out and they both fell silent as if attending a funeral. A marriage funeral.

Rachael came to, shaking her head back to reality. 'You're right, you know. It's only become obvious lately, but Sam's way of loving always made me feel like conjoined twins, like we share the same organs and I'd never survive without him. Through his affairs, I'd never seriously considered leaving him until recently. I called a real estate agency about a lease, but the leap from my life to that one was too great. He's spent our marriage surreptitiously making me feel incapable of it, which in itself is just such a nasty, disrespectful thing to do to someone you've shared a life with.'

Gertie thought she wanted Rachael to see reality; now she felt guilty for wishing this cold realisation on her dear friend.

'So,' Rachael paused for thought, 'if what you suspect is true about Ed, maybe it's time we both got out of this state of limbo and left our rotten husbands.'

'Better still, let's throw them both in the drink!' Gertie cackled, laughing in that maniacal manner that spontaneously flipped to crying without warning.

'Mum?' Abe's half-closed eyes spied them through the dark hallway. 'Who are you throwing *where*?'

Gertie had never sobered up so quickly, shepherding her son back to bed, reassuring him no one was throwing anyone anywhere.

'How would Dad fit inside a drink, anyway?' her little literal prince murmured as she gestured to Rachael that she'd be a minute, returning him to bed a little reluctantly. She was enjoying herself, plotting away with a like-minded girlfriend. Where was Fred? Wasn't he meant to be the kid wrangler?

Rachael said she'd leave her to it and let herself out.

Gertie blew her a kiss. 'It's just a silly expression, Abe. Mummy's just a bit sad.'

'About Daddy being away?'

Gertie nodded as she tucked him beneath his fire-engine quilt.

'He's okay. He's got that woman, Sian.'

Gertie's breath caught in her lungs. 'Daddy introduced her?'

He nodded. 'She's always around. Her English is getting better. She makes us laugh.'

186

'Does she just?' Gertie's throat swelled as she lay with Abe.

'Was Harry right? Are we going to have to have two Christmases?' Abe asked.

Gertie pulled him close, breathed in the musky scent of his glossy mop of dark hair, and let out a little sob. Everything Gertie wanted to offer to reassure him – *we'll work it out, don't worry we'll be fine* – felt like a lie.

Ed had been her husband for twenty years. He'd seen her vomit into a pot plant, picked the splinters out of her feet, and woke next to her killer morning breath day after day. But now the thought of seeing him IRL after months apart made her stomach flip. Flip and churn.

And even if she could forgive whatever it was going on with this woman, what if Ed didn't like *them* anymore? What if he remembered and didn't want to deal with Harry's meltdowns, Abe's anal insistence, Kat's millennial disinterest? What if his life of bachelorhood suited him? Gertie had gotten used to not having Ed in her life. Her pride had forced her to become accustomed to his loss. It had been a little like phantom pain for an amputated limb – awful, but not insurmountable. But she wasn't sure she could do it again.

She wondered how far back she had to erase to know for sure what was left was real.

How long, Ed? How long were you living a lie?

Chapter 21

Rachael

Rachael knew Gertie hadn't meant anything by it – she wasn't the kind of wife who tolerated cheats – but the concept had wormed into her mind since their talk. By the next day, it had shocked her into learning a different truth about herself. Rachael had thought she wasn't that kind of wife either, the kind to model to her young sons that it was okay to treat women badly. But here she was, rocking, changing, feeding the daughter of a man who constantly disrespected her. Rachael had grown so accustomed to the fact, it had become like a pebble in her shoe that, when felt, she told herself to ignore.

Her friendship with Gertie had been slowly preparing her for something, she was certain. Sure, his adoration through the highs topped up her confidence, but was it real enough to shield her through the lows? She felt the friction, the burden of this knowledge, but for once she didn't want to deny it, she wanted to be free of it. Rachael wasn't sure if it was hormones, lack of sleep or simply being fed up with Indy's incessant crying, but she felt something shift inside.

Sam had been loafing in boxer shorts eating his weight in bacon for most of his week of parenting leave, but he must have seen the desperation in Rachael's face, the resentment bubbling in her eyes, as his brow furrowed.

'How can I help, babe? Want me to try to get her to sleep?'

She desperately did, could barely see straight she was that tired, but what chance did he have?

'I have the right smell and she still won't settle.'

'Maybe that's the problem? Maybe the milk is distracting her.' He scooped up his daughter and she followed him as he took her to their bedroom, and sat down on the wing chair nestled in the corner. The bawling grew louder.

Rachael shook her head at him. 'She knows if you sit.' Rookie error. *I thought a father of three would know that.*

'Bollocks. How? I didn't even change my hands ...'

'It's like baby sixth sense.'

He stood and the incessant high-pitched cry slowed to a grumbling rumble. He started jiggling her like a football and Rachael winced, imagining all those little plates in her head like loose tiles waiting to be grouted. She should trust him, but trust and her husband were still becoming reacquainted. They'd almost got back to normal a few times – shared a memory over breakfast or a smile of pride over Indy's adorableness – when she'd think of him, with *her*, and realise the lack of respect that act of betrayal took, be hit with a pang of repulsion and be almost unable to resist hitting him over the head with one of his thick-bottomed omelette pans. Now she was allowing herself to acknowledge her resentment, the ugliness was invading every cell. It's not what you looked at that mattered but what you saw.

'Maybe you need to pump. Let me take the next feed and you have a kip.'

'She won't take a bottle.' Her eyes filled with tears. 'Even if you could feed her, I can't sleep when she's crying.' Not to mention she leaked milk in a warped synchronised dance when she did.

Sam left their room, Indy's incessant crying growing blissfully dim, then returning with vengeance as he came back with a set of his noise-cancelling headphones and placed them carefully around Rachael's neck, calming music billowing from each ear.

'Sleep.' He kissed her gently on the forehead, guided her down to rest and took Indy with him.

His thoughtfulness unravelled her. Why had she been worried only moments before? There was no way he would ever hurt her or her children. He could be kind, and he tried to help. They'd done this before. They'd survive again, wouldn't they? Rachael replayed the reel of excuses for his failings: his insecurities about her leaving him were the basis of his need to check where she was at all times – that was not his fault; years in the public eye had overfed his ego, of course he struggled to adapt to normal life – that was not his fault; he had women throwing themselves at him, he was human, occasionally things would get out of hand – that was not his fault. She kept the reel running, and eventually, she slept.

She could never sleep properly in the afternoon and when her bloated breasts woke her an hour later, Rachael was alone. Indy was not in her bassinette beside her.

She paced to the nursery. Not in her cot.

On the way to the living room, she glanced at the laptop on the kitchen bench, the screen lit with a list of websites. Sam was probably tracking his share-portfolio earnings again. Moving closer, she recognised it was her search history, various parenting sites offering sleep strategies, nappy services, Uber Eats. She thought little of it but then spotted a realestate.com.au listing, dating back to her foiled escape plan the day Sam had left for his trip. Her spontaneous, rushed rental enquiries before Indy was born. *Two-bedroom townhouse, Western Sydney.*

Everything clenched.

She retraced Sam's mood merely an hour before. Her husband had appeared calm, supportive and kind before her nap. Had he noticed this since? Or at all? The thread of worry unspooled in her mind. Had Sam taken her baby somewhere, in fear she planned to leave him? How could she be so careless? She quickly deleted the offending rows relating to her moment of madness. News stories of unwell fathers murdering their children to spite their wives slid into her thoughts, but she shut them away, unwilling to put her loving husband in the same category.

Panicked, she checked Ethan's room – he was engrossed in a game with his headphones on and didn't even hear her speak. She rechecked the nursery, the baby swing – no Indy.

She crossed the hall to the lounge to see if his car was still garaged and finally found Sam asleep on the couch, snoring contentedly. He held a half-empty cup of tea in one hand and cradled Indy in the other, snuggled deep in the crook of his arm with her head barely visible. After her initial relief that Indy was still under her roof, still hers, she imagined all the things that could have gone wrong – scalding, smothering, cot death, falls.

Indy was frozen still.

A wave of panic coursed through Rachael's limbs. Was she still dreaming? She ran to her baby.

'Jesus, Sam,' she whispered to herself, picking up the warm bundle to check she was breathing. A curt grumble confirmed she was, and Rachael had never been so happy to hear her cry. *A flash of cracked purple tiles, an overflowing bath.* Rachael shook her head to fight off the image.

Sam stirred as Rachael wrenched their daughter to safety from her sunken position between the nest of pillows.

'Rach?' He rubbed his eyes, coming to. 'What's wrong?'

Rachael soaked in Indy's sweetness with a shudder of relief and something uncoiled inside. 'Really, Sam? You couldn't have transferred her to the cot?'

'I tried.' He stretched out his neck. 'She stirred every time I edged my arm out.'

Rachael shook her head with a scowl.

'C'mon, don't be like that. The boys let me put them down when they were bubs, but you know what she's like.' His implication that women were the crotchety ones wasn't lost on her. 'At least I managed to get her to sleep.'

More blame. But he didn't seem alarmed, didn't interrogate her about the context of her rental search. Had she got away with it?

Rachael huffed. 'You're lucky you didn't smother her to death!' Tears welled. Frustration surged. She couldn't live like this – seesawing between too good to leave, too bad to stay.

'What bollocks, she was never in danger. Hon, you always think the worst. I know you were dealt a rough hand as a kid, but not everything is a catastrophe.'

She thought of all the milestones robbed from her brother in an instant. He'd survived, but never rode a bike, never kissed a girl, never earned a pay cheque. *Life can change, things can turn in a moment.*

'Maybe I'd be less of a worrier if I didn't have good reason not to trust you. I can't even rely on you to take care of our daughter.'

'Trust?'

Sam was finally awake and geared for war, but Rachael realised she was up for the fight.

'*You* don't trust anyone,' he went on. 'Never have. Ask your staff. You're so run off your feet because you never delegate. Even on leave you need to control everything because you think no one can ever do anything as good as you. Ask your kids. You continually check up on them as if you expect them to fail. Guess what, Rach? I did fuck up. I failed you, and sometimes they do too, but that's not the worst thing that can happen to a kid. The worst thing is knowing you don't have faith in them, in me.' He gestured to Indy, now resettled in Rachael's arms. 'You barely let me hold her. You never trust *enough*, Rach.'

'No, Sam. I trusted too much when I shouldn't have.'

He's never violent.

His arm flexed in a burst of anger and he groaned in frustration as he pulled back. 'Bollocks.'

No one is, until they are.

'I trusted you when you made marriage vows, I trusted you to stand by me, I even trusted you with those stupid role-plays you insisted would add spark to the bedroom, but you still cheated. Oh, I trusted you, too much. Over and over.'

'And that's all on me, you reckon? Your trust problems. Not what happened with Liam?'

She swallowed hard, disgusted he'd even breathe her brother's name to deflect blame.

'Do you even trust yourself, Rach? You're not coping with another kid and you think even that is my fault.' Sam's mug smashed to the tiles in pieces, spraying cold tea over the bamboo floorboards.

She couldn't help but flinch.

The fire in his eyes returned as he stomped towards her but stopped short of touching her. That's when he said it. 'Is that what you tell yourself to justify why you're leaving me?'

She swallowed hard. 'What?' Rachael flung away from him and stood in the hall, unsure where to go or what to do, feet stuck as if the floor was wet cement.

'Don't act like you don't know.'

Indy's cries escalated as their voices rose. It was so clear to her now. Rachael needed to get the kids away for good. Away from this toxic home. She turned to leave.

He'd never hit us.

Chapter 22

Gertie

When Gertie first moved to Apple Tree Creek, it had felt as if they lived in a garden labyrinth. She'd weave the kids in the pram, ducking around tight corners in suspense of what they'd find, being frustrated by dead ends as they searched for the thrill of solving the puzzle – finding their way back home. With just thirty-two bespoke homes, it was an intimate affair, full of hidden alleyways and secret paths, with everything wedged in close to use every skerrick of reclaimed land. Ed had often resented all the rules and had opposed the back-to-base security drones when they'd been suggested, but Gertie was of the view that surveillance (government, or otherwise) was only a problem for those with something to hide.

'If you want to record me unloading groceries – knock yourselves out!' Gertie had said at the body-corporate meeting.

But there were times the shrubbed enclosure and the CCTV made Gertie feel like she was an exhibit at a human zoo, or her family the subjects in some second-rate reality-TV show.

The Rainworths had won their place, but Gertie had quickly realised her rich and famous neighbours had picked this estate to spend their millions – a village completely enveloped in a ten-foot hedge, shut off from the world by security-patrolled gates. For what purpose? What secrets were they guarding?

Gertie thought back to Rachael being convinced a stranger had snuck through the gates just to get up close to a once-famous person. The layers of security had been little help there. Rachael had explained the history, but something didn't sit right. Was Rachael paranoid? Sure, Sam was a household name years ago, but he wasn't exactly celebrity royalty. Gertie found the business card the stranger had given her when they'd met by chance at the playground – *Blooms and Living Gifts by Rosa*. Rosa, or Annabelle, whoever she was, had a store nearby. Gertie pressed the card to her lips. She worried about Rachael's state of mind. Rachael had said no one ever answered when she tried the number, but maybe they were blocking her. Without contemplating why, Gertie called the mobile. Rosa answered.

'It's Rachael York's friend, Gertie. We briefly met at Apple Tree.'

'I know who you are. I'm glad you called. Can we meet?'

'Meet with *me*? No, I just wanted to clarify something – Rach wasn't sure she knew any Rosas, but you told me you knew her, that you spoke to her children.'

'I do know her family, but it's you I need to speak to.'

'I don't even know you.' Gertie felt disloyal even talking to her.

'I know you care about Rachael.'

'Sorry, I don't know why I called,' Gertie said, about to hang up.

'—she's not safe.' The woman sounded a little unhinged.

'What do you mean? You could tell me, but you'd have to kill me?' Gertie laughed. It felt as if she was on a YouTube prank video.

'You seem kind, Gertie. Please meet with me.' She gave directions to a nearby cafe.

Returning to the estate after meeting with Rachael's 'stalker', Gertie's mind was overflowing with allegations she wanted to verify, but she didn't know where to start. How much of it was true? Had she ignored the red flags her training had taught her to see, or was that woman the clever manipulator Rachael had painted her to be? Either way, she would not let Kat near that house until she understood the truth. Who knew what went on there if what she'd been told in that cafe was real? Gertie had to confront Sam, get to the bottom of these allegations.

She stopped her car outside the Yorks' place. She had no clue what to say, how to approach this predicament, but knew she had to figure it out, and rang their bell. When there was no answer, she peeked through the small windows running along the top of their garage door and saw Sam's Porsche parked inside. It was then she noticed the number plate for the first time. Personalised, clearly spelling 'Yorky'. The contact Kat had been texting.

Gertie fell forward and puked all over Rachael's agapanthus.

Her hands were shaking, her eagerness to know the truth so palpable she wanted to burst into her daughter's room, but she knew she had to tread lightly. Kat had been even less forthcoming since Gertie had accused her of plagiarism – now she understood why.

She knocked on Kat's locked door. Nothing. She wanted to break it down. She took a breath, cursing the ridiculous lock.

'Honey, your dad's flight arrives tonight and I really don't want him to think I broke you. Can I please help you try to find your smile?'

No answer. Calm and cruisy hadn't worked, so Gertie moved on to desperation. 'Sweetheart. I really need to chat to you before your dad gets home – this might be our last chance for a few days to talk girl to girl.'

A pause.

A red-eyed Kat swung the door open.

Gertie was horrible at keeping secrets and couldn't be fake if she tried. The sight of her daughter, so miserable, ended her. It came out in a blurt of sincerity and concern. 'Sam bloody York – what's going on?'

They locked eyes and Kat caved.

'Oh, Mum.' Kat bawled into her arms. 'I did something horrible.' Gertie saw by the depth of sadness in her daughter's eyes that this wasn't about plagiarism, and she feared her suspicion was real. *Yorky. Those messages on her phone were from fucking Sam York, not his son.*

'You know, don't you? You have that look. It only happened a few times, at school mostly – but I let it.'

Gertie wiped a tear from Kat's face, tucked her hair behind her ear.

'He was so sweet at the start, said we could move slow and just kiss …'

Gertie's breath caught as if she was being choked.

'… and I kind of wanted it to happen at first, but then' – she sobbed – 'then I changed my mind. It was too full on.'

Gertie tried with all her might not to scream. Scream and rage over whatever this dirty-pawed married man had let happen with her seventeen-year-old daughter. It didn't feel real. Gertie had assumed Kitty-Kat was too good a girl, too clever a girl to get mixed up with this sort of scandal – but that sort of thinking assumed her daughter had any control over it. The power had all been his.

'And this is Sam you're talking about, not Ethan?'

She nodded and Gertie died inside.

Kat straightened up, looked at her mother with a little more hope, a little more light in her eyes. 'I know it was wrong, but I just couldn't think of anything but him, his beautiful face, the way he moves – everything about him is just so smooth and perfect.' She sobbed, folding her arms. 'He said not to tell, that no one would believe me, anyway ...' Kat locked eyes with her, chin trembling. 'I know, he's like old, and a teacher and—' She was bawling now, like a pressure valve had been released, howling with regret and shame, 'I'm a total cow and Rachael's so lovely, I couldn't do that to her.'

Gertie shut her eyes. A good mother would have picked up on the signs of this sort of exploitation telepathically. An even better mother would have protected her daughter from it in the first place. But Gertie missed it. Too worried about her own problems.

She opened her eyes. She had to stay calm, keep Kat talking, keep her in focus. 'Right, good, that's good you were thinking of the bigger picture, hon. That doesn't sound too awful. So, ah, you said you wanted some of it to happen but then it got too much? Can you tell me about that?' Gertie stroked Kat's hair, calm and careful as if her world wasn't ending. *Oh, please, God don't let her say she's pregnant to Rachael's arsehole husband.*

'I said I wasn't ready, and he didn't force me to or anything – he's not like that.' Her lip trembled. 'But he got angry when I said we should stop ... that's when he started failing me and now he won't return my texts. He said it would just make matters worse if I told, and now I've broken that rule, too. I've wrecked everything and now everyone's going to hate me even more for what I did.' The sobbing returned.

Gertie's chin quivered and she tried to make it stop. Tears fell down her face.

'Oh, my darling, this is not about what you did – you're so young. It's about him and what he did to you.' Gertie held Kat's clammy, miserable face in her hands. 'This is what predators do. They manipulate your mind into believing things you wouldn't ordinarily even consider. You did the right thing speaking up. It's only when brave people like you find your voice that we can stop it.'

'I thought I was better than this. I feel like one of those desperate housewives sucked into giving their fortune to some Scandinavian prince online. How could I be so stupid, Mum? So gullible?'

'Oh, hon, you are so far from stupid. If anything it's your strength and your spirit that made him interested in you in the first place. And from what I hear, you're not the first victim of Sam York.' Kat's chest rose and fell against hers as she sobbed. 'I'm so sorry this happened to you, but we're going to work through this together.' She hugged her tight, and Gertie wasn't sure if the dampness on her shoulder was from her daughter's tears or her own.

It was torturous, getting through the afternoon's routine with the image of what Sam York had done flashing in her brain. But she baked the tacos, fried the mince and mashed the guacamole like everything was right in the world. As soon as Fred skulked in the front door from lectures with his laptop bag swinging, Gertie explained she had an errand to run, and left him with the dishes and the kids.

It took exactly two minutes to walk to Lavender Lane and establish through the top window of Rachael's garage that the prick's Porsche was still there, so he likely was too. It took another thirty seconds to text him.

Unless you want your wife to know what you've been doing with my daughter, meet me at the playground.

It took another five minutes for the six-foot-six fuck-knuckle to arrive at the fort, his taut calves disappearing into sporty drawstring shorts, his strong shoulders firm beneath his polo. He was relaxed, as if he had nothing to be ashamed of, nothing to fear.

'Is this about the plagiarism? Because I thought we'd covered that.' His smile was no longer warm, the act no longer convincing.

She told herself she would not be intimidated by him, but her words came out sounding like that was not entirely the case.

'How dare you?' Gertie growled, pointing her finger at him. 'Parents trust you with their kids and this is how you behave? Failing a girl for not sleeping with you. Could you be more clichéd? Shame on you!'

'That is total bollocks. Is that what she told you? As if in this post-MeToo age when every bloke's got a camera in his pocket I'd be daft enough to have a go at a student. On Indy's life, nothing untoward happened. I caught her having a gander a few times and told her to knock it off, and now she's mortified from me rejecting her. Why do you think she doesn't hang around anymore? I've got the messages to prove it.'

Gertie swallowed hard, her confidence shot. There was something about his pommy accent that made it sound feasible. Even Kat had admitted she was attracted to the lout, that he didn't physically force anything. No, she wouldn't get sucked into his game. Men like him were experts at twisting things to make you feel incompetent.

'That report was a fake – she'd never cheat. You'd better fix her grades or I'll inform the school you did more than blackmail an under-aged girl.' Gertie's chin was high, her gaze firm.

'Sod off. What more could I do to discourage her? I kept trying to give her the hint, but she still didn't accept I'm a married man and not up for it.'

'Hasn't stopped you before, so I hear.' Gertie folded her arms. 'How 'bout we let the police decide, then.'

That made him think. Gertie exhaled. She told herself she was strong and brave and a better human than this moron, but as he approached her, the shadow his shoulders cast over her made the feeling so precarious that a whiff of breeze could blow it down. His intent to intimidate was clear.

'Sure. And they can assess the damage bill from your little vandal slashing my artwork. Valued at ten thousand quid last time I checked. Could do with the cash after Cueball Crawley roped me into that bloody investment scam.' He towered over her like a giant. A smirk changed his features, made his eyes dark and cold, and Gertie couldn't believe anyone found this version of Sam York anything but bullish. 'Perhaps we'll just call it even, then? Besides, if you want to go with your version, I think you'll find she's legal. I'll just say she was looking to pull, that I didn't hear her complain at the time. And I'll make sure all the blokes at college remember about Kitty Rainworth is how she lost her free ride to a school she was never good enough for, for being a dirty skank.' He wandered off, indifferent.

Gertie's knees felt weak. *He'd called her Kitty.* Her disgust at the implied intimacy made it feel even more personal. The bravado and bluster she'd brought to defend her daughter had been quashed by his vile words. She waited until the monster was out of view before she crouched on the rubber playground floor and cried like a child left too long after the bell.

Sheets of peach and orange splashed across the evening sky as the birds sang in the cool evening air. Gertie was exhausted and emotionally stripped bare. She scurried through the perfect paths towards Lily Court without a backward glance towards Lavender Lane, where that arsehole lived. Did Rachael realise the kind of monster she slept next to at night? As she approached the roundabout that led to the estate entry, she heard the buzz of the automated gates closing. A Yellow Cab crept towards Lily Court and Gertie was sure she recognised the wide shoulders and strong jaw of her husband chatting away to the driver.

Ed was back.

'Great timing as usual, Eddie.' Gertie hid from view and called her sister. She couldn't face him, couldn't find the words to explain what had happened without having a plan to fix it. 'Lou? I need you. Are you free?' Gertie sensed she'd caught her sister in traffic.

'I'm ovulating and on my way home to make a baby. Can it wait?'

'Everything's falling apart, Lulu.'

Lou paused, letting Gertie spill it all in a torrent.

'Fuck, that's a total shit-storm. Just give me an hour … don't do anything rash.'

Gertie stood still among the mondo skirting the roundabout and caught her breath. As she paused, she heard something. Muffled, angry words billowed from the direction of the Yorks' house. Had Rachael finally confronted her husband's bullish ways? Or were they echoing from Penny and Martin's place. What had Sam said about losing money with him? Gertie's gaze shifted to her toy-scattered yard and watched her husband's cab pull up. Was that his tail between his legs? Gertie was hemmed in by bonfires and about to soak them all in gasoline.

What could possibly go wrong?

Chapter 23

Rachael

The electronic click of the front door chimed and Rachael flinched. Moments later, Sam paced down the hall. When their words had got too heated, Rachael was relieved when he'd thrown his hands in the air and yelled, 'I need some air!' But despite his walk around the block, Sam was still on edge, raking his fingers through his thick hair, deep in thought. He pocketed his phone and exhaled.

'Did your girlfriend call?' Rachael was only half joking, and as soon as the words were out, she wished she could shove them back in.

'It was yours, actually. That wet-nurse, throwing a wobbly. I told you she was too thick too quick. She's bloody psycho.' He chopped the air with his hand.

'Don't call her that. Don't call anyone that.' Where was this bravery coming from? Indy continued to cry. Rachael could barely concentrate and tried to zone her out.

'Would you prefer "fucked in the head"? She messaged me about Kat's marks and when I agreed to meet up to calm her down, she gave me a right bollocking, threatened to report me if I don't change her little charity case's grades.'

Rachael felt an uneasiness settle in her stomach, but at least they'd moved on from him catching her planning to leave him. 'Kat's grades? Since when did she get anything but As.'

'Since I caught her plagiarising. I guess we know how she got that scholarship. All the knobs in the staffroom think she's ace – overrated, if you ask me.'

Rachael shook her head. She was sure the growing tension between her parents wasn't helping the poor baby in her arms settle, but her instincts told her not to let her go. 'I know the Rainworths well. That doesn't sound right, Sam, not about Gertie or Kat.'

Gertie wouldn't get involved unless she had to, unless Sam had done something seriously off. Rachael trusted Gertie more than her husband.

'What did you do?'

His hazel eyes darkened. 'What did *I* do? I'm not the one telling pork pies. That little tart's the problem.'

'C'mon, Sam. She's a polite, clever young woman.'

'Those skimpy shorts – asking for trouble.'

Anger curled up her throat. 'Don't you dare. She's got a right to wear whatever she wants without men like you saying things like that.'

'Well, she's no wall flower, loitering around the pool in her bathers, sending me suggestive texts. It's not proper. Now the nurse thinks I had a crack at her!'

Rachael held the edge of the couch, her eyes wide with alarm. She swallowed hard. 'Please tell me you didn't try something with that girl, Sam.'

'For fuck's sake, no.'

Rachael's brow furrowed. She waited for the 'but'.

'She got a little handsy a couple of times and I shut it down.' He cut the air with the heel of his hand. 'If she says otherwise, she's talking tosh. Why do you think we've heard bugger all from her this week? She's got the message finally.'

She wasn't convinced by his words. He saw it.

'Rach, on Indy's life, I never slept with that girl. C'mon, hon. I've done wrong by you in the past, but haven't I always told you straight up? I might have trouble saying no, but I'm not a fucking liar. As if I'd touch a kid. Christ.' He huffed, disgusted by the thought.

Even for him, the idea did seem too low an act. Her mind travelled back to the few occasions she'd seen Sam and Kat together. She was a little quieter around him, he seemed a tad indifferent – no red flags. And Rachael knew what effect Sam could have on young girls – a schoolgirl crush on her hero coach seemed the likeliest story.

He continued. 'I told you that American was the last time. I've been doing everything I can to help us get through this. Hoovering. Shopping. Everything possible to support you, show you that was a one-off, not who I am anymore.' His neck muscles strained like thick cords beneath his skin.

Rachael's heart raced. She knew she was crazy to push, but she couldn't stop. 'A one-off? Aren't you forgetting the first time you risked your family for a moment with a certain journo?'

The first time. The unmentionable time. Other than tiptoeing around her name when Gertie saw the 'friend' Rachael believed was Annabelle talking to Ethan in the playground, they hadn't spoken of her since. The affair might have been long ago, but the fallout was ever-present. In every whirr of the video, every blink of the lens watching every corner of this place, and the reason they needed it to. Rachael's instinct pushed her away and her legs carried her further down the hall, cradling a still-crotchety Indy in her arms. She placed their daughter safely in her cot and her screams grew louder. She left anyway, closing the door as she re-entered the hall.

'Rachael, wait,' Sam said, grabbing his wife's arm and begging through gritted teeth. 'We've started this now. Can we just, finally, talk about this?'

Rachael's slight frame stood in his shadow, an overwhelming surge of anger pulsing through her bones. She became aware that Noah was well outside on the tramp, Ethan would still be on his game, headphones numbing real life. They were out of hearing range. Her breaths were rapid, her nostrils flaring as she gathered strength.

He beckoned her closer. 'Bring it, hon! I deserve it,' Sam yelled, the tendons in his neck tightening as his jaw tensed.

The light was fading outside, but Rachael could still see his face, the determination to resolve the friction and mistrust that had been building ever since he loosened his tie and confessed what he'd done in that carpark. He was huge and he was strong and he was pacing towards her.

'C'mon, throw it at me!'

Her instincts screamed run, but her heart told her to stand firm. Rachael sniffed, tears flowing. 'You're a total arsehole, a self-indulgent prick who can't keep it in his pants.' She realised she'd been preparing these phrases for weeks. They were prepped, waiting to be freed, and it felt exquisite.

He cheered. 'Excellent, it's about bloody time we had it out.' He egged her on, arms open wide, welcoming her torrent of abuse. His presence was overbearing, encroaching on her personal space.

'You show no respect to me or the life I've built for our family. I can't even leave the house without you monitoring me like a prisoner.' The anger she'd lodged inside for years spewed forth, discharging in the air like gas.

'Nice one. Keep going.' He nodded he could take it.

'You think because I'm a strong woman, these betrayals don't hurt – well they do, Sam.' Rachael wiped tears away, her chin wobbling, thinking of all the nights she'd cried herself to sleep over him. Wondering if he was with someone else because he wasn't in love with her. Doubting her desirability, his attraction towards her, every last decision she'd made that had led her to this life. Degrading herself with his ludicrous, domineering role-plays just to keep things interesting. 'Every time you cheat you whittle away at the trust we have, make a mockery of the times we shared. There's nothing left now. I have no faith in you being able to do what you promise.'

His head dropped, his own chin wobbling in shame and regret. 'Okay, right. I get it. I'm sorry. Come here.' He exhaled as he approached her, arms wide.

But the thought of touching him made her shudder and she retreated further down the hall. 'No.' Rachael pushed him away. 'Get away. I'm not finished.' She'd waited for this chance. To feel ready to fight. She needed to purge it all.

'Okay.' Sam looked towards the kitchen window, hearing Noah in the yard. 'Keep your voice down, we don't want the fucking Crawleys calling the cops.'

Maybe it was time the world was told what sort of man he was. She wouldn't protect him anymore.

Sam's arrogance deflated and regretful Sam skulked closer to her. 'I'm so sorry. I mean it this time. I've seen how much this impacts you. My eyes are wide open. You're the only one that lights up my room.'

Her pre-formulated rebuttals had dried up, but the anger still bubbled. Sam continued to edge closer, his arms attempting to envelop her.

'No!' Rachael forced the heel of one hand into his ribcage to keep him away.

'I love you.'

'No! Don't say that, it demeans the word. This isn't love.' She started punching, and with each burst a tiny spurt of anger dissipated, transferred from her fists to his torso. He was solid and strong and barely noticed the pitiful whacks of her tiny hands. She kept retreating at the same rate he edged closer until she was wedged against a tall side table that wobbled and tipped, the pot plant it supported crashing to the floor. And still, Rachael pummelled him with her knuckles, balled and fierce and completely ineffective. It made her realise why most women were forced to grapple for weapons against their partners. Against their size, their strength – they simply had no choice.

What Gertie had told her was true: men don't have to hit to hurt. Now it was Rachael who felt the need to hit. Hit back at the years of belittling her into thinking she didn't deserve respect, for the thousand tiny seemingly inconsequential acts of influencing what she wore, what she ate, whom she spent time with, that formed a critical mass that now left her broken, feeling powerless to do anything to change her life.

But she wouldn't allow him to steal her light, not anymore.

A slideshow of images. Kat's flushed cheeks as Sam guided the young swimmer's arms to demonstrate the perfect, streamline dive in their kitchen. His willingness to walk her home when she lived a well-lit, security-monitored block away. Ethan's bitterness towards his dad since Kat had entered their home. *Was it possible?*

'If I find out you so much as winked at that schoolgirl, I'll make sure you never set eyes on another woman again!' Rachael yelled, having now grabbed one of Ethan's drumsticks and aimed to thrust it firm into his eye.

'Okay! Okay!' he said, his tone now firm as he grabbed her forearm, stopping the wooden stick from piercing his pupil.

She persevered, inching the weapon closer.

Sam's huge hands gripped tighter, till she winced.

Chapter 24

Gertie

Husband and wife stared at each other in awkward silence.

Face streaked with mascara, the memory of Sam's calm indifference of her accusations still fresh in her mind, Gertie Rainworth approached Edward Rainworth on their doorstep with consternation. Had it only been a couple of months since an Uber stole him away? She felt something shift inside that, at first, she gauged as relief – she wanted to fold into him, blurt out all her woes about their daughter. But was this the dependable Ed she'd married, or the new version she didn't trust?

The door burst open in front of them, two grinning faces at waist-height.

'Daddy!' Harry and Abe called in unison.

Gertie was not sure why it peeved her, seeing them frolic freely towards Ed. But part of her felt he didn't deserve to see their cherub faces, feel their sausage arms curl around his neck. He hadn't done the time. Not lately, at least. Kat stood behind her brothers with less enthusiasm for the visitor. She gazed at Gertie with a face of mixed emotions, as if asking permission to approach the enemy. Gertie smiled. Whatever their marriage woes, he had a right to see his children. They hugged him hard – never having been apart for so long.

'I think I really underestimated how much I'd miss you guys.'

'But you rang me every night!' Abe said, returning to the lounge.

Unbearably polite, Ed said to Gertie, 'After you,' and they followed the kids through to the family room – cluttered with piles of washing she was yet to put away, the newcomer bearing presents from his cabin bag like Santa Claus. Ed had lost weight. His clothes were different (ironed shorts sporting a belt!). Just the fact that he was wearing shoes Gertie didn't recognise raised a barrier between them. It felt wrong. Gertie had hoped there'd be a sign – a big neon one saying all was right in the world now that *GertAndEd* were reunited. But all she could think was, *He was my husband and he's wearing someone else's shoes.*

'Thanks, Dad!' the boys beamed, flushed with delight over their new gaming headphones.

Gertie saw Kat setting up a new iPhone with glee – seemingly distracting her from the mind-blowing confessions she'd shared that afternoon. Gertie sat in a dizzy haze without comment, watching her family reunite, bouncing stories naturally between each other as if Ed had never left. The chuffed look on Ed's face said, 'Can we just pretend I never did?' He had tears in his eyes as he planted a kiss on his daughter's forehead. Kat was beaming at her dad, stoked at her present.

'I thought you'd need a reliable phone,' Ed said. 'Especially with uni next year, my scholarship girl.'

Kat's face fell. She looked to her mother, then bolted to her room.

'Ah, Ed? I kind of need to catch you up on stuff ...'

'Me too ...' Ed replied, nodding seriously. 'We'll get these boys off to bed first.'

They remained exquisitely polite that evening as they tucked kids in bed in a well-rehearsed routine, but all the while something built inside Gertie. Adrenalin? Fear of how they'd be together once the kids were out of the picture? How to admit to Ed what she'd let happen to their little girl? There was so much he'd missed, so much he didn't know. Whatever Ed might have done, he had a right to be part of Kat's life.

'Where's Fred?' Ed asked, as if delaying the conversation even longer with more tedious chitchat.

'Lectures till late on Wednesdays.'

He nodded, seeming disappointed. 'I got him a present, too.'

Gertie's lips twisted as she saw another iPhone box in the bag. 'You bought our manny a phone?'

Ed waved her away. 'Two-for-one deal at the airport – thought he might like the second.'

'Generous. They must've given you a good raise.' Where was her frugal Ed? She was reminded of the PA's comments when she'd phoned his work, of her surprise she had not joined Ed in Singapore for the transfer he'd requested *on purpose*.

The hurt came back in a flood.

When her husband turned to her, she couldn't meet his eye. Couldn't face what she might see there. Guilt? Awkward indifference? Was he sizing her up right now, comparing her to that blonde bit sashaying around his apartment? And to think of how she'd looked when he arrived – broken and spent, with a house still in the usual disarray.

Big, fat tears flooded her eyes that she was too proud to let him see. She snuck to the bathroom to splash water on her face, in an attempt to feel normal again. Ed followed, hovered awkwardly as if he needed to be invited into his own bathroom, then started rummaging through drawers for a toothbrush. Gertie realised he was rustling through Kat's drawer (she refused

213

to use the bathroom the boys weed all over) and gestured to show his error, but not before he revealed a pill strip: twenty-eight little white lumps with teeny arrows showing the way forward from the red section. Gertie hadn't seen the likes of them since pre-Ed's vasectomy.

'Something you're not telling me?' Ed asked accusingly.

'They're not mine!' Gertie threw at him. The hurt quivering on his face distracted her from the fact that their seventeen-year-old daughter, unbeknownst to her, had started taking the pill. 'Oh, Jesus, Ed.' She spat the toothpaste in the sink, wiped her mouth and settled in on the side of the fancy bath. Before today, Gertie would have assumed they were prescribed to regulate Kat's cycle for swimming comps or acne control. But now the obvious answer was likely the right one.

He joined her on the cold bath's edge, elbows to knees, hands to temples. He swallowed hard. 'Well, let's not overreact. At least she's being responsible. Maybe it's just *precautionary*. We don't know for sure that she's ...' Gertie could see the picture he was painting in his mind, the disgust he had for the very idea of his daughter in bed with any bloke. '... using it. Who could she be interested in? Someone at school?'

'Kind of. That's the news I said I wanted to catch you up on ...' Gertie winced at what she had to reveal, then, like a bomb, exploded it in his face in one loud blurt. 'Kat had a crush on her swim coach and she started something with him – and when she refused to do more, he started failing her in PE, made up evidence she'd plagiarised and now she might lose her scholarship.'

There. She'd said it. He was all up to speed. She felt better.

His eyes flared for a second. 'Whaaat?' His face reddened. 'She's sleeping with her teacher? Perhaps you could have led with that!' He paced across the bathroom floor and back. 'That utter bastard. I'll kill him! Where does he live?'

'In the estate, actually. It's my friend's husband.'

'Husband? Bloody hell. How old is the prick?'

'Too old. The bright side – I'm sure the text I saw on her phone said she was a virgin, so the pill thing is new to me.' Gertie's face twisted.

'You're snooping now? Since when do you micromanage the kids like this? We always said we'd trust them. They were fine when I left!'

Her eyes narrowed. 'Don't you dare!'

'What?'

'Don't you judge me! Like this is my fault!'

Ed flinched. 'I didn't say that.'

Gertie was surprised it had taken this long for the night to have gone belly up.

'No, but you're thinking it. Your eyebrows are saying it. That our daughter wasn't on the pill when you lived with her, and now she is. That she wasn't being harassed by a married man, now she is. I wasn't spying on her then, now I am.'

Gertie filled her husband in on the how and why, the ins and outs of what Kat confessed to her that afternoon, perhaps without the high drama and confessions of love. *Was that really just today?*

'Don't judge me, Ed. You have no idea how hard this has been for me, while you swan around in Bachelor Land doing God knows what with God knows who while I raise your family for you! Did you even miss us, Ed?'

'Gertie – look at me.' He held her shoulders, pulled her chin up so her eyes met his gaze. 'I've been a total mess, G. You didn't return my calls all week since you texted me all that stuff the other night about knowing what I've done.

I can't eat. I can't sleep. I've got a rash, for Christ's sake – then the fog closed the airport. I became one of those vagrants sleeping across chairs in boarding gates waiting for a flight. The thought of losing you – I just couldn't bear it. If anything, it made me see what a total arse I've been – how important you are to me. And the kids – it physically hurt being away from them.' He was baring all, as honest and open as she'd ever seen him.

She wasn't mad anymore but wasn't feeling the love. He still didn't seem like her Ed.

'Wait – I prepared a speech.' He fished what looked like an airsickness bag from his pocket, then cleared his throat and began. 'So, it's not gonna be easy. It's gonna be really hard, and we're gonna have to work at this every day. But I wanna do that because I want you.'

Gertie felt a rush of emotion begin to swell, but then recognised she'd heard the words before, from Ryan Gosling. She frowned. 'Isn't that from *The Notebook*?' Ed had always struggled to articulate his emotions. Had he resorted to stealing lines from on-screen heroes?

He waved his hand at her to hush, and continued, turning the paper bag sideways to follow the trail of his mid-flight biro scrawl. 'You said you couldn't be with someone who didn't believe in you. Well, I believed in you. I just didn't believe in me,' Ed said, quoting *Pretty in Pink*. This was getting old, but then he looked at her longingly and said, 'I'm just a boy, standing in front of a girl, asking her to love him ...'

Her chin wobbled a little without her permission. 'The Notting Hill bookshop. That's my favourite.'

He nodded. 'I know.' There was silence for a beat before he spoke again. 'Remember that breakfast in bed when we spoke only in film quotes?'

She nodded.

'You're my world, love. You always have been.'

Gertie couldn't place that one in her film-o-file. 'Which flick was that?'

'No, that's just Ed, your real-life hero who lost the plot for a bit. I'd never try to hurt you, you have to know that.'

Did she know that? Gertie was no longer sure of anything. She thought of Rachael and Sam York and the tales he must tell her daily to keep her on side. Gertie refused to live like that. She'd never seen marriage as work – it shouldn't have to be if you marry the right one. And it never had been, until this year.

'I saw you were upset when I arrived,' Ed said. 'I got the impression you didn't want me here, and I guessed why, but then Kat said you saw some woman in my room. Is that what you think I've done?' Gertie realised with all of Kat's dramas she'd forgotten about the Zoom woman who had plagued her thoughts for days.

Ed fumbled with his phone, scrolled and showed her a picture – a curtain of silvery hair framing the lovely, weathered face of his housekeeper Sian, he explained, who must have been not a day younger than eighty.

'Eighty-three and she thinks it's time to learn English – crazy old bat.'

Gertie was speechless. She felt ridiculous. She looked up at her husband's kind eyes, more crinkled than the last time she'd seen them in the flesh. Was the utter despair Gertie had felt, that sense of betrayal, really just a misunderstanding? Her gut told her it was, but was that wishful thinking? She thought of the sinister way Sam York had denied involvement with his student, compared to Ed's explanation now.

No. They were not cut from the same cloth.

Gertie perched uncomfortably on the end of the tub – the always-wet bath where they'd supervised tired, squealing kids for years, shared their days, planned their new adventures. Under the bright light of the bathroom vanity, husband and wife locked eyes.

Wordlessly they told each other, *Now what?*

The thread between them snapped. He'd made her like this – untrusting, insecure. This wasn't her.

She shook her head. 'I believe you, Ed. But I'm still hurt.'

He tilted his head. 'Honey ...'

She stepped through to their bedroom. A bedroom he hadn't set foot in for two months.

'You still ditched us, Ed! Are you forgetting that? You gave up. You say you wanted to go back to when the kids were little. That we were good back then even though some bits were hard. That we were always tired, but we always tried. The thing is, Ed, we never gave up with the kids, and we never gave up with each other. From the moment you decided you were moving out, the man I thought I knew ceased to exist. This other man was born that I didn't recognise, that I couldn't trust. Marriage means not piking when things aren't perfect. Requesting to live away from your family isn't love, Ed. It's selfish. And there's no room for that in any relationship.'

'You're right. I did seek out that branch transfer. But I've worked hard to financially provide for this family for nearly twenty years without a break. I figured that bought me a bit of me time. Time to think, to sort out what I wanted for the rest of my life. To give you space to make sure you still wanted me. Then I figured you could get to know Fred while I sort out my mess.'

'Huh? If you're not having an affair, what mess do you speak of? And what's Fred got to do with anything?'

'You were right in your text the other night. There is something I need to come clean about, but I had to do it in person.' He held her hands firmly together.

Gertie was horrified. 'You *did* have a fling?' She couldn't bloody believe it. 'She's a colleague, isn't she? I knew it!'

'Huh?' Ed said, confusion playing on his face. 'She's a horticulturalist. One of the best in the country, actually.'

Gertie's throat tightened. There it was – confirmation that he was a rotten cheat. 'A horticulturalist! Whoever she is, she's not me, your wife.' She wanted to scream, but her kids were just outside, and the thought reined in her white-hot anger.

'So, Fred worked it out, did he? About me and his mother?' Ed shook his head, angry at something. 'I thought he might – we kind of look alike in the eyes.'

Now Gertie was utterly confused. 'Fred? What has our manny got to do with you having a fling in Singapore?'

'I thought you'd realised.' He braced like a mangy dog awaiting a beating. 'He's my son.'

'What the *hell*?' Gertie's tongue barely formed the words. 'Fred's your *son*?'

'Shh, he doesn't know yet. That's the other reason I wanted to come home. To get it all out in the open. He thinks he's just here for work experience and free rent while he's at uni.'

She couldn't take any more surprises today, but she had to know how bad this news was. The kid had only just started uni – was barely older than Kat.

'How old is he?'

'Just hold your horses – he was the product of a rather short encounter with one of the church auxiliary ladies at boarding school in Toowoomba. It was more than two decades ago, and Danielle was a happily married woman and never had the courtesy to tell me I was a father until last Christmas when

I bumped into her by accident – you know, when I had that conference in Dalby. She wants nothing from me, just thought it was time I knew Fred.'

'Fred. Your son.' Gertie sat on the edge of their bed, as dumbfounded as she had been three months before when he'd said he was moving to Singapore. She was seeing a pattern here.

'I'd already arranged the work transfer when I found out about him, and I didn't want to tell him I was his dad and leave him again, so I didn't tell him who I was. Danielle said he needed a job and a place to stay and I thought it would kill two birds ... and he could get to know his half-siblings. I was so lost, before, hon. You know how hard it is for me to admit things like that.'

Why didn't you just stay. Stay and talk to me?

'I know it's a lot for you to take in – I'm still processing it months later. But, hon, I promise you, that is the only wrong I'm guilty of and I'm ready now to be a proper father to all my kids, and a proper husband to you.' He stood on the other side of the room, alone, his face crestfallen.

Gertie shook her head. 'We've been together since we were sixteen, Ed. You still cheated on me.'

Gertie began walking towards Ed, who held out his hands like a hostage.

'We weren't engaged. God, we hadn't even said we were in love, then. Okay, we might have technically been going steady, but we were kids! And I had no idea Fred was the result of a rushed session behind the cemetery garden shed with one of the Sunday-school ladies.'

'You impregnated Fred's mother in a cemetery?'

His face fell. 'It was my first time. She was older. It lasted about three minutes.'

'We lost our virginity together – it was in your parents' caravan in your backyard after renting *Pretty in Pink* on a scratchy VHS. It had a porthole for a window and you kept your socks on. Remember?'

Ed's face flushed. He always was better at having sex than talking about it (which she'd figured was better than the other way around).

'I had no idea, that day at the church, that I'd even' – he coughed – 'made landing. Hon, put it in perspective, it was a long time ago and I was young and clueless. I wasn't even sure it counted.'

Gertie felt the sob gathering force and surging up her throat, out of her mouth. *Why can't men just keep it in their pants?*

Ed sat beside her on the bed, deflated, then placed his hand on her shoulder. She flinched.

'Don't touch me!' She rose from the bed, grabbed his unpacked suitcase from the hall and kicked it across the carpet. His recital of a Google search of favourite movie quotes would not undo what he'd done. 'Get out!' Disappointingly, it didn't slide far. She needed a show of strength. Gertie spied his golf clubs in the walk-in robe. 'Go!' Next, she hurled a handful of clothes from his side of the wardrobe at his head, showering him in shirts and pants. He shielded his face with his forearms as she kept flinging clothes, hangers poking at him from every angle. Her finale – she yanked the suitcase to the front door with attitude and launched it, it unzipping midair and raining clothes across the lawn.

'Strewth, Gert. It was a lifetime ago. It was one mistake in a moment. I would never break my vows.'

'But you have, Ed. You left us. You lied to me about why you were leaving. You lied about why Fred was living with us. You lied to Fred about who we are. You didn't involve me when you found him. You chose to shut me out and lie. Now get out!' Gertie felt her wrists dig hard into his chest as she pushed him into the hall, down the steps and out to the street.

'Honey, c'mon. We need to deal with the Katerina situation. Where does the prick live? Deviant. 'Bout time we met, I reckon.'

'You want to win me over with quotes, Ed? Well, frankly, my dear, I don't give a damn!' She opened the front door wide, planning a good old-fashioned slam before she took in what he'd said. 'Don't you dare! Do what you do best and stay out of it.'

He stopped gathering the scattered shirts and scanned the street as if looking for clues to Sam York's whereabouts. He was shaking his head, red-faced and fuming. 'I'll flatten the son of a bitch for laying a hand on my daughter.'

'Enough. If you make this worse for Kat, I'll do more than that to you, man formerly known as husband!'

A moment later, Fred's ute stopped in their driveway. He got out and surveyed the clothes strewn over the yard. 'Man, did Abe have another meltdown?'

'Nope,' Gertie replied. 'Today it was my turn.'

The door slammed loudly, but gave no satisfaction.

Chapter 25

Lou

Louise Underwood's decidedly lovely husband, Tim, propelled his muscled torso back and forth towards her. He tried his best not to look positively bored, and as he fell into the familiar rhythm of 'Staying Alive', Lou tried just as hard not to picture the Bee Gees. As this was the sixth time they'd made love in three days, it was getting harder to feign enthusiasm. The fertility experts had warned Lou and Tim not to confine sex to ovulation, that spontaneous lovemaking should be maintained, but it seemed the couple's eagerness (desperation?) at critical times made the act oh-so-less appetising later on.

In Tim's defence, he'd always tried his best not to look alarmed when Lou nudged him on the couch, noting the subtle cues that alerted her to the fact that her ovaries were ripe for the picking. She was sure Tim knew what having a baby meant to her. He saw it on her face when she gazed with envy at her sister, Gertie's flock of kids. He'd never refuse his wife an opportunity to become a mother, and he didn't even know about the boxes of adorable baby clothes she'd been saving for years, waiting for the day the world deemed her worthy of the only thing she'd ever wanted.

People judged her. Assumed professional women chose their career over motherhood, or simply had no maternal instinct to speak of so there was no choice to make. But Lou would have given it all away in a second for the chance to have a pudgy-fingered little person hand her a heart-rimmed, misspelled card on Mother's Day. And yet, all she heard from parents was bitching about drop-offs or tiredness. She'd never sleep again for a moment of it.

Lou focused on Tim's eyes, tried to imagine their baby with those lovely grey eyes, imagined his seed being planted in her fertile garden, just like a footballer pictured the ball reaching its mark. But that strategy only made Lou miserable. She'd been a lawyer for nearly nineteen years. She knew enough to accept there were no guarantees in life. That juries surprised you. That key witnesses changed their testimony. Shit happened. Maybe they just weren't going to be parents. Maybe Lou would just have to settle for being the favourite aunt of Gertie's three, and the quicker she realised it the better.

Tim and Lou had started their baby-making voyage when they were first married years before, cheeky with the knowledge that they were having unprotected sex, egged on by the baby-making works package – candles, theme music and a lacey twin set. They'd lie in a sweaty twist of limbs for hours telling their stories, looking up at the ceiling fan, dreaming about the family they'd create together. Sometime last year, that adorable baby-making routine had declined to a perfunctory, sock-wearing affair that Tim had once described as 'making him feel like a stud dog servicing his bitch', followed by a desperate hope that maybe this time, deep inside, human life would click into being.

Lou tried not to think of her approaching birthday. She smiled at Tim, focused on his ears, bobbing up and down as he thrust away (while she tried not to hum the chorus), before she noticed the news headlines on the TV in the background and squinted to read the scrolling text.

Man suffers life-threatening stab wounds inside exclusive Apple Tree Creek Estate.

'Oh, God!' Lou screamed so loud she scared herself. The voice of her unhinged sister babbling on about Kat being in trouble and Ed being back and some teacher being a turd – it all came back to her in a torrent. Had shit actually got real?

'Yes, baby!' Tim offered, mistaking her cry as enthusiasm, and sped up his rhythm.

'Stop, stop!' Lou tapped his sweaty pecs. 'The news!' she said, easing his motion to a quick stall. 'My sister!'

Confusion played on his face as Lou robed up and lurched for the TV remote on the bedside to increase the volume. An aerial shot of Gertie's ridiculous estate – a hexagon of copycat houses encircled by a tall hedge, like the setting of a weird cult on *60 Minutes* – filled the screen, followed by a flash of one of those cold cement boxes like Gertie's, swarming with media and police.

But then again, they all looked the same in that place.

Tim got the message that their baby-making session had ended abruptly, a slightly pained look on his handsome face.

'Sorry, hon. It's my sister … something's happened. I just know it.'

Louise Underwood called Gertie's number with no response, called her niece and got her voicemail. Desperate for knowledge, she searched online for news, but no results were found.

Channel 7 fleshed out the broadcast with stock advertising images of the estate when it was first developed seven years ago, before a journalist read out: *'A father of three is being rushed to hospital with life-threatening stab wounds. Police are yet to release the identity of the victim, but* 7 News *are first at the scene so stay tuned for the latest developments …'*

Louise thought back to Gertie's last tearful words. *Ed's on the doorstep, Kat's told me she's had a thing with Rachael's husband. Ed's going to flip when I tell him.* Had Ed attacked Sam? Had Gertie attacked Ed over his affair? Had Kat attacked the dodgy teacher? Lou had thought it was all rubbish – as if Ed would cheat on her. He didn't have it in him.

'Oh, Jesus, Gertie … please tell me none of you did anything rash.' Lou's hands fumbled to redial her sister's mobile, her landline, but they rang out and she huffed in frustration, opting to text her.

Gertie. Don't say a word. I'm on my way.

Ever since she was a girl, Gertie had been a blurter. She'd confess everything before even being asked. Lou rushed to find clothes, eager to get to her crazed sister before she did anything stupid. *Please let this one not be about us.*

Louise Underwood had raced to a hundred crime scenes in her career as a defence attorney, usually with a rush of adrenalin and shameful sense of voyeurism. Now the only thing she felt was fear.

Chapter 26

Gertie

Gertie stood alone, leaning on the kitchen bench. She stared out at the early-evening sky that was alight with brilliant peach and tried to let her brain catch up. Ed was MIA. He'd gathered what he could of the clothes strewn across the yard and trundled his case along the street, cursing the uneven cobbled surface despite the neighbours peering through matching plantation shutters. Harry, already bored with whatever bribery his father had dished out, was lurching crazily through the house with the golf clubs Gertie had thrown about mid-meltdown. Kat, freaked out from their arguing, had skulked off somewhere with her new phone. Abe was conspicuously absent, but as it was rubbish collection day she figured he was busy straightening wheelie bins down near the janitors' shed. Fred was off being Ed's offspring somewhere. Her ruminating thoughts halted.

Ed had a son to another woman. They were no longer the two virginal childhood sweethearts, destined to be together forsaking of all others, she'd always believed they were. And that orange-looking, rather pleasant teaching student who had made mini muffins for her kids was, in fact, Kat, Harry and Abe's half-brother.

Gertie started to laugh, it was so preposterous, but the heaves soon turned to sobs. The fact that Ed himself was unaware of this until recently, and that this betrayal happened long before they were even married, should have lessened the hurt, but it didn't. It was still *her* he'd cheated on – and a firmer, slimmer version at that.

She rang Kat to check she was okay (and nowhere near That Bastard) when she heard Kat's old phone vibrating on the coffee table. Her daughter had escaped without leaving her new number. Gertie was uneasy about the idea of not being able to call her, given her fragile emotional state. She'd vowed to protect her better, and she'd already misplaced her.

The kitchen security phone buzzed. She figured it was Ed, ringing to continue his defence campaign, perhaps from the entrance gates. But when she glanced over, it was Rachael's address displayed on the digital screen. She hesitated – how could she sound normal without coming clean about Sam and Kat? She answered anyway.

'Hey—'

'Gert! Thank God.' She barely recognised Rachael's voice, it was so panic-stricken. 'There's so much blood and I don't know what to do!'

Gertie's mind raced. The last time she had heard that from a new mum was when her baby soaked his nappy red after tasting his first beetroot.

'What's wrong? Is Indy sick?'

'Just come quick, please!' Her voice was rushed, clipped. 'Eth's on the mobile with the ambos. They're saying fifteen minutes!'

'Just breathe, hon. What's happened?'

'It's Sam. He's been stabbed in the chest and is struggling to breathe.'

'Okay, just stay calm.' Gertie had always worked well under pressure. She had been known to lose her shit if the boys left pee puddles on the toilet seat but was level-headed in an emergency. 'Is the wound sucking in air when he breathes?' she asked, grabbing her first-aid kit from under the sink.

'I don't know what that means!' Rachael cried.

'It's okay, I'm on my way.'

The thought circling through Gertie's mind as she scurried, heart racing, along the cobbled path to Lavender Lane wasn't about tending to Sam's chest wound – whatever her feelings towards him – and it wasn't fear of Sam being in danger. She couldn't care less. It was about who had put him there.

Pacing through the open door into the Yorks' house, the metallic odour of blood was her first concern. The size of the crimson circle expanding on Sam's shirt was her second. A shell-shocked Ethan was on the phone to the ambulance officer while Rachael pressed a soaked towel against Sam's chiselled chest. Gertie swallowed hard then focused.

'You guys are doing so well.' As she gloved her hands, she heard the hiss as Sam inhaled and exhaled. Gertie didn't have time for the who, how and why, but had to know the basics to do her job. 'You said he was stabbed?'

Awash with the brightness of fresh blood, Rachael wiped her brow as she crouched on the floor beside Sam and quickly nodded. 'Ethan found his dad like this after the intruder left.'

Intruder?

'I need to see the wound. Let's cut this off to minimise moving his spine,' Gertie said as she grabbed scissors and sliced a once-white polo shirt free from the pale, floppy patient.

She quickly removed the blood-soaked towel and wiped the gurgling chest wound clean.

'They said to keep pressure on it!' Ethan said, red-faced and exasperated.

'You're right, that's so important.' She hurried to open sterile pads and swabs. 'How far away?'

'Ten minutes now,' Ethan said.

'Great.' It wasn't great. He wouldn't live that long at this rate of blood loss. She cleaned the wound long enough to see it was more puncture than slice, before it flooded with pink, frothy blood once more. Gertie plugged the flow, sealing off the wound with her gloved index finger. The hissing sound eased. The gushing pulse of blood stopped.

Sam opened his eyes, gasped air and filled his lungs.

She wasn't sure he was conscious but spoke like he was. 'That's good, Sam. Just don't try to move or my finger can't do its job, righty-ho?'

'Is he going to be okay?' Rachael asked, eyes wide.

'He's lost a lot of blood ...' Gertie had come to think of Rachael as her rock, her sounding board, her best friend. She was also intensely private. Did she realise in minutes she'd be the first suspect of this crime, questioned to the edge of her life? She tried to prepare her, meet her eyes, but Rachael's only focus was Sam. 'The cops will secure the scene, look for the weapon ...'

'It's not here, they must have taken it,' Ethan said, holding the landline in the kitchen.

They? If he hadn't laid eyes on the intruders – was he just assuming there had been more than one? The wound was bullet-sized. Should she look for an exit wound? 'Honey, you're a good lad, helping your dad, but you also need to be sure of what you tell the police. Are you sure it was a knife, not a gun? The doctors will know soon, anyway.'

Ethan and Rachael glanced at each other. Were their eyes saying more than their lips?

'We would have heard that,' Rachael said.

Gertie checked her patient's pulse, kept her finger plugging the wound. Precious minutes passed as the burnt-orange sunset turned to a tawny twilight. Ethan had Barry on the landline and the ambulance on the mobile, relayed messages between Gertie and the crew, constantly checking the road for the ambulance.

Ethan's eyes lit with relief. 'I can hear sirens.'

Gertie exhaled, the gravity of the scene hitting her now that help was imminent. He might just have a chance. Thoughts filled her mind of where Kat was, and Ed and his illegitimate son, for that matter. What if there had been an intruder and her boys were home, alone? And brilliant Lou. What would she advise Rachael if she were here?

'The cops will be asking questions, Rach. My sister's a lawyer. I think you need one.'

Rachael blinked in quick succession. 'Why would I need a lawyer? We're the victims here.'

Does she mean Sam's victims? Was this self-defence? Gertie wasn't sure what Rachael was capable of, but after that day, she had a fair idea of what Sam was. Gertie locked eyes with her friend, but Rachael's face gave away nothing except her fear. She was on tenterhooks, the loyal wife stroking his hand with love, genuine concern in her eyes. Something wasn't adding up and Gertie worried she knew why.

Was it possible?

She retraced her day's discoveries, all the evidence of Sam York's errant ways, all the people she knew who had grievances with him – Annabelle, his ex, Kat, even Penny had him in her bad books for some reason. Then there was Sam's mention of Martin and money.

Her thoughts turned to Ed. *I'll flatten the son of a bitch for laying a hand on my daughter! Where does the prick live?* Gertie shook the idea from her head. It couldn't be Ed. He was all talk. He'd be drowning his sorrows at a sports bar in town by now.

The sound of sirens closed in. Lights flickered across windows. Whatever Rachael had done, Gertie had her back.

'I'm here for you, hon.' Still plugging the nick in Sam's chest with one hand, Gertie touched the trembling hand of her friend with the other. It was clammy. Rachael had paled, her skin papery, her eyes glassy and distant. 'Ethan, you're doing so well. Can you get your mum a blanket? I think she's in shock.'

Did she love him? Did she kill him? It was possible that both were true.

In Gertie's mind, Rachael's slightly slowed country-girl drawl spoke to her.

I'd imagine all the ways I'd kill the bastard.

And if wasn't her, then who?

Chapter 27

Penny

Penny thought she was hearing things. They never had sirens around here. It wasn't until she flicked the water off in the shower that she confirmed it – that whirr of sound that signalled no good was closing in on her lane – and a thick layer of dread formed in her stomach. A moment later, a sweep of red light dipped across her bathroom mirror. An ambulance rushed by in a flash of glorious living colour. 'Fuck.' She dried herself quickly and robed up.

She told herself it wasn't about her, or her bugger of a husband. Where was Martin? Penny couldn't get onto him when she'd called the office to see if he could give Spencer a lift on the way home. She hesitated, then looked in the mirror. Her face wasn't on, but this was an emergency! A flick of the shutters confirmed there were police cars in the street! *There goes the neighbourhood.* Maybe it wasn't the end of the world that they had to sell up.

The vehicles stopped right outside Rachael's place.

He's killed her. That sex pest has killed his wife. 'Oh, my God, poor woman.' She felt awful for all the judgemental thoughts she'd had about the working mother and her skinny jeans. Penelope hurried to pull on whatever was quickest – leggings and a hoodie. Cars, lights, a scrum of locals huddled on the verge of Rachael York's pristine yard.

Edging the front door open a crack, a rush of night air prickled Penny's skin as two more police cars arrived in convoy.

Movement at the Yorks, their door open wide. The warm glow of the internal downlights made her privy to private spaces, the lavish master bed, the ornate lamp and to-be-read pile. All so benign and full of optimism. Minutes later, an endless parade of police wearing disposable shoe covers passed by the windows. Crime-scene LEDs like she'd seen on TV were being rolled in.

She thought of Martin, his face red with fury as he'd explained Sam York's ridiculous tip-off and how he had trusted him. How it had ruined their lives. Where was he? She needed the silly idiot.

A scrum of locals gathered behind the line of cop cars that filled the narrow street just as the fancy sprinkler system hissed into action, as if it were any ordinary Wednesday. As if an ambulance wasn't blinging in their drive like a beacon.

'A stabbing!' Penny heard. A sinister cloud floated through the vocal mob, all voicing expert opinions. 'This is why we pay ridiculous body-corporate fees – to have twenty-four-hour security that keeps the riffraff out. And look, the iron gates are still wide open! It's a media circus in here!'

'A stabbing?' she echoed. 'The bloody swimmer must have stabbed his wife.'

Mrs Harris nodded. 'Anyone is capable of pulling a trigger. But a knife at close range – to feel the tip pierce the flesh of the mother of your children.' The old bat seemed enthralled.

Penny knew the Yorks had been married long enough to accumulate more than a few reasons to feel like killing each other.

The paramedics were tending to someone on the floor, crouched over for what seemed like too long. The body from the floor was lifted onto a gurney and carefully lowered down the driveway; a man, thank God.

'It's him, not her!' Mr Harris announced, as if he'd appointed himself to give a running commentary. The theories adapted to the new fact.

'A robbery gone wrong? They did have some fancy things, not to mention gold medals in frames – have to be worth something on the black market.'

'Had to be her. I overheard Barry tell the police no visitors were brought through the gates all day, only residents and the usual contractors. Footage proves it.' Mrs Harris seemed almost pleased, as if the storyline on a soap opera just turned for the better.

The ambulance skidded away, taking out a row of mondo grass.

'I heard Barry was adding guests without proper checks. Something like this was bound to happen.'

As the sky glowed orange between the roof lines and fairy lights began to wink along garden edges, the neighbours came in droves. Penny decided to shut up for once and listen to everyone's take on the drama.

'Clear as day it was the wife – heard their barnies? He was in the doghouse. Heard her call him a selfish prick on the weekend, among other things.'

'Well, the poor woman does have three children and no help.'

'Oh, no, didn't you hear, they got that hot young nanny who looks like snow white from down the street a while back. If you ask me, that's what started all this …'

A voice from behind her – Irish, unmistakably. 'Ma'am? You live next door?'

She nodded and turned, smoothing her wet hair. She felt a royal mess, and now she was being interviewed by police!

'They're only new here, right? How well do you know Rachael York?'

Another voice from the crowd interrupted him. 'I don't think that woman is capable of *stabbing* someone.'

The detective shrugged. 'I think we all are, under the right circumstances.'

Penelope Crawley thought of all she knew. He was probably right.

Part 2
The Motive

Chapter 28

Rachael

Arms stretched microphones towards Rachael as the detective guided her down to the front gates. She hunched under the Irish detective's shoulder – so close she could smell his aftershave. A torrent of overlapping words from the crowd combined to an indecipherable rumble, but the focus of the journalists' questions was clear. *Why?* What had transpired in the days before to force a loving wife and mother to go to such extremes? The probing questions revealed the story angle, and their intention shocked her – firstly, that they'd assume she was guilty, and secondly, that they believed the answers were simple ones.

Cameras flashed. Pupils flinched. The swarm shuffled left as she did, like a thousand-armed octopus after its prey. 'What triggered this callous act?' an anonymous voice asked. But Rachael was barely processing the what, let alone the how or why.

Triggered. The word itself implied suddenness, a cause and effect. In reality, there was no isolated event, nothing to warn her of the bedlam that was soon to unfold in their home on an ordinary afternoon among tree-lined streets. Even if her mind could focus, her mouth form words, she couldn't answer. There was no single cause, just five hundred bad decisions, missed opportunities and errors of judgement, tossed together with exhaustion that had crept their family towards this – this death by slow, incremental change.

The police officer driving waved a friendly salute to the estate's security guard – good old Barry in his pompous hat and jacket – who obliged him and opened the iron gates. Barry who always played the ukulele and delivered her parcels with a smile. Barry who let her in when she lost her keys, even looked after her kids when she needed a moment. Now Barry's kind eyes dropped with shame as they met hers, as she slumped in the back seat of a police car that smelled like stale grease. She wondered how much he'd pocketed in bribes for letting those reporters through the gates. And who else?

The driver made eye contact via the rear-view mirror. 'You're going to need to tell us what happened, love.'

Rachael continued to rub her chafed hands and focus on the thin line of dried blood still present in the quick of her thumbnail. Instinct took over once more and she remained silent. She had nothing to say.

Nothing that would help, anyway.

Fluoro light, burnt coffee and overheated air was all Rachael noticed as she shuffled inside the station in a cloud of whispers. It was modern – pale woodgrain benches, wide windows and chrome – not like the country cop shop where she grew up, where the policeman lived out the back.

Two detectives Rachael recognised from her home earlier ran through the obvious questions anyone would ask given the scene they'd discovered her in. It wasn't the Irish one, O'Sullivan. It was the other two. Their tone was direct, professional, yet with thinly veiled contempt, and she guessed she couldn't blame them – the way it looked. Rachael's mind was dusty, her emotions extra raw, and physically she was exhausted. But through the fog, she knew she could have prevented this chaos if only she'd made better choices.

Gertie told the paramedics all she knew before the police interrogated them – even Noah and Ethan were questioned like criminals. They'd taken swabs of their DNA, imprints of their shoes to match with the tiny blood splatter that held a partial imprints and lists of people who had valid reasons to be in the house to rule them out. Sniffer dogs had arrived within half an hour, circling the premises before they got too hot to sniff, and cleared out. Gertie's sister had called her before she was taken to the station, like she'd promised she would.

'I don't want a lawyer,' Rachael had replied.

But the fast-talking Louise soon convinced her she needed one.

'Rachael,' Lou reassured, 'don't take it personally – the first suspect is always the fucking spouse.' Rachael knew Louise was a sought-after partner in a prestigious law firm so knew her stuff. 'It's procedure. It doesn't mean anyone thinks you did it.'

But the contempt in the cops' fleshy faces told Rachael otherwise – they were not thrilled about her taking Lou's advice of, 'Say nothing until I get there.'

Even Gertie thought she'd done it. She could tell by how protective she'd been while the cops repeated the same questions, as if trying to trip her up.

'The neighbours spoke of a disturbance late this afternoon. An altercation between yourself and your husband. Can you tell me about that?' The cop gestured to her wrist, fading finger marks bruised into her forearm like a smudged tattoo. 'That bruise came up fast, or is that last night's effort?'

Another hopeful pause.

He continued to patronise Rachael with a 'there, there' tone. 'Even a continuing threat of family violence is enough of a defence. Strong fella, your husband. Olympic champ. Six foot six. Nothing you want to tell us?'

Rachael sat and stared, unaware of how much time went by, disbelieving this was real. Twenty questions in, they quit asking, left her alone with her over-sweet tea and her ragged breaths, picking beads one by one off the lip of a Styrofoam cup. She couldn't slow her thoughts or settle the thump of her heart, not with that mirrored-glass panel leering at her on behalf of the people-watchers skulking behind it. She adjusted her weight on the hard, plastic chair. She felt collected by loneliness, lost and afraid.

The chrome door handle lowered, and a man in navy cotton slacks and polished leather shoes stepped closer to the table Rachael was seated at. She recognised the Irish voice. They'd swapped cops on her.

'Rachael?' The cadence of his accent made her stock-standard name sound romantic. *So, he's their good cop.* 'Is there anything I can do for you? Get for you?'

Silence. She swallowed hard. Her eyes, fixed and emotionless until now, betrayed her and welled up at the first shred of humanity she'd felt since everything she'd known to be real broke to pieces.

His eyebrows threaded together. 'I've got kids, too. I get it. Me missus and I have a six-month-old terrorist and a three-year-old I'm just starting to like again.'

That lilt – it got to her. Tricked her into thinking anything he said must be true.

'You know what they want, Rachael – just the truth. Tell them your story. We don't want to be here all night, do we?

You've had the worst of days. So, if we're barking up the wrong tree, with fingers pointing your way, a simple explanation would be fine.'

She broke her silence. 'Is he …' Her hand covered her mouth, too afraid to ask, to hear the answer she dreaded. 'Is he still alive?' There'd been talk of a drug-induced coma to keep him stable. Had his heart arrested? Was this now a murder charge and that's why they'd refused to let her go home? The agony of not knowing was stronger than her resolve to keep quiet.

'Aye, he is. Is that the answer you wanted?'

'Of course.' Rachael felt the tension unspool, triggering the let-down in her breasts. Two circles of wet blotted her shirt like headlights. She braced her aching chest with folded arms. 'Oh, God, I need to feed her. Can I go?'

He didn't stir or blush with embarrassment like most men would.

'I didn't plan on being away from her, and my pump's at home.' Tears trickled down her face with the fear that this arrangement may be permanent, if they proved she was involved. A spell of dizziness coursed through her. Rachael realised she looked tired, unkempt, emotional. She always thought a love like theirs to be a unique kind of madness, and just as unhealthy. Was this the only way it was ever going to end?

He sniffed, looked at his shoes. 'You know, if those clowns in that filthy room get their answers, we could see about getting you home, solving that leakage problem for you?' His words reminded her that he batted for them, that this charming Irishman was merely part of a ploy to make her feel secure enough to talk herself into trouble.

Rachael's eyes narrowed. 'You have no proof. There was no weapon found. Cameras prove I never left.'

'We haven't checked them all yet.'

'I know I didn't leave. You have nothing substantial. I'm just the only one you've got.'

He stroked the stubble on his chin and considered her answer. 'Was it more of a domestic issue? We all know most blokes are pretty keen to fob off what we can to our better halves, hey? The division of labour, stress of a wee one – I've seen people threaten lives over less. Gets pretty ugly at my place.'

Silence.

'Perhaps it was an accident? He's a handyman, your bonny husband. Bit of a do-it-yourselfer by the look of the tools everywhere when the incident occurred.'

Rachael had thought of explanations. Stories she could run with if she needed an alternative hypothesis to the reality. The Stanley knife slipped when he was cutting carpet. He was wrestling with the kids when a tool in his pocket slipped and lodged in his chest. He fell? None sounded remotely plausible. Rachael thought again of Lou's recommended response.

'On the advice of counsel, I decline to answer.'

'You see, these lads are pinning it on you. No signs of forced entry. No evidence of outsiders getting in that Fort Knox of yours. Neighbours heard a rather vocal barney between you and the victim not long before. And there's also this recent movement of significant funds from your joint account. Anything you want to tell me about that?'

What funds? Rachael dredged through memories – a casual conversation where Sam said he was chatting to Martin Crawley at the tennis club.

'Sam controlled the finances. He said something about throwing a few grand with Martin Crawley's firm for some investment portfolio, but I don't know the details nor see how that's relevant.'

'I'll look into it, shall I?' He paused, then tilted his head. 'One clean pierce. The very tip of a knife was all it took. Nicked the chest to a depth of fourteen millimetres – not exactly a full-forced attack by a strong-willed opponent who meant business. Not like a revenge attack or crime of passion after years of bitter physical abuse as one would expect with DV. Almost as if the attacker wasn't exactly committed to their rage. I disagree with my colleagues who have it all wrapped up as a marital spat gone wrong. My money's on a third party. An amateur. Hazard a guess?'

Stony silence. Rachael could only manage to inhale and exhale. *Just Breathe. In. Out.*

'Let's brainstorm the possibilities. Assuming you're not about to confess, is there anyone you think might have even the slightest motivation to hurt your family? Anyone even remotely capable of stabbing your husband? Any bad blood with neighbours?'

Her brain was too tired to form words, and Rachael felt anything she said would be held against her, so what was the point?

He exhaled, frustrated, and pulled out his notebook. 'I spoke to Gertie Rainworth. She told me she tracked down her daughter, Katerina, not long after this all happened. She was at her friend Sienna's house at the time of the attack. Can you confirm you definitely did not see her in your home today?'

'Today? No. Not for the past week. She's been sick, didn't want to give it to Indy.'

O'Sullivan made a note, seeming a little annoyed. Rachael was desperate to know what secrets that book harboured.

'Can you tell me more about Katerina, Rachael?'

What could Rachael even say about her? That she smelled like lilies and Ethan couldn't take his eyes off her. That she had the confidence of someone older but still showed a vulnerability that was becoming. *Overrated, cheating tart, according to Sam.*

'She's seventeen, a scholarship kid, great with children.'

'How is she with husbands?'

'Shy, actually. Sam's too much for most people.'

'But not you? Strong, successful career woman ...'

Rachael shut down again.

Detective O'Sullivan exhaled louder. 'The thing is, Rachael, if you won't tell me what happened, we're gonna have to rely on your neighbours' accounts of what they heard, piece this puzzle together without you. And you know how neighbours get. I've had a whole team interviewing the street all night. Vocal lot. Still haven't found Ed Rainworth, but I hear he flew in today, coincidentally.'

Rachael's jaw dropped. 'Gertie's husband has never even met Sam – or me. What on earth would he have against either of us?'

'Maybe he thought his wife knew your hero husband better than they let on? Saw some pretty heated footage of Gertie and Sam this afternoon.' The detective's lips thinned. 'Everyone's got a theory. Especially the judgemental ones, like the Crawleys. Crammed in like sardines in those fancy houses. They're not your husband's biggest fans, are they? Not so cosy, that estate you've moved in to, is it?'

Chapter 29

Gertie

Gertie Rainworth woke to the sudden clonk of her sister's forearm across her face. Lou had on one of those eye masks rich people with poodles wore, and was unapologetic, nor understanding, when Gertie woke her on purpose, and asked her to explain her presence in the bed. There was a distant sound of outrage billowing from the living room, which Gertie took to mean the boys were up and absorbed in watching some brainless twerp on YouTube preaching about something, and she hoped it wasn't *How to Make Slime at Home!* again.

'I'm staying here.' Lou's usually perfect hair was birdsnesty, and Gertie loved the sight of it. It made her appear far less uptight. 'That's okay, isn't it? These overpriced villas aren't that fucking big, are they? And since your husband is MIA and your redhead farm boy is in your spare room, here I am.'

'I can see that. The question is *why* you're here, exactly?' Gertie prayed Tim hadn't found Lou's credit-card statement and finally left her for obsessive shoe procurement.

'The friend you begged me to represent called. I met with her and I was too lazy to drive across town only to come back today in fucking peak hour to meet with her again.' Lou pulled her shoulder-length bob into a quirky pigtail with a band that miraculously appeared from nowhere. Resourceful should have been Lou's middle name.

'Thank you!' Gertie whispered.

Lou grabbed her arm. 'I thought Edward was coming back yesterday?' She gestured to the Ed-less bed.

'He did.' Gertie could not fathom telling her about what happened, so she left it at that. 'Don't ask.'

Besides, Gertie's head was full of Rachael. Of Rachael and those comments she'd made about making a hobby out of ending her cheating husband's life. She had been kidding that night, surely? They had been deliriously tired! There was no way her lovely friend had *stabbed her husband*. But the scene Gertie was faced with last night – Sam bleeding out on the floor, Rachael and Ethan nervous as thieves – told a different story.

'You didn't tell me you stuck your fucking finger in the victim's chest. That's the stuff of legends. Always so modest.'

'You've spoken to Rach?' Gertie felt her left eyebrow lift and ask on her behalf, *she didn't do it, did she?* Gertie felt sick to the stomach thinking about that man, that awful look in his eye when she'd tried to confront him about whatever was going on with Kat. But the idea of sweet Rachael charging at someone with a knife was totally incongruous with the person she'd begun to genuinely care for.

Gertie waited for the 'client counsel privilege' lecture her sister usually offered when she pried into Lou's more gossip-worthy criminal cases, but Lou said, 'Your guess is as good as mine. She's not talking.'

Gertie nodded. 'Probably wise. That was your advice to me in your text last night. The text you sent when you thought *I had tried to kill Ed*.' Gertie glared just in case her loudness didn't communicate her outrage.

'Sorry about that. It did look like your house on the news – freakish *Edward Scissorhands* place you live in. And you were rather pissed at your husband, fired up about the handsy coach. That kind of stress can result in these sorts of lash-outs.'

'You don't know the half of it.'

Lou shook her head. 'She was out of it when I saw her – some sort of shock-induced trance, unless she's an exceptionally good actor. But that will serve us well until I figure out how to angle this.'

Gertie took comfort in the fact she'd done something to help her friend (she was still not convinced she'd saved Sam's life, nor if that was even considered a good deed for the world), and her big sister was the best in the business. From about the age of eight, Lou Rainworth wouldn't lend so much as a scrunchie without a formal contract. She could argue permutations of the same point for weeks without drawing breath. She was anal about housework, a formidable opponent in Monopoly, but a great advocate. She swore like a death-row prisoner but regularly used words like 'fiduciary', 'chattels' and 'impignorate'.

Kat bounced into Gertie's room, flopped on her bed and hugged a pillow to her chest. Gertie noted her daughter hadn't piled on thick eyeliner and perfectly straightened her hair like she usually did before facing the day. This whole York thing was hitting her hard.

'Have you heard if he's going to be okay?' From the way Kat asked, she wasn't sure if she was upset that Sam York was hurt, or disappointed that he'd survived.

'He'd stabilised after surgery, last I heard,' Lou reassured. 'I'm sure they'll look after him, hon.' Lou then turned to Gertie, mouthing she had no idea about his condition. 'You were close with the family – any ideas on who would do such a thing?'

Kat shrugged. 'Some random meth head? Who knows? He's kind of famous, so your guess is as good as mine. Aren't they loaded? Maybe it was a burglary that went wrong?'

'The disturbing part is that they got a warrant for the security CCTV downloads and no visitors entered the grounds that day. They're still trying to work out what happened to the Yorks' entry camera, which was conveniently down, but the footage from the entrance was clear, so unless they arrived by helicopter or scaled a ten-foot barbed-wire fence, it wasn't some random intruder. It had to be someone from the estate.'

Kat seemed concerned by this. 'You guys are so naive. There are ways.'

Both women glared.

'I've been using different entries for years. It would be so easy for anyone to get in here without Barry noticing.'

Lou turned serious. 'How? You should tell the police. It might help them exonerate Rachael.'

'Wouldn't all the cameras detect anyone lurking in the estate, anyway, even if they got in without authority?' Gertie said.

'Ask Ethan, he's right into his tech stuff – only ninety-two per cent of the estate has coverage.'

What was the point of all the bells and whistles if a kid knew how to bypass them?

She had to admit, she needed Ed to navigate this one. It was too big to map out in her mind, and perhaps she had been a little rash to ditch her co-pilot over a transgression twenty-three years ago. She realised whatever happened with their marriage, Ed was in her life for good. Was that the obstacle Rachael faced? Divorce wasn't enough distance from Sam York and his evilness? It was nearly impossible to disentangle yourself from an ex and still be a parent, to pull your own thread from the twisted mess and expect it to slip free without fraying.

Even for someone as committed to marriage as Gertie, there'd be a line she couldn't cross and still uphold an acceptable level of self-respect. Had Rachael seen something go on between Sam and Kat that crossed a line of no return? But if Rachael had done this, if she had finally had enough and brutally stabbed her husband in the chest with a knife, and Gertie failed to share this knowledge with the police, did that make her complicit in the crime?

An unknown number called her mobile. She stepped into the laundry to answer. 'Hello?'

'Gert. It's Rach.'

'Rach!' All the unsaid pulsed in her throat.

'Sorry – on a burner phone. It's a media circus here. I need to talk to you – can you meet me at the meadow?'

'Meadow?' Was that code for something , a safe word she'd forgotten?

'Ask Kat. She showed Ethan the trick, apparently.'

Gertie found Kat in the backyard, forlorn and looking younger than her seventeen years. 'You okay, kid?' Gertie thought of the issues her daughter had faced – dealing with a man twice her age who may have been grooming her for months, her academic future, her dreams, in jeopardy. Despite her clever mind, Kat had limited exposure to how unfair the world was.

'You were there. You saw how much blood he lost. Is he, like, brain damaged?'

'It sounds like he's pulled through the surgery – they often place them in an induced coma afterwards just to let the body recover.' Gertie wondered how appropriate it would be to ask one of her ICU colleagues about his prognosis. 'You sound really worried about Sam, even though he wasn't exactly treating you with respect.'

Kat bit her lip, threw Nacho's ball across the yard and folded her arms. Gertie knew to tread lightly or she'd clam up, and Gertie really needed her daughter to know she was on her side. That she would be her voice.

'I'm proud of you, hon. For how you handled your dilemma – we can't let issues like that lurk in shadows. There were lots of ways that could have gone. I think you chose the right way by telling me the truth. That's all I ask.'

A funny look warped Kat's features. 'It doesn't feel like it's finished. My marks are still shot. Ethan hates me because he knows about what happened with his dad, Sam's in hospital and what if Rachael found out, Mum?'

'It'll take some time to process, but this is not your fault, hon. And by no means is it dealt with. But there was so much going on in that house. Even if Rach did suspect, it was just a small part of a big puzzle. And you didn't ask for any of it.'

'What if I did, though? What if I wished for it at the start? I'm such an awful person. Who does that to another woman?'

Gert could see the conflict in Kat's face, the confusion.

'Honey, men like that mess with your head, make you feel the way they want you to feel, the way that meets their needs. If you were a consenting adult, I'd agree – I'd say you should take responsibility for your choices and learn from it, but you're a school kid and he was your teacher. It's not only unethical for him to take advantage of that power imbalance, it's against the law. This is not your fault. If Sam harassing you indirectly got him hurt, then that's on him.'

Gertie gave her a hug, fighting back sobs of regret that she hadn't clued to it earlier. 'Tell me, this secret way out – does it involve a meadow?'

Kat narrowed her eyes at her mum. 'Did Ethan blab?'

'Rachael needs to escape without a media tail. Be a sport and let your old mum in on it.'

Gertie walked a few hundred metres to the far eastern corner of the estate boundary and there it was, a thinning of the leaves, a loose panel of fencing hidden behind the janitors' shed, just as Kat had described. Gertie winced as she manoeuvred her frame (somewhat wider than her daughter's) between the branches and the iron sheeting, and arrived at a wedge of forgotten land just outside the perimeter of the village. Unlike the precise formal gardens and golf-course-standard lawns of their estate, the forgotten triangle of fenced-off field was perfectly untouched with scattered leaves and sticks speckling the fresh wild grass. Huddles of mossy stones flanked the banks of a clear, flowing stream – the estate's namesake that rippled through the perimeter and fed through to the harbour river system. Tiny yellow butterflies hovered over sprinkles of wildflowers.

'Pretty, huh,' Rachael said. 'Bloody kids – we pay a fortune to maintain security and they find a blackspot.' Her voice tried to be flippant. Her expression was anything but.

'Rach.' Gertie walked across the long grassland to her friend and hugged her. 'God, what a shitstorm. Are you holding up okay?'

Rachael nodded, but her face didn't match her answer. 'Mum's here. She's home with the kids, so I don't have long. Sorry for the secret location, couldn't handle being followed again.'

Gertie smiled. 'Gave me a good excuse for Kat to spill – she's been escaping for years, by the sounds.' The events of the past few days had taken their toll on her friend – puffy eyes, blotchy skin, and worry lines etched across her forehead. 'How is Sam?'

'He pulled through the surgery, which is a good start. How can I ever thank you enough for what you did?' Rachael held her hand to her trembling lips. 'Still not conscious.'

She still loves the stupid bastard.

Gertie wondered if it was convenient, him being unconscious and all, then felt awful for thinking such a thing about her lovely, confused friend.

'They've stripped away the crime-scene tape, removed all traces of fingerprint dust, but it still doesn't look or smell like home.'

Gertie felt the same. Even walking down their street – all she could see was that ambulance. That stretcher. The blood.

'This – this awful thing. It feels like it's been building, like a crescendo. That it was inevitable. That all the smaller disasters that had been coming through were warning waves. How did I allow my family to unravel like this?' Rachael shook her head, as she wiped a tear from her nose.

Gertie folded her arms and waited for the confession she feared – why else had Rachael suggested meeting in such seclusion.

'I did this. I did this to us,' Rachael said, nodding knowingly. 'This is my fault.'

Gertie exhaled, bracing for a confession.

'But it's true, what I said when you came to help. We were the victims, this was done to us.'

She was talking in riddles. Gertie led her towards two wide boulders, speckled with purple petals, nestled beneath a shady tree.

'I know things were complex, with Sam. You know you can tell me, whatever happened last night. I've got your back, same as Lou.' Gertie had seen Rachael when treating Sam, but so much craziness had gone down just before, she hadn't been able to unload it. She wanted things to go back to normal between Rachael and her, though she didn't know what that looked like now.

'Well, as you guessed, we had the inevitable fight about his affair.' Rachael's eyes were red and swollen as if they'd cried every last tear. 'It did get out of hand, so I'm not surprised the neighbours heard.'

Gertie eyed the finger-shaped bruises on Rachael's wrist. 'I can see he hurt you, honey. Are you physically okay?' Gertie turned her wrist to inspect the damage.

'Yes, that was my fault, really.'

Gertie shook her head, sickened that she hadn't done something before now. He'd clearly brainwashed Rachael into a distorted reality of their relationship. 'Honey, you must never blame yourself for acting in self-defence, for protecting your family. If you were scared for your life, if he threatened your kids – that's a defence.' Anger clawed at Gertie's throat. *And this is not the first time, you arsehole. I wish I'd killed you myself.*

'On Indy's life, I swear I didn't touch him, Gert. We fought, it was awful, but we made up, and he promised to turn things around. You have to believe me. I can't bear you thinking I could do this. Someone came into our house and hurt my husband.' Rachael looked her straight in the eye as she said it, without hesitation.

Gertie dropped her head and exhaled. 'Well, that's a fucking relief.' She slapped her hands on her knees, putting an end to one problem. 'So, let's figure out who the hell did.'

'I've been trying but can't think straight. I'm just so worried about Sam. Noah's quiet and clingy. Ethan – he's taking it pretty badly, won't come out of his room, hardly saying anything.'

'God, you can't blame the kid for being traumatised, finding him like that, but he was so great that night.'

Rachael nodded. 'I'm sure he knows more than he's letting on, covering something for Sam. He was forever guilting him into things. The cops think there was an outage on our front camera, but I reckon Ethan's deleted the footage and I think I know why. I can't help but feel it's more than a coincidence that Annabelle Alesi gave a false name to get inside the estate, and I know she's met with E even though he denies it, and now Sam's in the ICU.'

Gertie adjusted her weight on the hard stone and tried not to cringe. She knew why the woman spoke to Ethan, and she knew why he'd feel the need to say he didn't. 'About that ...' She swallowed, wishing she'd had a chance to share this earlier, but she'd had to confirm her facts. Now there were things Rachael deserved to know. At first, Gertie wondered if Rachael had been right about the woman being a stalker. Her paranoid demeanour, her constant checking behind her back as they spoke in the crowded cafe, suggested she was a little unhinged. But after chatting for over an hour, her outrageous claims about her ex-partner Sam York were too detailed, too in line with the misogynistic way he had treated Kat, to be false. And what she said was terrifying.

Gertie huffed out her concern and began. 'You were right about the woman I saw in the playground with Ethan – her name isn't Rosa. It was Annabelle *Rosa* Alesi – Sam's ex-partner, who, as you know, he met about eighteen years ago when she was a journalist. That part is all true, like you said, she just avoids using her first name in her business, given she once was a controversial public figure. She wanted a fresh start.'

Rachael seemed almost relieved someone believed her, but then became puzzled. 'How do you know? Barry said her car was registered to a Rosa – that I was paranoid.'

'Did Barry tell you that, or did Sam? I don't believe this woman, whatever you want to call her, is who Sam made you believe she was.'

Rachael rubbed her brow with her fingers. 'Annabelle followed us all the time. I saw her with my own eyes. She'd wait outside our last school at pick-up just to catch a glimpse of Sam, always trying to meet with me to 'talk', slip notes in my bag, bother the kids – especially Ethan. She'd gaze at him like she was deranged, because he looks most like Sam, I presumed. We had to put a restraining order on her – for God's sake, she baited our dog!'

Gertie squeezed Rachael's hand, regretting the timing of sharing this knowledge with her already emotionally vulnerable friend. But she had to be told. 'Rachael, try to think back. Is that how Sam painted the picture of her to you, or do you have proof she killed your dog?'

Rachael huffed. 'So, you're on his side – you think I'm the delusional one. I don't have time for this.'

'Oh, hon, no.' Gertie swallowed hard. 'I think you're an amazing, resilient, kind and clever woman – remember that when I say this next bit.' Gertie winced. 'I met with her.'

'You *met* with her?' Rachael shook her head in disbelief. 'How did you even find her?'

'She didn't answer your call as she knew you'd just shut her down. I found her card, rang her – mostly to tell her to leave you alone – but she scared me, told me you were in danger. I was curious, I had to check you weren't at risk.'

Rachael shot up and paced towards the creek. 'I can't believe this. Why would you do that after I told you how she ruined our life? We moved here to escape her.'

'Have you ever wondered why she's been so persistent for all these years? To be fascinated with a man for a decade – that's longer than most marriages.'

'This isn't a joke! He has a way of taking hold of women, even strong women.' Rachael stepped away, crossing her arms. 'You don't get how stalkers think – they fixate on celebrities. She's unwell.' Rachael was not buying her story.

'She *was* unwell. She was treated for depression and anxiety, went off-grid, led a simple life for years afterwards before starting a florist.' Gertie approached Rachael staring blankly out at the creek, hating every minute, hating having to explain the deeds of a monster for the second time that week. 'But the woman I met in the cafe was a beautiful, articulate, woman whose only concern was making sure I helped you get out of your marriage with your life. She said she gave Ethan your first dog when he was little and months later when she wouldn't back off, Sam killed it as a warning to her to stay away.'

Rachael laughed. 'Now you're the one hallucinating. Do you really believe I could stay married to a puppy killer? Sam bought Boof!' Her jaw dropped. 'Get away from me! I thought you were my friend.' Rachael held out her hand to stop Gertie's attempt to comfort her.

Gertie's chin started to wobble, but she would not back down. She had to get to the main event. 'She told me she'd investigated the woman Sam was with before they were a couple – the one you were told overdosed from drugs.'

Rachael exhaled, looking small and frail beneath the speckled shade. 'Charlotte, yes. She was a troubled young girl, an addict. From New Zealand. That's why Ethan's family aren't in his life.'

'Annabelle researched what really happened, interviewed the family about the cause of death.'

'Oh, let me guess, Sam killed her? He's not only a dog killer but a murderer?' Rachael sniggered out loud, but there was no humour in it.

'No, not exactly.' Gertie huffed out her frustration. 'Charlotte's sister said Sam controlled and belittled Charlotte so much, sapped her confidence and will to live, that eventually she ended her own life.'

Rachael shook her head, laughing it off as total lies. 'No, she had post-natal depression – it wasn't Sam's fault. Yes, he can be controlling and does tend to make you doubt yourself, but he's got good qualities, too. Look at how he took Ethan in when she died. He adores us.'

'It wasn't PND as Charlotte wasn't Ethan's mother. He lied about that, too, Rachael.'

'Oh, I see, now you know all about my son, as well. Did Sam conceive him all by himself?'

Gertie tilted her head. 'Annabelle had photos of Sam and her holding Ethan as a newborn, as a toddler. A birth certificate. Annabelle Alesi is Ethan's biological mother.' Gertie scrolled to a photo on her phone of the document she'd been shown in the cafe.

Rachael's eyes swelled with tears. 'No, that's not possible. She must have photoshopped his name in. She was a TV anchor, it would have been in the papers if she'd had a child.'

'She was just a young weather girl back then, a no-name.'

'We took her to court for stalking – there was no mention of any child. She's an unwell woman, Gertie, but she's clever – she's got you fooled.'

'Sam had us fooled, Rachael. He is so good at what he does, so charming, that he has been feeding you and Ethan lies about this woman's continual presence in your life for years. The court case – did you ever sit in on the hearing?'

Rachael shook her head, exasperated. 'I was never allowed in sessions. It was a closed court – no public, no press – because of Sam's notoriety.'

Gertie nodded, letting Rachael's words hover for a moment. Rachael's face was pale, but Gertie sensed that it wasn't from hurt over how her husband had deceived her. It was disbelief, and a sense of betrayal by Gertie, the woman who had delivered her baby, who claimed to be her friend. And she didn't know the half of it.

'Rachael, I found the listing in the court records. No details were made public, but it was a custody hearing, during which Annabelle claims Sam said she was too unstable to take care of baby Ethan. He said she had mental-health problems. He had local cops testify that he'd called them, warning in advance that Annabelle was psychotic and off her meds and would likely front up at the police station and falsely accuse him of domestic violence. When she came in with bruising on her wrists a week later, they arrested her for making a false claim. He was going to be the next Olympic champ – the cops wanted to believe their upcoming national hero, got him to autograph their coffee cups. He even managed to have Annabelle committed to a mental-health facility and gained full custody of *their* son.

'There are other lies. I'm not sure what he told you, but he hasn't had a speaking gig in over three years, Rachael. His agent refused to represent him after he sexually harassed her and accused her of sabotaging his career. This rings true with the stories Annabelle told me, such awful stories, how he'd continually humiliate her, belittle her abilities as a parent, as a journalist, lock her out of the house, tell her the cops wouldn't help her. Tell me he's not a narcissist, Rach. Tell me he's not dangerous.'

'It's not his fault, it's a sickness.'

Gertie exhaled. She was getting somewhere.

'Then we need to get him help. He can't keep hurting women. He tried something with Kat, too. Did you suspect?'

Rachael shook her head in disbelief. 'Now he's unconscious, you're accusing him of assaulting a schoolgirl when he's unable to defend himself, fighting for his life?'

'Hon, I know it'll take a while to process all this, but Kat admitted starting something with Sam, but when she wasn't up for it he threatened to fail her unless she changed her mind. He's been distorting your reality for a long time. If you disregard what he's told you, do you really have any evidence to support his version of things?'

Rachael looked at Gertie, her breaths ragged and shallow. 'I loved you, Gertie. I thought we were real friends. The kind of friends that grow old together. Now you wait until my husband has life-threatening injuries to tell me he's a dog killer, a child abuser. You've gone behind my back to meet with a woman who told you complete and utter lies about my family. That she's Ethan's mother? For Christ's sake! If she's willing to go to such lengths, I'm certain it was she who attacked him.' Rachael's tears had dried, her worry lines smoothed over. What was left was scepticism. 'You're asking me to believe the word of that unhinged woman over the man who's fathered my children, who I've loved for over a decade.'

Gertie shook her head. 'You asked me to believe you when you said you didn't stab your cheating husband, despite finding you covered in his blood, and I did.' She placed her hand over Rachael's. 'Now I'm asking you to believe me.'

Chapter 30

Penny

The police station smelled like cheap aftershave and new carpet.

'I knew she was going to try to kill him one day, and I'm not sad that she did,' Penelope Crawley exclaimed to the detective. 'But a stabbing!' It made her shudder. She'd heard enough dreadful alley fights as a little girl – over-zealous debt collectors, scuffles when her father's hairbrained business deals turned sour. 'To think such evilness had been living right next door!' She may as well have stayed in their housing-commission dump with a broken front door and permanently blocked toilet.

'And by evilness you mean Mrs York stabbing her husband?' O'Sullivan asked in a disbelieving tone.

Hadn't all women felt like killing their husbands now and then? She could have killed Martin when he lost all her money, broke that vase against the wall, but then she made a cosmopolitan and ran a bath and bloody well got over it.

'Him, I mean. I don't blame the woman for fighting back. Show them, Martin.' She elbowed her round ball of a husband sitting uselessly beside her and wished she'd done more about it at the time it was unearthed. Perhaps if she had, it would have prevented all of this ugliness.

Martin passed over a flash drive to the detective. A flash drive with the footage of Rachael and Sam participating in rather violent intercourse on their back deck – metres from the Crawleys' home. Footage they'd since confiscated Spencer's drone because of, not to mention spent a fortune in therapy that they could no longer afford. Penny had lost so much sleep over that child (and, if she were honest, a lot of Smirnoff).

The detective watched it, blank-faced, said he'd tag it for evidence, but given the breach of privacy – neither party filmed was aware of the camera – it would be inadmissible.

'That video goes for more than fifteen minutes. Must have a rather good drone. The cheap ones barely have the battery power to last as long as the Rio Rocket obviously can.'

Penelope scoffed at his inappropriateness. 'Surely, it's clear evidence that our Olympic hero is not the charming boy next door the media would have you believe – that he's actually a violent aggressor – and proves Rachael attacked him out of self-defence!'

Detective O'Sullivan remained blank-faced. 'I'm afraid all this footage proves is that a married couple had some sort of role-play in the privacy of their own home, and your son invaded that privacy with an illegal monitoring device. Have you ever had any concerns about possible partner abuse before this?'

The arguments next door had become muffled since they began shutting their windows at night as it got cooler. Not that she went out of her way to pry, but she liked it better when she could keep up.

'As I told you, I definitely heard angry shouting as I left to pick up Spencer around five, along with the usual carry-on that afternoon from Kat and Noah on the tramp, but that was after I got home and before my shower – half an hour prior to the ambulance.'

'You mean Kat as in Katerina Rainworth, their childminder?' He flicked through documents. 'My partner's notes indicate you saw Noah with a cat – as in a pet. We have no record of Katerina being at the premises. Did you actually see her or just hear her?'

'Well, I can't honestly say I saw her, I was in the shower just before all this happened, but I definitely *heard* them playing that lava game that makes Noah sound like a galah.'

'She babysits for them frequently, doesn't she?'

'She did, then they sacked her, apparently. That's why I was surprised to hear her there again.'

'Sacked her?'

'Not sure of the details … Rachael can be rather controlling though.'

'And you're sure it was the afternoon of?'

'Yes, as I went to get Spencer from his friend's, came home, showered for dinner, then heard the ambulance when I got out.' Penelope hoped it wasn't as serious as the media had them believe – a knife through the heart! How monstrous!

'Rachael always came across so measured. At the one body-corporate meeting she bothered attending, she was such a skilled facilitator – reframing people's views, moderating flare ups, helping parties at odds to reach agreement. She exuded patience and unflappability – she runs that successful business. It seems so out of character for her to lash out with a knife. The only way it could have been her is if he threatened her life. Tell him, Martin.'

'He was a piece of work, that swimmer.' Martin finally chimed in, adjusting his pants. 'Arrogant, bit of a womaniser, I hear. I have no doubt he was not a nice man, no respect for women. Wouldn't trust him as far as I could throw him.'

The detective raised one eyebrow. It was very disconcerting. Penny wondered if they taught them that at the academy.

'What I *did* want to ask you about, Mr Crawley, is one of the neighbours seeing you and Sam sharing a lemon squash at the tennis club a few times – overheard something about an investment you were both keen on,' Detective O'Sullivan said. 'Was he one of your clients?'

Martin blushed, his face beetroot from the tips of his ears to the folds of his chins. 'Well, yes, I've got quite a few clients in Apple Tree.'

'So, any outstanding debts between you and the Yorks? No disagreements over commissions or anything of the sort?'

Martin went all blotchy, the way he did when he watched sex scenes at the movies – part of the reason they'd stopped going. He was easily flushed. 'Well, I can assure you I've always been upfront about my fees and never had any complaints. Of course the details of all transactions, and my client's investments, are completely confidential – pretty private bunch, as you can imagine.'

'Nothing a warrant won't fix,' O'Sullivan threw in. 'And, just out of interest, Martin, were you home? I don't recall seeing you out on the footpath.'

A cough. 'I would have been at the business until at least seven.'

'Right. And someone can corroborate that?'

'Well, for a short while, but I'm usually the last there, locking up. The joys of being the boss. What are you insinuating, Detective?' The blotches were turning purple and Penny watched him loosen his collar.

'Just ruling out all the residents. Security footage of your office might do it, perhaps, if no one was there to verify your alibi?'

'Oh, this is getting ridiculous,' Penny piped in. 'Martin is an upstanding citizen and has a flawless reputation as an investment consultant – some rather famous clients which of course we can't disclose – but I can assure you he had nothing to do with this.'

Penelope had the sense to end the fight that had lasted between Martin and her all the way home from the station before opening the car door. She didn't want the neighbours hearing her private pain. She stomped up the drive, annoyed they couldn't park in the garage with Martin's Cobra parts scattered all over the floor (it had broken down, again).

Through the upstairs bay window, a dim glow from the computer screen in Spencer's attic room distorted his features. His expression was blank and joyless. Penelope wondered how well she really knew that young man of hers. The missing money from her emergency stash came to mind, and now that she knew what Spencer was capable of, she was convinced he'd stolen it. Was that how he'd bought that expensive drone? Penelope would never tell Martin, just like she'd never tell him she caught Spencer filming himself mocking his wheelchair-bound grandfather for his bladder incontinence, not to mention whatever he'd been doing to that poor rat – she was glad Ethan put it out of its misery. She couldn't bear to think what enacting that sort of cruelty unveiled about the kind of person her son was. The kind of person *she* must be to have made him. She wasn't a saint, sometimes she thought she wasn't even nice, but she wasn't cruel. How did she produce a cruel son? She'd always tried to raise her boys with such clear boundaries, firm discipline, consequences for their actions with absolute authority, none of this fuzzy parenting by consultation 'let's-be-friends' bizzo the young mums went for these days. It had been good enough for her, growing up.

Penelope peeked through the hedge buffering her from the Yorks'. Rachael was on the porch, Indy nestled in her arms, a soft sprinkler mist glossing the ferns flanking the path to her front door. Baby's breath and petunias overhung the terracotta pots lining the verandah, and Rachael herself, with her willowy limbs and sharp green eyes, fitted into the scene perfectly. She didn't *look* like a typical 'battered wife'. Or maybe there was no such thing? Penny glanced at Rachael's face through the thinning leaves. That pretty, little, elegant-nosed face. *Are you the culprit, Rachael? Did you discover Sam had lost all your hard-earned money? Were you the one who sank that knife into his heart?*

Penelope realised she'd had good intentions as she left the car, but they'd been eaten by the evening breeze. She couldn't work out what she actually wanted to be true. An intruder angle was so sinister, so random. At least if it was a marital dispute gone wrong, it would mean she wasn't a potential target. Maybe someone got the address wrong – she'd wandered up the wrong driveway after a few too many. Identical bloody doors didn't help.

It *was* odd having houses all the same, but she believed the homogenous designs gave a sense of belonging, like a uniform. She'd always wanted a proper school uniform as a girl. She'd had the op-shop version – the same colour as the real one and two sizes too big so it would last longer. Penny made sure her sons never felt like the financial burden she had. Nothing but the best brands, the latest gadgets. Was that her mistake? Martin was right. She was consumed with money. Penelope had always tried to position herself a peg above the common folk, but lately that ambition had felt lonely and pointless. And despite jostling for a place at the head of the body corporate, did she ever really feel like she fit in here? Her son was a bit of a shit, if she was honest, and even her husband who always 'had an eye for figures' had let her down.

She stopped procrastinating from her real concern. Now she was out of view of that detective, she finally allowed herself to accept she'd called her husband at the office the afternoon of the stabbing, but his secretary advised that Martin had left early. He wasn't at work like he'd said to that awful detective. He'd failed to disclose critical information and lied to the police about his whereabouts. What possible reason would he, such an honest, decent man, have to do such a thing?

She felt dizzy as her stomach lurched and she puked all over the agapanthus.

Chapter 31

Rachael

Rachael knew she had asked Gertie to believe the impossible; that despite having told her all the ways she'd planned to kill her husband, a random intruder had snuck into the secure premises and done the deed for her. The evidence was stacked against her. The cops knew it. She knew it. In low points over the years, Rachael had wished Sam gone, and now he was. It seemed like more than a nifty coincidence.

It was true, they had fought. Gertie had made her see Sam through a different lens and Rachael had finally found the courage to broach the issue. She'd wanted to confront the affair, but it had quickly got out of hand. In hindsight, perhaps keeping the lid on her anger for months hadn't been the wisest move.

Rachael remembered grabbing one of Ethan's drumsticks and aiming to thrust it firmly into Sam's eye. 'I'll make sure you never see another woman, you bastard!'

'Whoa, whoa,' he'd said, his tone firm as he'd grabbed her forearm, stopping the wooden stick from piercing his pupil.

She persevered, inching the weapon closer, and he gripped tighter till she winced.

'The subtle way you make me doubt my own mind – it's like lacing my coffee with arsenic every day for years. You're slowly killing me.'

'Okay, hon, c'mon. I get you're angry about the affair, I totally deserve that, but this bullshit – you can't really believe that. Is this about making sure I know where you are? I care about you so much I want to make sure you're safe. All I want is to make you happy, but you're so hard to please, it's like you're incapable of being happy.'

He was right. She was rarely happy. Hadn't been for years. Rachael started to believe it had to be about her, not him. It had to stem back to Liam, her inability to trust, like Sam had always said. It was then she gave up.

'I'm sorry,' Rachael said, crying uncontrollably.

Sam pulled her close. 'It's okay, hon. It's all said now, we can move on. I love you.' He held her until her tears had stopped, and her breathing had returned to normal. Sam raked his fingers over his face. 'Sure you're okay?'

Rachael took a deep breath, relieved that she'd finally screamed out the anger she'd felt for months. 'Yep.' She checked to make sure Noah was oblivious, out on the trampoline under a setting sun, and Ethan, with his noise-cancelling headphones wouldn't have known if the house had caught fire.

'Look, I've got to clear my head, get some air.' He kissed her forehead and left. 'I'll get some takeaway and we'll just have an early night.'

She just wanted a second to breathe, find some equilibrium, but the moment he closed the front door, there it was again, Indy's witching-hour cry. After Gertie had mentioned something about white noise reminding newborns of the womb, Rachael had brought in a box of old tools from the shed, to see if she could create the same effect with an analogue radio. She found the old paint-splattered thing, tuned it off station and held Indy close in her sling. Indy cried louder.

She checked on Ethan again, mostly to make sure he hadn't heard their raging argument. He seemed oblivious, his only concern being his screen time running out. 'Mum – why'd you only give me an hour?' He muted his microphone. 'My friends are on! They'll think I'm a pleb if I say Mummy won't let me play.'

She tried to ignore his patronising tone. 'I'll add another hour, then. I'm just worried you're becoming antisocial.'

He grimaced as if her very existence pained him. 'You really don't get it, Mum. This is *how* we socialise and you're wrecking it!' Already his eyes had darkened, sucked down a porthole into the depths of the cyberworld like digital cocaine. Rachael tried to remember where she'd left her phone so she could extend his screen allowance one more bleeding hour.

Starting a hot shower, she tried not to think of Indy crying alone – maybe Sam was right and the women of the family were hard to please and never happy. She stripped and stepped into the cube of fog. For what seemed like forever, she let the heat numb the tension in her shoulders, the steam clear her mind, and the rush of water drown out her baby's gut-wrenching pleas.

But, finally, the guilt thrummed inside. It had been too long. Her mum was forever telling her how important self-care was – to 'fit her mask first before helping others'. She told herself Indy was safe, she was entitled to have a shower, but it was no use. Rachael had to check on her.

As soon as she shut off the tap, Indy's monotonous cry pierced through the quiet. Hastily, Rachael dried off before realising she was sobbing. She dressed in a clean cotton dress, drips from her hair dampening the straps, and inhaled a deep breath.

'I can do this,' she told herself, padding down the hall towards the nursery, her daughter's cries louder with each step.

Her eye caught a flash of red against pale bamboo boards. Two fat dots reminded her of when Ethan was little and had broken a bottle of Grange.

'What on earth?' Rachael whispered to herself in a shaky voice. Had Noah had another bloody nose? 'Noah, hon? You okay?' She could smell the lemongrass even before she saw the bag of takeaway Thai abandoned on the kitchen table.

Then she saw him.

Sam. Her Sam lying along the hallway floor. His checked blue shirt stained by a small circle of rich red.

'Oh, God.' Rachael inhaled sharply, slid on her knees over to him. She slipped in a small puddle of blood and panicked, speckled fingerprints like preschool art mixed with confused footprints.

'How did …?' she asked, hands splayed out, hovering above him, unsure. The blood. Thick. Warm. But her focus stayed with her husband. 'Oh, Sam, it's okay, don't try to speak. I'm here.'

'I can't breathe …' Sam gurgled. His face was deathly pale.

In the periphery she noticed Ethan, racing towards her from the hall linen cupboard carrying a towel. That's when the horror registered. Blood all over his hands.

Rachael stumbled after him. 'Ethan? Are you hurt too? What's going on?'

Ethan shook his head as if the answer was too unreal to utter. 'I was on my computer and when I came out – he was just like this.' He started to cry, his hands trembling. 'I went to get something to stop the bleeding.'

He held out a towel, which Rachael took and pressed on the spreading stain of blood on Sam's shirt.

'Is he okay? What do I do? Tell me what to do.' Ethan sobbed, completely overwhelmed.

Adrenalin kicked in. An action plan formulated. Ethan waited motionless against the wall in a state falling between shocked and dazed. Rachael demonstrated how to hold pressure on the wound, then found her phone and called an ambulance. 'An intruder – my husband's been stabbed in the chest. Please come quickly!'

The officer talked her through the process, asked her to stay on the line.

'Fifteen minutes?' He could bleed out by then. She thought of Gertie, called her to come quickly.

Rachael exhaled, took a moment and returned her focus to Ethan.

'Did you see who did this? Was it a stranger or someone we know?' Then asked again, her frustration growing. 'Ethan? C'mon, it's important, the police – they're going to ask questions ...'

Ethan shook his head, tears flowing, snot dripping, still trying his best to keep it together. 'Don't blame me.' He paused, his glare accusatory. 'Where were you? Why didn't you hear me screaming! It's not like I can't hear you two arguing, but somehow you can't hear me calling for you?'

A rush of regret floored her, of prioritising her sanity, blocking out the world in the shower like a selfish cow while chaos reigned.

Ethan's fear turned to anger, the red beast inside lashing out. 'I hate you for letting him do this to you! This is your fault, Mum! Pay attention to what's going on in your own house!'

You're right, Ethe. This is on me.

Chapter 32

Gertie

The mystery of where Ed scurried off to with a half-empty bag was solved when his sheepish face appeared on Gertie's security panel as he knocked on his own front door. 'Hello? G?'

Seeing Rachael in shock the other night had made Gertie realise how distraught she'd have felt if it had been Ed lying in his own blood. The fragility of life was ever present in nursing, but seeing it play out in her private life gave her clarity. Gertie still loved the silly man, even with this ridiculous news about Fred. Could she really be angry about something that happened two decades ago? She'd never actually considered how Ed must have felt being denied any chance to parent his own child. Gertie had offered no support when he'd obviously needed it, back when he was plotting his escape. While his method of coping wasn't ideal, she had no doubt that his struggle was real. Perhaps he'd been right about her being more mother than wife, having him at the end of a long list of priorities.

'What's with the fuss at the gate?' he asked into the security speaker. 'Who died?' Ed laughed.

Gertie pressed to talk. 'I called you. Everyone called you.' She watched him yank his phone from his cabin bag while jostling to hold a box of something.

'Oh, bugger, it's out of juice. I checked it constantly at the pub, hoping you'd call, but stopped around the sixth beer.' Surprise brightened his face when she opened the door. He was holding a box of doughnuts wrapped like a bouquet. Sugar mingled with Nutella filling and remorse. 'I was a bloody idiot. Forgive me.'

At last, they were his own words.

He held up a sheet from a hotel notepad with more of his man-scrawl. 'I've listed …'

'No more monologues, Ed.'

That was three days ago.

Slowly, snippets of the topics they were meant to broach butted into their stilted conversations. Gertie continued to ignore his passive-aggressive comments about how sore his back was from sleeping on the couch. She didn't want him in her bed. Yet. But that didn't mean she wanted him to leave.

She woke to the repeated chord progression in Green Day's 'Good Riddance'. In a sleepy, mildly hungover daze, she kept listening, remembering a certain mosh pit at a certain concert in another life, her skinny legs wrapped around Ed's gyrating shoulders, her wearing nothing but a red string bikini and a grin. It had been the time of her life. Then reality hit. It was her ringtone, her grown-up life. She fumbled to answer.

'G?' It was her sister.

'Why are you ringing me? Aren't you in my house?'

'I'm at the fucking Apple Tree Creek Developers suites, rushed here from your place after spitting my coffee down my shirt. I take it you haven't looked at your security panel today?' Lou's voice was short, sharp and formal. 'There're pictures on the estate community page.'

Gertie yawned. 'We have a community page?'

'Yeah – the purple house icon on the security panel? Posted last night by someone whose alias is EyeInTheSky. Anonymous as whoever posted it had a VPN.'

'What are the bloody pictures of? And speak English, please,' Gertie said.

Gertie's phone pinged.

The images were grainy, the light in the school aquatic centre patchy in places. But it was clear what was going on. In bathers, they were technically clothed, her wet hair dripping, her toned arms wrapped around his broad shoulders as he pressed her against the rollerdoor behind the counter of the closed pool canteen. What was taking place was clear as the stream in the meadow. Sam York was snogging her little girl.

'It's okay,' Lou said. 'I've ordered management to pull them, which they're more than happy to do straight away – claiming someone hacked into their system. I checked no one downloaded them – old farts probably don't know how on that antiquated system they installed years ago when they built this weird-ville, but there're twenty-five views, so someone saw them and may have manually taken pics.'

'Who? Media? Police?'

'Thankfully, it's only accessible to people on your server – your neighbours. It didn't help that it was the wallpaper on this morning's welcome message – little slimeball.'

'Thankfully?' *Rachael's my neighbour.* Gertie had already assumed the fledgling friendship they'd started had rotted to the core in a big festering heap since that awkward bear-all by the stream, which stole another piece of her already broken heart. 'Is Rachael completely murderous? Sorry, wrong choice of words.' *Though if she didn't want to kill him before, I'm sure she does now.*

Lou continued. 'I haven't shown her yet. The other problem is who took them and what else is in their arsenal? Know any perverts who could access Apple Tree's server? Rachael's son – the gamer – what's his name?'

'Ethan – he's got the skills, but what would be his motive?' Gertie replayed her conversation with Kat. 'Pretty sure Kat said Ethan knew, not sure how.'

'If he liked Kat and found out she had a thing with his dad instead … That would totally fucking motivate me.'

'He's not his father. He'd be mortified if everyone saw that.' She thought about Kat's other confession – that she and Ethan had used the old bird cage to save Spencer's rat from YouTube humiliation. That reminded Gertie of all she knew about Spencer and his hobbies. She groaned. 'Creepy Bloody Crawley.'

Ed paced the room, raking his hands through what little hair he had left. He found his commanding voice and directed it towards Gertie's phone, which was on speaker on the bed.

'Louise, tell me you've ordered these to be pulled down and someone charged over it.'

'We have no cause.' Her voice was apologetic. 'You signed for her image to be used on estate marketing when you won the house.'

'But they didn't put it on there, surely? Didn't someone hack it?'

'The content is not indecent.'

'It is bloody indecent!' Ed shouted. 'She's a student! He's a teacher! Isn't that against the law?' His face twisted with outrage.

'She's over the age of consent, but you're right, it's an offence for people like teachers, priests, doctors, to sexually engage with someone under their care.' Lou asked, 'Gertie, you told me on the phone she had a crush or something? Was that the same day he was stabbed? I didn't realise they acted on it. How did I not link that before?'

Even with forewarning, Gertie was grappling with the fact that people in her village were discussing intimate things about her little girl. It felt like only yesterday that same little girl was chasing lizards through the garden beds and reading *Babysitter's Club* books on the sun loungers in this place.

Ed's face was flushed red, his eyes wired, fearful, disappointed, the whole gamut of emotions. He huffed. 'If that bastard isn't cold by the time I get to him, I'm going to make sure he is.'

She forgot her sister was still talking to them on speaker, asking about the Kat and Sam connection as if it was relevant to the attack.

Gertie looked at it objectively. 'Well, he was also blackmailing us, threatening to continue giving her bad marks if we told anyone.'

'Are you joking?' Lou asked. 'Ed, did Gert tell you all this the night you came home?'

'Gertie did mention it when I got back, yes. Eventually.'

They looked at each other, confused.

'Please tell me you two didn't confront Sam about it, because you know that would make you suspects.'

Gertie's face pinched. 'I may have ...'

'Please tell me you didn't do it in that freakshow estate with a camera on every corner?'

'It was the playground, a few hours before everything happened ...' Gertie hadn't even considered how that made things look. 'Are you asking me if we did this? Because I certainly didn't.' *Though I did kind of wish it on the scumbag.*

There was silence. Gertie looked at Ed.

Ed looked incredulous. 'You two seriously think I stabbed the stupid prick?'

The thought of Ed, who was so angry when she'd told him about the swimmer taking advantage of Kat, doing this in some fumbled testosterone-fuelled marking of territory had crossed her mind, but her instincts had shut the thought down as laughable.

'He's right, Lulu. Ed doesn't even complain at a cafe when they bring him the wrong order, that's how averse he is to confrontation.' *It took him years to tell me he wanted out.*

Ed still looked offended, as if being capable of physical assault was a preferred trait in a man than being content to let things slide.

Lou huffed. 'Leave it fucking with me.'

Her sister's brilliance was as sharp as her mouth and Gertie knew they were in safe hands.

By the time Gertie and Ed rehearsed how to approach things, Kat had seen the image for herself and was in full meltdown. Gertie let the boys go nuts with screen time, enabling her to focus on Kat, who was bunkering down in the bathroom.

'My life is ruined! I can never leave the house!' Kat yelled through the door in hysterics. Gertie worried about what Kat had access to, given her fragile mental state (a few strips of Panadol? Her razor?). She wasn't a little kid anymore, but she hadn't locked herself in the bathroom since Year 2 when Nicoletta Roundtree invited the entire class except Kat to her My Little Pony party.

Gertie's heart was pained by her pride and joy being at the centre of all this. Her eyes couldn't stop tearing, her mind couldn't stop wishing she could weather the storm for her daughter. She saw Kat's shadow break the line of light beneath the bathroom door. She slid down her side of it, needing to be as close as she could. She pressed her palm on the smooth oak finish, hoping her fierce love would flash through the door between them and penetrate the parts that needed it most.

'We're here for you, Kitty-Kat. What can we do for you? I'll do one of those TikTok dances you love if you come out?'

More sobs. Chest heaving, guttural wails. 'You don't get it. I really thought I liked him, Mum, so how can I trust my own feelings if they were so misguided? My emotional intelligence must be like, imbecile level. And now everyone knows.'

'Sweet pea, you were dealing with a master manipulator. Look at Rachael. Despite awful things happening to her as a child, she started an empire from nothing to help people celebrate their differences, and now she can afford things like truffle oil and organic sourdough. Just like you, she's brilliant and yet still got sucked into his orbit.'

'You don't get it. He was my chance. Everyone's got a boyfriend, got someone to love them – I'm the only virgin in my class.'

Thank the Lord.

'Maybe I should have just got it over with! There's so much pressure, like the world revolves around sex. Is it really worth all the fuss?'

'Um ...'

'And why can't I meet someone who likes me for me?'

Ed hovered behind Gertie like a shadow, still pacing, still fuming. Gertie couldn't help but think of a red-faced cartoon character with steam clouds puffing from each ear.

'Oh, my darling girl. Clever and kind and full of spirit. What's not to love? You've been loved since before you were born.'

'Not like that, Mum,' she scoffed. 'He made me feel like the only woman in the world for him. A love so ardent … when he kissed me it was like nothing else mattered.'

Gertie threw up a little in her mouth. Lou should never have bought Kat that Jane Austen box set.

'Hon, have you forgotten he threatened your entire future because you wouldn't let him control you? That he was put in charge of caring for you and he took advantage of that trust? Does that sound like love?' Kat had no concept of just how far that man was out of line. Gertie hadn't pushed her for details about exactly what happened between her and her swim coach on the bench of the canteen at the aquatic centre, and she had to trust that things had stayed as chaste as those period novels.

A scrum of angry villagers gathered on the eastern block. Gertie hadn't seen this many neighbours together since snooping around Gozer's place when Dave Grohl visited his fellow rock legend in Iris Street. It wasn't until Gertie scurried down the oleander-flanked pathway to overhear snippets of their complaints that she realised they were gossiping about her daughter. Words like *teacher's pet* and *deflowered* hissed in her ears. Mr Harris was the ringleader, generalising that the photo on the intercom that morning was further evidence of the moral decay of modern society. Beatrice and Eunice were less dramatic – being broadminded lesbians who just wanted the man castrated. Penny and Martin were there, too, voicing their disdain for Sam York.

'We've already taken steps to have him suspended from staff at school,' Penny told the angry mob.

Martin took things further, suggesting the 'paedophile should be stripped of his medals, a disgrace to the country.'

'That's enough, people. You can all go on home – nothing to be gained from turning on each other,' Gertie said. 'And can I just remind you folk that there's an innocent young girl living here that had no say in any of this.'

'Innocent!' one of the older men scoffed. 'She didn't look so innocent in those pictures!'

'Can I ask all of you to please respect her privacy and keep the content of those images to yourselves. It really is a matter for the family to manage and has nothing to do with any of you.'

Mr Harris fired up. 'It has everything to do with us! We have a right to know the calibre of the men in our community! He's already lured an axe murderer into the estate – what next?'

Ed appeared. Bare-chested and wearing thongs, he thrust himself into the crowd like a warrior in a bucket hat and started defending Kat's honour, pleading with the residents to think of the little girl they'd watched grow up, to imagine it was their own daughter and to respect her privacy, which Gertie loved. He then mentioned something involving a baseball bat, threatening anyone who even thought of posting it online, which Gertie was less impressed by, and she pulled him towards home. But as they retreated, the residents fired up again.

A man Gertie had never seen before piped up. 'The media already know he lives here, so there go our property prices, not to mention the sex pest being a danger to other children!'

Gertie rolled her eyes. 'Well, he's currently unconscious, and I very much doubt he will be coming home anytime soon.'

Silence.

The crowd parted, and there she was – Rachael standing still, alone at the back of the scrum, on the outer rim of the circle of neighbours. She looked small and defenceless, and Gertie felt partly responsible. Gertie swallowed hard. Ever since she'd told Rachael about meeting her 'stalker', she hadn't replied to any of Gertie's olive branches – texts, emails, even the old-fashioned skulk around her driveway hadn't elicited a response.

Rachael was silent, perplexed, and looked awfully vulnerable above the fray. Gertie wanted to run to her, hug her tiny shoulders till she found her smile.

'Rach?' Gertie stepped towards her and the crowd hushed once more, waiting as if an oracle was about to speak.

But before she could break her silence, necks craned towards the sky, towards the source of an almost imperceptible hum. Over near the hedge stood Spencer Crawley, tongue lodged in the corner of his mouth as he directed his wicked camera drone over the disgruntled crowd.

Penny and Martin appeared horrified as they noticed their son.

'Spence, that's enough of that for the moment, honeybee …' Penny quickened her pace as she approached her son, who either hadn't heard her or didn't care to comply. 'Spencer! That was in the confiscated cupboard!' Her embarrassment made it clear who the source of the 'Rio Rocket snogs student' image was.

Without a word, Rachael charged over to Creepy Crawley, still flying his contraption high above their heads. 'Give it to me, you brat,' she ordered, grabbing the controller and fiddling with the buttons until the drone wobbled and bent mid-flight and crashed straight into a cement pylon securing the fence, the casing splitting open, leaving electrical components twisted and exposed.

'I was aiming for the creek, but that will do nicely.' Rachael pegged the controller in the compactus full of ground branches left by the janitor and pulled the handle to start the grinder. A satisfying crunch was heard.

'You've wrecked it!' The redheaded beachball cried like a toddler as he realised his electronic partner-in-crime was now in pieces. He turned to Rachael. 'Have you any idea how much that was worth, you bitch!?' Spencer Crawley spat.

'How dare you!' Rachael was seething. 'Don't even think about invading people's privacy ever again or I'll report you to the police.' She shook her head in disgust. 'You have no idea what pain you've caused!'

Spencer's lips pursed as he considered something clever to say, and finally came out with, 'You can't talk, your husband stole all our money – we have to move thanks to that arsehole. He deserved what he got.'

Rachael looked more confused than hurt as Penny and Martin raced after their son to pull him into line before their reputation took another fatal blow.

Fred turned into the street from the games court, bouncing his basketball up the road. He paused and frowned at the mob on the footpath. 'What'd I miss this time?'

The day raced by in a cloud of misery. Gertie, Ed and Kat sat for hours, working through the details of how to approach this, calling Lou for updates on exactly how far the images had been leaked – had anyone from the school found out? Ed worked details out methodically, delegating tasks and assessing risks like a work project, calming his daughter's panic when it expanded in her chest and exploded out of her mouth in a torrent of fears. As night fell, things felt less chaotic than Gertie thought possible after those images had turned their world upside down. Somehow, they had made her daughter's trouble all the more real.

Hesitantly, Gertie edged closer to the truth about how misguided the relationship became between her daughter and Sam York.

'A first-base affair physically, by the sounds,' she summarised for Ed later that afternoon.

'We can cross off STD test, then?' he said, only half joking. 'What a bloody relief.'

'In a way.' Gertie felt no such relief, slumped in a heap on the couch.

'You're still worried, aren't you?' Ed asked, passing her a cup of English Breakfast just the way she liked it.

Gertie had treated victims of far more violent assaults, but often found the deepest scars stemmed from the mind games the girls became unknowing participants in. 'I fear the real damage was the undermining of her ability to trust her instincts. It's like' – she fought back tears – 'he's clawed at her belief in herself and ripped it to shreds – the very antithesis of what we entrust teachers to do. I mean, I knew something was off with her, but why did it take me till now to see her light was slowly being stolen by that man?'

Ed sat beside her, but his mind was elsewhere. 'I blame myself. Where was I?'

Gertie sipped her tea – the best cup she'd had since he'd moved out. 'You're here now.' She reached over and brushed his fingers with her own, the first touch of her husband's skin in months.

After being banned from social media in an effort to shelter her from any further fallout, Kat had started gracing them with her presence. She wandered into the lounge and perched on the arm of the one couch Gertie insisted Ed cart to the 'good' house six years before, back when Kat's dilemmas revolved around saving for unicorn slippers rather than being 'stuck' with her virginity. The couch sported scribbles of a stick-figure family surrounded by a lollipop-shaped palace with heart-shaped flowers. Gertie prayed her daughter's extraordinary ambitions were untarnished by all this.

'I figure you girls aren't up for stepping out, so I've ordered Uber Eats – schnitties with chips times five, all on the corporate account.' Gertie kissed Ed's scratchy cheek, knowing in her heart of hearts that this crisis would work out better with him here, and couldn't help but notice the blueprint he devised to navigate this drama pivoted on him staying home for longer than a few days.

Gertie watched in wonder as her confused seventeen-year-old daughter, lost to her just a week ago, nestled in between Ed and her in the bed, and finally slept.

But sleep evaded Gertie. She stroked the silky strands of French-braided hair, wondering how she'd failed to protect her precious girl. She tried to put a positive spin on the chaos – that this was something Kat had to learn for herself, that it would make her more wary with men. *The only way to learn is to live.*

But your digital imprint was forever. How easy would it have been for Spencer to copy that file to social media? Gertie was worried that every employer in Kat's future would google Katerina Rainworth and be confronted with that image. Not to mention how this awful abuse of power would impact her sense of self, her trust of men. Was it a parent's role to protect children from the evils of the world, or raise children resilient to them? Gertie was no longer sure you could do either.

Ed looked over to her. 'I'm supposed to go back to that cauldron of loneliness in two days, Gert.'

'Oh, God, Ed. Aren't you supposed to be on a course?'

'There was no course, Gert. I just needed to be home.'

Gertie was so emotionally spent she didn't have time to be angry at him anymore. She didn't have time to think it through, she just had to go with her gut. And she found she trusted it. It had always served her well. The vast majority of men were not like Sam York, and she still believed Ed was the most decent man she knew.

'You don't know how sorry I am, Gert.'

'Oh, enough already. You had me at "hello".'

Ed looked over, pulled her into their bathroom and locked the door. Her slightly balding, dependable, threaten-neighbours-with-a-baseball-bat-for-his-daughter Ed. The Ed that held her hair when she puked with a fever, the Ed that pulled the bins out for twenty years and separated crusts from pizza boxes for recycling. He had explained his way out of that stupid overreaction with his old housekeeper on the Zoom call. He'd come clean with the reason he sent a twenty-two-year-old dusty redhead to nanny for them in his absence. Could she really blame Ed for a three-minute lapse of judgement when he was younger than Kat? Their daughter had demonstrated very clearly that kids got pulled into misguided stunts all the time. It was part of their job description. And that was why they needed parents to pick up the pieces when their instincts failed and love them, anyway.

'Come here, you silly, silly man.' She held his strong arms, smelled his musky scent, and felt a heavy load fall from her shoulders.

'And I do remember that caravan, with the porthole ...'

His look was so familiar, yet strangely different enough to be a little more interesting, and a pang of longing ripped through her. With Kat snoring in their bed, Ed fired up the en suite exhaust fan to mask any noise. It was the best they could hope for in a full house, and for a moment they were the couple they used to be, spontaneous and in sync.

Gertie Rainworth forgot about the months of resentment, and her doubts about his love for her. All she thought about was Ed, and that caravan.

It had been a while since they'd done that anywhere but on a bed. It was surprising in a good way. But what was more surprising was the talk that followed as they were in the bathroom. Talk about their daughter and the muddle she was in. Talk about Singapore. About his running course around the zoo that he did each morning (Gertie had felt a few abs she was sure weren't there the last time that sort of thing happened). About teaching English to his old housekeeper because it was never too late to learn. About how Ed yacked all over the Uber as he raced to the airport with the very thought of what he was leaving behind – puked his way to a seventy-five-dollar clean fee. About how he'd texted each child every night, passing messages to Harry via Abe. How he'd never been so lonely. Ed had always been open but economical with words – Gertie often joked that he ran out by lunchtime. Especially words about things like *feelings*.

'You're different, and not just in the abdominals,' Gertie said to him, lying on the bathmat, staring up at the curved ceiling beams, transfixed by the spin of the fan blades. 'I'm not sure I am, Ed. And isn't that what you wanted me to do? Change?'

But then she thought of the new her, a working parent, a Pilates attempter, braving new friendships, taking on vile men who threatened her daughter. She'd recognised her fear of the unknown and plodded on regardless. She'd taken on battles outside her comfort zone and backed herself to manage them – and mostly she had. Perhaps she *was* a different woman? A more independent one. A woman who didn't rely on anyone else for her happiness, her security, her sense of self. She realised all that was too much for any one person to give – no wonder Ed felt he was struggling to keep her happy.

'That's the thing, Gert ...' His eyes were full of regret. 'I was the one who needed to change. You are perfect exactly as you are. You complete me.'

Chapter 33

Penny

She watched Martin chew his lamb chop, watched the way his top jaw slightly misaligned with the bottom. He held his cutlery in the wrong hands, too, when they weren't in public, said it was more comfortable that way. She'd forgotten how that used to irk her. It irked her now. Everything about him did.

Spencer sat at the dinner table, too – Penny had demanded he join them tonight. She thought it might be their last supper. Who knew when the police would barge down the door like they did in the movies, those fit, assassin-looking SAS crowd with their black, bulletproof vests and tasers? She was kind of looking forward to the wait being over. For the relief.

She'd cooked her husband's favourite meal, Frenched lamb with rosemary butter, corn and truffled broccolini. She'd cleaned the benchtops in case tonight was the night they closed in – nothing worse than being arrested with dishes filling the butler's pantry, what would the neighbours think? She'd even got her botox done, just in case. Might as well spend it before the dregs of their estate were garnished.

Even if Detective O'Sullivan hadn't put two and two together about Martin Crawley's motive to harm Sam York, how he ruined them, financially and emotionally with that dodgy advice, the tax office would come, start selling off their things. The yacht. The beach house. The Tesla. Those diamonds from that Caribbean cruise in her jewellery bag shoved in her knickers drawer. Penny hoped they were fake.

She watched Spencer eat with his mouth open, focused intently on some game on his phone. He acted like any attempt at conversation was a chore, distracting him from his true life's purpose playing out on that tiny screen. It would have been better if she'd let him eat in his room. But this meal, it might be the last time, so together they ate.

Sadness. That's all she saw in Martin's eyes as he picked at his food. No guilt or repressed rage. He hadn't admitted anything to her. He was a bit of a bore, but always a gentleman – he wouldn't incriminate her, involve her in his dark-web-worthy behaviour. That way she'd have plausible deniability – she'd looked it up on the internet (at the library, of course, so they wouldn't trace it). But why else had he lied to the police? Said he was at work the time Sam York was attacked? They all knew he wasn't at work – so, where was he? Was it shameful that she thought it more likely he had stabbed someone, than was off having an affair?

If he'd asked her, she would have helped.

But he hadn't.

Perhaps, that was the hardest part to deal with. Not the money, not him lashing out with violence, but that he had acted alone, when everything they'd done up until the night of the ambulance, they'd done as a team.

She'd end up alone, and poor, again.

Chapter 34

Gertie

Rachael had refused all forms of contact, offers to help – until this afternoon. One word: meadow.

Gertie found the secret path once again and squeezed through the hole in the fence. She admired the casual grace of the quiet meadow, brilliant with all the hues Mother Nature could muster but with only a peripheral awareness of its beauty. It reminded her of Kat – elegant and bright yet unaware of her gifts.

Gertie didn't want an apology, she just wanted Rachael to realise her only wish was to keep her safe, to let her know she had her back. To help her reframe events without the distorted commentary Sam voiced over her life.

Rachael stood taller than she had the first time they'd met that horrible day when she refused to believe the truth about Sam. The past few days would have been a grief-stricken hell, but Rachael's shoulders were straight, her eyes clear, her skin flushed with colour. Perhaps the time away from Sam had been the detox her mind needed. She hoped it was the seed of confidence, that would grow and bloom with time. That one day Rachael would shout at the world, '*I am so much more than he told me I was.*' She offered no greeting as Gertie approached her on the creek bank. Standing in a tiny field speckled with colour, Rachael could have been part of a model shoot, and Gertie felt frumpy in her shorts and T-shirt.

'Hello, Rachael.' Gertie wanted to play it cool, be mature about this awkward predicament, but instead she gushed an incoherent apology for not seeing what was happening with Kat, how her role in this made the shitstorm worse than it already was. 'I'm so sorry, Rach. I had no idea anything was festering with those two until the day he was attacked.'

'Please, Gert – it's not your fault, or hers. If anything, it was what I needed to see the truth. I mean, I knew he was a womaniser, but she's just so young ...'

Rachael glanced back at the mirrored surface of the stream and started to tell her story. 'The first time I knew things were not quite as they seemed was about a year in. He locked me out of our house, too. It was mortifying. I had no idea he'd done that sort of stunt to anyone before me. He was angry when I'd suggested moving closer to my mum, thought making me sleep on the landing would change my mind. He only let me in the next morning when Ethan needed breakfast and I was the only one who knew how he liked it. Then he started doing random crazy things like dangling Ethe over the balcony and driving erratically in the car just to remind us who was in charge. Of course, it didn't start out like this – there were good times, too, perfect times to keep me in love with him, hours of great sex, incredibly kind gestures and romantic weekends, but between them were ... problems. They grew like mould. The way he monitored me, vetoed any friends I made that spoke a bad word about him. There was always an undercurrent of abuse, I was just too close to see it until you pointed out what he'd done to others ...'

Gertie crept forward and sat on the boulder in the shade, her hands clasped on her lap in front of her.

A brightness lit up Rachael's face. 'I'm not defending him, and what he did with Kat was absolutely wrong, but he's not a wife basher, Gert. I'd never have stayed with him so long, never put the boys at risk. I never wanted to put myself in the same category as those women who are hit, who suffer so much more. He never actually hurt us.'

Gertie frowned. She still didn't get it, but perhaps they'd move forward a small step. 'Not with his fists.'

A towel wrapped around his waist, Ed treaded sloshy footprints from the foggy bathroom through the house as Kat was hogging their en suite again. Fred was loafing on the lounge watching *Stranger Things*. Gertie was getting the firm impression he believed his services were no longer needed now that Ed was in town, and figured that attitude would only deepen when Ed broached the issue about his parentage. Gertie couldn't stop herself staring at the kid, noticing the similarities and points of difference between Fred and her husband, Fred and her sons.

Fred looked up from the TV and skidded into the hall just as Ed paraded through, half naked, and they almost barrelled each other over. 'Dude, you've got the spare, too?' Fred asked Ed, gesturing to something on Ed's chest.

Gertie approached her husband and her eyes grew wide. A tiny pimple-like rise sat on Ed's hairy chest – had that always been there?

Fred lifted his T-shirt, pointing to his own third nipple-like dot. 'We could be twins, bro!'

Ed's face became determined. He stepped over to his son, sat down and said, 'About that ...'

Gertie's trips between her house and the Yorks' felt like walks of shame.

'First you get that murderer a lawyer, and now you're running her errands!' Mr Harris had scoffed at her one morning when she'd been preparing to deliver Rachael groceries, coffee and bagels. She kind of wished they could regress to the good old days of his complaints focusing on Harry's meltdowns interrupting his Sunday pot of Earl Grey.

'Firstly,' Gertie pointed out, 'no one has died so there is no homicide to speak of, and secondly, if you do believe this woman capable of killing a man, you'd better watch yourself!' Gertie waved a French stick in his direction, to which Mr Harris, paper rolled in hand, had backtracked quicker than she'd ever seen him shuffle.

Just as Gertie had grabbed from her boot the last of the groceries Rachael had asked her to pick up (the public interest in the case was so high she couldn't even make it to the supermarket without being photographed), Detective O'Sullivan and his partner were seen stepping down the sleek driveway of Penelope Crawley's house. Gertie could barely contain her curiosity for the twenty seconds it took to scurry back in to Rachael's and ask, 'WTF are the cops doing next door?'

'Oh, God, it's happening already?' Rachael's eyes had black circles from tiredness, but she had a spark about her Gertie hadn't seen in a while as she peered through the plantation shutters at the street. She was perched on her couch and a longer, jigglier Indy was nursing off Rachael's left breast, tapping her feet and looking around as she drank.

'What's going on?' Gertie asked.

'I need to catch you up. But first, tell me, how well do you know Martin Crawley?'

'I know enough to never get stuck sitting next to him at the estate BBQs 'cause you'll consider peeing your pants just to escape his breathtakingly boring investment stories.'

'Don't joke, I peed my pants jumping on the tramp with Noah yesterday. When does that stop?'

Gertie shrugged. 'Maybe never. Depends. Are you good with your Kegels?'

'I'm better with bagels.' Rachael smiled. She hadn't smiled in weeks and Gertie felt warm (and hoped it wasn't pee). 'But back to Martin, I meant in terms of his character – is he shady at all, or has, like, an aggressive streak?'

'Penny's husband? Have you met him?' Gertie laughed but then saw she was serious. 'The only aggressive thing about Martin Crawley is his investment plans – and perhaps his salami breath. He's a pussy cat – and an unfit one at that. Always a bit shiny from sweat.' Gertie shook her head with mild disgust. 'But he's actually rather good with Penny – she likes a drink, you see, and he's very sweet with her.'

'Sweet?' Rachael furrowed her brow.

Gertie felt she'd given the wrong answer.

'You don't think there's another person living with them? They just have Spencer, don't they?'

'And the tarty dog. Why?'

'Her early blogs refer to more than one child. I thought maybe they'd lost a baby – but you'd think there'd be a blog about that, if that was the case – probably got it wrong.'

Gertie was confused. 'I've known her for years. Pretty sure that would have come up.'

Rachael nodded then swapped boobs, Indy cooing and moving her hand in what Gertie was sure was a wave. She waved back.

'Anyway, your mud-mouth sister is a miracle worker – the cops have been trying to trace withdrawals from our account in case it was relevant to the attack but had no luck until now. Remember when Creepy Crawley mouthed off about Sam being the cause of them having to sell up? Turns out Sam invested with Martin Crawley's firm just before all this happened – some sort of promising pharmacological startup that went belly up after they injected all their saving in it.'

'Which means what? Aren't they loaded anyway? How much did they lose?'

'Well, we don't know for sure, but way more than the half a mill Sam sank, by the sounds.' Rachael's eyes widened as she bobbed her head a little with the severity of the situation. Even Indy stopped her feed in interest, gazing up at her mum.

'Jesus.' The only time Gertie had seen numbers that big on a bank statement was the mortgage on their old house.

'The bastard organised it all behind my back, totally stripped us bare. Everything we'd been saving to put in a trust for the kids – gone.'

Rachael was rather calm about hundreds of thousands of dollars. Gertie had expressed bitter hatred after realising one of her kids stole her emergency chocolate hidden inside the Weet-Bix packet.

'Yet somehow you don't seem as troubled by that fact as I would've thought?'

'Well, my business revenue is safe – something inside me always kept him separate from that. And in terms of the police investigation, it's a good thing.'

'Wait – doesn't discovering your cheating husband also cleaned out your bank account give you more motive?' Gertie winced, disbelieving they were chatting so casually about Rachael's potential arrest.

'Yes, there is that, but get this – Martin Crawley brokered the deal, invested a ton he was so keen on it, and lost the lot. Apparently the tip-off was Sam's idea, which also gives *Martin* a pretty strong motive to have attacked him. They're even pointing the finger at him for leaking that footage of Kat to show the world the real Sam York, and involve her in the scandal.'

'You mean frame Kat as a suspect? That's crazy. And they believe Martin did the hacking, not Spencer? I don't know, I just can't see Cueball Crawley hurting Sam. He can't even stand up to his wife, let alone a muscle-bound athlete.'

Rachael handed Indy to Gertie and continued to unpack her eggplant, tamarillos, kale and other produce Gertie had never before bought in her life with an almost joyous energy.

'You wouldn't think so, but it gets worse. Crawley lied about where he was the night Sam was stabbed. CCTV footage of his office had him leaving at about three in the afternoon, yet he told the cops he was there till seven. We're unsure if he was in the estate, though – Penelope's car entered the gates before the incident, but it was hard to see on the footage how many occupants were inside. Lou said she thought the investigators would ask the Crawleys to provide DNA and fingerprints today.' Rachael's tone went all deep and serious. 'To eliminate them from their enquiries, of course.'

'Bloody hell, Rach.'

'The sniffer dogs traced an unknown scent from our laundry door through the yard, through to the janitors' shed near where we've been sneaking out – little of it covered by CCTV, so they're interviewing the janitor, Lou tells me. She's an expert at muddying waters, that woman.'

'Charles – the gardener who spends hours scrubbing bird shit with a toothbrush?'

'That's the one. The detective also said something about checking phone records during that time again through the closest towers, if the intruder was silly enough to call an Uber or something. They wanted Kat's new number.'

'I really can't see Charles as a violent attacker, TBH, but anything that takes the heat off you is good, right?'

Rachael squeezed Gertie's hand. It was only then that Gertie realised it was shaking.

'Either way, I think I'm in the clear, G.'

Gertie thought of her confronting Sam in the playground over Kat's marks that afternoon and breathed a sigh of relief that neither her nor Ed's name came up, crossing her fingers that her sister was clever enough to have slung enough mud on the rest of the estate that they never would.

After a couple of days' shock over the whole family being informed that Fred was Ed's son, it was like he'd always been there. The kids were surprisingly modern about it, punching his arm like he was already part of the family, anyway. Lou seemed to take that as a cue to expand Fred's job description to 'Boy Friday' for her office errands, and by the end of the week the two unlikely allies had morphed into an old married couple bickering over who hadn't put out the rubbish.

The boys flopped on the couch and fought over the Xbox. Ed scurried to make toast. Rachael had needed to meet her accountant early, so Gertie had offered to let Noah play with

Harry at their place until she left for her shift at the hospital. Noah had eyes only for the pixels on the screen, pulling his controller left and right, dropping blocks and crafting potions.

Gertie watched in wonder. 'How pretty is that?' There was a hidden gate on Minecraft that ported him through to a beautiful green meadow with flowers and boulders bordering a flowing stream. It was undoubtedly the field outside the estate. Rachael's six-year-old had named the world 'Secret Meddoowe'.

'That looks familiar, buddy. Did Kat or Ethan take you there?'

'Both. The day Daddy got hurted. He's still asleep so he can get better.'

'Oh, yes that was an awful day.' Gertie frowned. 'But Kat wasn't around that afternoon. Are you sure it was that Wednesday?'

He nodded again, but Gertie was unsure he was even listening, eyes fixed on the screen. Kat was wearing earbuds, loafing on the couch near the boys listening to a podcast on her phone. Gertie tapped her on the shoulder.

Kat pulled an earbud out and said, 'What?'

'Honey, you were at Sienna's the day of the home invasion, right? That's what you told me and the police. But Noah here's saying you and Ethan showed him the meadow that day.'

Kat's face went blank, then she squinted. 'No, that's total BS.'

Noah's little face lit up. 'Nah, it was that day. Ethan gave me cake to shut me up about you two sneaking me to the secret meadow.'

Kat honed in on Noah. 'That was another day, dude. Remember?'

'Ask Abe if you think I'm lying, he saw us walking back. He was lining up the bins when the sirens went woo woo!'

Kat elbowed him hard. Noah's face fell and he went back to building flowers in his online garden.

Gertie didn't know what to make of the comment – her Harry was the same age and didn't know what day it was half the time, but that day was distinct. Noah would have remembered.

Fred sheepishly wandered out from the spare room. His hair looked redder than before, as if it had come into its own. He was wearing boxers, scratching and yawning simultaneously, and it reminded Gertie of a game of Simon Says. He and Ed greeted each other in awkward, manly, grunty ways and Fred finished off the toast and tea orders like a well-programmed assembly line.

Is he my stepson now? And does that mean we don't have to pay him?

Gertie snuck into the study that now resembled a police headquarters. Charts. Evidence. Papers. A stack of takeaway containers and coffee cups overflowed from the bin. 'Have you actually left this room this week?' she asked Lou.

Lou locked the door, and as if that wasn't secure enough, pressed herself against it. 'I've got Kat's new phone triangulation data. I don't know how to say this. She was in the Yorks' home between 5.33 pm and 6.15 pm on the Wednesday of the attack. The ambulance call was at 6.23 pm. Kat was there. Her phone records prove it. Why would she lie about not being there if she wasn't involved?'

Gertie's stomach flipped. 'Or her *phone* was. She leaves it everywhere.'

'Not likely the first day she got a new iPhone. This is a big problem, Gert. They had the details of her old phone, which was left at home and not at the scene. They never looked at her further as she wasn't seen on any footage and her alibi of being at Sienna's place to study, like she told us, checked out, but those photos of her and Sam change everything. They give her motive. She could have easily avoided the drones, she could even be the scent the sniffer dogs traced to the janitors' shed, hiding evidence. The weapon still isn't accounted for – probably at the bottom of that stream you talked about. Rachael told me she sees Abe rearrange the bins every week on collection day, so I asked him if he was out that Wednesday. He confirmed he saw Kat return from the east corner of the estate about the same time you were treating Sam.'

Gertie didn't want to tell Lou that Noah also said he saw Kat. She didn't want to tell Lou that Abe was missing when she left in a rush to help Sam. That it all fit. She just sat, stunned.

Lou went on, trouble etched on her face. 'I know you're pretty free and easy with where the kids are in this little bubble you live in, and I get maybe you were too busy throwing your husband out to know where your kids were. But, hon, the cops will have all this, too, soon enough. She was there, Gert. The question is why did she lie?'

Gertie sat on the swivel chair, the worry that had swirled in her mind for days now sunk like a stone in her stomach.

'Gert – if this evidence makes it to discovery, I think we have a big problem.'

Gertie felt the pressure of elephants' hooves stomp across her chest. 'What do you mean, if it makes it to discovery?' She fanned her face. 'Is it hot in here? I need some air.' She opened a window. 'Have they even arrested Rachael yet? Or anyone, for that matter?'

''Course not. I'm better than that.'

'So, there's no case yet.' If she said it out loud it must be true. 'Anyway, you're her aunt. Can't you make sure it doesn't come to any of that? Can't you just drop the case, conflict of interest or something?'

'I'll do all I can, you know that. But I'd be disbarred if I failed to disclose key evidence, especially evidence that helped my client, even if I withdraw from representing her. And there's no point if they'll find it, anyway. And this evidence – this is strong evidence that there's another person of interest in this assault.'

'You mean Kat?'

Lou softened her voice. 'G, I'm not seeing this as an aunt. I'm seeing this as a lawyer. If Pencil-dick Sam York was telling you he'd tell the world she was a little tart, that he'd make sure she'd never get into uni, he was probably threatening Kat with that, too. I don't think his type like it when the victims they groom find courage to leave them. He would have escalated control. Raised the stakes. Kat probably thought her life was over, but you know Kat, she's fearless. He probably didn't expect that. I think she's confronted him as you did – as you taught her to do,' Lou said.

Gertie stilled. A seriousness laced her sister's voice and it terrified her.

Lou went on, but Gertie was still processing the first part. 'You told me what sort of man he is – she may have had to fight him off with whatever she could find. We can work with that. No jury will convict a kid in those circumstances.'

'My girl, facing a jury?' Gertie shook her head to clear the thought from her mind and let herself return to denial that any of this was real.

'G, I don't know how else to put this without freaking you out. I'm afraid I really do think something happened between Sam and Kat that afternoon that ended with him getting a knife in his rib. Some sort of sordid scuffle – it might not have even been intentional. But, Gertie, the cops may not continue to consider Rachael their key suspect, with this evidence. You need to prepare yourself.'

Gertie's heartbeat pulsed in her throat. 'I'll talk to Kat. She'll explain all of this, I'm sure. She's not capable, Lou. I know it in my bones.' Gertie's chin wobbled and she knew she was about to lose it. She let her legs go limp and crouched on the floor of the study, using all her mental energy to conjure up alternative explanations to what she was hearing.

Lou sat beside her on the carpet, touched Gertie's knee like her actual sister would, instead of this ruthless finger-pointer that perched before her. But she took it. She took it because she couldn't believe this was happening. Her only daughter. She'd been her pride, her joy, the source of so much happiness. Kat was her grown-up kid. Her responsible, book-reading, rule-follower.

'And, Gert, what if he wakes up? Can we be sure he won't say her name?'

'He may never speak again, and if he does who'd believe a word?'

'A jury just might. You know how good he is. It has nothing to do with truth.'

Gertie blinked to fend off the tears welling. 'You think my Kat, our Kitty-Kat, stabbed a man in the heart?' Gertie laughed, but even as it fluttered up her throat and out of her mouth, she knew something was very wrong. Yorky had still been a mirage back then. Kat had convinced herself she loved him. It just might sound plausible to a jury.

Katerina Rainworth was a scholarship student, never had so much as an overdue library book. How could she become a suspect in an *attempted murder*? Even if it was quashed as self-defence, it would stain her record forever, her view of herself. Gertie couldn't let this happen, she just couldn't.

The level of love of a parent changed you irrevocably. It made you responsible for everything your child did because you'd made them from scratch.

Gertie made Kat. She knew her to the core. But did she know her mind back on that afternoon when she was lost to her?

I'll stand in front of the bus for you, Kat. I'll do anything.

Chapter 35

Penny

'I know where you were the night of the stabbing,' Penny declared as her husband returned home from the office in his grey trousers and navy shirt. She wasn't even sure why he still bothered; no one was going to invest with a bankrupt. Was he busy shredding evidence?

'What?' He scraped his hand over his bald head, deep in thought.

'You're visiting him,' Penelope accused.

'What? Who?'

She knew her husband had a lot on his mind, but she could not let this rest. 'You got a speeding ticket. It came in the post today.' Penny pointed to an official envelope, jiggered at the edge, as ripped open as their lives.

'So, we're opening private mail, now?'

'You lied to that rotten policeman about where you were. What's more, you lied to me. I thought you'd killed him, Martin. You think an envelope was going to stop me?'

His jowls shuddered a little as his jaw dropped. 'Come off it, Pen.'

'I'm not sure if the truth of where you were that night is any better. The speeding offence' – she grabbed the letter, trying to read the small print without her glasses – 'one hundred and ten kilometres an hour in a one-hundred-kilometre-per-hour zone in that bloody Cobra.' She threw it at him. 'Down the freeway near Long Bay.'

'That doesn't mean—'

'You were going to the *jail*. To visit Tyson. To visit our son.' It had been years since Penelope had referred to him as that, even within the privacy of their home.

At least Martin had the decency not to deny it, and collapsed into the wing chair, eyes closed. 'I was.'

Her eyebrows adjusted into a thunderous frown. 'For how long?' How long had he been betraying his wife, betraying his promise to let their eldest son serve his time, repay his debt to society? They had agreed that then, and only then, would they, as loving parents, welcome him back into their home and their hearts. Tyson was the reason they'd come to this place – to hide from the shame of what he did. Because, as a parent, everything your child did reflected on you. 'How long have you been seeing him behind my back?'

'The whole time.'

Penelope gasped audibly. 'But he's served five years of a seven-year sentence! And you've kept this quiet, for years, without telling me?' Her belly sank to her toes.

His lip twitched at the side, Martin's tell-tale sign of regret, of fear of what came next. Penelope fell onto the bed, every muscle feeling like jelly, like her bones had collapsed, leaving nothing but a sack of flesh that could no longer sit upright.

'We agreed.'

'I know,' he cried. 'I just couldn't do it. I'm not as strong as you. I wanted, I needed, to still have both my sons in my life,' Martin admitted, the pain in his voice deep and resolute.

'But – what he did to that girl!' Penelope cried. 'How do you forgive him for that?'

'I haven't. Not yet. And I dare say he hasn't forgiven himself, nor should he. But we're working on it. I just don't think punishment should mean the withdrawal of love. He's still our son, whatever he did. And I still love him, and I'll welcome him back into this home as soon as he has served his time.' He ended the statement with a nod, as if it made sense. As if they were indisputable facts to be believed.

Penelope was torn between wanting to know everything about Tyson – *Is he well? In good spirits? Are they feeding him properly? Are his teeth still straight from those bloody braces he hated?* – and not wanting to feel weak for caring.

'Why didn't you tell me? Why go behind my back?'

Martin had answers ready, as if he'd rehearsed these lines for this inevitable scene. 'Every time I mentioned him, you'd shut down, refuse to have his name uttered under this roof.'

Penelope's lips pursed together. 'You heard her testimony. You know what he did to that girl.'

Martin's chin trembled. 'I'll never unhear the pain in that woman's voice, and I'll never stop wondering what role we had in the assault. In making Tyson the impulsive, flawed man he is. But the state is punishing him. He's lost his freedom. Isn't that enough?'

A burst of disbelief, a sense of utter betrayal from the one person she'd always relied on. Penelope's jaw felt too tight to let the words out, wired shut with anger. 'We agreed.'

'Pen – the prison doctor rang me about six months in. Tyson attempted to take his own life. I tried to tell you. You didn't want to hear it.'

She inhaled sharply in shock, her legs folding under her as she collapsed lower, onto the bedroom carpet. It was true, she didn't want to hear it. Not then, not now. Because hearing anything about him, being reminded of what he did, only cut deeper into the wounds and encouraged the voice that screamed in her mind that she was his maker, his mother, his nurturer. She was to blame. She may as well have assaulted that poor girl herself.

Penelope launched herself at Martin, bashing his chest with her fists, and he held her until she stopped and the tears took over.

'I'm the mother, it's my fault our beautiful little boys turned out the way they did. Remember when I sewed matching red cord overalls for them? Tyson hated it – Spence was so much younger. They weren't bad boys, they didn't so much as shoplift, had everything they asked for.' Penny paused, her hand to her mouth. *Was that why? I gave Tyson everything he wanted and he grew up feeling entitled to take whatever he needed from that woman?*

'Oh, darling. If it's anyone's fault it's mine – it bugs me every day, especially with all this Me Too stuff coming out. Did I show disrespect to you? To women in general? Or behave in some way that meant he grew up with the notion that women aren't deserving of respect?'

Her breath caught. 'No, I don't think so. You were a good provider, you never hit me or cheated or treated me unfairly. Oh.' Penny clicked her fingers as she recalled another key bit of evidence. 'You even did that International Women's Day walk, remember?'

He scoffed at her and it made her feel small. All she was trying to do was build him up, build up all her boys. 'Penny, it's not that simple. After we caught Spencer making those movies the other week, it really disturbed me, the thought that it could be happening again. Have we done enough? I mean, he's in there now, on that computer – doing God knows what. We wouldn't have a clue.'

It was strange, it felt so natural to blame herself, but hearing her husband take responsibility for something she knew deep inside was not his fault, she had clarity. 'You're not exactly one of those alpha males with nude posters on your walls who catcalls girls on the street. We taught him about consent and that no means no.'

His cheeks reddened as he grabbed her shoulders. 'It's not enough, love. We should have taught the boys to wait for a yes, not simply stop after a no, that nothing entitles a bloke to have his way with a girl – not paying for drinks or being invited up for coffee.'

'You're right.' Penelope swallowed hard, wiping a tear from her eye. Her gaze wandered down the hall, to the dusty, disused room where Tyson's things were pointlessly displayed in anticipation for his parole, to Spencer's room, where he slumped, alone, every night and obsessed over his video games and whatever else. 'But it's not too late. Spence is still under our roof. We can start right now.'

Chapter 36

Rachael

Antiseptic and bodily fluids and too-far-gone flowers; that's all Rachael could smell as she sat and watched her husband in bed 10 of the ICU. Sam didn't look real – thin and pale on the stark white sheets, not a force to be reckoned with. Indy cooed from her sling. She'd only had a few weeks of knowing her dad – would she ever see him again? Was a questionable father better than none?

Machines beeped, drained, sucked, filled and exhaled for him. Each time someone arrived through the heavy door, the air pressure changed like an air lock in a plane. The rooms were partitioned by curtains, each pool of light containing another poor critical patient like him, plugged in, sedated, waiting to see if they would live or die.

Rachael York felt a cold shiver inside as the doctor explained Sam's prognosis. She would never forget the acrid smell of the ward as the neurologist uttered words like aphasia, cognitive deficits, limited baseline functioning – a well-rehearsed, even casual iteration of the cold, hard facts of her 'loved one'. *'Loved' is one big assumption.* The words terrified, but also sobered Rachael to the reality of what lay in store.

Because of the blood loss from the attack and the fact that Sam had been too unstable to undertake scans since his emergency surgery, the prognosis was unclear. He was likely to suffer substantially reduced functioning once he woke up. Just how substantial was a mystery. Rachael was left feeling more cut off than she'd ever felt. Sam's actions were unforgivable — even if he did recover, he was lost to her forever.

Arriving home from hospital, Rachael considered trying to eat to settle her churning stomach when Detective O'Sullivan arrived with an update on the investigation. It was cold and wet, with rain chipping the front windows either side of the entry door as O'Sullivan paused to take off his wet shoes. Rachael placed Indy down on a giant lady-beetle-print playmat, with a scattering of mirrors, chew toys and textured patches to keep her entertained. Lying on her tummy, Indy lifted all four limbs off the floor like a jet that intended to fly away at any moment.

'No luck with the Crawleys, I'm afraid.' He perched himself on the edge of her white leather chaise uncomfortably, as if he didn't want to dirty it. 'Penelope was accounted for, picking up Spencer, and Martin — while having a strong motive with the lost-money angle, was caught on CCTV at the Long Bay prison visiting his son.'

'Spencer's in jail?'

'No — but give him time. Penelope and Martin have an older son, Tyson.'

'Wow.' Rachael thought of the bedroom Ethan had spied in their home that didn't seem to have a clear owner, and the references to another child in Penny's earlier parenting blogs.

'And following the sniffer dog lead has reached a dead end, too, I'm afraid. All landscaping staff gave strong alibis and no clear motive for such a crime.'

'What are you saying? There're no other suspects? You're back to little old me again? What about the motive for publicising those photos with our babysitter?' Rachael tried to keep her face from showing the hurt, the disgust she'd felt, seeing those pictures, imagining what else might have gone on in her house.

He cleared his throat. 'The images of your husband and the young lass did come from the son's drone – he seems to be known for this sort of behaviour.' The detective blushed and coughed again uncomfortably. 'We've interviewed Spencer again and he admitted he did it to get back at your husband for what he perceives as "stealing his inheritance".'

'Doesn't that also mean he had a motive to attack him?'

'Firm alibi with CCTV of him arriving home, I'm afraid. I was hoping to speak to Ethan again to go over his statement – with you present, of course. There has been one development – we do have Kat's new phone signal placing her at the scene on the day. She hasn't been questioned – that lawyer of yours won't let us near her niece without an arrest.'

'Wait. You mean, arrest *Kat* for the attack? Surely not.' Had she been wrong about that girl? Could she rely on any of her instincts anymore?

O'Sullivan looked apologetic. 'May I ask if their relationship was a surprise?'

'I had no idea. I was under the impression Kat and Ethan had a budding romance. Her mother's a good friend. It's been pretty full on for all of us.' Rachael stifled a sob. *Just when I thought life couldn't get any worse.* 'Sam wasn't known for his fidelity, but she's half his age – a schoolgirl. He isn't that sort of man.'

The detective raised his eyebrows, and Rachael felt stupid. *Evidently, he is.* Her doorbell rang and saved them both from the awkwardness. Gertie's face on the security panel with a tight smile, Noah bouncing happily at her feet on the porch with his rainbow gumboots and umbrella. 'Speak of the devil. Excuse me one sec, Gertie's just bringing my son back.' Rachael went to the front.

'Thank so much for having him,' she said to Gertie as she opened the door. 'My sweet boy, how was your play with Harry?' She bent to kiss her son who said, 'Good' and ran in his wet shoes up the stairs. Rachael gave Gertie a tight smile. She'd been keeping it together inside with O'Sullivan, but seeing Gertie allowed the panic in her stomach to rise and form a lump in her throat. The police focus was narrowing, and no other persons of interest were likely.

Rachael whispered to Gertie that Detective O'Sullivan was inside. She subtly pointed at the camera mounted above her front entry and gestured they should sidestep left a few metres out of view.

'Sorry, they called me into the ward early to relieve tea breaks.' Gertie's frazzled look as she shimmied down the porch seemed to match how Rachael felt.

'They're waking him up.'

Gertie looked at her feet as if the answer to their dilemma was etched in the paving and Rachael was unsure if she'd heard, if she realised the implications.

'Gertie? What if he talks?' The chance of Sam regaining consciousness with no memory loss and his speech intact was slim, but Rachael still found the possibility frightening.

Silence.

Gertie's jaw set hard as she gazed out at the rain. 'Kat was here that day. She lied.'

Rachael took comfort in her honesty. 'Yeah, I just worked that out, too. Ethan told me he overheard Kat tell her friend she wasn't interested in a grade-ten geek like him. It broke him. I never saw her here, but he said she snuck in the back that afternoon to make up, but he fobbed her off. Now the cops have phone data to prove it. Maybe she just took Noah away to keep him safe when she saw the intruder, or maybe she was complicit somehow, I don't know. Ethan's sticking to his story, saying she was only here a few minutes and left long before it all happened.'

Gertie didn't seem relieved to hear it.

Rachael sat her down on the seat on the verandah, the scent of lavender sweet in the air with the rain. 'It's so crazy, I spent the first week worried Sam was lost to us forever, that he'd never wake up. Now I'm petrified he will … I can't live in a world where he exists anymore, Gert. And that's not even the worst bit.' Rachael exhaled. The next thing she said in a whisper barely audible over the roar of the rain pelting on the roof, over the thump of her heart.

'G, I think it was one of our kids.'

Rachael found Ethan alone but for a rat named Bartholomew. She tried her best to explain the specialists' imminent plans for his father.

'I don't want to scare you, love,' Rachael told him, 'but we just won't know how much damage was done until we wake him up. He might be fine, but we can't promise anything.'

'When will we know?' Ethan emphasised each word as though frustrated.

'I saw him today. The neurologist said she'd confirm after rounds tomorrow, but your dad's vitals look promising, stable enough to bring him out of the coma.'

'Tomorrow?' His voice was high-pitched, alarmed.

Rachael nodded with a teary smile, expecting him to be relieved, to be happy that soon they would have certainty, would know if his dad was lost to them. 'We may even get answers to who put him in that damn hospital bed in the first place. If you've been trying to protect Kat, hon, I understand she's your friend, but this is serious. There are police hovering, and they won't stop until they solve this.'

Ethan sprang up and shoved his desk chair sharply, sending it skidding into the skirting boards. Rachael stood in surprise as he punched a fist-shaped dent in his metal bin. He slid his bony back down the wall, folded his impossibly long legs beneath him and sobbed.

Rachael lowered to a squat, crawled over to him and sat at his side. 'I'm sorry this happened to your dad, Ethe, that we don't have more answers of why. I'm sorry I wasn't more present that day, and all the days before. I can't help but feel partly to blame that I let things get out of hand.'

Bart the rat scurried across the floor and stopped with intent at the skirting that had partially dislodged when the chair scuffed the wall in Ethan's outburst. The rat pressed its head between the gap, nibbling intently. Had Ethan stashed food in there?

'What do you mean?' Ethan said. 'This isn't your fault. It's mine.'

He tapped on the jutting edge of the skirting board. A foot-long section slid out, revealing a brick-sized cavity. The rat ran in, gnawing at the floorboard beneath the cavity that seemed to be stained with rust or paint.

'Ever wonder where the knife went, Mum? The Stanley knife from the tools left on the bench.'

The stain. It was blood. His father's blood. Blood that he lost such volumes of that he nearly died, could still die.

'You hid it. To protect Kat? Is it in there?' Rachael pointed to the hollow in the wall, where chocolate wrappers and what looked like pot and a cigarette lighter were also tucked inside. She tried to piece it all together. 'Did she confront him? Was she forced to use it on him to defend herself?'

Ethan yelped in a manner that was part cry, part laugh.

'Was it Annabelle, then?' Rachael asked. 'Gertie saw her with you at the playground. Did you recognise her as the woman that used to lurk around when you were little? Just tell me the truth and I'll do everything I can to help you fix it.'

Rachael remembered her training in communicating with people in the midst of mental-health episodes, which was clearly the terrain they had wandered into. *Never ask why. Never judge. Just listen.*

'He's going to tell you anyway, tomorrow, when they wake him up. When he talks.'

Rachael stopped breathing. 'What happened that day?'

He looked her straight in the eye. 'It was a total clusterfuck …'

Chapter 37

Ethan

Ethan York waited for the Fortnite lobby to load on Battle Royale. Spencer, the hypocrite who gave Ethan shit for still playing the game 'only homos and seven-year-olds play' was actually in the Fortnite lobby. *Yes. Game on, arsehole.*

He needed an escape from Annabelle Alesi hovering in his life, telling him things down at the meadow that put everything he knew to be true in doubt. He needed an escape from life to forget about Katerina Rainworth's lips. Forget they'd talked till dusk crept in and they had to use their phones as torches to scurry their way home. He needed to enter a realm where pretty girls didn't kiss you back like she had that day months ago in the meadow, moments before spouting to her friends that he was a loser she only tolerated out of obligation.

The frigging screen-time limiter warned him he had thirty minutes remaining in that day's allocated time. Ethan pulled his headphones down and screamed out to his mum to extend it.

He hit the desk, spilling jars of pens on the table, and they rolled onto the floor. He let them scatter and reminded himself to deal with that mess, and his mum, as soon as the storm died down on the battle. Anxiety swelled in his throat. If he lost this, he'd never live it down. His eyes watered, but he told himself it was from the screen, not from crying like a wuss.

'Fucking hell!' A fifteen-minute warning before the screen-time bullshit would cut him off. 'Mum! I said to give me extra time. Are you even listening?' Ethan texted her phone as he couldn't afford the few minutes it would take to find her IRL. No response again. 'Where the hell are you? Mum!' He was embarrassed by the crack in his voice. This was ridiculous.

The player pack was down from ninety-eight to five. *Megadestroyer9000* was still alive, chasing *BoofBoy17* through the open fields like the bully he was. Spencer Crawley knew that was Ethan's tag as he used to give him shit about it, but he didn't have the heart to change it after Boof#1 died. It wasn't like Ethan wanted to be Spencer and his minions' friend. He just didn't want to be the butt of every joke, the topic of every meme they posted, and tagged him in, of course. He'd changed his name, blocked them, but they kept making new fake social-media names in his honour. There was no escape. He thought Kat was different, that she'd given him a chance and saw the real him, but even that turned out to be fake.

Final four. One toxic noob decided to kamikaze-bomb himself and another player. It was just Ethan and Spencer. Final two with a gold scar and a rocket launcher. Ethan totally had this victory in the bag. His fort was impenetrable. His health and shields were full. He had two med kits and a clear view to his opponent. Ethan had to stop himself jumping on the spot with absolute delight.

But then the unthinkable.

You have lost connection.

Just as the screen limiter activated, Ethan saw: *Megadestroyer9000 won the game. You placed 2nd.*

He yanked the keyboard from its jack and hurled it against the wall, denting the plaster. His mind was imploding, every neuron fizzing as if exposed to the world with no protection, and for a moment, he wondered if you could die from this vile feeling grating and thrashing and messing with his senses. The sound in his head – like a ratchet tightening, higher, higher.

Ethan's phone beeped. He sobbed with the anticipation of what insult it would hold. Some dig at his gaming ability? But Ethan could not have been more wrong.

'Don't cry *BoofBoy17*. All is not lost. At least we know your dad's not a homo.'

An attachment brightened Ethan's mobile screen.

The school pool, two entangled bodies.

Vertigo body-slammed him, making the room spin.

Katerina Rainworth and his father were kissing at the pool, his filthy grown-man hands just inches from her nipple, on her inner thigh, smiling at her as she walked away. Spencer had even drawn an arrow to highlight a boner in his father's pants. *Had he photoshopped them? Was it some sort of sick joke?* The sound of blood pounded through his ears. Ethan collapsed on his bed in anguish. Heat crawled up his neck, clawing at his senses. His dad pashing his girl, barely dressed in her swimmers. Worms prickled through his limbs, crawling, spreading like fleas, and he was forced to move to make it stop.

Ethan burst out of his room and thundered down the hall but felt lost, disorientated.

The walls bent inward, swaying like palm trees.

The strange, animalistic groan he could hear began to really grate, and he hunted it down, pinballing against walls to balance himself as he moved in and out of the lounge, in and out of the bathroom, landing in the kitchen. The howl. It followed his every move; it was coming from him. This terrified him more. Ethan hoped he was dreaming. Nothing looked right. Nothing felt real.

Kat's face was at the window, eyes wide with fear.

Was this chick for real? Get out of my house, you two-timing whore!

'Ethe!' She tapped on the glass, urgently. Ethan could barely register what she was trying to tell him. Grief of what he'd lost – with her, with his father, and who he thought he was.

'There's someone out here. That woman we saw with the red car – from the playground.' Kat pointed to the yard and she yanked on the door handle. Ethan glanced to where she pointed.

Now he was sure he was in hell. Annabelle, the supposed dog-killer, was here again. But now, after that photo showed what his dad was capable of, he was convinced it was his dad telling lies, not her. Could this get any worse?

That picture would go viral. His life was over.

Everything was pixelated, but his eyes made out a dusty old box on the kitchen bench, an old radio, paint-splattered, cobweb-covered tools strewn everywhere among the breakfast dishes and crumbs. A hammer. A paint scraper. A Stanley knife called to Ethan to grab it. He picked it up, felt the familiar grip under his fingers from cutting cartons at the deli.

Maybe he could use it on himself, make this feeling permanently end. It was tempting. It seemed so simple. So instant. To fall into that unknowable darkness. He gave a silent scream as he looked at the blade.

The front door clicked open.

Dad?

His father appeared as if he'd respawned from nowhere. His words were slow and deep and distorted like his health-pack needed recharging. 'Eeeeettttttthhhhhhhhaaaaaannnnnnn?'

'I know who my real mum is, you liar!'

At first Ethan had assumed the woman was another of his dad's whores, another thing he'd have to hide from his mum. He hated his father for that. But then the woman had told Ethan things she couldn't know unless she was his mum. About his birthmark. His scar from hitting the coffee table when he was learning to walk. Ethan turned away from his father and ran to find his mum. He couldn't keep Annabelle's version of events secret anymore. He had to tell his mother everything his dad had done. That Sam had lied about who his real mother was. That she wasn't dead. That Annabelle wasn't the witch he painted her as.

'Mum!'

He tuned in to the sound of water running through the walls near his parents' room. His mum – in the shower. The water stopped. He'd tell her about Annabelle, about Kat, tell her to leave his dad, that she deserved more.

Ethan continued up the hall with purpose, with clarity. He would reveal everything, every secret his father made him hide. But what would become of his father?

The ping. Everything in Ethan's brain was so laggy he couldn't make sense of it. Everything was stilted and stuck, the room spinning in slow motion like a cheap virtual-reality experience. Time seemed to buckle and bend.

His dad lunged forward as if he'd guessed Ethan was about to ruin his gambit and tell all. Ruin his marriage. Ruin his life.

His father pushed between him and the door and pressed close.

'Don't do this, Ethe, I can explain.' His words were garbled, but Ethan had heard them before. For years.

Then the ping fell away. Everything raced at double speed.

Ethan didn't even realise what had happened until his palm filled with warmth. He'd forgotten he'd held the knife at his chest.

The sharp, coppery smell of his father's blood smothered his senses, stole the breath from his lungs. He did this.

It barely went in, he swore.

Chapter 38

Rachael

'It was me, Mum.'

Rachael gagged, tasting vomit on her tongue as she slid away from him.

Did she know this already? Had she always suspected? She'd certainly turned the possibility over in her mind, but had not let herself entertain the thought that it could be real. What sort of mother would? A tangle of mixed emotions battled inside her, voices told her she was a rotten mother to have suspected all along, and surely only a rotten mother would raise a child capable of this violence? But another part of her wanted to hold him, protect him, understand the how and why like only a good mother would. She couldn't be both good and bad, or perhaps she could. Perhaps every mother was.

'Annabelle asked to drive me home from school. Something about her made me believe her, but I wasn't convinced Dad could have lied to me my whole life. Then Kat came over to say sorry about bagging me to her friends. I couldn't deal, told her to go, then I heard Noah begging her to play with him before she left. On top of that shitstorm came the photos of them.'

'Wait – you mean the photos with Katerina on the estate page? But that was only this week.'

'Nah, I got an advanced screening. Spencer sent them to me that day.' He hung his head in his hands. 'I really liked her. Then to see her sucking face with my dad! She heard the carry-on, saw me flipping out from the deck, freaked and took Noah away.'

'To the meadow?' Kat was just trying to keep him safe.

Ethan nodded. 'Yeah, after they took fingernail samples and stuff, I said I needed a shower. They took my clothes and I changed and snuck out quickly after the ambulance arrived to find Kat and Noah, stop her from dobbing.'

He walked her through the bullying from Spencer, the betrayal from the girl he liked, the confusion over who to believe about his real mother. Rachael shook her head – even adults couldn't have handled that level of emotional turmoil all at once – and those photos on top. She wasn't surprised it had ended with blood.

'Ethan, I'm sorry.' Rachael wanted to comfort her hurt young son, but she was still reeling from the confession. From what he'd done. From knowing for sure.

'I didn't plan to hurt anyone. It was an accident, Mum. You have to believe me. I was just running up the hall to you – to tell you everything he'd done. There was a fumble. Dad pushed in front of me. It was just the tip, I swear, it barely broke the skin.'

A shudder coursed through her. Fourteen millimetres deep, the report said, with little force, leading them to think it was not a crime of passion, but the position of it, sneaking between two ribs, was amazingly unlucky.

'It pierced his left atrium, Ethe. He nearly bled to death.' *He was evil, a predator in many ways, but he didn't deserve to die for his crimes. Did he?*

'I don't know how you could trust him, Mum, he was such a prick. I heard all your arguments, how he had those other women. I even suspected he was spending time with Kat – she knew him too well. He was so moody I was sometimes scared to come home, not knowing what version of him I'd get. I hated him, hated what he did to you, but I still didn't mean for it to go down that way.'

A wave of something she could now recognise as shame pummelled her. The shame of how she could have been attracted to someone she now saw as an illusion. She couldn't understand how she was blind to the impact his presence in their home had on her kids. On her.

'Annabelle was here, too, after school, after she told me she was my mother.'

Rachael had been toying with that piece of information, wondering when to involve Ethan. Now it seemed like the least of her problems, but it was the focus of his.

'Oh, hon. What did you say?'

'I told her I already had one.' Ethan hugged Rachael so desperately she had no choice but to reciprocate. 'She doesn't matter. You raised me.'

'Honey, she made you, she's always going to matter.'

'You're the one that did all the hard yards. I'm, like, in the final level before finishing a game, she shouldn't come in and claim victory. It's not fair.'

Rachael's face lost some of its tension. 'There are lots of ways of showing love, no limit to the number of people you have in your life, and I think you should think about getting to know her – the real her, not the version your dad painted. I can't imagine not knowing my child.'

It would hurt like fire.

She felt Ethan's pain, shared his conflicted emotions, but she could not let her son off that lightly.

'The weapon?'

'I was still in a, like, a fog, like I was in a strategy game. Part of me thought they might point the finger at you if they found it, so I knew I had to get rid of it. I slipped the knife in our wheelie bin, but I knew if I wheeled it to the footpath the street cam would see me, and if the cops checked it later they'd see me taking out the bins straight after … after what happened. But it was bizarre. Abe was in the street, lining up the bins the way he does on bin day. You can see the footage of the little weirdo. He noticed ours wasn't out and wheeled it to the footpath just before the truck arrived, churned it all up and compacted it. That knife – it's landfill.'

A parent's love was whole no matter how many times divided. But there was a limit to how much a parent could protect their child, and – accident or not – Ethan's actions had exceeded it. A surreal, otherworldly feeling clouded the night as Rachael left her garden and crossed the street. She wandered around the estate, down the cobbled lane in a surreal daze, only half aware of where she was heading. She heard the whirr of the cameras as they moved as she did and wondered why she ever thought that was necessary – they'd caused nothing but trouble, offered no control. She followed the bordering hedge of the estate, overbearing in its size, useless in its intent.

The real danger to her family was already inside.

Ethan's confession ate at her. She contemplated how culpable she was in this crime, having failed to make her husband responsible for the wrongs he'd bestowed on her throughout their marriage. If she'd thrown him out long ago, would Ethan have found himself forced into that frightening position, caught between his father's lies, Kat's betrayal, his mother's identity, under intense pressures on all fronts? Had her bubble-wrap mothering protected him too much to let him learn what he was capable of?

She turned into Lily Court. Rachael was desperate to purge the truth to her lawyer before she moved the kids to Nepal.

Lou answered Gertie's door and led her through to her makeshift office. The lawyer moved a briefcase off a chair so Rachael could sit.

'I know what happened to the weapon.'

Rachael retold Ethan's story to Lou in one tearful, vulnerable gust, with the hope the woman would sprinkle her fix-it dust all over it and make things come out the way they should – being with her kids, and with Ethan accepting responsibility for what he'd done but with the support he obviously needed.

Lou rubbed Rachael's back. 'C'mon, Rachael, this is not your fault. It sounds like Ethe had some sort of psychotic episode – that it was a combination of his intense screen addiction temporarily dissociating him from reality, along with the bullying, the unthinkable happening between his father and Kat, not to forget this woman from the family's past casting doubt on his parentage all in one afternoon. Who could have foreseen that shitstorm?' Lou squeezed her hand, but it did nothing to dry the well of guilt. 'I know Ethan's confession is a little terrifying, but this is also good news for you.'

'My son is more troubled than I ever imagined, has confessed to stabbing his father, who was harassing and blackmailing a young girl for sex. How could any of this be good?'

Lou took her hands, and Rachael realised there were tears in her eyes, too. 'He's not legal age. He's admitted it and will cooperate. He might get some time in juvie, but that also means support services.'

'What will happen to Annabelle? She's another victim, a mother unfairly refused entry to her son's life.'

'That's up to Ethan. The family court considers the minor's view at his age.'

Rachael's handbag rang but she ignored it.

Lou's mobile chirped the macarena. She assessed the caller ID, gestured an apology and answered. 'Detective O'Sullivan. What's up?'

Rachael wondered if the Irishman's ears were burning from all this talk of weapons and confessions and motives.

'She's actually with me now,' Lou spoke into her phone. 'You want to speak to her?' Hesitantly, she handed the phone across to where Rachael rigidly perched on the office chair, concern closing over her face.

'Detective?'

'Rachael. There's been a development. I need to speak to you.'

'Is this about Ethan?' Rachael's voice shook along with her hand. *Had he called the station, already confessed?*

'Ethan? No. It's about your husband, I'm afraid. The hospital called. I have awful news ... Is Lou still there with you?'

Rachael heard it, without processing the words.

A fatal heart attack.

Despite the medical team's efforts to bring him back, Sam York was declared dead at 6.42 pm.

Rachael later processed what that meant.

Not only was her husband dead, she was living with his killer.

Chapter 39

Lou

This was why Lou avoided doing work for people she cared about. She heard Gertie click her fob at the front door of 12 Lily Court. Gertie, still in her scrubs, looked slightly deranged, tired and confused as she threw her bags on her kitchen bench.

'Did Rachael call you?' Lou asked. She hoped she had so she didn't have to say it. It had been a long day. Her sister looked like she'd had one just as long.

'Why? What the hell's going on, Lou?' Gertie stepped towards her with a finger-pointing tone in her voice.

She summarised all that had transpired. 'We have both knowledge of the weapon and a confession. Kat's in the clear.'

'*What?*' Gertie kept stepping forward as Lou backed away, palms raised.

Lou was confused. 'Why are you angry? This is good news!'

Gertie edged closer, an unhinged quality to her voice. 'You make me think my only daughter knifed someone and now you tell me you were *wrong*? Who was it, then? Who killed Sam?'

'So, you heard he's dead?' Lou asked.

Gertie swallowed hard, then nodded. 'Word travels.'

'Mum?' Kat stepped down the stairwell, all innocent in her Minnie Mouse nightie and wet straggly hair. She crossed the open-plan living room to the kitchen. 'Who's dead?'

Gertie and Lou glared at each other, mentally jostling for who would inform the love-struck teen that her Olympic hero was now likely being toe-tagged in the morgue. Gertie walked to the lounge, sat down and patted the seat next to her. Kat flopped beside her mum, who tucked her damp hair in a twist in such a familiar way it made Lou yearn to have that sort of relationship with her own daughter one day. She pressed her stomach and wondered.

'Sam suffered a fatal heart attack. The team did all they could, but he didn't survive, love. I'm sorry. I know you still had mixed feelings about the bloke.'

Kat's eyes teared up, and she nodded, cowering under her mum's outstretched arm.

'Tests indicated such a miniscule chance of him waking up. He'd lost so much blood it was almost impossible that he'd regain consciousness without life support.'

Kat's chest shuddered with each new morsel of information. Lou sat and waited and watched her sister, her warm, big-hearted sister have the most difficult conversation with her daughter. How was it that Gertie cracked it over Lego left on the rug but calmed in a crisis?

'I'm not upset about him. I'm upset about Ethan – he's lost his father. How's he going to cope knowing ...'

Gertie leaned in. 'Knowing what?'

'I lied about not being there. I was, I'm sorry. I went there to ask him to the formal – to show him I wanted to tell the world I was confused, that it was him I liked not his arsehole dad.' Kat inhaled, hesitating. 'I saw him flip out. Spencer had sent him one of those photos of me and Sam and he lost it. He had the knife. I took Noah through the hole in the fence to the creek to get him out of the way.'

Kat went on to tell them how the stabbing was an accident – a fumble that ended tragically. That Ethan slipped out later and came to find them, colluded not to tell anyone she was there that day. It was easier than having to lie about not seeing what she saw. The knife was slipped in the rubbish just before Abe took the bin to the kerb for collection. He had no idea he had helped hide the evidence.

'Ethan didn't mean it, Mum.'

Gertie's eyes widened and she sat silently, mouth open.

'You were the scent trailing to the janitors' shed,' Lou realised. 'This whole time, you knew?' The kid was good.

She really needed to improve her questioning techniques. It would have saved her a week of hard work and a whole lot of heartache.

'*Ethan* stabbed Sam?' Gertie's face pinched. 'You're telling me the boy you asked to the formal stabbed his father?'

Kat's tone was a little patronising. 'Yeah, Mum, keep up.'

Chapter 40

Penny

Womb with a View – Final Blog Post

My eldest son was charged with sexual assault. There, I said it.

Tyson turns twenty-one next month. He's in Long Bay jail, repaying his debt to society. I know what it's like to live each day, and wonder how a person you love, a person you raised, was capable of doing such a horrible thing. I never visited him, I shut him out. I couldn't reconcile the man behind bars with the boy I used to tuck in wearing Cookie Monster pyjamas. I couldn't stop feeling like I should be the one being punished. It took me three years to accept that it wasn't my hands that held that poor girl down. That our children are not extensions of us, but independent beings we can't control. That we are not our children.

The hardest lesson I've learned as a mum is how to discipline a child while remaining loving. Of showing how we feel anger at their actions, but still care for them. I admit, I fucked it up.

My husband taught me something recently – that when we withhold love as punishment no one wins. I've learned that the hard way and hope this, my final post, helps you to avoid my mistakes. Or that one, at least.

Chapter 41

Gertie

Earlier that day …

Gertie Rainworth was not one of those women who got off on signs from the universe. She didn't believe her future was preordained, nor did she think she had to sit back and wait for it to reveal itself in stupid, subtle ways like through a song lyric, or a flock of ducks. But if she *was* that kind of woman, she'd certainly feel the universe had been telling her to take matters into her own hands that blustery afternoon.

First sign, it rained. Sheets of silver rain zigzagged down the windows of the ward. Staff absentees always rose a little when it rained – nurses got stuck, car batteries failed and trains broke down. And whenever they were understaffed, they stole from the general wards to cover their tea breaks.

'Gert – ICU needs help,' said Betty from St Peter's when she called. 'I know you're just back from personal leave, but could you pop in before your shift for an hour or two? Help 'em out, huh? I know you used to supervise in that ward, so you're our first choice. You're a darl!' Betty was so effective at rostering because she had a way of asking that sounded like you'd already accepted her request.

Second sign, it was Sam's ICU.

The ICU had an allocated nurse for every bed. Most were filled with post-op patients who were simply under observation until they stabilised. Others were gravely ill, requiring precise care. As Gertie made her way through the nursing staff, getting the rundown on each patient, she tried not to think of the last on the list – Samuel York in bed 10. A slideshow of images flashed through Gertie's brain: him cornering her daughter in the dressing room, having his way with an innocent teenager. She didn't need a heart-rate monitor to know hers was climbing.

'I've got Dreamboy,' Sally declared, wiggling her eyebrows as Gertie entered the crowded nurses' station. 'Hope they do wake him up tomorrow. Then I might get his autograph. Anyway, G, he just needs a central line flush sometime tonight if you get to it ...'

'No probs,' Gertie answered, her hand shaking. *He could wake up. He could talk. He could say my daughter's name.*

Third sign (if she were into that), he needed a line flush by one Gertie Rainworth.

Gertie breathed, steadily placed one foot in front of the other in a trancelike state out of the cubicle and down the corridor. She stared at the sign. Bed 10. *Stop me now, Universe. It's about to get ugly.*

The fourth sign. The sound of her pulling the privacy curtain closed did not wake the guard, his girth overhanging the tiny chair, there to ensure no unauthorised visitors harmed the Very Important Patient.

It was unlikely Sam would ever speak a word again, but Gertie Rainworth couldn't take that chance with her child's life. She pictured Rachael, lumbered with caring for the bastard for life, and she knew it was in everyone's best interests to act now.

I spent the first week worried Sam would never wake up. Now I'm petrified he will.

She couldn't act too soon, or she'd still be on duty when the consequences of her actions became clear.

Kat was there. Her phone records prove it. Why would she lie about not being there if she wasn't involved?

His central line flush was due.

It was her! Katerina Rainworth stabbed me in cold blood out of jealousy!

A three-port line. Three vials.

Katerina Rainworth, I am charging you with the murder of Samuel Marcus York. You have the right to remain silent.

Ten millilitres of KCL in each would stop his heart.

Gertie took three vials of saline and emptied them into a disposable coffee cup she'd found abandoned at the feet of the sleeping security guard, making sure to dispose of the empty vials in the pedal bin as she normally would after a central line flush.

Her gloved hand found the ten-millilitre ampoules of potassium chloride containing twenty millimoles of potassium per ampoule – so powerful they were only available on special order in the ICU.

Gertie flushed the central line, hiding the three empty KCL vials (taken from storage to reduce suspicion) in the coffee cup.

She didn't look at his face as she left.

Gertie returned to the nurses' station to see Sally had returned. She smelled of nicotine.

'Oh, you're a naughty girl, Gert, what have you done!' She tut-tutted at her.

'Sorry?' Gertie asked, an adrenalin rush flooding her brain.

Sally pointed to the disposable cup she'd stolen from the guard. 'No hot drinks in the ICU – remember the rules? You'd be shot if Matron saw you. You'll be allowing durries next!'

'My bad!' Gertie offered, tossing the cup in the rubbish bag hanging from the cleaner's trolley just as he pulled it shut and took it out for the compactus. Gertie casually mentioned, 'Flushed Dreamboy's lines, nothing else of note, Sal.' She was surprised the words formed in her mouth, she was so petrified.

Was it really killing if the person was dead already?

Gertie felt like there was a big neon sign blinking above her murderous head, but no one was paying attention. Everyone was in their own world, chatting about their lives, their frozen-dinner choices, their Netflix binges.

'If that's everything, I'll head off, then, folks!' Gertie said as a chorus of goodbyes and thank-yous followed her out.

She was already at the lift when she heard the code called to bed 10, telling her that her handiwork had kicked in. Just like it worked on the monsters on death row, the potassium had stopped his heart. Gertie thumped the button to close the doors and pressed herself against the lift wall before the panic stole the breath from her lungs.

Epilogue

After the rain, the wildflowers stretched and raised their heads towards the light. Some might call them weeds, growing however they pleased, but the three women admired the flowers, an eclectic carpet of yellow, magenta and lavender sprawling towards the creek.

The meadow was where Gertie and Rachael, and now Lou, swapped their secrets, but it could also be said that they knew of them before the confessions left the others' lips.

Gertie sized up her sister with suspicion. 'You're pregnant,' she said as they sucked on mini plastic spoons over kid-sized gelato cups.

'You guessed.' Lou beamed with happiness. 'I'm hurling all day, but I'm so happy.'

Rachael smiled and offered her congratulations to her friend.

Gertie's eyes closed and she exhaled in a relief she'd waited years to feel on her tormented sister's behalf. 'It's not Tim's, though, is it?'

Lou shook her head. 'He knows though. He agreed to try a donor. He was willing to try anything to start a family. Don't worry, I got contracts signed covering all scenarios.'

'A lawyer at heart, huh?' Rachael laughed.

Gertie nodded, then brought Lou in close in a tearful embrace. 'I'm happy for you, hon. You'll be as good at mothering as you are at every bloody other thing.' They released from their hug and Gertie licked gelato from her hair that had managed to dip in Lou's pistachio 'n' cream.

The Apple Tree Creek Scandal had fizzled since the headlines named and shamed Sam York as being a serial womaniser, including charges of indecent assault of a minor, various claims from former ABC anchor Annabelle Alesi, sexual assault of his publicist, and involvement in an offshore performance-enhancing-drug scandal.

The police were no longer pressing for a criminal conviction, since the circumstances in which a minor accidentally hurt his father in an emotional scuffle became clear.

Lou glanced over at Rach. 'How's Ethan going since the hearing?'

'He's good, actually. Doing his hours at the garden centre, taken up boxing, getting some intervention for his gaming addiction and anxiety. He's started emailing Annabelle – tells me all these stories about her amazing war reporting. And I think he's even started to forgive Kat – although apparently they're still in the friend zone.'

Lou's tone became serious. 'The reason I got us together was to let you know I got Sam's COD report from the pathologist.'

Gertie's stomach clenched.

Rachael's eyes locked with Gertie's and the gesture was not lost on Lou.

'Natural causes,' Lou announced.

Gertie failed to hide her reaction, a shuddering breath cascading from her throat.

Lou went on so casually Gertie thought she'd misunderstood the results. 'I had my suspicions, G, that you helped the process along a little …' Lou said.

Gertie scanned around the empty meadow, the thick hedge of the estate casting an unnerving shadow. The only witnesses to the three women's secrets were a few bees buzzing above dandelions.

'You knew?' Gertie asked her sister.

'Oh, c'mon,' Lou replied, then looked over at Rachael. 'I suspected you were in on it, too, but I wasn't one hundred per cent sure until I saw the look passing between you both at the funeral.' Lou glanced over to Gertie. 'Took me a few days to figure it out, I won't lie. Did a bit of investigating. Didn't think you had it in you, sis, oh proud giver of life. But yeah. Ballsy. Jesus, Gert. You're a fierce mama-bear when someone pokes your cub. Except, he kind of didn't.'

Gertie's only visible reaction was to sip the dregs of her melted gelato, but inside she was still disbelieving how she let protectiveness of her child overrule all sense of right and wrong. The love of a mother was a form of madness. But did she regret it?

Rachael gave her a knowing smile, and they spoke without words, just like they had that dreary afternoon on her rain-speckled porch.

No, not a bit.

Lou paused, leaned over the boulder she was perched on and threw up her pistachio 'n' cream. It dribbled down into the green, green grass.

Rachael laughed at the first-time mother's shock at the power of morning sickness.

'You just wait for motherhood, sis,' Gertie warned. 'That mess there – it's just the beginning.'

Acknowledgements

This book could've been written a whole lot quicker if it wasn't for my three spirited sons, who apparently require feeding every single day. But without said offspring, it would not have been written at all. This one's for you, my kind, clever sons. Being your mum is the best thing I've ever done, and brought me the most unbridled joy (remember that when I yell at you!).

To the much-loved girlfriends who've guided me through 'when to drop a bottle' to 'how not to lose your shit at teens' – the chosen few that have had me snort-laughing in coffee shops till closing time for years, sharing the highs and lows of this outrageous thing called motherhood.

To the inspiring folk at Pantera Press who continue their midwifery of stories, especially Managing Editor Lucy Bell and Publisher Lex Hirst for their word-wrangling experience – this book baby was a long labour requiring several interventions, so I appreciate your patience. I'm so glad my tales of motherhood did not scare you away from it.

To Lauren Finger and Alex Nahlous, for their wise and wonderful editorial work. I'll never stop being grateful for the generosity of spirit of all editors working backstage to make the author's writing sing. I see you and appreciate you.

To my first reader and biggest fan – Mum. Without you, I would not have had the gumption to think I could write. You made me believe I could, and here I am getting away with it.

My husband, Jamie, for dreaming that one day I'd write my way to a beach shack somewhere for us, and dealing with the kids' shenanigans more than he'd like while I chip away at that dream.

My Beta readers (and even 'better' people) Carolyn Martinez and Lily Malone for cheering my head talk on when it needed it, and praising my undeserving dirty drafts.

Detective Sergeant Andrew Self, Queensland Police Service, for keeping my crime scene within the realms of possibility.

My friend, writer and nurse Amy Andrews for sharing with me how to murder without a trace, and not reporting me to authorities.

My readers – I think of you often, anonymously lurking in my mind, and hope you enjoy this one.

And to all those friends and relatives who became unwilling contributors to this story via inadvertently sharing an anecdote or concept. (Leanne Keane, credit to you as the creator of the Lock Box as a sanity preserver – PS: readers, it also works for snacks). Sorry, not sorry.

Thank you, all you lovely humans.

PS: If this story prompted mixed emotions or concerns for you or someone you know, information regarding intimate partner abuse can be found at www.reachout.com or 1800RESPECT (1800 737732) 24/7 within Australia.

About the author

Kylie Kaden has an honours degree in psychology, was a columnist at *My Child Magazine*, and now works in the disability sector.

She knew writing was in her blood from a young age when she snuck onto her brother's Commodore 64 to invent stories as a child. Raised in Queensland, she spent holidays camping with her family on the Sunshine Coast.

With a surfer-lawyer for a husband and three spirited sons, Kylie can typically be found venting the day's thoughts on her laptop, sometimes in the laundry so she can't be found.

Kylie is the author of *Losing Kate* (2014), *Missing You* (2015) and *The Day the Lies Began* (2019). *One of Us* is her fourth novel.